FIRESTORM

Acclaim for Radclyffe's Fiction

2010 Prism award winner and *ForeWord Review* Book of the Year Award finalist *Secrets in the Stone* is "so powerfully [written] that the worlds of these three women shimmer between reality and dreams… A strong, must read novel that will linger in the minds of readers long after the last page is turned."—*Just About Write*

Lambda Literary Award winner *Stolen Moments* "is a collection of steamy stories about women who just couldn't wait. It's sex when desire overrides reason, and it's incredibly hot!"—*On Our Backs*

Lambda Literary Award winner *Distant Shores, Silent Thunder* "weaves an intricate tapestry about passion and commitment between lovers. The story explores the fragile nature of trust and the sanctuary provided by loving relationships."—*Sapphic Reader*

Lambda Literary and Benjamin Franklin Award Finalist *The Lonely Hearts Club* "is an ensemble piece that follows the lives [and loves] of three women, with a plot as carefully woven as a fine piece of cloth." —*Midwest Book Review*

ForeWord's Book of the Year finalist *Night Call* features "gripping medical drama, characters drawn with depth and compassion, and incredibly hot [love] scenes."—*Just About Write*

Lambda Literary Award Finalist *Justice Served* delivers a "crisply written, fast-paced story with twists and turns and keeps us guessing until the final explosive ending."—*Independent Gay Writer*

Lambda Literary Award finalist *Turn Back Time* "is filled with wonderful love scenes, which are both tender and hot."—*MegaScene*

Lambda Literary Award finalist *When Dreams Tremble*'s "focus on character development is meticulous and comprehensive, filled with angst, regret, and longing, building to the ultimate climax."—*Just About Write*

Applause for L.L. Raand's *The Midnight Hunt*

"Thrilling and sensual drama with protagonists who are as alluring as they are complex."—Nell Stark, author of the paranormal romance *everafter*

"An engaging cast of characters and a flow that never skips a beat. Its rich eroticism and tension-packed plot will have readers enthralled. It's a book with a delicious bite."—Winter Pennington, author of *Witch Wolf* and *Raven's Mask*, the Kassandra Lyall Preternatural Investigator paranormal romance novels

"'Night's been crazy and it isn't even a full moon.' Who needs the full moon when you have the whole of planet Earth? L.L. Raand has created a Midnight otherworld with razor-cut precision. Sharp political intrigue, furious action, and at its core a compelling romance with creatures from your darkest dreams. The curtain rises on a thrilling new paranormal series."—Gill McKnight, author of *Goldenseal* and *Ambereye*, the Garoul paranormal romance series

"L.L. Raand's vision of a world where Weres, Vampires, and more co-exist with humans is fascinating and richly detailed, and the story she tells is not only original but deeply erotic. A satisfying read in every sense of the word."—Meghan O'Brien, author of the paranormal romance *Wild*

"While *The Midnight Hunt*…is a gripping story [with] some truly erotic sex scenes, the story always takes precedence. This is a great read which is not easily put down nor easily forgotten."—*Just About Write*

By Radclyffe

Romances

Innocent Hearts

Promising Hearts

Love's Melody Lost

Love's Tender Warriors

Tomorrow's Promise

Love's Masquerade

shadowland

Passion's Bright Fury

Fated Love

Turn Back Time

When Dreams Tremble

The Lonely Hearts Club

Night Call

Secrets in the Stone

Desire by Starlight

Honor Series

Above All, Honor

Honor Bound

Love & Honor

Honor Guards

Honor Reclaimed

Honor Under Siege

Word of Honor

Justice Series

A Matter of Trust (prequel)

Shield of Justice

In Pursuit of Justice

Justice in the Shadows

Justice Served

Justice for All

The Provincetown Tales

Safe Harbor

Beyond the Breakwater

Distant Shores, Silent Thunder

Storms of Change

Winds of Fortune

Returning Tides

Visit us at www.boldstrokesbooks.com

FIRESTORM

by

RADCLY*f*FE

2011

FIRESTORM

ISBN 13: 978-1-60282-232-0

This Trade Paperback Original Is Published By
Bold Strokes Books, Inc.
P.O. Box 249
Valley Falls, NY 12185

First Edition: July 2011

CREDITS
EDITORS: RUTH STERNGLANTZ AND STACIA SEAMAN
PRODUCTION DESIGN: STACIA SEAMAN
COVER DESIGN BY SHERI (GRAPHICARTIST2020@HOTMAIL.COM)

Acknowledgments

This book is dedicated to the men and women who risk their lives to keep our homes, our land, and our wildlife safe. The wilderness that remains preserves the free spirit of us all.

Someone recently asked why I decided to write a series about first responders. Heroes come in many forms, from those who fight on the home front to raise and protect our families to those on the front lines who do battle for our freedom. I've always been fascinated by individuals who give of themselves for the benefit of others, whether they are medical professionals, law enforcement agents, soldiers, search and rescue workers, firefighters, or all the others who protect our waters, our shores, our wilderness, and our lives. The dedication to duty and the cost to the individual are common themes in my work and this series seemed a natural extension of that exploration. In addition, it's just fun to write high-impact, adventurous, exciting stories that also create a perfect backdrop for romance. While the books in the First Responder Series are not connected by character arcs, they are connected by theme, and the possibilities are limitless. As always, my deep appreciation to the readers who take the journey with me.

A special thanks to my incomparable Admin, Sandy Lowe, who understands me and my work, and whose diligent research has infused authenticity into this story. All the errors, omissions, and inaccuracies belong solely to me. Also my thanks go to editors extraordinaire, Ruth Sternglantz and Stacia Seaman; to first readers Connie, Eva, Jenny, Paula, and Tina for suggestions and support; to Nell Stark for her discerning comments from an author's viewpoint; to Sheri, who knows what I want in a cover before I do; and to Cindy, who gets the work out month after month; and never last—to all the readers who stand by me.

And always, gratitude to my own personal tour guide and fellow adventurer in life, Lee. *Amo te.*

To Lee, every day is an adventure

CHAPTER ONE

Mallory rolled out of the rack at 0445—a good half hour before anyone else was likely to be up. She wanted to beat the guys who slept in the barracks across the yard to the showers before hot water became a premium. Then a nice quiet, solitary breakfast. Fifteen minutes of privacy was worth a lot when she'd be spending the next four weeks with them twenty-four/seven. Assuming all four rookies made the cut. Odds were they would—she'd handpicked them over the winter, combing through the applications for just the right fit. When you lived with a person for six months and put your life in their hands every day, fit mattered. They were all experienced wildland firefighters, each had a critical secondary skill, and she'd gotten good personal references. Still, things could change in the off-season. One broke his leg skiing over the winter, and she'd been lucky to get a qualified last-minute replacement. Another had suddenly transferred to a station closer to his home just the week before, so she was still a man down to start.

She always hoped the new guys would make the grade. Usually, rookies flunked out of basic training because of poor conditioning. They all thought they were in great shape coming in—but one or two always discovered differently after a few days of lugging an eighty-five-pound pack over dense mountain terrain. She'd find out soon enough. Boot camp started at 0600.

The loft was chilly verging on frigid, and she quickly pulled on jeans and shrugged into a heavy sweatshirt with a United States Forest Service emblem on the chest over the thermals she'd worn to bed. Unlike the seasonal guys, she was a year-round forest ranger, wildland firefighter, and smokejumper. Most of the year, this station was her home. Impatiently she freed the thick waves caught in the hood at the base of her neck. Damn it, she needed a haircut, and when was she supposed to find time to do that? Not that her appearance was going to matter to anyone, but she hated when her hair got in her way when she was working, and it was getting too long to pull back in the short ponytail she usually wore. Something else to put on her endless to-do list.

Grabbing her shower gear, she headed for the ladder at the far end of her sleeping loft over the hangar deck that housed the twin-engine C-23 Sherpa jump ship. The minute she climbed down, the colder air in the cavernous space practically frosted her lungs. Probably in the thirties outside. The Montana mountains were still snow-covered in early May. Her breath hung in clouds as she hustled across the gravel yard toward the standby shack, a low-slung, metal-sided building with haphazardly arranged extensions that housed the sleeping quarters, mess hall, equipment and locker rooms. No one stirred around the barracks. Guys were still sleeping. Oh joy.

"Mallory," a gruff male voice called. "Hey, Ice! See you a minute?"

So much for the leisurely shower. Mallory hadn't counted on Sully being up so early, but she should have. He was as much a workaholic as she was—although she preferred to think of her work ethic as thorough, rather than obsessed.

"Yo, Sully. On my way." Abandoning her visions of hot steam and suds, Mallory reversed course back to the ops room next to the hangar and stopped in the doorway. Her immediate superior, Chuck Sullivan, was bent over the desk in his cramped one-window office, his arms braced on either side of a haphazard pile of papers and file folders. A huge bulletin board covered with aerial and terrain maps occupied the far wall. A rickety stand in one corner held a Pyrex coffeepot in a dingy white coffeemaker. The room smelled of burnt coffee. He'd been there a while.

Mallory suppressed a twinge of guilt. She knew what this was about—she'd been dragging her feet sorting through all the paperwork that went along with her new job as ops manager of the Yellowrock interagency smokejumping unit. It wasn't like she hadn't told Sully she was terrible at desk work when he asked her to take the position suddenly vacated when Tom Reynolds couldn't jump anymore. A bad landing had ended Tom up in the hospital with a crushed lumbar disc. She had seniority after eight years spending May through November fighting wildfires with the USFS, and she had plenty of experience directing activities as incident commander in the field, but ask her to fill out a timesheet—she'd rather spend two weeks sleeping on the ground during the height of mosquito season. "Look, Sully, if this is about filling that last position, I read through the applications last night. I think there are a couple of good candidates—"

"Yeah, about that," Sully said, looking up. His smoke-gray eyes were hooded, the furrows extending out from the corners paler than the rest of his tanned skin, even though summer was still more than a month away. Something in his look made her stomach tighten.

"What?" Mallory said, leaning her shoulder against the doorjamb.

"The last position has been filled."

"That's interesting. How come I don't know about it? I thought the training manager chose the crew." Mallory clamped a lid on her temper. Something was off, but whatever it was, Sully wasn't likely to be responsible, so venting at him wasn't going to help. Sully had been supervisor at the Yellowrock station for fifteen years, and they got along well. Never had any problem communicating. Now he was uneasy and had made a decision that directly affected her for the next half a year without consulting her. She didn't like surprises. Anticipation was her holy grail—she planned, studied, considered contingencies. Orderly, well-thought-out plans brought the team home whole. Fire was unpredictable. Fickle and frivolous. She couldn't afford to be. Not when lives were at stake. "What's going on, Sully?"

"We've been assigned a transfer from Grangeville to fill that vacancy."

"A hotshot?" Mallory tried not to grind her teeth. Hotshots usually worked as part of wildland fire suppression teams on large, long-term fires. They were used to performing as units and often had difficulty making the transition from field-based firefighting to the rapid deployment into remote areas that was the daily fare of smokejumpers. "Geez, Sully. How come I'm just hearing about this?"

Sully straightened and jammed his hands in the pockets of his khaki work pants. His jaw worked like he was still chewing the tobacco he'd given up the year before. Yeah, he was definitely unhappy. "Because I'm just hearing about it myself. I got a call from regional headquarters informing me of the posting. The whole thing was handled a couple levels above my pay grade."

"I've never heard of the higher-ups getting involved in something as basic as hiring a crew member."

"Well, she's not just any crew member."

"She?" Mallory raised an eyebrow.

Sully laughed. "What? You think you and Sarah are the only women capable of doing the job?"

"I know we're not. Except I know all the other female jumpers, and most of the women on the field crews too. None of them said anything to me about wanting to come on board. What's her name?"

"Jac Russo."

Mallory frowned. "Why do I know that name?"

"Maybe because her father is Franklin Russo?"

Mallory stiffened. "Oh, you gotta be kidding me. The right-wing senator from Idaho? The right-to-life, anti-gay, anti-affirmative-everything guy?"

"That's the one. The rumor mill says he's going to give Powell a run for his money for the White House come election time next year."

"Just gets better and better," Mallory said.

Sully smiled a little grimly. "Never knew you were political."

"I'm not. Usually." Mallory shook her head. Sully knew she was a lesbian—so did everybody else she worked with. She didn't make an issue of it, she didn't hide it. She was who she was. In the air, in the wilderness digging a line or setting a burnout, no one cared who you slept with. All they cared about was how well you did your job and looked after your buddies. Most of the time she was too busy working to think about what bureaucrats were doing, but she couldn't turn on the television or pick up a magazine or read the news without hearing something about Russo and his campaign to turn the country back to a time when straight white men held all the power. And his vitriol turned her stomach. "This posting is politics, right? Somebody owes somebody a favor and we get to pick up the tab?" She raked her hand through her hair. Her too-damn-long hair. "Does she even know anything about firefighting? This is crazy. I don't want some pampered politician's daughter, who probably thinks spending six months in the mountains with a bunch of men will be fun and look good on her résumé, on my team. Hell, if she doesn't get herself killed, she'll get one of us killed."

"Slow down, Ice. She's not a rookie. Not quite. She worked part of a season with a Bureau of Land Management hotshot team in Idaho." He fished around on his desk and came up with a dog-eared file folder. He flipped it open, turned it around, and held it out to her. "Besides, real-life experience is an acceptable substitute for the usual field training, and she's got that covered."

"She's still a rookie as far as I'm concerned." Mallory regarded the folder as if it were a rattler coiled in the brush trailside, waiting to strike. There couldn't be anything good inside that file. Smokejumpers returned year after year to the same crew; vacancies were few, and the waiting list long. She hadn't seen Russo's name on any applications, but somehow, Russo had managed to leapfrog to the head of the list, and that could only mean someone had pulled strings. Anyone qualified for the job didn't need to do that. "Come on, Sully. You know this doesn't make any sense. If she's already on a crew, why move her over to ours? We'll have to train her to jump—"

"You'd have to train whoever joined us to jump, Ice."

"Still, I don't get it."

"Neither do I." Sully gave her a wry shrug and waggled the folder. "I wasn't given the option. She'll be here this morning. You might as well look at this."

Reluctantly Mallory took the folder and glanced at the typed application and the color photo clipped to the top of the page. Jac Russo. Twenty-seven—well, at least she had a couple of years on Russo in age and quite a few more in experience. At just thirty, she was young to captain a jump crew and wouldn't have wanted to start out the season breaking in a hotshot who discounted her authority because she was younger or less experienced. The photo was a good one. Even the Polaroid head shot couldn't dampen the appeal of bittersweet-chocolate eyes and thick black wavy hair—true black, not dark brown like her own—and also unlike hers, neatly trimmed above her collar. Russo's face was a little too strong to be pretty, with bold cheekbones and an angular jaw. A decent face, nothing out of the ordinary, really. Mallory got caught in the dark eyes that almost leapt out of the glossy surface of the photo—intense, unsmiling, penetrating eyes. Eyes that held secrets and dared you to reveal yours. Okay, so maybe she was a little bit good-looking. The guys would probably be happy to have her around as long as she had even marginal skills. Mallory didn't agree. She couldn't afford to have anyone jumping who couldn't carry her own weight. No one was coming out of the mountains on a litter on her watch. Not this year. Not ever again.

"I'm telling you right now," Mallory said, flipping a page to look at the work experience Russo had listed, "if she can't cut it, I'm not putting her up in the air. I'm not going to let her endanger my team. I don't care whose daughter she is."

"I wouldn't expect you to," someone said in a husky alto from right behind her.

Mallory spun around and went nose to nose with a woman about her height, their bodies colliding hard enough for her to feel firm breasts and a muscled torso press against her front. Molding to her—except that had to be her imagination. She pulled back, and the black-haired stranger took her in with a slow up-and-down perusal and an expression that was half-arrogant, half-amused. Her lips were full and sensuous and unsmiling—like in the photo.

"Jump to conclusions much?" the woman said.

"Sorry," Mallory muttered. "I didn't realize you were behind me."

"I gathered that." The really nice lips smiled, but the eyes were cool. "I'm Jac Russo."

"Yes." Mallory indicated the folder. "I saw the picture."

"Did you also see the part that said I've got search and rescue experience? Can handle explosives? How about the part—"

"I noticed you're short on field experience," Mallory said tightly, "and this isn't remedial class. Basic training starts"—she checked her watch—"in forty-five minutes."

"I'll be ready," Russo said. "And I'm a fast learner."

"We'll see," Mallory murmured.

"What—you've already made up your mind?" Jac's expression tightened and her eyes went flat. "Let me guess. Something you heard on TV, maybe?"

"Sorry, I must have missed the bulletin," Mallory shot back. She lifted the folder. "I was talking about what *isn't* in here."

"Don't be so sure you know all about me from what you read," Russo said.

"I'll reserve judgment till I've seen how you run. You'll be first up this morning."

"Good enough."

Sully cleared his throat loudly. "Russo, I've got some paperwork for you to complete."

"Yes sir, I'll be right there." Jac didn't shift her gaze from Mallory's. "I didn't get your name."

"Mallory James." Mallory smiled thinly. "I'm the ops manager and training coordinator. You can call me Boss. Or Ice."

"What do your friends call you?"

"Mallory." She made sure Russo got the message she wasn't planning to fraternize with her. Not that she ever really did with any of the crew. She hung out with them, swapped stories, but she never really shared anything personal with anyone. Breaking away from Russo's probing gaze, Mallory turned and tossed the folder onto Sully's desk. She wasn't sure what besides anger might show in her eyes, and she didn't want Russo to see past her temper to her worry, or her fear. "Roll call at oh six hundred. Don't be late."

"Can't wait."

Mallory snorted and strode away.

Jac watched until the ops manager disappeared into a building across the tarmac. *Well, that was a great start.*

She'd been hoping to slide in under the radar, but that obviously wasn't going to happen now. She couldn't tell from the conversation exactly what was behind Mallory James's animosity. Most of the time, a cold reception had little to do with her and a lot to do with her father. The higher he'd risen in national politics, the more airtime he got and the more controversy he stirred up. He seemed to thrive on the reactions his often extreme positions evoked—even death threats didn't bother him. Unfortunately, the more visible he became, the more his notoriety overflowed onto his family. Her mother was an anxious wreck who didn't want to leave the house past the line of protesters lined up across the street and the reporters in the driveway. Her sister Carly was generally humiliated by her parents anyhow, the way all seventeen-year-olds were, and was trying even harder than Jac had to prove she was nothing like their ultraconservative right-wing father. She'd started running with a tough crowd of dropouts and delinquents.

Jac had been hoping to escape some of the recent fallout here, but no such luck. She was used to being judged on the basis of her father's latest sound bite, and usually that didn't bother her. Today it did.

She squared her shoulders and faced the guy watching her speculatively from behind the desk. She'd been proving herself all her life—or more accurately, disproving the assumptions everyone made about her. In high school all she'd had to do was demonstrate her willingness to break the rules to crack the mold her family had created for her. Considering that breaking the rules usually involved sex, drugs, and rock 'n' roll—all the things her father railed against—divorcing herself from her family's politics hadn't been all that hard. Most of the time rebelling had been fun, but she wasn't sixteen anymore, and while she still chafed under the weight of rules and regs, she'd pretty much given up all the rest. The drugs and rock 'n' roll for sure, and the sex most of the time. But then, it didn't take a whole lot of sex to get her into a whole lot of trouble.

Realizing the guy was still watching her, still waiting, she said, "I guess you weren't expecting me."

He grinned fleetingly. "You're quick."

Jac shook her head and muttered, "Damn it, Nora, thanks for warning me." She walked forward and held out her hand. "Jac Russo. I take it you got that part already."

"Chuck Sullivan. I'm kind of the overseer around here, but Ice calls the shots."

"Interesting nickname."

His gaze narrowed. "None better at the job."

Jac held up her hands. "Hey, I don't doubt it. She just seemed a little fiery there for a minute."

Again the fleeting grin and a shake of his head. "Not much riles her up."

"I'm not sure I'm happy about having that privilege, then." Jac sighed. "I didn't know about this myself until yesterday when someone on my father's staff told me, but I thought you'd been contacted. I don't blame you for being pissed."

"I'm not pissed," Sullivan said quietly.

Jac tilted her head toward the door behind her. "She is."

"Don't worry about it. Pass basic training, you'll be part of the team."

Too bad it wasn't that easy. Being good at what she did, being qualified, pulling her own weight—all those things helped her fit in, but they never helped her to be accepted. When she'd been younger, she'd desperately wanted to be accepted. Now she didn't care. At least that's what she told herself most days. The freeze in Mallory James's eyes was nothing new, although usually the disdain was motivated by something other than her showing up where she wasn't expected or wanted. All the same, for the first time in a long time, she'd wanted to melt the icy reception she'd gotten used to receiving.

She wanted this job, sure. She'd wanted it for a long time, but she hadn't planned on getting it this way. But now she was here, and she wanted to stay. She wanted Mallory James to admit she was good enough to stay.

Chapter Two

M allory about-turned out of Sully's office and steamed across the yard to the standby shack. The barracks in the back, adjacent to the locker rooms, held twenty single, plain, metal-framed beds, ten to a row down each side. She chose to sleep in the hangar loft, not out of modesty but just for a few moments of peace and quiet at the end of the day. The guys would be stirring any minute. No time now for anything but a quick shower and a hurried breakfast, but it really didn't matter. She was too aggravated to relax anyhow.

She cut through the main equipment room on her way to the locker room. Orderly rows of jump suits, helmets, and gear belonging to the crew on the jump list she'd made up the night before hung from pegs on the wall. Her Kevlar jacket and pants hung closest to the door. She was the IC when she jumped, and as incident commander, she was first in and last out of the hot zone.

A windowless swinging door on the left side led to the women's locker room, where she and Sarah Petrie, a veteran jumper and her best friend, stored their extra gear and clothes, and shared a six- by-six-foot communal shower. The plywood walls didn't do much to mute the noise when all the guys were next door, and any conversation was easily audible. Not that the illusion of privacy really mattered. They lived together for six months straight, eating and sleeping and sweating and risking their lives together. Privacy took on a whole new definition under those circumstances. The only truly private place was in her head.

She peeled off her clothes, piled them on the bench running lengthwise between the row of gunmetal gray lockers and shelves holding towels and cubbies for gear, grabbed a towel, and walked naked to the shower. After twisting the dial to hot on one of the four showerheads, she stepped under the water. Standing under the pounding spray, she replayed the meeting with Jac Russo. She couldn't quite put her finger on what annoyed her, and that annoyed her even more. Sure, Russo had circumvented normal channels in getting the posting, and that offended her sense of order. Maybe her sense of fair play too. All the same, she didn't usually vent her feelings out loud, particularly in front of people she didn't know. Or in front of a coworker like Sully. She prided herself on being in control, on being cool, on placing reason ahead of emotion. It'd earned her the nickname Ice, and she liked it. Some people extended the name to Ice Queen, but she wasn't bothered by that. If she did keep her feelings under wraps, what of it?

Perfunctorily, she squirted shampoo into her palm and lathered up her hair, turning, eyes closed, letting the heat smooth out some of the tension in her back. So why was she bothered so much by Russo? Because she hadn't picked her? That seemed a little bit petty, and she didn't like thinking of herself that way. But Russo was an unknown, and unknowns made her uneasy. Fire was enough of an unknown, appearing on its own timetable, spreading at its own rate, jumping lines where least expected, blowing up, cresting a ridge where it never should've been, trapping eleven wildland firefighters in a clearing that should've been a safety zone. A safety zone she'd picked. Nine of them had walked away.

She closed her eyes tighter, trying to forget the anguished faces of the families waiting to see who walked out of the forest alive, and who did not. Looking to her for information, for answers, and her having none.

She shuddered and opened her eyes, waiting for reality to drive the memories away, and all she got was tears in her eyes. Tears that had to be from soap, nothing else.

This year everything would be different. This year she was in charge from day one—ops and training manager. She'd see that the rookies were hammered into shape and the vets honed to razor sharpness. She'd picked her new guys so carefully. They all had the goods, they were all young and healthy and strong. And then along comes Russo. The outlier, the unknown. Sure, Russo had some firefighting experience, but the details were pretty thin on paper. Russo was still practically a rookie, and the way she'd been appointed suggested she didn't have the skills to make it on her own. That was a real problem.

Mallory sudsed her breasts and torso, bending to finish the rest of her body in quick automatic swipes. Russo. Maybe she'd wash out. One thing was for certain, Russo wouldn't be jumping if she didn't make it through basic training. Mallory was going to be sure Russo's month was every bit as rigorous as she could make it.

Mallory flipped off the shower, wrapped the towel around her chest, and knotted it above her breasts on her way into the locker room. The four metal lockers against the wall were an optimistic number since even two women stationed in the same place was unusual. Out of the three hundred smokejumpers in the country, less than one-tenth of those were female. Sarah should be arriving the beginning of June. If Russo was still here, that would make three, with a locker to spare. Sarah slept off base whenever she could and usually bunked in the main barracks when she couldn't. Russo would have to as well. Mallory considered the extra bunk in her loft and discarded the idea. No way was Russo sleeping in her quarters. A clear picture of dark challenging eyes and a sinful mouth, just a hint of a mocking smile turning up one corner of full sensuous lips, shot through her mind. Oh hell no, Russo wasn't sharing her loft.

Mallory opened her locker, pulled out a clean white sleeveless tank, a short-sleeved navy T-shirt, and navy cargo pants from the stack on the top shelf, and tossed the pile onto the bench. After dumping her dirty clothes into the laundry bag in the bottom of her locker, she toweled off her hair and lobbed the damp towel into the hamper, feeling her skin pebble and her nipples tighten in the cold room. The slight scuffling sound of the door opening behind her brought her whipping around, flinging wet hair from her eyes. Russo stood framed in the doorway, her duffel dangling from one hand.

"You have a bad habit of sneaking up on me," Mallory said, feeling her nipples tighten even more under the unabashed scrutiny.

"Sorry about that," Russo said, her husky voice deeper than Mallory remembered.

"You want to close the door?" Mallory said.

Russo pulled the door shut, closing them into the cramped space. "Sully told me to bring my gear over here. I guess he didn't know you'd be naked."

Russo wasn't much taller than Mallory, five ten or so, and rangier. Lean where Mallory had a bit of curve even when in hard, summer shape. Russo's gaze was direct and unapologetically appraising. Mallory's breathing kicked up, and she willed herself not to grab for her shirt. She'd been naked with Sarah thousands of times and never given it a thought. Sarah was straight—at least she'd never indicated otherwise—but even if she wasn't, Mallory wouldn't have thought anything of being undressed around her. Work and sex never crossed paths in Mallory's consciousness.

Odds were, Russo was straight too, but Mallory was glad for the bench that bisected the space. Her skin felt hot, and Russo seemed to take up more space than she ought to. Maybe it was her eyes—they never wavered once they looked at you. Like you were all she saw.

"I don't think whether I'm dressed or not is really on Sully's radar." Nonchalantly, Mallory reached into her locker for a pair of navy bikini briefs, pulled them on, and slid the tank over her head and down over her breasts. Russo's gaze followed her movements, and Mallory had a second's flash of Russo's hands tracking where her gaze had just gone. Her stomach tightened. What the hell?

"Ought to be on someone's radar," Jac said.

Damn it, Mallory felt herself flush. Annoyed with herself now, she jerked on her pants. Turning her back to Russo, she quickly finished dressing and clipped her radio to her pants. Good. Ready to go. Ready to get to work.

She wasn't used to anyone putting her off stride, not in the field and not in her personal life. The women she dated, when she had time to date—which this time of year was practically never—were always self-sufficient women with busy lives of their own who wanted good company, interesting conversation, and undemanding sex if the mood was right. If sex didn't happen, an enjoyable evening with someone who wasn't on the job was satisfying enough for her. Women just didn't occupy a big place in her life, and never disrupted it. Russo had done nothing but disorder her usual calm routine just by breathing the same air. Being around Russo made her feel as if she was missing a layer of skin, and she never felt that way. The tingling in her belly was unfamiliar too. No, that was a lie. It was very familiar, just not very frequent. Double damn her body for having no sense of discretion whatsoever. Russo's sexy dark gaze heated her beneath her skin, in a place she couldn't control. No matter. No problem. Maybe her body was reckless, but her head wasn't.

Mallory picked up her watch, strapped it on, and headed for the door. "You can use that locker on the end."

"Thanks." Russo unzipped her gear bag and stowed her gear quickly and efficiently.

"If you plan on getting anything to eat, I'd hurry if I were you. Now you've only got twenty-five minutes."

"I'll be there." Jac paused. "How about I buy you breakfast? Boss."

"Breakfast is free," Mallory said, walking out.

"Figure of speech," Jac called, hurrying after the woman she had to impress. She hadn't done a very good job of that so far. Not that sucking up to anyone was part of her repertoire, but Mallory James was her boss. Mallory would decide when she jumped and what she did when she landed. Since she planned to pull her weight on this team—hell, she planned on doing more than that, she wanted on permanently at this post—she'd have to prove herself. And that meant convincing Ice James she wasn't just some appointee getting a free ride, courtesy of her father's connections. Just the opposite—her father hadn't been doing her any favors, but Mallory wouldn't care about her problems. Why should she? "Keep you company, then."

Mallory hesitated, looking as if she might say no.

"Might be our only chance," Jac said hurriedly, lengthening her stride to stay by Mallory's side. "Seeing as how you're going to wash me out later today."

"You so sure I won't?" Mallory asked, her green eyes snapping.

Jac grinned. "Pretty sure."

"Like I said. We'll see."

Mallory kept walking, but she hadn't said no, so Jac fell into step with her. Outside to the east, the first ribbons of dawn purpled the sky over the mountaintops. Base camp was situated in a dip of flat land between towering crags of rock face and dense evergreen forests. At eight thousand feet, the crystal-clear air shimmered with the whistle of the wind, always the wind slicing down the mountainside, and the chatter of daring early birds. Then testosterone-infused laughter laden with the energy of a dozen men eager for adventure erupted in the yard.

Calls of "Hey, Boss" and "Morning, Ice" floated their way, and Mallory waved, a slight smile softening her full lips, turning her classic features from distant to beautiful.

"Ready for a workout, Cap?" called a wiry blond in a green flannel shirt and jeans, his mustache and rough stubble tinged with hints of red.

"That's my line, Bowie," Mallory responded. "Hope you didn't get too soft over the winter."

"Still hard, Ice." Bowie patted his belly, and the other guys hooted good-naturedly.

Mallory just shook her head.

"How many rookies besides me?" Jac asked, noting that a lot of guys shot appreciative glances Mallory's way, though she didn't seem to notice. Why wouldn't they? She was a knockout. Thick, wavy chestnut hair just kissing her shoulders, deep-set almond-shaped green eyes, elegantly carved cheekbones saved from appearing delicate by her strong chin and direct gaze. Great body—loose and strong and full in all the right places. Athletic and fit with undeniable grace. Jac's mouth actually watered, and she nearly laughed out loud at her pathetic musings. Mallory James, if she even liked women in bed, was more likely to give her twenty-five push-ups than the time of day.

"Four."

"Huh?" Jac said.

Mallory cut her a bemused stare. "Four other rookies. Although I suppose technically you're a snookie."

"I'm pretty sure I don't like that idea," Jac said. "Sounds like one of those chocolate-covered marshmallow things." She patted her stomach, mimicking Bowie. "Pretty hard myself."

Mallory gave her a flat stare. "Snooks are second-years. And this isn't day camp, Hotshot. This is make-or-break time."

"I got that message." Jac grinned when Mallory's gaze lingered on hers. "Loud and clear, Boss."

"Enough with the *Boss* already." Mallory opened the door to a long, narrow room that smelled of coffee, eggs, and bacon.

"Oh man," Jac moaned, "when you said breakfast I thought you meant vending machines and microwaves."

"We're lucky to have on-site meals. Luckier still to have Charlie

Awita as a cook. This used to be an auxiliary Air Force outpost, so there's a kitchen and dining hall."

"Does everyone live here full-time?"

"Mostly—a couple of the married crew keep apartments in town."

"How about you?"

"How about me what?" Mallory grabbed a dented stainless steel tray from a stack at the end of the food line and handed it over the counter to a middle-aged Native American wearing a Grateful Dead T-shirt and a white apron around his portly waist. "Hey, Charlie, fill it up."

Charlie smiled. "Good morning, Captain Mallory."

Mallory smiled back. "Don't call me Captain, Charlie. Ice will do just fine."

He shook his head, his dark eyes shining. "Oh no, I don't think so. It's an honor to lead the team. You should be proud."

"I know and I am, but it doesn't change anything else." Looking uncomfortable with the praise, Mallory took the tray heaped with scrambled eggs, bacon, and biscuits and moved quickly on down the line to the coffee machine. She grabbed an extra-large cup and filled it to the brim.

Jac followed her lead. "So?"

Mallory sat at a square wooden table in front of a window with a killer view of the long valley that narrowed into a pass between two towering peaks. "So...what?"

"Are you married?"

"No."

"So no apartment in town?" Jac blew on her steaming coffee and tried a sip. Excellent.

"No." Mallory paused, studying Jac through narrowed eyes. "What are you doing here, Russo? I assume you could have had your pick of places to go—so why here? We're remote, we see hard time all season, we never get any filmmakers or writers wanting to do documentaries about us. We're just not high profile."

Like you. The words hung in the air unspoken.

Jac set her fork down and lifted her coffee cup, buying a few seconds. She'd expected the question but didn't know how she wanted to answer. If she told Mallory James why her father had leveraged his political clout to get her a job in another state, a job he knew she wanted and would have a hard time turning down, she'd have to reveal a whole lot more about herself than she ever did to anyone. The silence lengthened and she met Mallory's gaze. Mallory's eyes were a darker green than they had appeared earlier, with flecks of gold glinting in the bright sunlight that had burst in the sky. Deep, intense, unflinching eyes that almost made her want to tell it all. Almost. "Maybe the same thing you are."

"Oh? And what would that be?"

Trying to prove I'm worth something to someone on my own. She opted for a safer answer. "Trying to make a difference."

"You don't know why I'm here, and you didn't answer my question. But it won't really matter if you don't make it to the end of the month." Pushing back from the table, Mallory stood. "Now you've got ten minutes."

Jac watched her walk away. Cold. Remote. Beautiful. Like the mountains. And probably just as unforgiving. But she'd never been afraid of a challenge, and Mallory "Ice" James was all that and more.

CHAPTER THREE

"Hey." A guy about Jac's age with linebacker shoulders and hair as red as his T-shirt flashed a wide-open grin and straddled a chair next to her. "You another one of the new guys? I didn't see you at the briefing yesterday afternoon."

"Just got here," Jac said, holding out her hand. "Jac Russo."

"Ray Kingston," the redhead said.

A thin African American with round wire-framed glasses and thoughtful eyes joined them, and a half minute later a husky middle-aged man with a thick mustache and a neck as wide as his head pulled up a chair. Anderson and Hooker, they supplied. Jac shook their hands.

"So where you from?" the redhead, Ray, asked.

"Idaho. You?"

"Texas. What's your usual gig?"

"Been in the Guard," Jac said, not offering anything else. The guys all nodded solemnly. "You?"

"I work on the oil rigs in the Gulf off Galveston the rest of the year," Ray said.

Jac laughed. "That's a big switch."

"You ever been in Texas in the summer?"

"Luckily, no."

Hooker was an out-of-work timberman. Anderson was a high school guidance counselor from Vermont with ten years' search and rescue experience.

"I've been trying to get a spot on one of these crews for a couple years," Anderson said, polishing his spotless lenses. "This is a real sweet post."

"Yep." When Nora Fleming, her father's campaign manager, had informed her of her father's request that Jac be less visible during his push to clinch the presidential nomination and told Jac about this opening, she'd jumped at it. It was what she'd wanted to do, and since her father wanted her to disappear for the "good of the family," meaning his campaign, she'd said yes. The next morning she'd been on her way to Montana. She was coming in the back door and she knew it. More to prove, another secret to live down.

"One of the busiest crews in these parts," Hooker said, smoothing his moustache. "I see you were getting acquainted with the training manager."

"Just met her," Jac said carefully. The guys all seemed friendly enough, but she was always cautious with personal information. And Hooker wasn't just fishing about her, he was talking about Mallory. Her stomach tightened with an unfamiliar sensation she finally recognized as protectiveness.

"The regular guys say she's really good," Ray said.

"That's what I hear too," Anderson commented.

"Guy I met who worked with her a couple of years ago says she's a ballbuster," Hooker said flatly, his gaze fixed on Jac.

A test to see where her allegiance lay—with her fellow rookies or with the only other female on the team? Jac raised her brows and eyed his crotch. "Well then, I guess you'll have to be careful, Hooker. Since I assume you have a pair."

Ray burst out laughing and the other guys joined in. "Man, you're right. Maybe you'll be luckier, Jac."

"Maybe, but I think she's probably an equal opportunity buster." Jac glanced at her watch. "And in about four minutes, we're going to find out."

Standing, she gripped her tray and Ray said, "Good luck today."

"You too," Jac said, but she didn't think luck was what she was going to need. The only thing likely to impress Ice James was a high score. Not just passing, not even good. The best. Just another thing she had to prove. What else was new?

❖

Mallory stood in the shadows inside the open door of the hangar, watching the rookies mill about, talking in low voices, jostling one another, sorting themselves out. She searched for signs of tension, rivalry, competition. Wildland firefighters were naturally independent free-thinkers, and inherently competitive. Those traits were important when faced with an emergency and quick action could be lifesaving, but teamwork was just as important. She watched them all, but her gaze kept returning to Jac. Even in the sweatshirt and cargo pants that tended to neutralize gender, Jac stood out. Her features were so bold as to be arresting, and she moved with confident, natural grace. She interacted easily with the men, responding when spoken to, but remaining just a little bit apart, watchful and appraising. Like she had appraised Mallory earlier. Obviously, Jac was a woman who sized up the playing field, studied the ground, assessed circumstances. Confident, aware. All quality traits for a smokejumper. But it took a lot more than confidence to be a smokejumper.

"All right everybody, line up." Mallory stepped out of the shadows into the early morning sunlight. The rookies instantly faced her, shoulder to shoulder. "I'm Mallory James, and I'm the ops manager for Yellowrock Station. I'm also the training manager. For the next month, we will start at oh six hundred every day. We'll stop when the day's exercises are over. If we're not finished, we'll sleep in the field. When we work a fire, we have to move fast. Sometimes to get out ahead of the fire front, sometimes just to get out. You'll be wearing your jump suits and humping your gear out there. Today you get a break—no packs, no equipment. Today will be the easiest run you'll ever experience as a smokejumper." As she talked, she walked up and down the line, watching the rookies watch her. They were similarly dressed—jeans, T-shirts and sweatshirts, work boots. "The designated course is three miles long and laid out with yellow markers. Secondary trails—the blue and the red—cross the main course. They're shorter but steeper, and the terrain is tougher. Stay off them." She smiled. "You'll need to complete your run in under thirty minutes to qualify. A helitack spotter will be stationed above the route. If you run into trouble and have to drop out, just settle down by the side of the trail and signal the spotter. One of us will be by to assist. Any questions?"

"No ma'am," a number of voices responded.

"There's no need to be formal," Mallory said. "Cap is fine." She pulled her stopwatch from her pants pocket, said, "Have a good run," and clicked the start button. She met the dark eyes that had followed her every step. "Russo. Lead out."

❖

Jac broke from the line and loped toward the trail marked by a yellow disk tacked to a pine tree on the far side of the yard. She wasn't worried about qualifying. Running came easily to her—she'd run track in high school and still ran for exercise and pleasure every day. Even in boots and heavy clothes, she covered the ground easily, jumping over fallen branches, dodging rocks, leaping over streams of snow runoff. After a few minutes she started to sweat, shrugged out of her sweatshirt, and tied it around her waist. Her lungs burned as the cold air flowed in and out, her skin flushed and dampened, and her heart pounded. Ten minutes in she heard footsteps behind her but didn't slow. Rhythmic breathing synchronized with her own, and after another few minutes as she raced up a rocky slope, she smelled honeysuckle. Mountain honeysuckle. The sweet fragrance made her smile—too early to be flowering, and she remembered when she'd smelled the scent earlier. In the locker room, wafting from Mallory James's damp, shower-flushed skin. Her heart rate kicked up, and it wasn't from the rigorous course.

"Keeping tabs on me?" Jac called without looking back.

"Just making sure you don't get lost," Mallory responded, running half a step behind Jac.

"No problems here." Jac glanced over her shoulder. Mallory had tied her hair back in a loose ponytail, and her face glowed with healthy exertion. Her eyes were bright, deep green, intense and focused. She'd shed her sweatshirt too, and her bare arms were sculpted and buff. Her white tank top clung to her chest and abdomen. Firm high breasts, long tight abdomen. Her breathing was steady, deep, unlabored. She was gorgeous.

"You checking up on all the rookies?" Jac started up a steep incline, looped an arm around a tree and pulled herself up the last few feet of the slope onto more level ground. She didn't slow for Mallory but kept on running. A few seconds later Mallory was just behind her right shoulder again. So was the smell of honeysuckle. Her stomach tightened, and a jolt of electricity shot up her spine, throwing her off stride. Man, she had to focus, or she was going to trip over her own feet.

"You're setting a pretty fast pace," Mallory commented. She wasn't breathing even a little bit hard.

"Feels comfortable to me," Jac said.

"Not trying to prove anything, are you?"

"Nope." Jac slowed on the downhill. Another stream, this one wider, rocks in the center, wet and mossy, slippery. A broken ankle waiting to happen. She glanced left and right, saw a shallower area a bit off the trail, and cut right. Splashing through the stream, she clambered back onto the trail on the other side. Mallory followed.

"All you have to prove is that you can handle the work," Mallory said.

"How'm I doing?"

"You haven't finished your run yet, Russo. Don't wear yourself out."

Jac ran on. Mallory's footsteps faded, then disappeared. An unexpected swell of loneliness filled Jac's chest, and she shook it off, uncomfortable with the unfamiliar feeling. She'd long ago gotten used to being alone.

❖

Jac skirted along the crest of a rocky ridge about three-quarters of the way through the course, starting to enjoy herself. Her time was good, the morning was brilliant, and the scent of honeysuckle lingered. A flash of red halfway down the craggy slope off to her left caught her eye before being obscured by trees. After running another twenty yards, she saw it again, and whatever it was, it had not moved. Curious, she slowed, then circled back and cut off the trail for a better look. She expected to see a piece of abandoned equipment, but finally made out a red T-shirt covering a broad torso. A still figure lay against an outcropping of rock forty feet below the ridge. She sucked in a breath and narrowed her eyes, memorizing the location. Picking a tall, bifurcated pine as a landmark to orient herself once she went off trail, she took one quick look into the sky, didn't see a spotter craft, and eased over the edge of the ravine. The steep terrain was rocky and densely forested. Without guidelines, the descent was tricky and slower than she would have liked. After a few feet she couldn't see the figure, but she spotted the pine tree and followed the trajectory she'd mentally mapped out. Two minutes later she found Ray Kingston sitting on the ground with his back propped against a boulder, blood streaking down the right side of his face from a gash in his forehead.

"Ray," Jac said, kneeling beside him. "How you doing, buddy?"

"Been better," he muttered, rubbing his face and smearing the blood onto his hand and neck. He looked around, his expression confused. "Never was much of a runner. Tried to cut some of the distance and took the red trail. Must've tripped." He squinted at her. "What are you doing here?"

"Got lonely up there. Let me take a look at your head." Jac gently cupped his chin and checked his eyes. Pupils were equal, but pinpoint. Adrenaline surge. Maybe a prelude to shock. The laceration was long and deep. He'd need stitches. "How are your arms and legs, Ray? Can you move them? Feel everything okay?"

"Yeah, yeah." He braced a hand on the rock behind him and tried to push himself upright. "I'm okay. I need to finish the course."

He swayed, his face graying, and Jac quickly jumped up and wrapped an arm around his waist. "I don't think you'll be doing any more running today, buddy. Let's just take it easy and get back to level ground. I'll flag down a spotter."

"No way. You need to finish the run. Go on, get outta here."

She grinned. "Oh no, I'm not leaving you. Hell, you'll probably try another shortcut, get lost, and I'll be up half the night looking for you."

"Frak you, Russo."

"Promises, promises." Jac slung his arm over her shoulders, gripped the waistband of his pants, and took his weight. "Let's go. Nice and easy now."

"Crap." Ray leaned heavily on her, his balance unsteady and his breathing labored. "James is going to fry your ass, you know, if you don't finish."

"You let me worry about the boss." Jac eased him down the slope toward a clearing in the trees, trying to ignore the acid burn of disappointment in her stomach. Mallory James had been right. She was going to wash out the first day.

❖

Mallory checked her watch and watched the trees, resisting the urge to pace. Three rookies were already back at base. Jac wasn't with them. Neither was Ray Kingston. The others had made it under the time limit, but Jac should've been in well before them. Mallory moved a little away from the group and radioed the pilot in the spotter helicopter. "Benny? You got anything?"

"Just sighted them, Ice. Looks like we got one down."

"Damn," Mallory muttered. "Where?"

She was already striding toward the equipment room for a FAT pack as Benny radioed the location. "I'll be there in seven minutes. Stay over them until I get there."

"Roger that."

Mallory shouldered into the field and trauma kit, mentally sorting down the emergency response checklist that was second nature to every paramedic. Firefighters got injured all the time—occupational hazard. Still, having a rookie go down the first morning was not how she wanted to start boot camp. Anxiety swirled in her stomach, and she pushed the feeling aside. She was just worried about one of her team, that's all.

But as she raced for the trail, the image of Jac running so effortlessly, her stride as smooth and graceful as a deer, flashed through her mind. She didn't want to imagine Jac lying injured somewhere. She didn't want her to be hurt. Warning bells clanged, too loud to ignore. She couldn't afford to have any kind of personal feelings for another firefighter, not even friendship. She couldn't take another loss.

CHAPTER FOUR

Mallory took the left fork off the yellow trail and cut cross-country, following her GPS to the coordinates Benny had triangulated from the spotter craft. Off trail, the groundcover was dense. Her Kevlar jump jacket protected her from the worst of the gouges and scratches that might have been inflicted by low-hanging limbs and broken branches. At home in the mountains, she moved as quickly and surely as a New Yorker maneuvering crowded midday Manhattan sidewalks—effortlessly dodging, weaving, and bounding over obstacles.

The squirming tension in her stomach was an unfamiliar background noise that she tried to ignore, chalking that unusual disturbance up to her new level of responsibility. Surely her unease had nothing to do with the identities of the rookies out on the trail. She let her mind empty. Speculating about what she might find when she reached the injured was pointless. Emergency triage protocols were so ingrained in her mind she didn't have to think about them. And she didn't *want* to think about the individuals. She ruthlessly obliterated faces and names. She was a paramedic and she had injured. She didn't need to know anything else and wanted to feel even less. Her mind settled into the zone, that place of ultimate focus, where her heart beating a steady tattoo in her ears and the sensation of her breath flowing in and out of her chest centered her, at once readying her for action and obliterating all distractions.

Immersed in this calm, focused energy was where she loved to be, sure of herself, in control, battle ready. Battle worthy.

She intersected the red trail fifty yards from her destination and sprinted north, covering the uneven, uphill terrain in long quick strides. As soon as she skirted a craggy outcropping, she saw them. Ray Kingston slumped by the side of the trail with his back propped against a broad pine. Jac knelt with her hand on his wrist and her eyes tracking Mallory's approach. Ray's face was bloody. Jac appeared unhurt, her expression steady and calm. Mallory held Jac's gaze, and her stomach settled for the first time since Benny had radioed they had injured. She couldn't think about that now, or what it might mean.

"What have we got?" Mallory asked. Jac, like every firefighter, had basic EMT skills, and as the first responder, her assessment was critical.

"He was alert and oriented times three when I reached him approximately ten minutes ago," Jac said. "By his account, he took a header. His memory for exactly what happened is vague. There's a full-thickness ten-centimeter laceration on his forehead. Moving all fours, he walked down here with help."

Mallory crouched in front of Ray and flicked her penlight into his eyes. Both pupils equal and reactive. "Hey, Kingston. Did you knock yourself out?"

Ray frowned. "I don't think so, but I don't exactly remember."

"Good enough." She palpated his carotid, noting a strong, rapid pulse. She pulled the blood pressure cuff and stethoscope from her kit and tossed it to Jac. "Check his BP, will you."

"Sure thing," Jac said, wrapping the cuff around his upper arm.

While Jac worked, Mallory slid her hand around the back of Ray's neck, running her fingertips over each spinous process in his cervical spine, searching for tenderness or irregularities. No evidence of damage.

Jac said, "One ten over eighty."

"Good." Mallory took her stethoscope from Jac and moved the diaphragm quickly over his chest. Heart sounds sharp and clear. Moving air through both lungs. After slinging the stethoscope around her neck, she ran her hands up and down both his arms, then both legs. "Give me your right hand."

Ray grasped her hand and she said, "Squeeze." When he did, she repeated the process with his left hand, then had him lift first his left leg and then his right while she pressed down on them. Good strength in all four extremities.

Leaning back on her heels, she said, "It looks like the head trauma is the worst of it, Ray. I'm going to have the helicopter drop a Stokes. I don't want you walking out."

"Oh, frak no," Ray protested. "No way am I getting lifted out of here. I'll never live it down." He glanced at Jac, his expression pleading. "Come on, buddy. Tell her I'm okay."

Mallory stiffened, waiting for a challenge.

"Have a heart, will ya," Jac said, sounding pained. "You don't really want me to buck the boss on the very first day, do you?"

"I'll never be able to show my face around here again."

Jac clapped him on the shoulder. "Sure you will. Go along with the program, and I'll let everybody know you would have beat my ass back to base if you hadn't had to follow me off trail to make sure I didn't get lost."

Ray studied Jac, a furrow forming between his brows. "Thanks, I owe you."

"Nah."

Mallory moved a few feet away and radioed for the litter. While she directed Benny to drop the long line down into the clearest part of the trail, she regarded the steep side of the ravine and mentally extrapolated where Jac had been running along the crest when she'd left her. Considering where they were now, Jac would've had no reason to deviate from the yellow trail.

"Russo," Mallory called. "You want to handle getting the Stokes down? Let's see what kind of retrieval skills you've got."

"Sure thing, Boss." Jac sprinted to the clearing and craned her neck to watch the slow descent of the lightweight metal stretcher from the belly of the helicopter. When the lower edge of the stretcher was just above her head, she caught it and guided it to the ground, released the winch hook, gave it two sharp tugs, and stepped back so the line could be reeled up and away. Once the heavy metal hook was above her head and there was no danger of it swinging around and catching her, she lifted the stretcher and carried it back to where Mallory crouched beside Ray.

"Nice work," Mallory said. Jac had been efficient and careful. Full marks. "All right, Ray, let's get you in here."

Grumbling, he started to rise, and almost instantly moaned, "Oh frak." Groaning, he lurched away and vomited.

"Okay," Mallory said briskly, grasping him around the waist as

Jac steadied him with a hand on his shoulder. "Let's get you horizontal again."

They got him stretched out on his back in the Stokes, strapped in with a cervical collar around his neck, within seconds. Mallory glanced at Jac. "Ready?"

"Yes ma'am," Jac replied and signaled for the long line. The winch played out, the hook swung into view, and she connected it to the O-ring on the basket. Two sharp tugs and the Stokes started to ascend, Ray gently swaying as the helicopter pulled him in.

Mallory stood, the tension draining from her back and shoulders, the exhilaration of accomplishment flooding through her chest. She'd never worked with Jac before, but they'd read each other well and functioned naturally as a team. There'd been none of the push-pull that often accompanied working with a new partner. Silently, she gathered her gear and started rapidly back up the trail to base. Jac wasn't her partner, she swiftly reminded herself. Jac was a rookie, and she'd just failed the first leg of boot camp.

❖

Jac jogged beside Mallory in silence, the drone of the helicopter slowly fading as it outdistanced them on the trip back to camp. She tried not to think about what came next for her. Ray still needed attention, and his welfare was a lot more important than her performance rating. Ordinarily, she didn't mind silence, most of the time she preferred it. The casual chatter around a TV set waiting for the next call or friendly ribbing over cards, whiling away sleepless hours in the middle of the night, was one thing—that kind of aimless conversation made it easy to avoid revealing personal information. The guys she'd worked with last summer, even most of the troops she'd been stationed with, didn't associate her name with her father. Some of her commanding officers had known of her family connections, but they were too short-staffed and too harried to care about anything other than what she could do with an IED. The anonymity was a relief after growing up in the spotlight.

Right at the moment, though, she would have given a lot to know what was on Mallory James's mind. The woman never even broke a sweat, all-out running with a pack on her back. Her smooth, unlined face was as calm and unreadable as a carved statue. Her focus was almost eerie, and Jac had the sudden, suicidal inclination to say something provocative just to see that cool façade crack a little bit. A smile. Hell, even a frown. Something to get inside, underneath that icy exterior. Never mind provoking James was probably a really bad idea. Delving into another woman's personal space really wasn't her thing. She could hardly ask anyone to respect her privacy when she didn't respect theirs, so she'd developed a hands-off attitude over the years. She accepted what was given, and never asked for more. She let it be known she wanted the same in return. She'd done really well with that approach until Annabel Clinton. Annabel had not only gotten her to break her own rules, she'd completely snowed her.

She'd met Annabel at a club in Boise right after she'd gotten back from her third ten-month tour in Iraq. She'd been more than ready for the company of a woman who didn't know her and who seemed to want nothing more than an uncomplicated physical relationship. Annabel had said she was a student at the University of Idaho, and Jac had never thought to question Annabel's appearance in her life until the first article appeared in the *National Enquirer* about Franklin Russo's lesbian daughter. Along with a photograph that made the claim pretty unassailable. In the photo, thankfully fairly grainy, she'd been sitting on the side of a bed naked with a woman straddling her lap. You couldn't see exactly where her arm was going, but it didn't take much imagination to know her hand was between the woman's legs. Annabel's face didn't show, but hers was recognizable. She still wasn't sure where the camera had been, probably in the closet of the motel room. Annabel had insisted the twenty-minute drive to her apartment was too long for her to wait to have Jac inside her, and she'd picked the hot-sheet motel. Maybe she hadn't lied about the not being able to wait part, though. Some things you couldn't fake.

When the picture hit the newsstands, her father had claimed Jac needed to disappear from public awareness for the sake of her mother's health. His political aspirations were not the issue, he'd said, and perhaps he hadn't been exaggerating too much about her mother. She had her sister to think of too, and Carly was already having a hard enough time in school without more familial notoriety. She'd disappeared all right, but now it looked like that plan was going to fall apart.

"What now?" Jac said as she and Mallory emerged from the forest.

"I need to check Ray," Mallory said. "But you go grab a shower. Join the rest of the group. Get something to eat."

"I'd rather tag along with you. See how Ray's doing."

Mallory glanced at her. "How is it you wandered off that trail? I didn't see any sign of Ray when I came up behind you this morning. Where did he come from?"

Jac shrugged and switched her attention to the other rookies clustered in front of the hangar, who pretended not to be watching them. "I don't remember exactly how it went down."

"Uh-huh. And it doesn't bother you that the other guys are going to think you screwed up?"

"Does it really matter?"

"Maybe not what they think. But it matters what I do."

"Look," Jac said, "I know I didn't finish the course and—"

"Let's get Ray squared away. Then you and I will have a sit-down."

"Okay. You're calling the shots." Relieved that Mallory was letting the subject drop, at least temporarily, Jac reached for the door of the standby shack and pulled it open, stepping aside for Mallory to pass through.

Mallory regarded her quizzically. "Thanks."

Jac realized what she'd done and laughed. "Sorry. My mother raised me to be chivalrous."

A smile flickered across Mallory's mouth, almost but not quite cracking her impenetrable cool. "Interesting fact."

"I'm just a mass of them."

"Really." Mallory kept walking, leaving Jac to follow in her wake.

The infirmary occupied a small room off the main building and held three beds, well-stocked equipment carts, and several locked medication cabinets. A Native American who Jac presumed was Benny, given his flight jacket, stood beside a bed where Ray now lay under a snowy white sheet. Another guy with curly blond hair and a slow grin who Jac recognized from the cafeteria that morning leaned against the far wall. One of the regular smokejumpers.

Mallory strode directly to the bed and leaned over Ray. "How's the stomach?"

"About like my head," Ray said, his voice tight and strained. "Both a little bit off."

"Headache?" Mallory shone her penlight into Ray's eyes again, and he winced, slamming his lids shut.

"Little bit."

"Got a little photophobia there too," Mallory muttered. She glanced at Benny, who had just taken Ray's blood pressure. "Vitals?"

"Nice and stable. One twelve over seventy, pulse is ninety."

"We're going to keep you here overnight, Ray," Mallory said. "I don't want you getting up and walking around. You've probably got postconcussion syndrome, and it may take a day or two for your stomach to settle and the headache to resolve. You know the drill. If anything changes—if you notice any weakness, alteration in sensation, worsening of the headache—let whoever is with you know right away."

"Can't I just—"

"No," Mallory said quietly. "You need to be here. Either that, or in a hospital."

"Jeez, don't do that."

"I won't, not as long as you're stable."

"Fine. Anything you say."

Mallory smiled. "Naturally." She signaled to the guy against the wall. "Cooper, can you pull a suture set for me. I want to take care of his forehead."

"Sure thing, Ice. I'll get everything set up for you. Hey, Ray. Any allergies or anything?"

"No," Ray said and started to shake his head. He moaned and went pale again. "Oh man. I hope this doesn't last long. I hate to puke."

"I'm with you there," Mallory said, giving his shoulder a squeeze.

Jac tried not to stare when Mallory rose, shrugged out of her pack, and removed her jacket and sweatshirt. Her throat went dry watching Mallory walk to a small sink in the corner and wash her hands and arms. The back of her tank was sweat stained, a vertical diamond between her shoulder blades a shade darker than the rest. Jac didn't see the outline of a bra, and couldn't help but check out Mallory's breasts when she turned. Not too big, firm and round. Tight-nippled. Damn it, she was so damn hot. "Ice" couldn't be further from the truth. Jac swallowed, her mouth feeling as if it were stuffed with cotton. She couldn't ever remember a woman affecting her this way, especially one who wasn't the slightest bit interested in her. She cleared her throat. "Can I give you a hand?"

Mallory regarded her in that implacable, unreadable way for a long second. "Sure. I could use an assist."

"Great." Jac removed her own sweatshirt, washed up, and sorted through the glove packs Cooper had placed beside the suture tray on top of a metal stand. "Sevens?"

"Seven and a half." Mallory's gaze drifted over Jac's hands. "Eights?"

"Yeah."

Mallory opened the suture pack and snapped on her gloves. After Mallory filled the syringe with local anesthetic, Jac handed her one of the Betadine swabs that came in the suture pack. Mallory efficiently cleaned the area around the laceration in Ray's forehead. "I'm going to anesthetize you, Ray. It'll sting for a few minutes."

"Yeah, sure, no problem," Ray muttered wearily, his eyes closed. He didn't budge when Mallory inserted the needle multiple times along the edges of the laceration, injecting the local anesthetic with epinephrine designed to decrease the slow trickle of blood.

While Mallory did that, Jac opened suture packs and loaded needle holders for her. Then she found suture scissors and waited to cut suture as Mallory tied.

Mallory was quick and adept, and within a few minutes the laceration was closed with a neat row of running black nylon sutures. Jac had assisted on or performed the same procedure a dozen times herself, but she didn't think she'd ever seen anyone look sexier while suturing. She felt dampness accumulate between her breasts and down the center of her belly and between her legs, and only part of it was from the heat in the room. Just being in the vicinity of Ice James made her unaccountably hot. Too bad she wouldn't be around long enough to try thawing out the ice.

CHAPTER FIVE

Mallory snapped off her gloves and tossed them into the wastebasket. As she taped a light dressing to Ray's forehead, Jac cleared away the instruments, working quickly and efficiently. That seemed to be Jac's modus operandi—quick, efficient, capable, strong. Capable? Strong? Now where did that come from? Most firefighters were competent and capable—you didn't last long in the job if you weren't. Male or female, it made no difference—all were skilled professionals. Jac was no different. Mallory was the one behaving differently, so hyperaware of Jac's presence her concentration was shot. While she'd been suturing and Jac had been assisting, Jac's shoulder had brushed hers, their arms had crossed, their hands had touched. Nothing that didn't happen all the time in close working quarters. Only her skin never tingled and her stomach never did slow rolls when she casually brushed against other firefighters.

Enough already. She had one goal and one goal only. To take care of her team. Nothing else mattered.

"Okay then, Ray," Mallory said, adjusting the sheet over his chest. "Get some sleep. Cooper will be here for a while, then I'll be back."

"Thanks, Boss," Ray muttered, keeping his eyes closed.

Mallory turned to look for Cooper, but her gaze landed unerringly on Jac. Her instinct was to look immediately away, but she couldn't. Jac stood three feet from her, watching her with a contemplative expression, as if waiting for Mallory to answer an unspoken question. Mallory wanted to say *Stop, don't look at me, don't ask me any questions, don't ask anything of me.* In the next breath she wanted to close the distance, obliterate the space between them. Say *See me, touch me.* That was completely crazy. Her imagination was out of control. Jac wasn't doing anything at all.

"We're done here." Mallory took a step back, needing to sever the connection she didn't want and hadn't asked for. When she looked away, the hypnotic pull of Jac's dark eyes broke, releasing her, and she was caught off guard by a swift surge of loneliness, as if she had lost something she hadn't known she needed. She countered the momentary weakness with a surge of temper. She did not want this. And she definitely did not need it. "Meet me on the hangar deck in ten minutes."

"I'll be there."

"Good." Mallory had to find her footing, reestablish control. She was the team leader. Her path was clear. All she had to do was keep her distance, and she'd be fine. This strange draw she felt to Jac Russo would disappear fast enough once they got back on the training schedule.

Mallory spun on her heel and left the infirmary as quickly as she could without seeming to flee. Outside, she found the other rookies still congregated in front of the hangar. Striding over to them, she answered their unspoken question. "Ray got a little banged up out on the trail, but he's stable now. You all made it in under the required time, so you're good. Everyone take a break. This afternoon, we'll work with full packs, so eat a big lunch."

Her announcement was met with grins and a chorus of approval.

"Sure thing."

"Roger that."

"Yes, Cap."

Hooker stepped a little apart from the crowd. "Russo find him?"

Mallory hesitated. She didn't buy Jac's story—the timing and terrain didn't support the sequence of events, but she wasn't sure why Jac had put forth the explanation. Until she knew more, she didn't want to lay responsibility on her. "The details are a little sketchy right now. Ray is sleeping."

"Are we going to evacuate Kingston to a regional medical center?"

"No need to. He's doing fine."

"If he goes bad, it's an hour to the nearest hospital."

"He was never unconscious." Mallory kept her temper in check. Maybe Hooker was just worried about one of his colleagues. Maybe. "There's no evidence of serious injury, and he's being carefully monitored. He doesn't want to go, and I don't see any reason to send him at this point."

"Sure thing, Boss," Hooker said, his tone just short of sarcastic. "Whatever you say."

He swaggered away, his tone and manner cocky. Mallory wasn't surprised or even all that bothered. She'd seen plenty of firefighters like him, guys who thought they knew better than all their bosses, male or female. Not that many females headed teams, but that was mostly because there just weren't that many in the system. The few ranking women were usually well respected and had no problems. But when you worked in a predominately male profession with guys who made the word *macho* sound prissy, you were bound to run up against some guys who resented female authority. Maybe Hooker was in that camp, maybe not. Right now, she couldn't worry about it. She had one injured rookie and another who by rights should be packing to go home. She should already have told Jac Russo to go home. Russo hadn't been her pick, and she didn't want Russo on the team. Boot camp was designed to root out the physically unfit and the psychologically ill-suited for smokejumping. The course was rigorous for good reasons and rookies didn't get second chances. She had a perfectly legitimate reason to let Russo go.

Mallory headed toward the hangar, wondering why she wasn't even certain what she was going to say when Jac showed up, let alone what she was going to do. Her avoidance of the simple, obvious decision couldn't have anything to do with the way Jac looked at her. She wouldn't let it.

❖

Jac leaned down over Ray and said, "Check you later, buddy." He was already asleep. Straightening, she said to Cooper, "I'll be by in a while, but if something changes, would you give me a holler?"

"Friend of yours?"

"He is now."

Cooper nodded. A veteran like him would appreciate how strongly and quickly allegiances were forged among those on the line. "Sure thing, rookie. See you in a bit."

"If I'm still around," Jac muttered. She left the infirmary and headed across the yard to keep her appointment with Ice James, trying not to dwell on what was about to come down. Nothing *she* could do to alter the facts. Whether she stayed or whether she left was completely up to Mallory. She hadn't passed the first leg of boot camp, and no excuses would be offered. The job was black and white. There was no such thing as a margin for error when fighting a fire. Errors meant injury or death. There were no second chances, no do-overs, no remediation. Mallory had made it pretty clear first thing that morning that she wouldn't make any kind of concessions for Jac, and why should she? Out here, Jac was the same as everyone else. A firefighter whose past was unimportant, whose place was defined by her performance and nothing else. She wouldn't have it any other way and wanted nothing more out of her life than to be judged by her actions, not by the words or opinions of others. So now, she could hardly argue that the verdict be based on anything other than her performance. Not her intentions, not her desires, not her needs.

Jac stared at the dark recesses of the hangar, feeling as if she were walking into the belly of the whale. Taking a breath, she entered the cavernous space. The jump plane occupied the place of honor in the center of the room, poised like a great beast ready to leap from its hiding place into action at the first sight of prey. Benches holding machine parts and tools lined the far wall. The air smelled like engine oil and metal shavings—tart and pungent. The space exuded an anticipatory feeling, as if waiting for the adventure to begin. She remembered Mallory saying she slept in the loft and imagined her asleep, surrounded by the scent of machines. She wasn't surprised Mallory slept just one step away from the aircraft that would carry her to the fire line. Mallory struck her as a woman who welcomed a worthy opponent. She liked that about her. Liked it a lot.

"Boss?"

"In the back," Mallory's voice called her.

Jac found her sitting at a scratched wooden desk pushed into the far back corner of the hangar. A bulletin board was nailed to the metal sheet siding above it, and neat stacks of paper sat in several black plastic trays along the back of the desk. A straight-back wooden chair was the only other furniture besides the swivel captain's chair in which Mallory now sat. She half turned as Jac approached and gestured to the chair beside the desk. "Have a seat."

Jac settled as comfortably as she could on the uncomfortable chair, crossed her left leg over her right knee, rested her hands on her thighs, and waited. The ball was in Mallory's court.

Mallory tapped a pencil on the faded desk blotter, its green surface covered with notes—mostly map coordinates, weather information, telephone numbers. Jac wondered idly if Mallory had made all those notes when talking to dispatchers about fire locations. She looked from the tapping pencil into Mallory's eyes. The green was denser now, shadowed with questions. Her tank wasn't all that tight, but Jac had no problem conjuring a mental image of her breasts beneath the thin cotton. She swallowed, looked away.

"You want to tell me again what happened out there?" Mallory finally said.

That wasn't the question Jac had expected. "Between us?"

Mallory's expression never changed, but the green of her eyes smoldered to almost black. "Anything you and I talk about is always just between us."

"Sorry," Jac said. "Force of habit."

"What do you mean?"

Jac shook her head. "It's not important."

"Why don't you let me decide?"

"Most people asking questions are in the market to publicize the answers."

"Reporters, you mean?"

Jac foundered in the conversation. Already the discussion had taken a direction she didn't anticipate and didn't really want to go. But she found herself going there anyhow. "Don't you read the newspapers?"

Mallory smiled. "I know who you are, if that's what you mean."

"Really? Who am I?"

"I see what you mean," Mallory said after a minute. "That was an asinine thing for me to say, wasn't it? Let me rephrase. I know who the newspapers say you are. I know who your father is. I don't know a damn thing about you."

"Well then, you're the first person I've ever met who feels that way."

"Actually, I misspoke. I do know something about you. You're a damn good runner. And you know something about helicopter evacuation. Why is that?"

Jac's head started to spin. Mallory's questions weren't linear. The conversation wasn't what she expected. Neither was Mallory James. "I was in Iraq. I've seen a lot of helicopter evacuations from some pretty tight spaces."

"Really. What did you do there?"

"I disarmed explosives."

Mallory flashed on all the news images and photos she'd seen of the horrors wrought by IEDs. She imagined defusing one, how vulnerable a person would be in the face of such massive destruction. Giving herself time to absorb the information, Mallory carefully set the pencil down in the center of the blotter, lining it up at perfect right angles to the edge. Jac wasn't the first vet she'd met; in fact, it seemed that a higher percentage of hotshots and smokejumpers were veterans than in many other professions. Maybe because service was part of their blood. She knew female vets, women who'd been bloodied in combat, but she'd never met anyone who'd been an explosives tech before. She only knew what she'd read about them. She almost smiled at that— more secondhand info. No wonder Jac was used to being judged by something other than herself. "Why did you choose to do that?"

"I have steady hands."

"I noticed when you were cutting sutures for me. Not even the slightest sign of a tremor."

Jac laughed. "I wouldn't have lasted very long out there if I had one."

"You're also really good at sidestepping questions."

"Survival skills. Although I'm not quite so good at that as I am at defusing improvised explosive devices," Jac said, bitterness lacing her voice.

"So what's the answer? Are you going to tell me it's because you don't fear death or because you don't care if you die?"

"Is this line of investigation germane to my position here, Captain James?"

"I think it is. It makes a huge difference to me whether I can trust you to take care of yourself out there, or if you're going to do something wild and crazy and get yourself or someone else killed."

"I don't have a death wish," Jac said.

"That's not quite the same as not caring if you die, though, is it?" Mallory was pushing and didn't care. She'd meant what she said about needing to know if she had a cowboy on the team. But she wanted to know about Jac—she wanted to know her.

"You're getting awfully personal."

"What we do, all of us here every day, is as personal as it gets. And you still haven't answered the question."

"I did it because I could," Jac said, realizing she'd never really answered the question in her own mind before. The job was there, she knew she could do it, and she wanted to be alone when she worked. She took a breath, decided not to second-guess her answer, and that was new for her. From the time she was twelve or so, old enough to understand who her father was and what that meant for her, she'd stopped having spontaneous conversations. He was a public person, and by extension so was she. She'd quickly learned to think before she spoke. Weigh her answers. Judge the impact of what she said. She almost never said anything that she hadn't mentally prescreened. After a while she didn't feel anything she hadn't examined, judged, assessed. Except with Annabel, and look where that got her. Here. Sitting in the hot seat across from Mallory James. She wanted to tell Mallory something of herself with complete and total freedom. She didn't ask why.

"Plenty of guys get shot over there, but warfare medicine—it's awesome. Most live. But the ones who die—most of the time they die in explosions. The IEDs are inhuman. The worst thing any of us have ever seen. Indiscriminate weapons designed for the greatest degree of destruction. Completely without honor. I hate them, and I wanted to be the one to take them out."

"The one," Mallory murmured. "You alone?"

"Yes," Jac said instantly. "Just me and the device. One on one. As personal as it gets."

"Some people would say that fire is personal," Mallory murmured. "But out there, Jac, you can't fight alone."

"I know."

"And I have to be able to trust you to remember that."

"I know."

"What happened out on the trail today?"

"Ray fell, I found him. I rendered emergency care and waited for backup."

Mallory nodded. "And what's the story you're going to tell the rest of the team?"

"What I told Ray I would. It doesn't matter to me if a couple of the guys think I screwed up. It matters to him. I don't know why, I only know it matters. He's a good guy, I like him."

"Why didn't you signal for a spotter? You must have seen them circling every few minutes. That ravine is tricky—even with guide ropes. Which you didn't have." Mallory spoke levelly, almost offhandedly, but her eyes were searching. "Why didn't you do the smart thing—the prescribed thing—and wait for backup up on the trail?"

Jac suppressed a shudder, her skin vibrating as if Mallory were running her hands over her the way she had Ray out in the field—examining, studying, weighing and measuring. Measuring her. She was used to being judged, but this time she wanted the opinion to be based on who she really was, not an assumption.

"I didn't know how seriously he was injured, but he appeared unconscious." She shrugged. "I wasn't going to stand up on that trail waving my arms in the air while a guy died from respiratory obstruction or bled out."

"Judgment call?"

Jac's jaws ached, and she made an effort to unclamp her teeth. "That's right."

"You didn't finish the course today," Mallory said in that infuriating calm tone.

"Are you gonna wash me out?"

"Why shouldn't I?"

"No reason at all." Jac sucked in a breath. She wouldn't make an excuse, but she wouldn't go quietly either. "Except—"

Mallory leaned forward. "Except what?"

"Except I'm a damn good runner, and I climb as well as I run. And if you'd been up on that crest today, you would have done exactly what I did. Any good smokejumper would have."

Mallory smiled but her eyes were flat. "You think you have me figured out?"

"I know I don't. But I know I want to."

Mallory leaned back in her chair, the cool mask sliding into place. "You've got half an hour to get something to eat, then you and I are going out for a run. Let's see if you make the time. Last chance."

"Why don't we run with packs this time?" Jac rose, wondering where along the trail this morning she'd lost her mind. Maybe when she smelled the honeysuckle.

"Ever run with eighty-five pounds on your back?"

"No, but I know I can do it."

Mallory stood, and they were very close together. Jac caught the scent of honeysuckle and saw a trickle of perspiration track down Mallory's neck. She wanted to catch it on the tip of her tongue. She raised her eyes to Mallory's face and wondered if Mallory could read what was in her mind, because the green of her eyes had changed yet again, brightening, gleaming, reminding her of a secluded forest glade on a spring morning. Ripe with invitation.

"All right, Russo," Mallory said softly. "Let's see what you're made of."

CHAPTER SIX

B y 1300, the early May day was as warm as late June, and Jac started to sweat a minute into the run. She'd stripped down to her T-shirt and cargo pants in anticipation of the long, hot, hard run, even though she knew the eighty-five-pound pack was going to chafe her shoulders without a jacket to cushion the weight. A calculated risk. She wanted to make good time. Hell, she wanted more than that. She wanted to beat Mallory back to base, fully loaded, running all out. Dumb, yeah, but she couldn't shake the feeling there was more on the line than a temporary six-month posting or even whether or not she moved on to the next round of boot camp. This felt personal—between her and Mallory. She'd gotten so used to others taking her at face value, or what they assumed to be face value, she'd long ago stopped caring what people thought of her. From the instant she'd met Mallory that morning, everything had been different. She'd felt judged, sure, but that was nothing new. What was new was she cared that the woman making the judgment know the truth about her. If she was gonna wash out, she was gonna make the decision hard for Mallory.

Not exactly a brilliant plan, and definitely not the best one she'd ever had. She was going to have to work to impress Mallory, because the woman was a machine. Mallory ran effortlessly beside her, a zip-up canvas jacket over her T-shirt. Standard field apparel under her pack, not as heavy as a Kevlar jump jacket but still damn hot, and not a drop of sweat showed on her forehead or her neck. Jac's T-shirt already clung to her back and between her breasts, wet through.

Mallory caught her looking and observed calmly, "You're flirting with heat exhaustion."

"I'm not the one wearing a coat." Jac wasn't breathing heavily and could still talk while running, which was proof enough that her cardiovascular state was pretty damn good. She tried not to look self-satisfied. "I think you're the one who needs to worry about the heat."

"You're running pretty close to a five-minute mile, which might be impressive on a high school track, but it's just plain stupid out here in the mountains," Mallory said, more worried than aggravated. She didn't need another rookie down, and Jac was setting a blazing pace over unpredictable ground. The trail was scarcely a trail, more like a barely trodden path through densely packed trees and heavy undergrowth. No point training on groomed trails—there wouldn't be any of those where the jump plane dropped them.

Jac was a smart runner, clearly gauging the terrain ahead in time to cut around fallen trees and other obstacles, skirting frozen patches of runoff in the shadow of boulders, at home in the mountains the way many rookies weren't. Experienced firefighters didn't always acclimate to mountain terrain. City fires held their own inherent dangers—burning buildings that collapsed in on themselves, trapping firefighters between floors, abandoned warehouses and garages filled with flammable chemicals, unstable rooftops that gave way underfoot. But the mountains waged war not with man-made artillery, but nature's most fundamental weapon—the earth itself. Valleys acted like funnels, propelling flames on downdrafts to flank firefighters and cut them off from their escape routes. Mountain ridges hid advancing fire fronts until a blowup surged over a crest, catching a team far from its safety zone. Timber went up like tinder, fire soaring from treetop to treetop, a juggernaut of annihilation. Jac needed to be more than fast, she needed to be vigilant, and caution did not seem to be in her vocabulary.

Mallory dropped back a step to watch her. The pack on Jac's back shifted a few inches from side to side with every long stride. Rookie mistake, running with that much weight and no coat to absorb the stress. Even so, she seemed comfortable, her breathing even, her stride regular. She was in excellent physical condition. Her shoulders were broad and muscled, tapering to a narrow waist and hips that weren't much wider. Even in her heavy cargo pants, her ass was tight, her thighs muscular and hard-looking. She had a great body. Heavy tension coiled between Mallory's legs.

Shock raced through her, nearly throwing her off stride. She didn't look at women that way. Not even when she was interested in a date, and never in the field, never a fellow firefighter. She dated women who were easy to talk to, women whose interests were as far away from what she did every day as possible—teachers or businesswomen or waitresses. She didn't date firefighters or forest rangers or cops or emergency medical personnel. She didn't choose dates for their looks and didn't care if they slept with her or not, as long as they were easygoing, quick to laugh, calm and steady. Jac was nothing like that. Jac was as tantalizing and dangerous as fire.

Mallory dropped back farther, needing space where there shouldn't have been any connection at all.

Jac glanced back over her shoulder. "Want to stop and unload that jacket?"

"Just keep running, Russo, and watch where you're going," Mallory said.

Jac flashed her a cocky grin, jumped over a nest of fallen logs, and raced on, leaving a trail of spice and musk. Mallory kept her focus on the trail, running in Jac's wake, Jac's scent sliding over her skin.

❖

Twenty-four minutes later, the end of the trail was in sight, and Jac slowed. She was ahead of Mallory, but she hadn't outpaced her and didn't want it to look as if she had when she reached the yard. Mallory could have overtaken her easily, but she'd never tried. Mallory ran right beside her, right where she'd been the entire run, still breathing easy, still cool and unruffled. Nothing to prove. Mallory knew how good she was. Another thing Jac liked about her, her self-assuredness. She wasn't arrogant, didn't need to throw her authority around. Confidence was sexy on a woman. But there was something, wasn't there? Something that drove her to drive herself—the woman slept with her plane after all. And whatever was driving her probably put that haunted look in her eyes when she didn't think anyone was looking. Jac had been looking, she just didn't know how to ask.

Now sure wasn't the time.

The last few miles had passed in total silence. All she'd been able to hear had been Mallory's deep rhythmic breathing, the sigh of the wind, and the call of birds she never saw. She'd run in and out of patches of sunlight that heated her skin, making the shadows and cool breezes under the heavy canopy all the more welcome. She loved running through the woods, cloistered in semidarkness, enveloped by the sweet allure of honeysuckle. The flare of artillery against the night sky, the bright bursts of camera flashes on a raised podium, the crush of crowds at a political rally all disappeared. She could take a deep breath. Out here she could relax her vigilance, she could be free.

"Good run," Jac called. She hadn't looked at her watch, she didn't need to. Her time was good, better than it would've been that morning. Running with Mallory inspired her. Her muscles felt looser, her blood richer, her mind clearer. "You're a great partner."

"What?" Mallory said, sounding shocked.

"Running. You're great to run with. You bring out my best."

Mallory laughed, an edge of disbelief or maybe denial sharpening her tone. "Do you always say the first thing that comes into your mind?"

"You have no idea how *not* true that is." Jac stopped at the end of the trail, raised her leg behind her, and caught her foot, stretching her quads. She repeated the motion on the other leg.

Mallory mirrored her stretches. "What do you mean?"

"Remember what I told you about reporters? I learned pretty young to think twice before I spoke. The older I got, the longer I thought."

"That sounds like a drag."

Jac nodded. "Yeah. It is."

"Well then," Mallory said, her voice oddly gentle, "I'm glad you seem to have forgotten to do that recently."

"Me too." Jac had enough sense not to say the change in her normal hypervigilance was entirely due to Mallory. Being around Mallory made her want to be real—whatever that was for her anymore.

"How are your shoulders?" Mallory asked, sauntering out into the yard.

Following, Jac grinned. Nothing got past Mallory. "Little bit sore."

"Uh-huh. I'll bet." Mallory narrowed her eyes at her. "Let's head for the showers, and I'll take a look at them."

"So what's the verdict?" Jac kept her voice low. The other four rookies lingered outside the standby shack, pretending they weren't watching, but casting surreptitious glances in their direction, no doubt hoping to psych out her fate. She'd rather tell them the outcome herself, especially if it was going to be bad.

"Your time is good, but you don't need me to tell you that," Mallory said.

"But it's not just about the time, is it?"

"You already know it isn't."

"But this morning, all that mattered was that we finished the course."

"A lot can change in a few hours," Mallory murmured.

"Yeah, I know." Jac waved to the guys on her way into the building and headed for the showers. A lot had already changed between this morning and now, and all of it had to do with Mallory James.

❖

Mallory followed Jac inside the shack, emptied her pack and stored her gear, and headed for the locker room to shower and change. She stumbled to a halt just inside the door, treated to the vision of Jac's naked back and her firm butt in tight black briefs. She hadn't considered they would be showering together, and if she had, she would've found some excuse to stop in her office first. She wasn't shy about showering with other women. Seeing women naked wasn't sexual for her, at least not when the goal was to wash away sweat and smoke in the aftermath of a long, hard shift. But then she hadn't anticipated the effect of Jac being practically naked just a few feet away, and she should have. She'd been nearly mesmerized just watching her run, completely clothed. The naked version was bound to be just as captivating. She just hadn't realized how *much* better.

Her throat was tight, and her heart pounded so hard she was certain her T-shirt was vibrating. To make matters worse, Jac turned around and caught her staring. Jac's eyebrows rose and her mouth lifted in an irritatingly knowing smile. And damn it, if she didn't just stand there, relaxed and naked and so damn sexy.

"Something wrong?" Jac murmured.

"No," Mallory said, relieved she sounded normal. At least, she thought she did. Her ears were ringing, so it was hard to tell. "I want to take a look at your shoulders. If you're blistered, you're not going to be comfortable in the safety harness, and you're not going to jump until you are."

"We're going to jump soon?" Jac's face brightened, her expression so innocently joyful, Mallory's heart actually gave a little tug. She wouldn't have believed that was possible.

"Like I said, it depends on your shoulders."

Jac seemed completely unperturbed by her nearly nude state and leaned back against the lockers, resting her hands on her hips. Her torso was even better from the front than the back. Her breasts were small and round and tipped with pale chocolate nipples, neat and very hard.

"If you're thinking about whether or not I can jump, does that mean I'm still in?"

"As far as everyone else is concerned, you're in." Mallory hoped she wasn't making a mistake, seeing as her judgment was warped by the strange fog that enveloped her brain every time Jac was nearby. Jac was a puzzle she wanted to unravel, an unmarked door that invited opening, a whisper of secrets demanding to be unveiled.

"What's the but?" Jac asked, her brows drawing down.

"But as far as you and I are concerned, you're on probation."

"Meaning what? If I piss you off I'm gone?"

"It's not personal, Russo. I'm not saying I agree with your judgment call this morning, but I can't argue with it either, considering that Ray got swift and appropriate treatment, and you're no worse for the wear." She peered at a red swatch she hadn't seen earlier on the side of Jac's neck. "Except for what looks like a pretty nasty scrape." She angled around the bench and cupped Jac's chin, turning her face away to get a look at the undersurface of her jaw. A half-inch-wide abrasion ran along the edge, the wound puffy and red. "Looks fairly deep. We'll want to get that cleaned up and some antibiotic ointment on it."

"I don't remember getting scratched." Jac reached up and Mallory caught her hand.

"Don't touch it," Mallory chided. "After you get showered, I'll take a closer look and put some bacitracin on it."

Jac laughed. "Does every rookie get such personalized attention?"

"No," Mallory said, her throat tight enough to make her voice hoarse. Jac's fingers closed around hers. They were warm, strong, surprisingly soft. Their bodies nearly touched. If she leaned forward another inch, their mouths would brush. Jac's pupils widened, the deep brown of her irises condensing until her eyes were the black of a moonless night. Dark and seductive, and Mallory felt herself falling. She let go of Jac's hand so quickly her balance shifted, and she shot out her arm to catch herself against the metal lockers behind Jac. Her breasts brushed over Jac's, and her nipples instantly hardened. She shoved herself back off the lockers. "Sorry."

"For what?" Jac asked, her voice low and husky.

Mallory licked her lips, her mouth so dry she wasn't sure she could speak. "Shoulders. Turn around."

Slowly, Jac pivoted and braced both arms against the lockers, spreading her legs slightly as if she were waiting to be patted down. Mallory had an image of herself pressing up tight against Jac's ass, slipping her hands around the front of her body and running them over her collarbones, down over the swell of her breasts, along the tight columns of her abs. By the time she reached her thighs, she'd be molded to the swell of Jac's ass, her breasts crushed to the arch of Jac's back. Oh God, she was losing her mind.

"They're red," Mallory muttered, stepping to the side to get a closer look at Jac's shoulders without touching any part of her body. She didn't think she could control herself if she touched her right now, which was as confusing as it was infuriating. Even in the throes of passion she'd always maintained control. Always aware of her surroundings, part of her ready to pull back, pull away, adjust if the intimacy became too personal. "I think you're getting a blister along the side of your neck." Gingerly, she brushed the dark hair away from Jac's nape. The instant she touched Jac's skin, Jac jerked as if Mallory's fingertips were electrified. "Sorry."

"No problem," Jac grunted, keeping her head down. Her arms were taut, the muscles banded in her biceps and forearms. Her shoulders were bunched, tight, anticipatory. Jac reminded Mallory of a jungle cat preparing to pounce, and she wasn't sure she'd resist. Disgusted with her unprofessionalism and lack of control, Mallory backed up so quickly her calves smacked into the bench in the middle of the room. "Ow, damn it."

Jac gave her a look over her shoulder. "Are you all right?"

"Dandy."

"So, am I going to jump?" Jac asked, starting to turn.

Mallory held up her hand, wanting nothing more than to get out of Jac's presence until she was able to rein in her runaway libido. "I want to take a look at your neck again later, make sure it's not blistering. But if it's no worse, yes, you can jump."

"It's nothing," Jac insisted.

"No heroics, remember," Mallory said. "Don't make me give you any more demerits today."

"Demerits? What is this, scout camp?"

Mallory laughed in spite of herself. "You're impossible, you know that? Are you ever serious?"

"Only in secret."

"What do you mean?" Mallory immediately regretted asking. The conversation had veered too close to home, like so many conversations with Jac seemed to do.

"If you don't let on you care, it's harder to get hurt, right?"

Mallory's stomach twisted, and like a coward, she ran. "Not if you don't want anything to begin with, and I don't. I'm not in the market for anything."

Jac regarded her steadily. "Then I guess you're safe."

"Take your shower, Russo, then come by the infirmary." Mallory stepped over the bench, and the tightness in her chest eased. The distance helped. "I want to check on Ray, then we'll do a little first aid on your neck and back."

"I can take care of it."

"Probably." Mallory pulled the door open. "But I'll do it better."

CHAPTER SEVEN

Jac waited a full minute before pulling off her briefs—still watching the door, half hoping Mallory would walk back in. Mallory had left so quickly, Jac was still trying to figure out what she'd said or done to spook her. Whoever had nicknamed Mallory "Ice" didn't know her very well, or maybe they did, but they just didn't pay enough attention to what mattered. Ice wasn't anywhere close to describing her. Mallory was cool all right, tightly wrapped and incredibly controlled, but there was fire licking at the undersurface of that ice. A pressure cooker of hot emotion, threatening to create a fissure where all that passion would come exploding out. The flames were there in Mallory's eyes if you looked, and Jac had been looking.

Mallory had been looking at her too. Jac shuddered. The way Mallory's gaze had tracked over her body had ignited her skin and turned her insides to molten lava. When Mallory had lingered on her breasts with her lips parted as if she couldn't catch her breath, a drumbeat of need thudded in Jac's stomach. She was glad she'd still had her briefs on, because she was instantly wet. Wet and hard and if Mallory had been any closer, she would have known. Any closer for any longer and Jac might've done something exceedingly uncool. Making a move on the training instructor was a really bad way to start boot camp.

Another minute passed and the locker room door didn't open. Mallory didn't come back. Jac's skin bumped up in the cold air, and she brushed her hand over her chest as if that would warm her. She was hot, burning on the inside, but she shivered. Her fingertips brushed her breast and her stomach hollowed. She let her fingertips stray to her nipple, brushing lightly, knowing she'd regret getting herself worked up even more, but unwilling to relinquish the memory of Mallory being so close, almost touching her. The drumbeat moved lower, focused between her legs.

"I don't need this." Jac dragged her hand away from her breast. She stripped out of her briefs, grabbed a towel from a stack on a shelf opposite the lockers, and padded into the adjoining shower cubicle. Standing to one side, she wrenched on the dial and waited for the water to heat. As soon as it was steaming, she got under, braced her hands on the wall, and lowered her head to let the hot water pound over her neck and shoulders. Facing the wall, she immediately thought of leaning against the lockers with Mallory behind her. She'd gotten harder then, gotten wetter. She didn't usually think about being taken, but she'd been thinking about it then. About Mallory's mouth moving down the center of her back, about Mallory's hands reaching around to hold her breasts and squeeze her nipples. She groaned and realized her fingers had found their way back to her breasts. No way she was going to get off in the shower when Mallory might change her mind and walk back in at any minute. That's all she'd need to really convince Mallory she had a control problem. Besides making her look like a kid in summer camp, what did it say about her ability to handle the pressure of the job if she couldn't control her own body after spending five minutes naked with a woman who hadn't touched her and barely glanced at her?

"All it means is she turned you on something wicked. Not something you want her to know," Jac muttered. She rubbed her hand up and down the center of her stomach, trying to coax some of the tension out of her belly. It didn't help. Her hips flexed of their own accord, and her clitoris pulsed, sending a silent request for a little relief. "Damn it."

"Oh hey, sorry! Didn't mean to surprise you."

Jac sucked in a breath and looked over her shoulder. A cute blonde, maybe ten years older, stood with a bar of soap in one hand and a towel slung over her shoulder. She was naked, toned, and smiling with a little bit of a question in her eyes. Jac hoped the sound of the water had drowned out her talking to herself.

"No problem."

"I just drove in from New Mexico, eighteen hours straight in the car. I really need to wash off the road, and my place in town isn't ready yet. Mind if I join you?"

Jac smothered a smile. Must be her day to be surrounded by naked women. Thankfully, her clitoris chose that moment to hibernate. "No problem."

The blonde hung her towel on a peg, turned on the adjacent showerhead, and stepped under the water with a gratified groan. "Oh my God, that feels good. I'm Sarah, by the way."

Keeping eyes up, Jac pumped some shampoo into her palm from the receptacle fixed to the white-tiled wall and lathered her hair. "Jac Russo."

"You must be one of the rookies," Sarah said. "I didn't know we were getting a woman. That's cool."

"I was a last-minute addition," Jac said.

"Mallory have you out on the trail already today?"

"Oh yeah, bright and early."

Sarah laughed. "Yeah, that sounds like her. Everybody make the cut?"

"So far. We got an injury, though." Jac turned to rinse her hair.

"Oh hell. What happened?" Sarah's smile disappeared, alarm flashing through her eyes and just as quickly extinguished.

"One of the guys fell, head injury."

"Serious?"

"He's in the infirmary. Not too bad, but Mallory thinks he has a concussion."

"Damn, just what she doesn't need, you know?"

Sarah's expression suggested Jac should know what she was talking about. She didn't, but her stomach squirmed uneasily. "How so?"

"It's just—she always takes responsibility for everything that goes wrong on her watch, even the weather, for cripe's sake. And after last year…I still don't think she's stopped blaming herself." Sarah turned off the water. "She doesn't need anything else to beat herself up about."

"What happened last year?" Jac tried to sound casual as she cut off her own shower and grabbed a towel.

"You weren't around?"

"Iraq. Didn't get back until the end of July."

"Oh, that explains it, then. We lost a couple guys the end of June. Mallory was the IC. Just about killed her."

Jac's jaw tightened so hard the muscles in front of her ears ached. "That blowup in northern Idaho?"

"Yeah, that's the one."

"It happened a few weeks before I got home. I never did hear all the details. Mallory was running that team?"

"Yeah. She spotted the safety zone." Sarah wrapped her towel around her chest, pushed wet blond strands off her face with both hands. "She blames herself for the guys who didn't get out."

"She would."

"You know Mallory from somewhere?" Sarah asked, cautious curiosity in her tone. "Because I know you haven't been up here. This is my eighth season."

Jac briskly rubbed her hair. "Just met her this morning."

"Oh." Sarah studied her, one hip canted. "You sound as if…"

"What?"

"Nothing. Just—most people don't see much beyond her hard-ass attitude. I thought the two of you might be friends."

"Nope. I'm just another rookie."

"You know, Mallory doesn't talk about Idaho. I probably shouldn't have brought it up."

"She won't hear anything about it from me." Jac had her own secrets in Idaho, and hurting Mallory was the last thing she wanted to do.

❖

Jac walked into the infirmary, wanting to check on Ray before lunch. Mallory was just walking away from Ray's bedside. He was awake and looking a lot better.

"You decide to join the land of the living again?" Jac said, squatting by the side of Ray's bed. Ray's color had brightened from clay to pinkish-tan, and his face had lost the pinched, pained look. His eyes were clearer too. Some of the roiling in her stomach settled.

"I don't feel like puking anymore, which, believe me, is all I really care about." Ray turned his head, trying to see the back of the room, and groaned. "Damn, I still get queasy every time I move, though."

"Well then, don't move, idiot." Jac rolled her eyes. "You heard what Mallory said this morning. It may be a few days before the concussion wears off."

"Yeah, and what's gonna happen to me then? You know she's gonna cut me loose."

"I don't know that. Neither do you. She seems to be pretty fair."

"Speaking of fair, am I remembering right? You told her you were the one who went off trail?"

Jac shook her head. "I told her the straight story, but I don't see as how it's anybody *else's* business what went down out there. That's between the two of us."

"I'm not letting you take the heat for my dumb-ass mistake," Ray whispered roughly. "I appreciate it, I really do, but—"

"Look, it's no big deal to me what anybody else thinks. Until you're up and around, I'm sticking to the story."

"What about you? Are you in trouble with the boss?"

Jac grinned. "Nope. She's crazy about me."

Ray laughed and immediately winced. "Geez, don't do that. It feels like the top of my head is coming off whenever I laugh."

"Russo," Mallory snapped. "Let him get some rest."

The woman was like a stealth bomber—you never heard her coming until rounds started landing all around you. Jac winked at Ray. "Take it easy, buddy. Talk to you later."

Ray closed his eyes. "Yeah, yeah. Have fun until then."

"Intend to."

Jac straightened and started for the door.

"I need you to sign some forms," Mallory said. "Come on back to the office with me."

"Okay," Jac said cautiously. In her experience, paperwork was not only deadly boring, it could be dangerous. Write something down, record it, and you lost control of the facts. People could distort your words, subvert your intentions, or publicize something you might prefer to keep private. Growing up in the limelight of her father's ambitions and serving in the shadow of Don't Ask, Don't Tell had taught her never to commit anything to paper, tape, or image that she didn't want coming back to ambush her sometime later. "What's up?"

Mallory walked slightly ahead, all business again. "Incident report. Just routine. I need you to sign off on the summary. Add anything you feel is important that I might have missed."

"Can't imagine there'd be anything." As they passed the plane,

Jac noticed a pair of legs sticking out from under the fuselage. Probably Benny, checking the craft. Otherwise the hangar was empty. The rest of the guys were probably in the gym, where smokejumpers tended to congregate in between calls. Working out helped dissipate the boredom better than sitting around watching television. The first thing she noticed when they reached Mallory's secluded corner was the FAT box standing open on her desk. Rolls of tape, gauze, topical antibiotic, and field dressing packs all lined up in neat rows, everything in its place. Just like her desk. Just like Mallory. Jac had a wild urge to get her messy—just to see the fire leap in her eyes.

"First, take off your shirt," Mallory said, her back to Jac as she pulled a tube of ointment from the bag.

"Here?"

Mallory looked over her shoulder at her. "I thought you'd be more comfortable here than in the infirmary in front of Ray and Coop, but we can go back there if you—"

"No, no, this is perfect," Jac said hastily. The less fuss over her nonexistent injuries, the better. Nevertheless, when she pulled her T-shirt up over her head, the stretch of her shoulders caused her to wince. The burning she'd ignored during her run seemed to have escalated now that her shoulders were pressure free. She didn't intend on letting Mallory know she was uncomfortable, because she planned on jumping with everyone when the time came. She balled her T-shirt up in her fist and turned her back to Mallory. Stealing herself for Mallory's touch, she concentrated on breathing evenly.

Mallory's fingertips were cool as they brushed over the back of her neck and the crest of her shoulders. Jac's stomach tightened instantly, and heat blossomed between her thighs. Damn it, she was never this susceptible to casual touch.

"It still looks pretty good," Mallory murmured. "Just a few tiny blisters by your hairline. I'll put some bacitracin and a Tegaderm on it. Ought to protect it."

The ointment was cool too—icy against her warm skin, and Jac almost laughed aloud. Ice applying ice, and she felt like an inferno.

"So I'm cleared to go?" Jac turned around when she felt Mallory's fingers slide away. Once again, Mallory faced away from her, almost as if she didn't want to look at her.

"As of now, yes."

"Good, thanks." Annoyed for no good reason, Jac jerked her T-shirt on and jammed it into her jeans.

Mallory held out a clipboard with several sheets of paper on it. "Take your time. Sign at the end."

Jac read quickly, skimming the standard incident information—date, time, individuals involved, summary of the event, immediate management, outcome, emergency treatment, estimated time of recovery. What really interested her was the box labeled Potential to return to duty.

It was empty. Ray hadn't automatically been disqualified, even though he would miss several days of training, at least. A ripple of irritation went through her. She'd almost gotten canned for helping him out. Mallory hadn't cut her a second's slack, but then Mallory had made it clear that morning she wasn't going to. Well, that was okay—she was looking forward to showing Mallory she was wrong about her. She might have gotten in the door on her father's connections, but she'd be staying because she could do the job.

She also noticed that in Mallory's recounting of the incident, Ray was described as having strayed from the trail, fallen, and sustained a head injury. Jac had assisted him upon noting his situation. Nothing in the report suggested that either one of them had deviated from standard protocol running the course or following the incident.

"You write this like a politician," Jac muttered.

"No need to insult me," Mallory shot back.

Jac grinned. "I just meant you don't give anybody anything to work with."

Mallory hitched her hip onto the desk. "Do you always look at every situation as if someone is going to make money off it with a front-page article in the *Star*?"

"Pretty much. The minute I drop my guard, someone usually bites me in the ass."

"You're serious, aren't you?"

Jac hesitated. Sharing personal information, especially humiliating information, did not come easily.

"Forget I asked," Mallory said brusquely, busying herself with the bandages.

"The last woman I...dated...sold some revealing photos to the tabloids."

Mallory swung around, her eyes blazing. "That's unconscionable."

Jac shrugged. "Doesn't say much for my judgment."

"Don't be ridiculous—no part of that could be your fault."

"Ah, well, I appreciate you saying so." No way was she telling Mallory that fiasco was what had ended her up in Montana, in Mallory's boot camp. She couldn't believe she'd told Mallory anything at all about Annabel's ambush. Maybe she had a secret desire to fail or something, because Mallory couldn't think much of her now. "Wasn't the first time, just the most dramatic."

"I'm sorry, that's hateful. I suppose there's no reason for you to believe me, but you're safe here."

"I'm not even sure I know what that means."

Mallory extended her arm, as if she were about to touch Jac's cheek, and then she drew back. "Well I hope you find out."

"Yesterday I would've said it doesn't matter."

"And today?" Mallory said softly.

"Today, everything feels different."

Mallory nodded, her eyes distant, unsmiling. She glanced in the direction of the infirmary, as if checking on Ray through the walls. "I think I'd have to agree with you." Her gaze swung back to Jac. "I just don't know whether that's good or bad."

CHAPTER EIGHT

Mallory concentrated on packing up the medical supplies. The cavernous hangar suddenly seemed way too small, and Jac was way too close. Even in summer, the hangar was cool, and this early in the year it was downright cold. But Jac's naked back had been warm. So very warm. Mallory glanced at her fingertips, half expecting them to be red. They still tingled from where she'd brushed them over Jac's neck. "You should get some chow, Russo."

"Are you heading over?" Jac asked.

"Not just yet." Mallory knew she sounded dismissive, probably downright unfriendly, but she just needed a minute or two by herself to recalibrate, get her bearings. She hadn't been herself all day, not since the moment she turned around and bumped into Jac. The world had angled to tilt, and she hadn't been able to right it yet. And she really needed to—the persistent churning in her stomach was a distraction. So was the low-level buzz of arousal slightly lower down that absolutely should not be there, not when she hadn't planned on it, not when she wasn't prepared.

"Mallory?" Jac's voice came from very nearby, soft, gentle, questioning. "Everything okay?"

"Of course. I've just got some things to do." She did have plenty to do before the afternoon's exercises, but that wasn't the reason she wasn't going to have lunch with Jac. Last year at this time she would've socialized with the rookies—lending moral support, giving them a few tips, answering their questions. She'd been closer to being one of them last year. Still senior, often in charge, but she hadn't been determining their fates. At least, not consciously. Now she couldn't afford to stop thinking about what she needed to do to keep them safe, and getting friendly with them wasn't going to help her do that. The realities of the job had changed—every smokejumper lived with the knowledge that the work was dangerous, life-threatening, and any call might be their last. No one spoke of it, and she doubted that very many thought of it. She had never feared for her own life. She'd also never considered that she would be the one to walk out of the mountains beside stretchers bearing two jumpers she'd been responsible for. She would have sworn on everything she believed that she would die before she would let one of her fellows perish. She'd been wrong, and she would never be able to make that right. She could only see it never happened again. Jac was a distraction she couldn't afford, and friendship was out of the question. "You go ahead, Jac. You'll need fuel for this afternoon."

"Okay." A whisper of heat brushed over her shoulder, Jac touching her ever so briefly. "You ought to take your own advice."

The caress was so butterfly light, Mallory might've thought she'd imagined it except for the tremor coursing through her body and settling in her bones. Resolutely, she kept her back turned as Jac's footsteps faded away. Taking a deep breath, she settled herself. Jac derailed her balance like no one else she'd ever met, probably because Jac was so unpredictable. Challenging and cocky one minute, incredibly tender, unknowingly vulnerable the next. Jac was nothing like Mallory had expected, considering her family, her father, and her reputation. And wasn't that exactly what Jac had been saying since the moment she'd arrived? Jac was a problem all right, but not because she was anything like the person Mallory had assumed her to be.

Mallory sighed. Expectations based on appearances were so very often wrong, and she'd fallen right into the trap. Jac was nothing like her aloof, condescending, virulently privileged father. Jac was, if anything, remarkably open considering how careful she apparently needed to be just to protect the privacy others took for granted. God, imagine having someone you'd slept with expose your intimate moments. Mallory couldn't imagine having something so private spread across the nation in a trashy newspaper. She'd had enough trouble dealing with the media notoriety after Idaho. At first she'd been too numb to really notice the intrusion, and after a few weeks, a new story came along, and she was no longer front page. Considering that Franklin Russo was a front-runner for the presidential nomination, Jac was likely to remain in the public eye indefinitely. Was it any wonder she was so vigilant? First a lifetime of scrutiny, then a lover using her for some twisted gain.

Mallory's hands shook as she closed the locks on the FAT box. How could Jac blame herself for that woman's betrayal? She wished she knew who the woman was. She wasn't prone to violence, in fact rarely ever lost her temper, but her blood burned with the desire to do something—say something—find some way to extract a measure of justice on Jac's behalf. She laughed bitterly, and the sound echoed like bullets ricocheting against the metal roof.

Justice. Where was the justice in two men dying while she walked away? Where was the justice in Jac bearing the pain of another's betrayal? Foolish to think justice was anyone's due. Mallory sucked in a breath. She was getting morose, and she didn't have time for self-indulgence. She quickly gathered the incident report, slid the sheets into a plain manila folder, and returned the FAT box to its spot on the equipment shelf. Time to bring Sully up to date on Ray's status. Time to focus on her mission. Jac Russo could take care of herself.

"Hey, Ice," Benny called from beneath the belly of the plane. "Some exciting morning, huh?"

Mallory slowed as he rolled out on a dolly. "I could've done without it."

"I don't know, that was a pretty slick and seamless pickup this morning." He rose, wiping his hands on an oil-stained rag he pulled from the pocket of his coveralls. "Didn't seem like a rookie down there with you. The kid's pretty solid."

The kid. Benny tended to see anyone under forty as a kid, her included until she was made ops manager. Now she seemed to have graduated into adulthood. Jac was anything but a kid—a combat veteran, a veteran of political wars from the time she was young, and bloodied on the field of personal battle as well. Too many battles. "She did okay."

"The rest of the group looks pretty good too," he said.

"So far." She grinned. "Then again, it's early days."

He grinned back. "Looking forward to getting them up in the plane."

"Soon enough." She thought ahead to the first of the requisite jumps. They wouldn't be going up in the plane right away—they'd start working on the mechanics by jumping from a stationary tower first. She was looking forward to the exercises, and if she was honest with herself, looking forward to seeing how Jac handled the course. She liked watching Jac work. And that was the last time she was going to think about that.

❖

"So what's the word on Ray?" Anderson said, sliding his brown plastic lunch tray onto the table across from Jac and settling onto the bench seat. Most of the guys had already eaten, and the mess hall was nearly empty.

"He's doing better." Jac brushed cornbread crumbs off her fingers and scraped the bottom of her bowl with her spoon. "Man, this is good chili."

"It's a good thing Ice is working us so hard," Anderson said, dipping cornbread into his chili. "If I show up at home at the end of the season ten pounds heavier, my wife will never believe I spent the summer working."

"Somehow I get the feeling we'll be burning it off pretty quick." Jac buttered another piece of cornbread. "Word is we're gonna jump soon."

Anderson brightened. "Yeah? Excellent."

Hooker thumped his tray down on Anderson's left and dropped onto the seat. His tight green T-shirt accentuated his muscled chest, and a day's growth of stubble added to his roughneck image. "Not a great way to start boot camp. Can't say I'm exactly surprised, though. I had my doubts when I heard who was running the show up here."

Jac chewed carefully and swallowed. "What do you mean?"

"A bad injury on the first day? Doesn't say much for the training manager."

"Accidents happen." Jac didn't figure Mallory needed anyone defending her, but she wanted to all the same. Hooker was opinionated and abrasive, although on the surface he wasn't all that different from a lot of guys. Most of the time, once all the posturing and jockeying for position was out of the way, everybody got along. Something about Hooker put her on edge, though. He wasn't just griping about authority, he had a target. And the target was Mallory. "I don't see how Ray falling could be put on anyone. Just bad luck."

"The training manager's responsible for laying out the trails. She ought to have known if one wasn't safe. We should have been told." Hooker slurped beans from his spoon and tore off a hunk of bread, waving it for emphasis. "She doesn't have a great track record. I'm surprised they moved her up after she fucked up last year."

Jac stiffened. Hooker had just crossed the line. "Look—"

"Nobody can predict a blowup," Anderson said mildly, disproving his own words by metaphorically getting between Jac and Hooker. He held Jac's gaze across the table, his steady gaze saying *Take it easy. Not the time or place.* She nodded slightly, acknowledging his support.

"Hey, I'm just saying," Hooker said gruffly, "spotters are supposed to pick safety zones that are safe. Those guys who died never made it to the safe zone James picked out."

"The fronts can shift out there in seconds," Jac said, fighting down the urge to leap over the table and strangle the asshole. "Especially on the slopes."

Hooker stared at her, and his mouth twisted into a smirk. "Got a hard-on for the ops manager, Russo?"

Jac slowly sucked in a breath. She'd been baited by the best, and personal insults rarely disturbed her. But this wasn't about her. He was taking shots at Mallory. "Getting a little personal, aren't you, Hooker?"

"Hey, I'm just saying. I don't care if you're looking for a little extra something after hours. She's got a great ass. I wouldn't mind having a piece of that myself, but out in the field—"

Jac's vision narrowed, and her ears filled with the rushing sound of a freight train barreling down in the dark. She pushed the bench back and stood, gripping her tray so hard her knuckles ached. "I'm going to suggest you not go there again," Jac said softly. "If you do, I'm going to shove the words back down your throat."

Hooker laughed as she walked away. Asshole. She'd lived mostly with men the year she was overseas. Crude talk, endless discussions of female body parts, graphic tales of sex and more sex, none of that bothered her. When there was nothing around you but sand and death, not much penetrated the numbness except your connection to your buddies and sex. You looked after your buddies and you shared sex stories. The guys didn't treat her any differently than they did each other. She didn't pretend she didn't like women, she just never gave details about anything. If the guys included her in their banter and their bravado, she never objected. But Hooker—that was different. He'd singled out Mallory, and he'd suggested he wouldn't mind putting his hands on her. The idea of him anywhere near Mallory sent blades slashing through her insides. She wanted to kill him.

Jac kept walking even though every fiber in her wanted to turn around and confront him. She'd started out on the wrong foot with Mallory and then compounded it by deviating from safe procedure, climbing down that ravine without backup or safety gear. Homicide was probably not a good idea as a follow-up. She dumped her food into the receptacle and piled her tray on top of the stack nearby. Stepping outside into the brisk spring afternoon, she tried to clear her head. She had time to get in a workout, and she needed it. Between lingering sexual frustration and the simmering urge to crack Hooker's skull, she felt like a short fuse burning too fast. She needed to get some calm going before she showed up for the afternoon session. Mallory would be watching her, and she wanted to be ready.

CHAPTER NINE

"Mallory! Hey!"

Mallory turned in the middle of the yard, a rush of pleasure loosening the fist of tension lodged in her chest. As her breath flowed a little easier, the tightness she'd been trying to ignore all day disappeared. "Sarah!"

Sarah grinned and hurried toward her, her blond curls escaping from under a navy blue knit cap. Even in her cargo pants and matching navy cable-knit sweater, Sarah looked thinner than usual. Mallory had just enough time to wonder about Sarah's state before Sarah threw her arms around her and squeezed every thought from her head.

"God, I missed you," Sarah exclaimed, kissing Mallory soundly on the mouth.

"Whoa, I'll say." Mallory laughed, a weight she hadn't realized she'd been carrying lifting off her shoulders. Sarah was a good friend—probably her best friend if she'd kept track that way, and a colleague she could rely on. Mallory hadn't realized just how much she'd longed for a friendly face, someone she trusted not to push her to go places she didn't want to go or to think about things she didn't want to remember. Unlike Jac, whose very presence seemed to propel her into the red zone. "What are you doing here? I didn't expect you until the middle of the month."

"Last-minute change of plans." Sarah wrapped her arms around Mallory's waist and gave her a tight hug.

"What kind of change in plans?" Mallory looped her arm over Sarah's shoulders. Sarah was deceptively delicate-looking, with finely etched features, a tiny waist, and luminous blue eyes. In fact she was anything but fragile—all lean strength and supple grace. Sarah never had a problem jumping into the roughest terrain or packing out her equipment. She could work a lot of the guys into the ground on a long call out. Her endurance was legendary. And right now, she felt good in Mallory's arms, warm and comforting.

"Got a minute to catch up?" Sarah asked.

"I was on my way to see Sully, but I've got time. Have you eaten?"

"Not yet. I've really missed Charlie's cooking."

"Come on, then."

They loaded their trays, and Mallory picked a table well away from the few guys talking over cups of coffee. Sarah sat down and Mallory said, "So?"

"I decided Mark didn't deserve me." Despite her nonchalant tone, Sarah's eyes looked unhappy.

"Oh, hey. That's hard. I'm sorry."

"No you're not," Sarah said, her smile stronger. "You always thought he was a world-class a-hole."

Mallory shrugged, grinning slightly. "I never thought he treated you the way you should be treated, and he sure as hell didn't know what a good thing he had in you. So what happened between you and mister anatomical part in question?"

"Remember how I used to brag about how supportive Mark was of me smokejumping? That he never complained about me being away for long stretches?"

"Yeah, I used to think that was out of character for him." Mallory forced herself not to gobble the chili. Charlie had outdone himself. "Mark always struck me as being high maintenance. I thought he would have needed too much attention to go without you for long."

"Well, he managed so well because he had a seasonal substitute. Some college girl who was keeping his bed warm between semesters."

"Oh, that really sucks." Mallory reached across the table and took Sarah's hand. "I'm really sorry. Really. I might not like the guy, but I know you did."

"Thanks." Sarah sighed and pushed her half-eaten bowl of chili away. "I kind of knew it was coming for a long time, but I just didn't want to admit it. The upside of the whole mess was I discovered his sideline just when I was making plans to leave for the season. It seemed ridiculous to ask him to move out when I was leaving in two weeks. He might as well stay and pay rent on the place until he finds somewhere else to live." Sarah grimaced. "I didn't much feel like seeing any of our friends or listening to my sister say I told you so. I just packed up the car and started driving."

"Well, I'm glad you're here. You don't have to work until you're scheduled—"

"No, I want to. Please, put me to use."

"You sure?" Mallory pointed to Sarah's chili. "You better eat that, then, because we've got another five or six hours ahead of us this afternoon."

Sarah nodded and dug in. "Believe me, long days of hard work are exactly what I need. I'll sleep at night, and I won't have time to think about him or what an idiot I was."

"Okay then. I can always use another training instructor. And you're not an idiot for being trusting."

"Maybe not, but I think maybe I stayed with him longer than I should have because it was convenient. Or maybe just easier. And he's not hard on the eyes." Sarah chewed her lip, her cheeks turning pink. "I feel a little shallow about that."

Mallory laughed. "Why? Because you've got a good, healthy libido and he fired you up?"

"Well, a little bit of heat might be a good excuse for a casual thing, but two years?" Sarah shrugged. "It's over and done, right. So, what's on for this afternoon?"

"I thought I'd see how they do off the tower. Most of them have no jump experience, and it may not be what they bargained for."

"It'll be dark in a few hours. We're gonna jump with lights?"

Mallory grinned. They didn't fight fires from nine to five. They jumped whenever the plane could get them to the front, night or day, rain or snow. "I thought we might as well see what they're made of."

Sarah laughed. "I'm in. Oh—my place isn't going to be ready for a couple weeks, so I was planning on bunking here."

"Well, that's no big—" Mallory thought about the sleeping arrangements in the barracks. Sarah's bunk was the only one secluded enough to offer some privacy. "Damn. We're not set up yet for more than one woman in there."

"Why do we—oh, right. The rookie." Sarah frowned. "Well, it's my fault for showing up early. I'll just have to—"

"Hey, that's your bunk and you have seniority. You're not giving it up for a rookie." Mallory sipped her coffee, sorting through options. "Besides, the reason we're not prepared for her is because she showed up off the books this morning."

"You didn't know she was coming?"

Mallory hesitated, her aggravation of the early morning having smoothed out some since she'd gotten to know Jac a little bit. Jac's circumstances were a lot more complicated than Mallory had first thought—maybe Jac's father had pulled strings, but she doubted that was Jac's doing. Cashing in on her father's influence just didn't seem like Jac's style. But then what did she know of Jac, really? All the same, she wasn't going to go off with half the facts. "No. She didn't come through usual channels."

"I'm not following."

"Someone at regional posted her here."

"Huh." Sarah raised her brows. "And what aren't you telling me?"

"I don't know all the details," Mallory said.

"She's got some pull somewhere, it sounds like." Sarah's eyes widened. "Oh! Russo. She told me her name was Russo. Her father… not…?"

Mallory nodded. "Yes."

"Wow. Who would've thought we'd end up with his daughter here." Sarah shook her head. "You know, when I first saw her I thought she looked familiar, but with her hair wet and—"

"I'm sorry?"

"In the shower. I ran into her in the locker room—in the shower, to be precise."

An image of Jac naked, water streaming down her face and over her chest sent a bolt of lightning down Mallory's spine. She felt her face color and caught herself before she twitched in her chair. "Oh?"

"Uh-huh. She seems nice."

"I guess." Mallory had a hard time thinking of Jac as nice. There were a lot of words she would use to describe her, but that was not the first one that came to her mind. Intense. Mysterious. Interesting. Gorgeous and sexy.

"You don't like her?"

Mallory blinked. "No. I mean, no, I like her fine. Why do you ask?"

"I don't know, I just got a really strange vibe—is something wrong?"

Mallory shook her head again. Nothing was wrong, only her. "Nope. Everything's fine."

"I wonder if the guys know who she is. That can't be pleasant for her."

"What do you mean?" Mallory's shoulders stiffened.

"Well she's kind of notorious, you know, what with the girlfriend thing and all—"

"You know about that?"

"Are you kidding me? You know I'm a *People* magazine junkie. They picked up the story after those pictures showed up in the *Star*." Sarah made a face. "I'd hate for the people I work with to have seen me naked. That way I mean."

Mallory's teeth started to ache they were so tightly clenched. "She was naked?"

"Oh yeah. Her and the girlfriend. The *Star* photo was grainy, but clear enough to see they were in flagrante delicto."

Mallory lost what was left of her appetite. When Jac had told her about revealing pictures, she'd imagined a heated kiss or a hand in a compromising position. She hadn't actually considered the photos were taken in the act. Was the girlfriend without pride as well as honor? She knew the seasoned veterans on the team, and trusted them to respect Jac's privacy. She didn't know the rookies.

"If you hear any scuttlebutt about her, let me know." Mallory stood. She needed some air. She needed to walk off her fury before she said something in front of Sarah she'd regret. Jac could look after herself. She wasn't responsible for Jac, not that way. Her only responsibility was to see that she was safe in the field.

Sarah collected her tray and walked with her. "So what are you going to do with her if I take the bunk in the barracks? Can she share your loft until my place is ready?"

Mallory's heart lurched. "Oh, I don't think so. No way. She's not sleeping with me."

Sarah's eyes narrowed. "Who said anything about sleeping with you, huh? I mean, she'd be sleeping in the loft somewhere but—"

"You know what I mean."

"I think I'm beginning to." Sarah's smile widened. "She is really hot."

"And you're really straight. Unless something else changed down there in Santa Fe." Mallory looked over her shoulder, hoping no one was within hearing range.

"Ho ho. You've got a crush."

"Oh my God, I do not. God. She's a rookie." Mallory stowed her tray. "I've got to get going. I want to talk to Sully, and then I need to check the tower."

"You're avoiding."

Mallory turned her back to escape toward Sully's office. "No, I'm not."

"Yes, you are." Sarah tagged along, laughing. "You're avoiding your best friend's nosy questions."

"I am not."

"So, do you think she's hot?"

"Geez, Sarah. Is this high school now? No."

Sarah grinned. "So where is she sleeping?'

Mallory imagined Jac's quiet breathing in the dark, pictured her moving around in the morning, her thick dark hair tousled from sleep. Her mind skittered away and landed on a grainy image of Jac on the smeared and rumpled pages of a newspaper, naked and defenseless and unable to protect herself. The rage in her chest turned to ice.

"In the loft." No big deal, right? She was way too old for a crush, and even if she wasn't, she had more sense than to be seduced by a cocky grin and soulful eyes. Dark, intense eyes that saw inside her.

Mallory shivered. The wind had picked up. Ought to make the jumps challenging. She'd have to adjust the tension on the guidelines to counter the shear forces. Plenty to do, plenty to think about. None of those things were Jac.

❖

"Hey, you want a spot?" Anderson peered down from the head of the weight bench. "You've got a fair amount of weight on there."

Jac pushed out a breath and shoved the bar up, feeling her deltoids and chest muscles start to quiver. "Yeah, thanks."

Anderson's hands appeared next to hers, under the bar, waiting to catch it.

"What's your count?"

"Ten," Jac said, lowering the bar to her chest, stopping it just inches above her breasts. She kept her breath moving in and out, oxygenating her muscles, and shoved it up again.

"Eleven." Anderson looked down at her, his expression calm and steady. "One more, and then let it rest."

"Fifteen," Jac grunted.

He grinned, looking amused even upside down. "I wouldn't push it, not if you want to have anything left for the jumps this afternoon."

"Blackmail," Jac muttered and let him guide the bar back onto the hooks. Her breath was coming fast and a little ragged. She'd already done two sets before he showed up, and she still had a hard time blocking Hooker's voice out of her head.

"I hear you did a solid with Ray out there today," Anderson said quietly.

Jac sat up and toweled the sweat from her neck. "What do you mean?"

"Just that you got to him first, handled things, and sent him up to the helitack like a pro."

"Word gets around fast." Benny. Must have been Benny, because Mallory wouldn't have said anything.

Anderson grinned. "Nothing else to do while sitting around waiting for a call. Don't worry, it was all good."

"If I worried about stuff like that…" Jac shrugged.

Hooker came into view, sauntering in her direction. He still wore the tight green T-shirt and had changed into sweats. He was husky, heavily muscled, and took up a lot of space.

Hooker gave her a grin as if they were best friends. "Got bad news for you, buddy."

"Life's full of it," Jac said as if she couldn't care less. Hooker was standing so close to the bench if she tried to stand her breasts were going to rub against his chest. His legs were spread, and she had no desire to end up with her crotch snugged up against his. So she sat, which put her eyes at about the level of his belly button. She tilted her head just enough to see his face. He was looking down at her, a look in his eyes that was all too easy to read. If the guy got a hard-on, she was gonna punch him in the nuts.

"I think you've missed your chance with the boss lady."

"I don't know what you're talking about."

"In case you had any ideas of getting over on her, I think somebody's got there first. Cute little blonde with big tits. I saw them getting cozy out in the yard before they went off together. Like lip-lock cozy."

"Not interested in what you saw, heard, or think, Hooker." Jac pushed up off the bench so fast, Hooker stepped back in surprise. Jac kept her hands at her sides, even though she wanted to slam him in the chest and knock him on his ass. Mallory and Sarah, it sounded like. Made sense. The two of them had worked together for a lot of seasons. If they were lovers, they'd want to be posted together. The two of them together—it shouldn't matter to her, but it did. She wasn't about to let Hooker know that. She looked past him to Anderson as if Hooker weren't there. "Thanks for the spot. See you this afternoon."

"Sure thing," Anderson said with his usual even tone.

Hooker laughed and clapped her on the shoulder. "Don't worry, babe. If things get really tough, I can take care of you."

"The only thing I'll need you to take care of is my back out in the field," Jac said.

"Anywhere, any time," he crooned. "I'm there."

Jac ignored him and headed to the locker room to grab a quick shower and change. Mallory and Sarah. She could see it, but she didn't want to.

Chapter Ten

Mallory strode into the main staging area in the central room of the standby shack and signaled for Emilio Torres, a thin, quiet man fifteen years her senior, to join her. Emilio was the loft master responsible for seeing that the necessary equipment was loaded onto the jump plane during a fire dispatch. He was also the rigging master, in charge of chute repair and preparation. She trusted him with her life.

"Ready, Emilio?"

"All set." Emilio gestured to the group of rookies gathered around one of the forty-foot-long tables in the center of the room where a chute was laid out ready to be prepared. "You want me to do the demo first?"

"Yes. Then while I take half over the obstacle course, you can have the rest for rigging practice."

"Sure thing, Ice."

Mallory walked around to the far side of the table and pointed to the chute. "After today, the only person who should ever touch your jump pack is you or Emilio. I shouldn't have to tell you that you can never check your chute enough times. During boot camp, you'll clear the chute with Emilio before every jump."

She stopped, judging their reactions. This was the point when rookies sometimes came to the realization that jumping out of an airplane with nothing but a bit of flimsy-looking nylon to break their fall was a lot less glamorous and a lot more daunting than they'd been willing to admit. No one spoke. "How many of you have ever jumped?"

Hooker was the only one of the six rookies to raise his hand.

"Where?"

"Skydiving," he said.

Mallory nodded. "You'll discover pretty quickly that we jump differently. Our landing zones are much smaller, our chutes are designed to float differently, the draft on your body when you're fully loaded will be different, your landing will be different." She smiled at him. "What I'm saying is, you're going to have to unlearn what you know."

He grunted and shrugged. Mallory held his gaze for a few seconds, then swept the rest of the group. "Those of you who have never jumped are not at a disadvantage. In fact, we generally prefer that you have no experience. No bad habits to unlearn."

A couple of the guys laughed.

"Every day for the next week will break down like this—morning run and classroom work before lunch. After, you'll run the obstacle course—standard setup. Rope climbing, clearing obstacles, climbing barricades. At the end of the course, you'll be climbing the jump tower for a series of simulated drops." Mallory checked her watch. Right on time. "Fit in your gym workouts when you can. Minimum requirement is forty-five sit-ups, twenty-five push-ups, and seven pull-ups. Questions?"

"How high is the tower?" asked Stan Rubin, one of the few professional firefighters among the rookies.

"Fifty feet. The cable lift is a hundred at its highest point."

"That'll produce a little speed on the way down," Anderson remarked.

"Because you'll be on a pulley rather than using a chute, you'll feel the landing impact much as you would when dropping from the aircraft," Mallory said. "I'll take Rubin and Russo on the course first. The rest of you stay here so Emilio can get you acquainted with your jump gear. Your partner assignments for the jump simulations are on the wall by the door."

Mallory took stock of the rookies. Anderson, as usual, appeared thoughtful. Rubin stoic. Jac was intense and focused. Hooker rolled back on his heels, bored. Mallory tried not to let her gaze linger on Jac's face, but it was hard. Hard not to look at her, even harder not to want to.

❖

"Ready for this?" Sarah asked as she and Jac got into line at the foot of the jump tower.

Jac looked up to the top of the platform fifty feet above her head. It didn't really look all that high off the ground. "Ought to be a piece of cake after the obstacle course."

"It's a bear, isn't it?"

Jac stretched her shoulders. "Forty-five feet of rope never looked so long in my life."

"Did Mallory offer to let you out of the rest of the course if you could beat her time up?"

Jac regarded the blisters on her palms. She could still feel the burn of the braided hemp rubbing on her wrists above her gloves. Mallory had gone up the rope like a monkey. Her legs had entwined with the rope as naturally as if it were a lover. The muscles in her arms and shoulders and back contracted and relaxed in the steady unbroken rhythm that propelled her to the top as effortlessly as if she were walking down the street. She would have been beautiful under any circumstances. Considering how Jac had been thinking about all that muscle moving over her, or under her, she'd been glorious. Jac swallowed hard, her throat so dry it stung. "I'm not dumb enough to bet against her. But Rubin was."

"After he saw her climb?" Sarah laughed. "How bad did he lose?"

"I think the performance anxiety really got to him. He almost fell off."

"What do you want to wager a few more give it a try next round?"

"Doesn't she ever get tired?"

"Not that I've ever noticed," Sarah said softly, glancing up to where Mallory was just a dark slash against the fading afternoon sun.

Sarah's face softened as she watched Mallory move around above them, and Jac wondered if she was reliving some intimate personal moment. She wanted to ask but didn't know how. It wasn't any of her business what their relationship was. She'd just have to go slowly crazy trying not to speculate. "What about you? You ever beat her time?"

"Not on the rope," Sarah said. "But I'm a mighty fine tree climber, if I do say so myself. I've never actually raced her up a pine, but I think I'd have a good shot."

"I think I'd much rather climb a tree than a rope."

"It's awesome. One of the reasons I can't wait to get back here every year."

"What do you do in the off-season?"

Sarah smiled. "Spoken like a true smokejumper. Most people consider this the off-season and the rest of the year their real jobs."

"What about you?"

"I guess I'd have to say this is what I really care about," Sarah said pensively. "The rest of the year I teach riding and train horses at a ranch in New Mexico."

"Sounds pretty interesting."

"It is. But out here"—Sarah shrugged and swept her arm toward the mountains—"when I finish working a fire, I know I've done something worthwhile. Made a difference. No question in my mind."

"And had fun doing it."

"Like you wouldn't believe." Sarah shot her a grin.

Mallory's voice came over the radio. "Five-minute warning."

"Okay," Sarah said briskly. "Give me a run-through of the drop sequence."

Jac repeated what Mallory had reviewed after they'd completed the obstacle course. "Jump, check the canopy, check the airspace, check the three rings, grab the toggles, disconnect the stevens, steer."

"You listen good, rookie."

Jac laughed. "I'd rather not fall on my ass first time out. I haven't exactly had a great start."

"Sounds like you did just fine," Sarah said.

"All the same, I can do without any more attention," Jac said. Especially not Mallory's. And especially not for something she'd screwed up.

"You're not actually jumping today, so you don't have to worry about the landing. Just the same, run the jump sequence in your head every time." Sarah looked Jac over. "You look good to go. The more times you do this, the easier it's going to be going out the plane."

The radio crackled again, and Mallory said, "Team one, climb up. Team two, on the approach."

Jac looked at Sarah. "Here we go."

Sarah grinned. "Remember to tuck your chin."

Up on the platform, Mallory gave them a perfunctory nod, then checked everything Jac was wearing—her boots, her pants, her jump jacket, the parachute pack on her back, the reserve chute across her chest, her personal gear bag underneath. Jac was loaded exactly the way she would be if she were ready to climb onto the plane for a fire call. Then Mallory tugged on the harness that crisscrossed her body and ran between her legs.

"Looks good," Mallory said.

Jac didn't figure an answer was required. The view was incredible. If she reached up, she was certain she could touch the clouds that had fluffed up in the heat of the midday sun into pillowy mounds. Mountains ringed the camp, unbroken by power lines or man-made roads, sweeping, majestic, wild, and awe-inspiring. Mallory looked good framed against the dark craggy peaks, her face as daringly sculpted as the line of mountaintops behind her. Her eyes were bright and clear and crystalline as the sky. She was in perfect harmony with the world around her—strong and confident.

"Repeat the jump sequence," Mallory said.

Jac hesitated for a heartbeat, still lost in Mallory's aura. Then she came to attention and automatically repeated what she had recited for Sarah a few minutes before.

"Good." Mallory clipped the pulley rig from which Jac would be suspended in air onto Jac's harness and then a second one to Sarah's. "Mount the ready stand."

Jac stepped onto the foot-wide riser at the edge of the platform, and Sarah climbed up next to her on the parallel pulley line. The slope fell away below her, much like the mountainside below a ski jump. Except there was no groomed surface to land on if the pulley gave way, only treetops.

"On the count of three," Mallory said.

Jac looked down the hundred-foot slope at the wall of sawdust at the end that formed the landing zone. She'd heard about it—some people called it the slamulator.

"Three, two…" Mallory's voice intoned.

Jac let Mallory's voice fill her head and emptied her thoughts of everything else.

"One. Jump."

Jac stepped off into nothing.

❖

Jac watched the door to the mess hall, waiting for Mallory to come in for dinner. She lingered over fried chicken and mashed potatoes as long as she could, making small talk with Anderson and Rubin. Finally, she accepted that Mallory wasn't coming.

"Okay, guys," she said. "I'm ready to surrender. I'm gonna get some rack time."

Anderson stood. "I'm with you. I'll walk over with you?"

"Uh, I'm actually headed over to the hangar. I'm bunking over there until Sarah's place off-site is ready."

Hooker looked up as they passed his table. "Sleeping with the boss already, Russo?"

Jac ignored him. She'd been as surprised as anyone when Mallory stopped her after the afternoon's workout and said, "Sarah's taking the bunk in the barracks. Bring your gear over to the loft." Before Jac could say anything, Mallory had spun on her heel and strode away. She couldn't tell if Mallory was pissed at having her private space invaded with no warning, or if she was totally indifferent. Jac had been hoping to see her at dinner and maybe get some answers, but no such luck. Since hiding out wasn't her style, she figured she might as well go find out what the story was.

Anderson looked over his shoulder as they walked out into the yard. When they were alone, he said, "I don't mind telling you, I'm sore all over. And I thought I was in good shape. I've been training hard for this all winter."

Jac rubbed her right shoulder where she'd banged into the not-so-soft sawdust wall on one of her last practice runs. "I was feeling pretty good after the obstacle course, except for a few blisters. But I felt like my brains were going through a blender after the third time into that wall."

"Yeah, I think they made their point. There's no such thing as a soft landing."

"Well, there's always landing in a tree," Jac pointed out.

"Oh yeah, that works. If you don't fall out and break your ass, you have to rappel down on a skinny little line fully geared up. No thanks. I'll take the good old ground, anytime."

"Yeah, me too." She cut right toward the locker room as he cut left toward the barracks. "See you tomorrow."

He waved and she went through the empty ready room to collect her gear. The hangar was dark when she let herself in through the side door, but she had a feeling she knew where Mallory would be and plotted a course from memory. After she circled around behind the plane, she saw a small cone of light edging out into the darkness. Mallory was at her desk, going through a six-inch stack of paperwork.

"I didn't see you at supper," Jac said.

Mallory glanced up. "Charlie sent over a sandwich for me."

"Too bad. The chicken was tear-inducing."

"I know." Mallory smiled. "Charlie does something to it—injects it with sugar or something. Once you've had his chicken, you're ruined for life."

Jac laughed. "I might have been ruined before I showed up here, but I'm definitely not salvageable now."

Mallory scribbled something on the bottom of a form and tossed it on top of the pile on her right. The right-hand stack was the finished pile, presumably. That stack was a lot shorter than the one she was working on. "I cleared out a space upstairs. There's a cot. It's rustic."

"Believe me, after today, I could sleep anywhere."

"That's good, because you're gonna have to."

"At least I won't be bedding down with sand and fleas." Jac hesitated. "Will I?"

"The field training is just like fire call…tents, sleeping bags, water and food rations, the whole nine yards. Enjoy the cot while you can."

"I appreciate you letting me—"

"Look, Jac," Mallory said without looking up as she scribbled something on another form, "there's nothing personal about this arrangement. You needed a place to sleep. That's all it is. You should go get some. Light switch is on a beam to your left as soon as you get up there."

"Right." She'd been dismissed. No reason to be bothered by Mallory's disinterest. Hell, she knew the offer of a room wasn't personal—Mallory obviously didn't even want her here. She shouldered her pack. "Night, then."

"Night," Mallory said, reaching for another piece of paper.

Jac climbed up the ladder to the loft and switched on the light. Mallory's sleeping space was neat and orderly. A tall, narrow, handmade bookcase of plain pine boards stood next to a cot with Mallory's sleeping bag on top of it. The shelves were filled with what looked like an eclectic selection of books. A familiar-looking dented green army trunk sat at the foot of the cot. For a second, Jac felt like she was back in Iraq. The place looked exactly like every barracks she'd ever slept in. Functional, sterile. A place to crash between duties. Come to think of it, Mallory reminded her of the soldiers who returned for second and third tours, who couldn't adjust to civilian life and preferred the controlled chaos of the battlefield. For a while, she thought she might be one of them, especially when it became real clear that having her around was a problem for her family. This posting had probably saved her from requesting another go-round over there. No time to think when you're defusing IEDs.

Another cot was lined up parallel to Mallory's about fifteen feet away, tucked under the eaves. A small rag rug sat on the rough wood floor next to it. A darker spot the same size marked where the rug had previously sat in front of Mallory's cot. That small kindness sent an unexpected shiver of heat through Jac's belly. She dumped the sleeping bag she'd been assigned along with her duffel onto the bottom of the cot and sat down, surveying the space. Despite its barren appearance, the place held a hint of Mallory. Honeysuckle. Smiling, she unrolled the sleeping bag, stretched out on her back, and closed her eyes. As she drew Mallory's scent deep into her chest, she couldn't think of any other place she'd rather be.

Chapter Eleven

Mallory leaned back in her chair and rubbed her eyes. After midnight, and the pile of papers in front of her didn't look any lower. Probably because she hadn't managed to complete anything in the last hour, at least. Ever since Jac had gone upstairs to the loft, Mallory had been aware of her, even though only silence drifted down around her. No matter how hard she concentrated on filling out work rosters, she couldn't keep her mind from wandering to Jac, lying upstairs asleep, breathing softly in the dark. She didn't want to go up to bed. Foolish. Nothing had happened between them and nothing was going to, but she couldn't shake the feeling that if she was that close to her, in the dark, in the night, alone, she would feel her in a way she'd never felt anyone before. Her skin disappeared when she was around Jac, and every sensation, every shiver, penetrated to her core as if she had no barriers at all. She pictured herself on her cot, listening to Jac breathe, and feared she'd imagine Jac lying next to her, naked. Her breasts tightened and her skin tingled. Oh no, she wasn't going upstairs.

She'd sleep in the damn plane before she'd let herself get any more crazy over Jac.

"It's getting pretty late," Jac said from very close to her.

Mallory jumped. "God! Where did you come from?"

Jac grinned and pointed upward. "Remember?"

"Forgot all about you," Mallory said through gritted teeth. Damn it. Jac was wearing a faded gray T-shirt with pinpoint holes over the belly, as if tiny sparks had drifted from the air and landed on it. Burning through. Faded letters said something Mallory couldn't quite make out—baseball, maybe—under some kind of college logo. And sweatpants, just tight enough to show off her muscular thighs. Jac was almost certainly naked underneath. Mallory's heart galloped and her fingertips almost vibrated, conjuring soft cotton over hard muscle.

"Want some company?"

"No. I'm working here," Mallory said grumpily. Jac's hair was tousled, just as Mallory imagined it would be, but she didn't look sleepy. Her dark eyes glinted, and her handsome face was smooth and unwrinkled. She looked young and vigorous and unbelievably sexy.

"Why aren't you sleeping?"

"Why aren't you?"

"Because I'd rather do anything except paperwork, and now I'm being punished."

Jac laughed, looked around the shadowy corner of the hangar, and pulled over a packing crate. As she sat down, she said, "Clear off a corner of your desk. You're not doing that stuff anyhow."

Mallory frowned, not bothering to debate the obvious. "Why?"

"Because," Jac said, holding up a deck of cards, "I'm going to beat you at gin."

The words were right on the tip of Mallory's tongue—*I'm not playing cards with you, go back to sleep, go away.* But those weren't the words that came out of her mouth. "Beat me? Oh, I don't think so."

Mallory heard the words and wondered what was wrong with her. Why couldn't she seem to say no?

"You're going to regret that, Mal."

"Excuse me? Mal?" Mallory's heart beat a wild tattoo against the inside of her ribs. "Where did that come from?"

"Ice doesn't suit you. Not really."

Jac watched her, searching, and Mallory couldn't escape. "You don't know that."

"Don't I?" Jac riffled the cards in one hand. "Ready?"

"You're incredibly sure of yourself."

"I didn't get the nickname Hotshot just last year, you know."

Mallory glared. "Oh, you're some kind of ringer, aren't you? What, did you put yourself through college playing blackjack?"

Jac grinned. "Nope. I put myself through college dealing stud in a casino in Reno."

"Same difference," Mallory muttered. "Well, gin isn't poker, *Hotshot*, and I'm very good at both."

Jac deftly dealt out a hand of gin. "I guess we'll see, won't we."

Mallory snatched up the cards. She had a good hand and allowed herself a moment of satisfaction. As she sorted her melds, she said, "How did your father feel about you being a card dealer?" Jac sucked in a breath, and Mallory mentally kicked herself. "Sorry. Out of bounds. I don't know where that—"

"No, it's okay," Jac said calmly. "I'm just not used to people asking questions because they actually want to know about me and not him. And he didn't like it—at all." Jac's smile was part pleased, part rueful. "He hated it, in fact, which is probably the reason I decided to do it in the first place. Then I found out I really liked it, it paid really well, and it was a great way to pick up girls."

"Aha," Mallory said. "Of course."

"You want the turn card?"

"No."

Jac took the upcard and tossed down a discard. "Of course what?"

"Nothing." Mallory picked up Jac's discard, pretending to shuffle the rest of her hand into a new order. "I'm sure you would have had no trouble getting girls even without the cards."

"You think so? Why?"

Mallory stopped herself from saying *You're sexy as sin and the devil rides in your eyes.* "Never mind."

Jac chuckled, took a stock card, and discarded one. After a beat of silence she asked, "What about you? Girlfriend?"

Mallory drew from the deck and fanned her cards. "Gin. No."

"Well hell," Jac said. "We keeping score?"

"Of course we're keeping score, Hotshot."

Jac passed the cards for the deal. "How come?"

"How come we're keeping score? Because I told you I was go—"

"No, you know what I mean." Jac studied her cards intently, seeming oddly uncertain. "How come no girlfriend?"

"Not that it's any of your business," Mallory said, completely at a loss as to why she was even answering, "but I live up here eight months out of the year. It's not conducive to relationships."

"What about dating?"

"What about it?" Mallory picked up her hand, feeling progressively more cranky. There were a million things she ought to be doing, and none of them included sitting up in the middle of the night with Jac Russo talking about things she never talked about. Not even with Sarah.

"We're not exactly in Antarctica," Jac said. "And although I haven't actually verified this, we do get some time off now and then, don't we?"

"If you make it through boot camp," Mallory said, "you'll be on rotation for fire call, and when you're off, you're welcome to go anywhere you want to." And do anything you want, which will undoubtedly involve a woman. Probably more than one.

"Well then, there's no reason not to have a date now and then, right?"

Mallory looked at Jac over the top of her cards, wondering where Jac was going with the conversation. Her expression was suspiciously innocent, but her eyes were anything but. If Mallory could only escape from Jac's eyes, she could get control of herself again. But looking away was so hard. Jac's gaze was so warm, so deep, so focused on her, the connection couldn't have been any stronger if they were touching. However Jac managed it, Mallory hadn't been able to break the link since the moment they'd met, and she was starting to get a little scared. Anger, she'd found, helped banish fear. "Is that your plan? Carousing on your off-hours?"

"I had thought of that," Jac said, her mouth curving at one end. "Only not quite in those terms."

"You're all set, then, aren't you?" Mallory discarded and immediately regretted it. She could have used the eight for a run.

"Looks like it," Jac said, picking up Mallory's discard. She laid her hand down. "Gin."

"You talk too much while you play," Mallory griped.

"Oh, that's lame." Jac scooped up the cards to deal. "An excuse beneath one as talented as you."

Mallory laughed. God, Jac was charm personified. "Go ahead and deal."

"Two out of three?" Jac asked.

Mallory got up, pulled two Cokes out of her tiny fridge in the corner, and set them down on her desk, one for each of them. "Best four out of seven. Be prepared to be humiliated."

"And the winner?" Jac asked, her voice dropping low. "What does the winner get, Mal?"

A kiss was Mallory's first thought, and she hoped to blazes Jac could not read her face in the dim light. "Coffee."

Jac frowned. "Explain."

"In bed. The winner gets coffee delivered in bed." Mallory picked up her cards and stifled a smile. She was so looking forward to her morning coffee, delivered while she was still warm in her sleeping bag.

❖

"It's almost two," Jac said.

"I don't think you want to quit now," Mallory said with just a hint of malicious delight in her voice. "Do you?"

Jac had been keeping score in her head. She knew the outcome. Ordinarily, she hated losing at anything. In the service, if she'd lost, she would have been dead. Tonight she'd been playing to win, and as far as she was concerned, she had. The score at gin wasn't what counted for her. "How do you like your coffee?"

Mallory folded her arms behind her head and leaned back in her chair, swiveling back and forth, looking supremely satisfied. She also looked totally hot. Sometime during the last game, she'd removed her sweatshirt, and her navy T-shirt clung tightly to her breasts as she stretched. She was the perfect combination of strength and beauty, and Jac's throat tightened. She could so easily see herself bracing her hands on the arms of Mallory's captain's chair and leaning over her, kissing her as she straddled Mallory's thighs. She could almost feel their breasts brushing. She pushed the packing crate back a few inches from the desk and stood, needing to move out of touching range before she did. Bad move on so many levels. Mallory hadn't given her the slightest indication she was interested, and even if she had been that lucky, there was the little problem of Mallory being in charge at the moment. Operative words, *at the moment*. Mallory would always be senior, but she wouldn't always be her boss. If she made it through the month, they'd be colleagues. Jac rubbed her stomach, and the muscles jumped under her fingers. Damn it, she was way too turned on. "So, the coffee?"

"A touch of cream. No sugar." Mallory sighed. "I guess we'd better pack it in. I've got training sessions to run tomorrow and you"— she pointed at Jac—"you have a course to pass."

Jac swept up the cards and slid them into their box, aware of Mallory watching her. She liked it when Mallory watched her. Right now she liked it so much her nipples were hard. "What time?"

"What time, what?" Mallory asked, just a hint of teasing in her voice.

"Coffee. What time tomorrow?"

"Oh five thirty. In plenty of time for me to enjoy it before I take a shower and have breakfast and start you rookies on your way."

"All right. You'll have it." Jac hesitated. As much as she wanted to escape, she didn't want their moment alone to end. Being with Mallory was easy—easy and comfortable, and that was odd. She'd spent plenty of casual time with women, but that was usually time spent over a few drinks in a bar or a few hours in bed. There hadn't even been much of that since she'd been home. But the past few hours with Mallory were different—their conversation had been real, as if what they were saying mattered. Like she mattered. Talking to Mallory had warmed her inside, surprising and wonderful, like receiving an unexpected kindness from a stranger.

"I guess I'll head up," Jac said, her voice husky.

Mallory rose, and she was suddenly very, very close to Jac. "I'm going to hit the head first. You go on."

They were almost exactly the same height, and Mallory's mouth was only a few inches away. Jac swallowed hard. Mallory's lips were moist, her breath spicy and sweet. Jac wanted to taste her. Taste her kisses. Taste her skin. Taste her everywhere. "Okay. I'll see you in the morning."

"Sleep well," Mallory said and then abruptly turned and disappeared.

Jac climbed back into the loft, a heavy thud of arousal beating between her thighs. She crawled into her sleeping bag, aware for the first time that the huge, nearly empty building was cold. She hadn't been cold sitting close to Mallory, talking, laughing, trading jibes. Her skin was chilled now, but she was burning on the inside. She lay awake, and a few minutes later Mallory climbed quietly up the ladder. Moonlight filtering through a small diamond-shaped window high above them, just under the dome of the hangar, provided the only illumination. Mallory's face was ghostly pale, and she might've been an apparition visiting Jac's dreams—except she wasn't. She was real. Alive and warm, and Jac wanted her.

Mallory kicked off her boots, and when her hands went to the waistband of her pants, Jac turned on her side, facing away. Mallory probably wouldn't care if she saw her undressing, but she would care. She wouldn't violate Mallory's privacy that way.

She prayed for sleep, but it was a long time coming.

❖

When Jac opened her eyes she wasn't even certain she'd been asleep. The loft was still cloaked in darkness, the chill of the not-yet-summer night having settled into the building, into her bones. She propped her head on her elbow and gazed across the space between their cots. Mallory slept on her back, one arm outside her sleeping bag, her fingers gently curled. Her face was soft, her regular breathing gentle and comforting. Jac turned her wrist back and forth until she caught a sliver of moonlight and checked the time. 0520. Smiling to herself, she carefully unzipped her bag, trying to be quiet. Soon she'd have the perfect excuse to wake Mallory. To enjoy a few more moments of stolen time with her. She climbed out of her bag and grabbed her boots and clothes to dress downstairs where she wouldn't wake Mallory.

Outside, the stars had not yet yielded to the rising sun, and the air was so crisp Jac's breath crystallized with each exhalation. She hustled across the yard to the mess hall. Charlie hadn't opened the chow line yet, and a couple of guys waited at tables, hunkered down over cups of coffee. The huge urn never seemed to be empty, the rule being when someone drank the last cup they made a new pot. Hopefully, the coffee was fresh. Jac wanted Mallory's coffee to be perfect. Laughing to herself, she poured two extra-large paper cups and added cream to both. She was looking for tops when Sarah walked up.

"Morning," Sarah said. "How'd you sleep?"

"Great. Thanks." Jac fixed the lids on both cups.

"You look like you're preparing for a long day," Sarah said, indicating the two cups with her chin as she poured one of her own.

"Oh. One of these is for Mal."

Sarah's lips parted and she let out a soft breath. "Really? Wow. She's got you running errands for her now?"

"Not exactly. I lost a bet."

"And payment is coffee?"

"Hand delivered. In bed."

Sarah sputtered on the coffee she was sipping.

"It's not as exciting as it sounds," Jac said.

"I don't know, it sounds pretty damn exciting to me."

"I better go. Not much time before we have to muster."

"Go ahead. Don't keep her waiting." Sarah shook her head. "She'll get grouchy without coffee first thing."

"See you," Jac said, wondering just how many times Sarah had seen Mallory first thing in the morning. Telling herself there was no cause for jealousy, and almost being convinced.

CHAPTER TWELVE

Mallory's heart beat so rapidly she was actually embarrassed by how eagerly she awaited a simple cup of coffee. Except it wasn't the anticipation of morning coffee making her pulse race. It wasn't the fun of winning a silly bet either. She was jittery waiting for Jac to climb into the loft, bringing with her that blazing smile and hot gaze. Mallory remembered stretching the kinks out of her back after the card game and the way Jac's gaze had dropped to her breasts and stayed there. Jac's expression had gotten fierce, and oh, but Mallory liked that. She *liked* knowing Jac liked the way she looked. And that was so not her. Half the time when she went into town on her nights off she did little more than jump in the shower, pull on clean clothes—the same clothes she would have worn going to work—and tame her hair with an unadorned band. Now she was practically purring because Jac Russo had cruised her with a hungry glint in her eye. And the longer she lay there waiting for Jac to come back and smile at her again, the more her brains were going to leak out of her ears.

Mallory yanked down the zipper on the side of her sleeping bag, threw it open, and swung her legs over the side of the cot. She'd slept in a T-shirt and panties, and her skin instantly pebbled in the cold air. Just as she was about to pluck her jeans from the floor, she heard activity on the ladder. Quickly, she slid her legs back into her sleeping bag and flipped the top flap down over her bare legs. Jac appeared, balancing a cardboard carrier in one hand and sporting that damn heart-stopping grin.

"Good morning." Jac presented the coffee cups in their cardboard holder as if they were flutes of champagne. "Would madam care for something to drink?"

"The gin rummy queen wants her coffee, you idiot." Mallory pried the cup closest to her free.

Jac set down the tray along with her cup of coffee and pulled a bran muffin wrapped in clear plastic wrap out of the right pocket of her cargo pants. Brandishing it with a flourish, she said, "Muffin, milady?"

"Will you stop." Mallory grabbed the muffin, her fingers tracing the top of Jac's hand. She couldn't see the sparks fly, but she felt them to her toes. "Thanks."

"You're welcome." Jac reached down for her coffee. "Hope I added enough cream."

Her voice was soft, free of any laughter, and the unusual, slightly uncertain note struck a chord in Mallory's heart. "This is nice. Thanks."

Jac looked up from her half crouch, her mouth gently curved into an incredibly kissable smile. "You're welcome again. I liked doing it."

"Where's your muffin?" Mallory asked, knowing she couldn't possibly swallow now. Not while her body thrummed with hunger all its own—a terrible ache no food was going to satisfy. If she hadn't been half-naked, she would have bolted.

"I could only fit one in my pocket."

Mallory patted the bottom of her sleeping bag. "Sit down. I'll share this one with you."

Jac's gaze went to the bottom of the narrow cot, then to Mallory. "All right."

Mallory pulled her knees up as Jac sat down, and her feet ended up resting against Jac's thigh. Even with the sleeping bag between them, when Jac shifted to face her, the muscles in Jac's thighs tensed, and Mallory had the urge to dig her toes into the firm flesh. She had the urge to do a lot more than that. She wanted Jac inside the sleeping bag with her, her hard body pressed close, her hands chasing the cold away. Mallory clenched inside and got very, very wet. Oh, this was bad. Very, very bad. Mallory broke off a chunk of the muffin and half sat up, extending the moist morsel on the tips of her fingers toward Jac's mouth. "Here. Have a bite."

Jac leaned closer, sliding one arm onto the cot next to Mallory's hips. Her chest pressed against Mallory's knees. Jac looked into Mallory's eyes and opened her mouth. "Sure?"

"I trust you not to bite," Mallory said, her voice an octave lower than normal.

"Really?" Jac's tongue swept over Mallory's fingers, and her lips closed around the small piece of muffin.

Mallory's clitoris swelled and her breasts ached and what was left of her senses dissolved like mist before the dawn. "Good?"

"Very good." Jac's tongue slid across her lower lip, catching a tiny flake of bran, and she nodded. "You should try some."

Mallory stifled a whimper. She'd never orgasmed without direct stimulation in her life, but she was close now. She couldn't let that happen. Even if she could hide it, and she didn't think she could, she couldn't bear the humiliation. "Jac, I don't think—"

"You said you trusted me." Without looking away from Mallory's face, Jac slid her fingers down Mallory's arm to the muffin Mallory cradled in her palm and broke off a piece. She held the fragment up to Mallory's mouth. "Taste it. You'll like it."

Mallory sucked the muffin from between Jac's fingers. She chewed and swallowed without tasting it, watching Jac's pupils flicker and dance, then licked the traces of butter from the tips of Jac's fingers. "Good."

"Yeah," Jac whispered, letting her fingers linger for a second against Mallory's mouth. She was crazy to touch her at all, but if she didn't do something, she was going to explode. Mallory looked so damn beautiful with her hair all wild and her face so unguarded. Mallory was different when they were alone—still wary, like a wild animal uncertain of a human hand, but still approaching. Cautious, but edging nearer. Jac didn't want to scare her away. She traced her thumb over Mallory's lower lip. Mallory's soft breath was hot in the chill air, her lips moist and a little swollen. "I'm glad you like it."

"Mmm. Yeah, I do."

Jac eased away until she was no longer touching her. Mallory's eyes had gotten hazy, and Jac was pretty sure if she kissed her right now, Mallory would kiss her back. And probably never do it again. "Now I need to go."

"What?" Mallory murmured. "Why?"

"I'd be happy for you to feed me all day, but you should finish your coffee. Oh six hundred is coming on fast."

"I know," Mallory whispered. "I need to get going."

"Yes."

Neither of them moved.

"Jac?"

"What?" Jac said softly.

"I can't get up while you're sitting on my sleeping bag."

Jac smiled. "That's a problem, then, I guess."

"It is, because I don't wan—"

A klaxon blared, the blast so loud, Jac's ears ached. Incoming. God. She bolted off the cot and spun around, reaching for something that wasn't there. Where was her weapon? "Mallory, stay there!"

"Jac, it's the fire call." Mallory threw back the sleeping bag and jumped up. "It's okay, but I've got to go."

Jac blinked and she was back. Hell, she'd blown it, but she couldn't worry about that now. "Where?"

Mallory jerked up her jeans and shoved her bare feet into her boots. "Doesn't matter. We'll get the information in the air."

"Is there something I should do—"

"No." Mallory hesitated. "I'll see you when I get back, Russo. You've still got the training course to pass."

"Right." Jac's chest ached. Mallory was heading out to fight a wildfire, and she was staying behind. "Be careful, huh, Ice?"

"Always." Mallory ran for the ladder, vaulted over the edge, and was gone.

❖

Downstairs, the hangar was controlled pandemonium.

"Five minutes, Benny," Mallory called as she raced by to collect her gear.

Benny waved and climbed into the plane. Caruso, one of the permanent crew, pulled the blocks out from in front of the wheels so the plane could taxi out.

Sully intercepted her in the middle of the yard, a printout in his hand. "Ridgeline up in Bitterroot. Regional fire management operator thinks the winds will push it down the mountain too fast for a controlled burn. He wants it contained."

"Got it," Mallory said. "I'll radio the status before we drop."

"Good. Safe trip."

"Right," Mallory replied automatically and hustled into the ready room with the rest of the crew. Her personal gear and chute were already packed and hanging from a peg just inside the door. Her field trauma kit was there too. All the firefighters had basic first aid training, but she was the only paramedic on the team. She kicked off her work boots, slid into her jump pants and jacket, and pulled on thick socks and her logging boots. After securing her hard hat to the side of her pack, she shrugged into her gear and jogged back across the yard to the plane. Benny had already taxied out of the hangar and Mallory waited at the cargo bay door to check each jumper as they climbed aboard, ensuring they had secured their chutes and loaded all their gear. She slowed as Jac and Sarah crossed the tarmac toward her.

"What's the word?" Sarah asked.

"Ridge fire at Bitterroot."

"How big?"

"Not sure yet. This early in the season, it's probably small. Pretty wet still."

"Probably," Sarah said.

Mallory shrugged. "We'll dig line, start a back fire, probably have it contained by morning." She glanced up at the sky where the sun was just rising. Cloudless. Cold. "If the wind doesn't rise."

"Uh-huh. The winds are tricky up there on Bitterroot." Sarah didn't need to say anything else. There'd been a near disaster there several years before. A smokejumping crew had been overtaken by a fire that had chimneyed up a ridge and caught them in a blowup. That team had been luckier than Mallory's had the summer before. They'd all gotten under their fire tents in time, and they'd all survived. Her crew hadn't. Phil Marcum never made it to the safety zone she had picked. He'd been caught in the blaze. His body had been nothing but cinders. Danny O'Donnell couldn't get his fire tent open in time. He had died of smoke inhalation a few feet away from where Mallory had lain with her face in the dirt, enclosed in her own fire-resistant cocoon, listening to the fire rage over her head. She'd never know if those men had died because she'd made an error in predicting the direction a blowup would take when she'd spotted the safety zone, or if they might still be alive if she had sensed the fire about to jump a minute sooner than she had. The after-operation investigation had cleared her of any error in judgment or execution, but she knew better. She had been in charge. Two men had died on her watch, and she would be forever responsible. Mallory shoved the guilt back down. "Ought to be an easy one."

"Uh-huh," Sarah said again, her solemn expression telling Mallory she knew differently.

"I've got to go." Mallory didn't have time to give assurances Sarah wouldn't believe. Sarah had as much as said at the end of the last season she was worried Mallory would take chances, trying to make up for something that wasn't her fault. "You're senior while I'm gone, Sarah. Check on my injured rookie, will you? Ray Kingston. Any problems, transfer him out."

"I will—don't worry about it."

Mallory couldn't pretend not to see Jac any longer. Jac stood next to Sarah with her hands balled in the pockets of her cargo pants, looking a little rumpled and a lot sexy. Had it really only been a few minutes since they had crowded together on her cot, pretending to feed each other but doing something far more intimate? Mallory's lips still tingled from where Jac's fingers had grazed them. She felt the weight of Jac's body leaning against her legs, and her belly quivered. Whatever had happened between them had been sidelined by the klaxon, and just as well. Jac's eyes were stormy now and every bit as hot as they had been upstairs. Mallory couldn't afford to get lost in those kinds of clouds, not with anyone, but certainly not with a rookie whose mere presence almost made her forget the cost of getting too close. She squeezed Sarah's arm and pointed at Jac. "Listen to Sarah. Don't screw up, rookie."

Jac stepped closer, then halted abruptly as if surprised she'd moved at all. "I'll wait till you get back to do that."

Mallory shook her head. "Then I'll try to make it quick."

"You do that," Jac said. "See you soon…Mal."

Hiding her smile, Mallory turned away and jogged to the plane. She climbed on, checked that all the crew were there and strapped in, and gave Benny the thumbs up. She slid the cargo door closed and made her way up front to the cockpit. Settling into the seat opposite

Benny's, she buckled in and didn't look out the window as they taxied away. Superstition, maybe. Maybe she just didn't want to see Jac's figure disappearing in the distance.

Once airborne, Benny said, "Sully radioed they've got a tanker dropping mud before you land."

"Good. The retardant along with the snow ought to make our job easier, even though it's hell to slog through that crap on the ground."

"Not to worry. I'll circle until the tanker leaves, and you can find a nice clean spot for your landing."

"Thanks." Mallory laughed. As long as no one ended up in a tree, she'd be happy.

Thirty minutes later she caught the first sign of the smoke column climbing into the sky. The fire stretched out along a quarter of a mile of ridge in dense forest. Snow still covered patches of ground, which would make clearing the line a little bit harder but might help contain the fire front. She pointed to a clear spot in the trees. "Over there."

Benny banked in that direction so she could get a better look. Mallory checked several spots until she found a landing zone close to the fire front, but flanking it and not littered with boulders.

"That looks good." Mallory radioed their position and reported the initial fire assessment to the local fire station.

The base supervisor radioed back. "Do you need ground support?"

"Not at this time," Mallory answered. "Will advise after we establish our control lines."

"Roger."

Mallory clapped Benny's shoulder. "We're out of here."

"Stay safe," Benny said.

"Right."

Back in the cargo hold, Mallory signaled for the team to clip on and prepare to off-load. She slid back the cargo bay door and waited while Benny flew over the landing zone, then tapped the first pair to go. On his fourth pass, she jumped with Cooper, and Benny headed for home.

In a matter of seconds, the frigid air whipped around her and numbed her face and body. She landed stiffly, jolting hard on the ground despite automatically flexing her knees and falling to her side at the instant of impact. Ignoring the bone-jarring pain, she jumped up, checked to see that the rest of the team had landed safely, and collected her chute. After a fast confirmation of the fire status, she dispatched the team and radioed the local base with a status update. Once done, she took her place on the line—farthest from the safety zone. If anyone got caught too far out ever again, it wouldn't be one of her crew.

Everyone knew what to do. They'd done it dozens of times before. Mallory set to work with her pulaski—part-hoe, part ax—clearing melting snow, clumps of ice, rotting leaves, and other debris along a ten-foot-wide line in front of the fire. She removed everything flammable down to the dirt—chopping roots, digging out stumps, scraping away undergrowth until nothing remained to feed the advancing flames. Men with saws took down larger trees and dragged them away.

Out on the line, her mind cleared and her body took over. She didn't think of anything as she chopped and cleared except the position of the fire and the location of the rest of the team. The day wore on, and she opened her jacket, letting the chill air dry the sweat soaked into her fire-retardant Nomex shirt. Smoke and embers drifted in the air, and she wiped her face with the bandanna she'd tied loosely around her neck. One of the times she stopped to drink water from her canteen, she pulled a protein bar from her PG pack and bit into it. As she chewed the mostly flavorless bar, she remembered the bran muffin and the soft caress of Jac's fingers on her mouth. Jac. How had Jac managed to get so close so fast?

Mallory shoved the wrapper in her pocket, grabbed her pulaski, and went back to digging. Thank God Sarah had shown up early. Sarah could take charge of Jac's training, and Mallory could get some distance. And some damn perspective.

CHAPTER THIRTEEN

Jac lay awake, listening to a light rain dance on the hangar's metal roof. The loft felt dark and close, growing colder every night that Mallory was gone. Almost a week that seemed like a month—endless hours stretching interminably from sundown until dawn. The shadows weighed more heavily on her chest, the empty cot across from her echoing the emptiness that hollowed out her bones. Tonight she'd never fallen asleep at all, lying on her back staring into the gloom, remembering all the nights she'd lain awake listening to the scratch of sand shifting against the sides of a canvas tent, surrounded by humanity and aching with loneliness. She ached tonight, but not in some vague existential way. Tonight she just missed Mallory.

Sighing, she punched her pillow and rolled onto her side. Mallory's neatly rolled sleeping bag mocked her. She'd straightened Mallory's bed the first night Mallory was gone. When she'd rested her hand for a few seconds on the spot where she had sat with Mallory's feet tucked against her leg, she'd registered that the bag was cool, but she'd imagined the heat of Mallory's body tucked inside it. She'd imagined herself spooned against Mallory's back, her arm around Mallory's waist and her chin tucked in the curve of Mallory's shoulder, her mouth close to Mallory's ear. Murmuring to her. Kissing her softly. The fantasy was exquisitely bittersweet, and when she crawled into her own cold sleeping bag, the pulse of desire hammering between her thighs haunted rather than tempted her. She feared an orgasm would taste only of ashes, reminding her of all the hopes that had vanished long before the desert winds had ground them to dust.

Each night, sleep became more elusive while her body strummed with anxious tension, but she didn't want the quick release and hazy aftermath of a solitary orgasm. While it made no sense, she didn't want to come fantasizing about Mallory when Mallory was fighting a fire on a mountainside somewhere. She had no doubt Mallory was sleepless, and it seemed the least she could do was to tolerate her own restless nights. At least she was warm and dry, and Mallory's team most certainly wasn't. Weather had blown in within hours of Benny's return from dropping the team at the fire front—an icy rain mixed with snow, nature's reminder that spring had not yet driven out the last breath of winter.

Jac had checked the satellite images of the burn area every few hours throughout each day, following the storm's path as it lingered over the mountains. She'd traced the topography of Bitterroot with her fingertip, climbing mountain peaks and descending into valleys, trying to place Mallory in that vast wilderness. Wishing they had radio contact. Wishing she was digging line and chopping trees by Mallory's side.

Sarah had opted to use the time Mallory was away to cover the mandatory didactic sessions, and most of the last few days had been spent sitting at a table with the other rookies in a cinderblock-walled room. While listening to Sarah talk about fire protocols and Sully discuss principles of fire management, her mind kept drifting to the realities of the job. She hadn't worked a full season, but she'd spent enough time on the line to know how easily the job could turn treacherous. Even when the fire wasn't bearing down, there were dozens of other potential hazards. Snakes, bugs, and terrified animals incited to violence were as dangerous as burning branches, falling trees, and blowups. And so many other ways to encounter injury—heat exhaustion, sun exposure, and always, always the fire.

Every firefighter recognized the dangers, guarded against them, trained to avoid them, and still, still, every year firefighters were lost. Everyone accepted the risks, no one dwelled on them. Jac tried not to. She'd spent enough time at the front—first when deployed, then on the fire line—to learn not to torture herself with what-ifs. She knew Mallory would be back, she just wished she knew when.

She'd skipped dinner earlier and opted for an extra-long workout, hoping to wear off her nagging disquiet. After too many nights with too little sleep, she'd turned in early, physically fatigued and mentally exhausted. If she'd been able to sleep propped up against sandbags in the middle of a godless desert, she ought to be able to sleep here. So she'd thought.

Now it was well into the deep hours of the night, and she was still wide-awake. With a sigh, she shoved aside the top flap of the sleeping bag and got up. Dressing hastily, she pulled on sweats and a navy blue sweatshirt, stepped into her unlaced work boots, and headed for the canteen. She expected the place to be empty, and she was nearly right. Sarah sat alone at a table with a steaming mug of coffee and a piece of pie in front of her.

"Tell me where you got that, and I'll be your slave forever," Jac said.

Sarah pushed a half-finished crossword puzzle aside and smiled up at her. "Really? And I could have your services for anything I desired?"

Jac felt a blush rise in her face, which was damn surprising. Ordinarily she'd pursue a harmless flirtation, just because bantering with a woman was pleasant. Instead, a vague sense of unease tripped her up, and she immediately thought of Mallory. Sarah was attractive, but she didn't want to flirt with her. Innocent or not. Quickly, she amended, "*Almost* anything."

"Well, I'm not so sure, then."

"Please," Jac groaned. "I'm in need."

Sarah laughed and pointed toward the double-wide swinging doors to the kitchen. "Charlie is still here. Ask him nicely, and I think you'll score a piece."

"Thank you," Jac said reverently and went in search of pie. Charlie was scraping down the grill when she found him. "If there's something you need done back here, I'd be happy to help out."

"Nice of you," Charlie said conversationally, his attention on the grill.

Jac laughed. "Not really. Sarah said there might be pie."

Charlie spared her a glance, his coal-black eyes studying her intently. Then he went back to methodically scraping the last of the oil from the gleaming surface of his grill with a flat spatula. "Not much left to do here. Go keep Sarah company, and I'll deliver that pie in a few minutes."

"You don't have to do that. I could get—"

"Go on now, out of my kitchen." His voice held no heat.

"Okay, thanks." Jac got halfway to the door and then turned around. "By the way, you make the best chow of any line cook I've ever run into."

He stopped scraping and straightened, his expression curious. "You know many?"

"I've done a few tours with the Guard. I've eaten lots of meals in lots of mess halls. Yours beats them all."

He smiled. "I did some Army cooking myself, back in Southeast Asia in the seventies."

"Then they were lucky soldiers."

"The apple or cherry?"

Jac grinned. "Any chance I can get a sampler?"

Chuckling, he went back to his grill.

"So? Did you talk Charlie into the pie?" Sarah said when Jac sat down across from her with her own cup of coffee.

"I think so. I sure hope so."

Sarah eased back in her chair. She'd changed out of the cargo pants and khaki shirt she'd worn earlier into black sweats and a soft, long-sleeved white T-shirt that was just tight enough to show off a very nice body. "It's pretty late. Can't sleep?"

A muscle jumped in Jac's jaw, and she consciously unclenched her teeth. "Not that tired. Sitting in a classroom most of the day just wound me up."

"Didn't work it off in the gym?"

"Not much gets past anybody around here, does it," Jac muttered.

"I saw you going over when I was on my way out for a run. When I clocked in for my own workout two hours later, you were still there. You didn't see me."

"Just felt lazy after an easy day," Jac said.

"Was that what it was?"

Jac ignored the gentle probing. She didn't want to talk about what was really bothering her. "Worked out good for Ray—all this class time."

"He's symptom free. He ought to make up the physical fitness part easily enough."

"Excellent." Jac asked as casually as she could, "Did you hear from Mallory?"

"No, but that doesn't mean anything." Sarah paused, looking

thoughtful. "She's probably in constant communication with the local station up there, but we won't hear anything, even when they've pulled out. If they're packing out, that could take a few days right there."

Jac massaged the back of her neck and winced. Her muscles were knotted and tender, and she rubbed her thumb over a sore spot at the junction of her right shoulder. "Waiting—I don't do it very well."

"That's a lot of this job." Sarah gestured to her crossword puzzle. "Long stretches of boredom interspersed with frantic activity. Then, when a crew goes out and you don't hear anything for days, sometimes a couple of weeks, it wears on you."

"Yeah." Jac rubbed her face with both hands and sighed. "A lot like the military."

"You served?"

Jac nodded.

"Then you know how it goes."

Charlie walked up and slid a plate with two pieces of pie on it in front of Jac. "Keep that to yourself, trooper."

Jac looked up at him. "I will. Thanks."

Charlie grunted and headed back to the kitchen.

Jac pushed the plate toward Sarah. "Want some more?"

"Yeah, I didn't get any of the cherry." Sarah picked up her fork and cut off a healthy piece from Jac's plate and slid it onto her own. "Thanks."

"So I wanted to ask you," Jac said, teasing a slice of apple free from the flaky crust.

"Yes?" Sarah asked absently.

"You and Mallory—" Jac looked up into Sarah's eyes.

Sarah regarded her curiously. "Me and Mallory, what?"

"Well, you know, the coffee the other morning—we were playing cards and we made this bet and I didn't want you to think—"

"Mallory is a really good friend, one of my best friends. It's probably dumb of me, but I don't sleep with my friends. Maybe if I did, I'd have better luck."

Jac grimaced. "Not too subtle, am I?"

"Subtlety is overrated. We're not lovers. I suspect she would've told you that if you'd asked her."

"I think so too." Jac stared at the table. "But I didn't want to ask."

"Why not?"

Jac traced the edge of her plate with her fork. "She'd run for the hills."

"Probably." Sarah sipped her coffee. "You know, Jac, Mallory..." She sighed. "I'm claiming best friend's right here, so I have something to say."

"Go ahead." Jac straightened. She knew the tone—she wasn't going to like what was coming.

"Okay." Sarah nodded, as if making a decision. "Maybe Mallory isn't such a good idea."

Jac pushed back a surge of anger and kept her voice even. Here came the "you're not the right person for her" lecture. "Oh? Why is that?"

"She's just...vulnerable right now."

"And you think I'll be bad for her? Hurt her somehow?" Jac carefully cut a wedge of pie with her fork but didn't lift it to her mouth. "Based on what? My reputation?"

Sarah colored. "I'm not going to pretend I don't know what you're talking about, but that's not what I meant."

"What, then?"

"I don't know you, and I'm not about to ask your intentions. But I know Mallory and I love her." Sarah bit her lip and let out a breath. "Since the incident last summer, she hasn't been herself. She still isn't."

"Maybe," Jac said softly, "she never will be. Not the Mallory you knew then. Wounds change us, but they don't have to destroy us. You should trust her."

"Yes." Sarah winced. "What I really should do is mind my own damn business. I'm sorry. I was out of line."

"No, you weren't. Mallory's lucky to have a friend like you." Jac couldn't resent Sarah championing Mallory—she envied their friendship. No one had ever stood up for her, and she'd learned not to hope for it. She finished off the apple and started on the remaining cherry. "Nothing has happened and probably won't. I just... If you and she were together, I didn't want you to get the wrong idea."

"So noted." Sarah waited a beat. "So, she's got under your skin?"

Jac put down her fork and rubbed her belly. She was so tight she could've bounced quarters off her abdominal wall. Massaging didn't help. "Yeah. Quite a lot."

"Well, maybe I'm completely wrong. Maybe a little shaking up is just what she needs."

"And you think I'm the one to do it?"

Sarah pointed a finger at her. "I think you very well could be. Hell, you managed to get pie out of Charlie. That took me three years."

"She's all right out there, isn't she?"

"Jac, you know the job." Sarah's face softened. "Things happen, but Mallory is really, really good. One of the best. She'll be fine. And she won't like it if you worry about her every time she goes out."

"I'll hide it."

Sarah rolled her eyes.

"You're right. I can see how good she is."

"You'll need to trust her, Jac. You'll both need that, in both directions, if you're working together."

"Trust." Jac had learned young not to trust, not to expect people to do what they promised or mean what they said. She'd learned not to count on anyone, and she'd learned not to be disappointed. "I guess that's the part of the training you can't teach."

"Nope." Sarah's expression brightened. "That you get from working your asses off together. You'll see what I mean when we head into the mountains to set up camp and field train."

If that meant living side by side with Mallory, Jac was all for it. She just wanted Mallory and her team to come home.

"You better get some sleep," Sarah said. "We're back on the tower tomorrow. You all have had enough class time for a bit." As if reading Jac's mind, Sarah squeezed her arm. "Mallory will be back soon, and you better look sharp."

"Right." Jac rose and grabbed their plates. "I'm gone."

Sarah laughed. "Keep your head on straight, rookie."

Jac wasn't worried about her head. She just wasn't quite so sure about her heart.

CHAPTER FOURTEEN

Mallory hung her gear pack on the peg inside the door in the equipment room and pressed both hands to her lower back, massaging the knots. She needed a shower to get the smoke out of her hair, the soot off her skin, and some of the kinks out of her muscles.

"See you in a few, Ice," Cooper said as he passed by on his way to the barracks.

"Yeah," she called, turning to wave good night to the rest of the crew. "Great job, guys."

The guys grinned wearily, muttered see you laters, and wandered away.

Before her shower, she needed to take care of essentials. She hoisted her chute onto her shoulder and trudged into the adjacent drying room. The partial ceiling had been removed and a series of pulleys set up to hoist the forty-foot chutes up into the air where they could dry without risk of damage. She unpacked hers, laid it out on one of the folding tables, and carefully checked it over for tears, weak spots, and other signs of wear. When she found none, she attached it to one of the pulleys and winched it high above the concrete floor. By tomorrow afternoon it should be ready to repack, and she would be ready to go back on rotation.

The important work done, she headed into the locker room, stripped off her smoky clothes, and stuffed them into a plastic bag. She tied off the top to contain some of the acrid odor, propped that in the corner to drag over to the do-it-yourself laundry room, gathered her toiletries from her locker, and padded naked into the shower. She didn't even bother to wait till the water was warm. She just wanted to be clean, cold water or not. Besides, the sun would be up in less than an hour, and she needed to see to the rookies. The cold water blasted into her face, and after the initial adrenaline shock, she got her second wind and started to feel halfway alive. She found the shampoo by feel, pumped some into her hand, and lathered her hair. The cleaner she got, the more human she felt. The icy water quickly became warm and then hot, and she turned and stretched and rinsed her hair. She was tired and sore, but satisfied. They had done good work, and she'd never found anything to make her happier. After switching off the water, she briskly toweled her hair and wrapped the slightly damp cotton around her body. The slamming of a locker door brought her up short.

Jac! Every fiber of her body went on alert. Her breath quickened and her fingertips tingled. She caught herself breathing quickly and forced herself to slow down. This reaction was ridiculous, and she definitely didn't want Jac to get any inkling of what her presence did to her. Tightening the knot on her towel, she cursed herself for not having brought her clothes into the shower room with her. She'd gotten out of the habit of doing that with just her and Sarah there most of the time. She and Sarah knew each other so well, she never gave any thought to being naked around her. Jac was another matter. She couldn't pretend they were just two women who worked together, not when the thought of Jac made her blood buzz, and actually *seeing* her made her downright stupid. She most assuredly was not going to be anywhere around Jac Russo naked. Quickly, she shoved her shower articles into their plastic case, zipped it up, and steeled herself for a brief, casual hello in passing.

When she walked into the locker room, her stomach sank. "Hey, Sarah."

"You're back!" Sarah threw her arms around Mallory, apparently not the least bit concerned that she was going to get wet. Keeping her arms looped around Mallory's waist, she leaned back and gave her a thorough once-over. "Well, you look all right." She ran her thumb over a bruise on Mallory's cheek. "Is this the worst of it?"

Laughing, Mallory lifted Sarah's hands from around her waist and pulled back. "I'm getting you soaked, silly."

"So? I was about to jump in the shower anyhow. A little more water isn't going to hurt. How did it go out there?"

"Pretty routine, except for the damn snow." Mallory grimaced as she stowed her gear and pulled a dry towel off the shelf. After wrapping her hair, she loosed the one from her body and began to dry off. "We had the perimeter set up pretty fast, and the front never really challenged. It was just rough going, a lot of snow and ice on the ground. No injuries, everybody did great. How are things here?"

"Fine." Sarah stripped off her sweats and underwear, threw a large towel over her shoulders, and stepped into flip-flops. "Everybody's bored to tears—we've been doing a lot of the classroom stuff while you were gone. I scheduled more time on the tower tomorrow—well, today, really."

"Good. Any problems? How's Ray?"

"You haven't been gone that long—what kind of problems did you anticipate?"

Mallory shook out her hair and ran her fingers through it to untangle the curls. "Well, considering the first day out I had a fairly serious injury and I'm not totally certain all the rookies are going to get along, almost anything could have happened."

"Ray is doing great. I don't see any reason he can't get back into the regular rotation now."

"Good." Mallory pulled on clean underwear and jeans and made an attempt at sounding casual. "How's Jac doing?"

"Jac? Jac who?"

Mallory felt her face flushing. "Sarah."

Sarah grinned. "Jac has been doing fine, if you don't count not sleeping and skipping meals."

"What do you mean?" Mallory's chest tightened, and an uncomfortable wave of anxiety fluttered through her middle. "Is she sick? Did she get hurt?"

"No," Sarah said, collecting her shower articles. "She's basically just been moping since you left."

Mallory snorted. "I hardly think I'm the reason."

Sarah looked at her as if she were dense. "Oh, don't tell me you haven't noticed she's got a major thing for you."

"I most certainly haven't and she most certainly does not," Mallory said hastily. "She's a rookie, for crying out loud, Sarah."

"Yes," Sarah said, "and the last time I looked, quite adult and hardly someone who's likely to be taken advantage of in this situation."

Mallory quickly turned her back, busying herself straightening her already organized locker. She was not going to discuss Jac and something that didn't exist and never would. "Well, I'm glad everything is stable around here. Thanks so much for taking care of everyone—everything—while I was gone."

"Trust me, if Jac had been able to think about anything except when you were coming back, I would've considered giving her a whirl."

Mallory whipped around. "You've got to be kidding me."

Sarah pointed a finger at her. "I'm not kidding. Mostly. She's really nice and really hot, and you know what, Mark *is* an a-hole."

"He is. But I'm not sure his being one warrants quite so big a change in your approach to dating."

Sarah shrugged. "I am bi-flexible."

Mallory choked on a laugh. "Since when?"

"Since Mark," Sarah said with a snarl.

"Well, if you don't mind, I'd rather you not drag one of the rookies away."

"Ha ha. Does it matter which one?"

"Any of them," Mallory said, only half-joking. She was pretty certain Sarah was kidding about Jac, but not entirely. And the image of Jac with Sarah, touching her, being touched by her, set fireworks off in her head. "I really can't think about this right now."

Sarah's brows drew down. "Think about what?"

"Never mind." Mallory grabbed a light windbreaker, collected her laundry, and started toward the door. "Enjoy your shower. I'll see you at roll call."

"Welcome back," Sarah called as Mallory went through the door.

"Thanks." She was glad to be back. Glad the call had been successful, glad for having done her job well. And glad that in a few minutes, she'd see Jac again. Pretending otherwise was silly. She didn't lie to herself, even if she wasn't about to admit how many times she'd thought of Jac while she'd been gone.

Mallory slowed in the middle of the yard. Jac was still probably asleep. Maybe going up to the loft right now wasn't such a good idea. Abruptly she changed course. No use complicating something that didn't have to be complicated.

❖

Jac woke at dawn to the rumble of a truck engine revving in the yard. A jumble of deep male laughter rolled upward on a gust of wind, then faded just as quickly, and silence descended. A quick check of her watch told her what she already sensed—she had a few minutes before she needed to get up if she wanted breakfast before reporting for roll call. She folded her arms behind her head and tried to quiet the rush of air in and out of her lungs, waiting for the soft fall of footsteps nearing the ladder. When none came, she pushed herself up and out of her sleeping bag. She had one leg in her cargo pants when Mallory climbed into the loft.

"Morning," Jac said, balancing on one foot.

Mallory's eyes swept down her body and then back to her face. The spark in Mallory's eyes stirred a fire in the pit of Jac's stomach, heating the places where she'd been cold for a long time.

"I got you coffee and a muffin," Mallory said, averting her gaze abruptly. She hesitated as if not quite certain what she should do with the items she held in her hands, staring at the cardboard tray as if not sure why she held it. "I was getting some anyhow and I thought…"

Quickly, Jac pulled her pants on and scrabbled around in her duffel for a shirt to cover the tank she'd slept in. She shrugged into a red cotton button-up and pushed a hand through her hair, trying for some semblance of composure. She took a step forward, intending to take the tray. "How are you?"

Mallory's eyes met hers, and the sparks intensified and broke free. Flames danced in the air. "I'm okay. Everybody's okay."

"Good."

"I really should go." Mallory looked down at the cardboard tray and the paper cups and the plastic-wrapped muffins, wondering how she'd come to be standing in the loft with a sexily sleep-tousled Jac Russo a few feet away. She hadn't meant to come here. She'd been on her way to grab some food, and then she'd heard Sarah's voice in her head, telling her Jac had been restless, sleepless, skipping meals. Because of her. And she'd wanted to see her. "I'm not sure what I'm doing here."

"Let me help you." Jac took the tray and set it down on a small packing crate between the heads of their two cots. She straightened and eased forward again, moving slowly, hoping Mallory wasn't going to bolt back down the ladder. She stopped a few inches from Mallory and closed her hands tightly before she put them all over Mallory. She wanted to grip her shoulders and pull her forward and kiss her. Simple and uncomplicated. Oh yeah, real simple. "I'm glad you're back."

"I ran into Sarah in the locker room." Mallory pushed her hands into her back pockets. "She mentioned you were worried, maybe."

"Maybe, a little. Yeah." Jac added quickly, "I know that's silly."

Mallory moistened her lips and took a deep breath. "Yeah, maybe. Not necessary. Nice, though. Thanks."

"You're welcome." Jac gripped her hair again, contemplating pulling it out. She felt about twelve, trying to figure out how to ask for her first date. "You want some coffee?"

Mallory glanced at her watch. "I should probably get going. I want to see Ray before roll call."

"Why don't I walk over with you?" Jac pulled the two cups from the tray and handed one to Mallory. She unwrapped a blueberry muffin, broke it in half, and passed part to Mallory. "We can save the other one for break time."

Mallory laughed, and the sound hit Jac like a flashover. "Thanks. They were out of bran."

"I'll put in a request. Charlie loves me."

Mallory's eyebrows rose. "Is that right? And how do you figure?"

Jac bit into the muffin and Mallory followed suit. Jac wanted to moan, not because the muffin was wonderful, which it was, but because watching Mallory eat one might be the sexiest thing she'd ever seen. "He gave me pie."

Mallory stopped chewing. "No."

Solemnly, Jac nodded.

"I never took you for a prevaricator."

"Oh." Jac slammed her hand against her chest. "You wound me."

Mallory narrowed her eyes. "Charlie really gave you pie?"

"Two pieces."

"Now I know you're lying."

Jac grinned. "I speak only the truth. Ask Sarah, she'll tell you."

"Sarah was there to witness this? When?"

"About three this morning."

"Really." Mallory's voice became a few degrees cooler.

"I was restless," Jac confessed. "I ran into her in the canteen."

"You're a puzzle, Russo," Mallory said softly.

"I don't think so."

"No, you probably wouldn't. You don't hide much, do you?"

Jac laughed at the irony. "God, Mallory. I hide everything."

"Why doesn't it seem that way to me?"

"I don't know. You make me want to tell all my secrets, and it's damn scary."

"I'm sorry."

Jac's heart beat so hard she wondered if she might be having a heart attack. "For what?"

"For making you think…" Mallory stopped, shook her head.

"I don't think anything, Mallory. I'm not after anything. Some things just are."

"And I don't know what to do with that, Jac," Mallory said helplessly. "I really don't. And I need to go."

"Yeah, I know." Jac felt Mallory leaving, even though she hadn't moved. She was helpless to hold her, knew she couldn't. Letting go felt like her heart was exploding. "So I'll see you at roll call."

"Don't be late, rookie," Mallory murmured and climbed over the side of the loft and down the ladder.

Mallory always seemed to be walking away. Jac glanced around, feeling Mallory's absence even more than she had the night before, and remembered the price of letting anyone close.

CHAPTER FIFTEEN

L isten up," Mallory called down to the group assembled around the wooden scaffold. "On my mark, you'll step to the edge, pivot with your back to the ground, tuck your chin, and drop."

Jac squinted at the six-foot-high platform and the hard-packed ground beneath. She was supposed to step off into nothing and land on the ground wearing a full pack and all her gear as if landing with a parachute. She glanced at Ray. "Is your head okay for this?"

"There's nothing wrong with my head, but I'm not sure about my sanity," he muttered.

Jac grinned. "Yeah. I'm feeling a little bit crazy myself right now."

Mallory glanced in their direction and raised an eyebrow. "Problems over there?"

"No ma'am," Ray said briskly.

"Not a thing," Jac said.

"Okay." Mallory stepped to the edge. "Don't hold your breath unless you want to lose it all when you hit." She grinned down at them. "And remember your chin."

She pushed off, seemed to turn in midair like a diver at the pinnacle of her leap, then fell gracefully, landed soundlessly, and rolled to her feet.

"Questions?" Mallory asked, unsnapping her helmet as she walked over.

When she shook her hair out in an unconsciously sensual move, Jac's heart went into free fall. God, she was every kind of beautiful.

No one had any questions, but a couple of the guys looked a little green.

"Hooker," Mallory said. "Why don't you go first and demonstrate. You at least know what the ground feels like coming up at you from your skydiving experience."

"Sure. No problem," Hooker said.

Mallory climbed back up to the platform and Hooker followed.

Jac didn't think she'd ever get used to seeing Mallory with the clouds at her back, sunlight glinting in her hair. Her face was flushed with exertion and pure exhilaration. She looked happy. Mallory hadn't looked happy in the loft that morning. She'd looked confused and uncertain and reluctant. Making Mallory unhappy was the last thing Jac wanted to do. Hell, she hadn't even gotten close to Mallory yet, and she was already screwing things up. What she needed to do was back off. Give Mallory space. That ought to be easy enough to do, if she could only figure out how to stop thinking about her. And keep her heart from stuttering to a standstill every time she unexpectedly caught a glimpse of Mallory out of the corner of her eye. If she could only manage not to tighten up inside at the mere sound of her voice. Then it ought to be easy to maintain some distance.

"You ready for this?" Ray said.

"Huh?" Jac said.

"This exercise." Ray gave her a look. "Where's your head at, Jac? You need to score some points with the boss."

"You can say that again."

"Huh?"

"Never mind."

Above them, Mallory said, "Hooker, take your place. On my mar—"

Hooker dropped off the edge, tucked, landed, and rolled.

"What the fuck was that?" Ray whispered. "Wasn't he supposed to—"

"Yeah," Jac muttered. "He was."

Hooker was testing Mallory, subtly ignoring her authority in front of everyone. Jac just couldn't figure out why. The guy must've known who was in charge of the station when he signed up, so if he had problems with Mallory, why didn't he opt out of the placement? What did he think he was going to gain by antagonizing her? She'd wash him out at this rate.

Hooker sauntered over, a satisfied smirk on his face. "Piece-a-cake, ladies. You all will be fine."

Mallory climbed down the ladder and walked over. "Too much wind up there, Hooker?"

He pulled off his helmet and shrugged his shoulders. "Nope. Felt great."

"So you weren't having a problem hearing me?"

He looked at her innocently. "Nope."

"Want to explain why you took off early?"

"Hey," he said nonchalantly. "You said you wanted me to demonstrate, I demonstrated. Any problems with my…technique?"

"The exercise isn't just about technique," Mallory said steadily, her gaze never wavering from Hooker's. "It's about performance. And part of performance out here is following protocol. Protocol keeps us all alive."

Hooker's jaw tightened. "Does it? That's real good to know. Considering."

Something hard stole into Mallory's eyes, and a wave of heat surged in Jac's chest. She clamped her jaws so hard, her ears ached. She wanted to challenge Hooker, hell—she wanted to kick his ass.

"Russo," Mallory said softly. "You're up."

"Roger that."

Jac waited for Mallory to lead the way up the ladder, watching the rigid line of her back as she ascended, knowing Hooker had drawn blood and wanting to filet him for it. Up on the platform, the wind blew Mallory's hair around her face, and Jac ached to catch some of those strands on her fingers and tuck them behind Mallory's ear. Any excuse to touch her. Maybe a futile gesture to ease her pain. Words, sympathy, even having been there herself, couldn't touch the private wound, and she knew it. Still, the helplessness ate at her.

"Questions?" Mallory asked.

"No."

"Repeat the sequence for me, please."

Mallory's tone was mechanical, remote, distant. She'd gone someplace inside, behind the barriers that helped deflect but never blocked the pain.

Jac did the only thing she could. Her job, just like Mallory. "Step to the edge. On your mark, step off, turn in the air, tuck my chin, land and roll."

"Good." Mallory rapped Jac on the back of her hardhat. "Don't forget your chin, Rookie."

The slight reverberation of Mallory's knuckles against the protective headgear shot through Jac like a hot caress. Her breath caught in her chest.

"Right." Jac stepped to the edge.

"Ready," Mallory said, her voice the only sound. "Go."

Jac pushed off and pivoted, searching for Mallory. She found Mallory's eyes fixed on her, steady and intent, and calm suffused her. The next second, she hit hard, harder than she'd expected, and the breath rushed from her chest. Coughing, trying to suck air back in, she immediately rolled onto her side, and some of the shock dissipated. Thankfully, she managed a breath and got to her feet. Her legs were still a little wobbly. She chalked that unsteadiness up to the hard landing. She wanted to pretend her moment of disorientation hadn't been all Mallory. But it was. Pretty pathetic that a casual rap on the head would turn her upside down. She hustled out of the landing area and made her way to the back of the line.

"Not bad," Hooker said.

"Thanks," Jac said, working hard to keep her voice steady. Her lungs didn't feel fully expanded yet, and she was still air hungry. Her right shoulder was a little sore, but she'd remembered to tuck her chin, and Mallory hadn't come down to criticize her drop. She'd take it for the first time out.

Hooker leaned too close to her, his big body crowding her. "Probably scored some points with James."

"That wasn't high on my list," Jac said, standing her ground. "I'd just rather not break both my legs the first time I jump from the plane."

"All the same," he said, "I get the feeling muffins aren't gonna get you where you want to go with her."

Jac tensed. She hadn't seen him on her coffee and muffin run, but he'd obviously seen her. Careless of her not to be on alert. "Hooker—"

"Hey, babe, good luck thawing that out." Hooker grinned

suggestively. "Whoever named her Ice wasn't kidding. I don't think you can get through with a blowtorch."

She wanted to take him on and she couldn't, for so many reasons. She'd get booted from the program. She'd probably make the news, and her family would have one more "humiliating escapade," as her father termed it, to suffer through. Mallory wouldn't want her to cause problems for the team. Mallory didn't *need* her to defend her. "Hooker, are you always such a moron, or am I just the lucky recipient of your idiocy?"

He chuckled. "You really think you're gonna get over on that one?"

"I don't think anything at all. What is your problem?"

"Not a thing." He turned so his back was partially to the platform, and his friendly expression went feral. "If you get a piece of her, congratulations. Maybe you'd even like to share. I've got plenty to go around."

Jac actually drew her fist back, and his gaze flickered to the movement.

"You really do have a hard-on for her." He laughed. "What are you going to do, hit me?"

Jac turned and walked away.

"Russo?" Mallory called. "*Russo*. Problem?"

"Just winded. Fell wrong," Jac yelled back without slowing. She kept going until she reached the shack. She hung her pack on the peg, put her gear away, and pulled off her jump suit. She jogged out of the building, across the yard, and into the woods. The cold mountain air dried the sweat on her skin, but didn't cool her fury. She had no destination. She only wished she had an IED waiting for her, anything to defuse her frustration and helplessness.

❖

Mallory finished writing her evaluations, stacked the forms neatly on the upper right-hand corner of her desk, and stared at the small brass wind-up clock that had adorned her father's desk until his death. Five o'clock. The sun would set in less than an hour, and the mountains would become a dense, dark labyrinth. No one ventured into the wilderness after dark unless life and limb depended on it. Jac hadn't returned to the loft to catnap or change clothes or unwind. She was probably in the gym or grabbing an early dinner in the canteen. Maybe playing cards or comparing war stories with the other rookies. Somewhere doing what smokejumpers did while waiting for the action, somewhere safe and sound.

The back of Mallory's neck burned, probably a bit of windburn from standing up on the tower most of the afternoon. She rubbed at the sore spot, but the niggling irritation didn't go away. Her warning antennae quivered, and she never ignored her gut.

"Damn it," she muttered, jumping to her feet. She pulled her sweatshirt off the back of her chair and shrugged it on, jammed her hands into the pockets, and stalked out of the hangar to the ready shack. She checked the equipment room first. Jac's gear was there, stowed neatly. She cut through to the hallway that led to the gym. The room was crowded, but a quick look was all she needed to know Jac wasn't there. Okay, so she was having dinner. But the canteen was nearly empty. Ray and Sarah sat with dinner trays in front of them, talking at a far table. Mallory walked over.

"Have you seen Russo?" she said to Ray.

He straightened in his seat. "No…ah. No."

The itch at the back of her neck spread like a rash, and she wanted to shake, twitching off the irritation like a horse shedding flies in the summer sun. "Sarah? Did you talk to her after the exercise today?"

"No," Sarah said in surprise. "I didn't see her. Sorry."

"Okay, thanks."

"Something wrong?" Sarah asked.

"No," Mallory said quickly, too quickly, because Sarah's eyes narrowed suspiciously.

"Sorry to bother your dinner." Mallory spun around and beat a quick retreat. She didn't want to discuss Jac or why she was looking for her. Back in the equipment room, she grabbed her field jacket and flashlight and headed for the woods. As soon as she ducked into the trees, the chill seeped into her extremities. Even in summer the sunlight rarely touched the ground under the canopy of evergreens, and in winter, the bone-deep cold hovered above the ice and snow like a malignant being, sapping body heat and distorting concentration. The snow was mostly gone now, but the soil temperature was still below fifty degrees.

It was damn cold. Anyone caught out overnight would be at severe risk for hypothermia. But she wasn't leaving Jac out overnight—she'd find her before then.

Mallory set off down the main trail, moving fast over familiar terrain, looking for signs of Jac, but not really expecting to find any. Jac was no inexperienced hiker. She wouldn't leave litter to mark her passing. What the hell was she doing out here, if she was even out here at all? Too late, Mallory considered that Jac might have left base camp altogether. Maybe she'd gone to town. Maybe she wanted to get away—or wanted company.

Except Jac wouldn't walk out in the middle of a training session without a damn good reason. A trip to town for a little recreation and company just didn't seem to be her style. Not that Mallory really knew what Jac's style was, but irresponsibility and flouting authority didn't seem to be her. Which meant something was wrong.

As soon as she let the thought in, her stomach churned. Not another rookie in trouble. Not Jac. By the time she reached the midpoint of the trail it was getting too dark to see, and she switched on her flashlight. She couldn't continue to search at night, alone. She'd be at risk herself, and if Jac was out here, possibly injured, then she needed to organize a full-out search and rescue mission. She ought to turn back. She stood in the center of the trail, searching the woods on either side. She couldn't leave her out here.

A branch snapped off to her right.

"Jac? Jac!"

She waited, heart pounding, and then heard a faint call. Maybe an owl, even a coyote, but she needed the sound to be Jac.

"Jac? It's Mallory."

"Hey."

Mallory spun around. Jac stood a few feet away. Mallory's heart leapt into her throat. "God Almighty. What in the hell are you doing out here?"

"Sorry," Jac said somewhat breathlessly. "I was on my way back and my flashlight batteries died. I was headed for the upper trail—better visibility. What are *you* doing out here?"

"What am I doing out here? What am *I* doing here." Mallory's anxiety morphed into anger. "You've got to be kidding me. I was about to pull together an SAR team to come after you."

"Why?" Jac frowned at her watch. "I've only been gone a few hours. I didn't realize that would be a problem."

"What the hell, Russo. You walked out of the session this afternoon, didn't leave word with anyone where you were going, and then didn't return with dark coming on. What did you think I would think about that?" Mallory was furious with herself for losing her composure, and even more angry at Jac, who stared at her with a confused frown. God damn it, she'd been scared Jac was hurt. She didn't need that.

"Hell, Mallory. I'm sorry. I didn't think—"

"You know, that seems to be a habit with you. You don't think."

Jac stiffened. "You don't know me well enough to say that."

"You put yourself at risk, Russo. Probably in the desert, that kind of behavior was necessary. I get that. I respect you for what you did over there. It takes incredible bravery to put yourself in front of one of those insane devices to save others. But you are not in the desert now. This isn't war. I can't have you going off like a loose cannon whenever the mood strikes you."

"Look, I'm sorry. I—" Jac clenched her jaw, biting off the rest of her sentence.

"You want to explain it to me, then? Why did you leave early today, and don't tell me it's because you were winded. You're in great shape. You took that fall fine. You weren't winded when you got up. You lost a little air, sure, but you would have been fine in a couple of minutes."

"You saw that?"

Mallory shook her head. "Don't change the subject."

"I was shaky after the drop," Jac insisted. "I needed to walk it off."

"For four hours?"

Jac looked away and Mallory's heart sank. Jac was hiding something. And that was another problem. "Jac," Mallory said, trying to be reasonable while frustration eroded what remained of her patience. "I need to know what's going on. If there's a problem with you, if there's something that's not working in the training, I need to know. I need to know that you're going to trust me to make the right decisions."

"I do," Jac said.

"Then what's your explanation?"

Jac looked away.

"All right. Let's get back." Mallory fished around in her pocket and pulled out another flashlight. She tossed it to Jac. "And don't wander away this time."

"Mallory."

Something in Jac's voice brought Mallory up short. Sadness, or resignation maybe. "What?"

"I know you don't have any reason to, but if I tell you the reason I left this afternoon has nothing to do with the training or the job, will you believe me? Will you trust me on that?"

Mallory considered. If it wasn't work, it was something personal. Something Jac didn't want to reveal. The options were few out here. "If there's a problem inside the team, that's just as critical for me to know as if one of the team members is having trouble with the training. It all comes down to the team, Jac. Not you, not me, not any one of us. Only the team matters."

"I know. I know I don't have any right to ask you, but I'm going to." Jac wanted to curse, but only a reasoned argument would win Mallory over. She couldn't tell Mallory about Hooker—she was not going to dump his bile on Mallory. The guy was a jerk, and she shouldn't have let him get to her. She sure wasn't dragging Mallory into it. "If you could just give me a little time to work things out, I promise I'll tell you if there's any problem."

Mallory drew a breath. Oddly, that nagging irritating sensation was gone. Her gut settled. Jac was right in front of her. Jac was fine. "There can't be a repeat of this, Jac."

"All right."

"And know this, Russo," Mallory said. "If you give me cause to question your judgment or your ability to function as part of the team again, I'm going to let you go. No questions asked."

"Fair enough," Jac said quietly.

"Let's get back. You've got a big day tomorrow." Mallory turned and walked away. Fairness had nothing to do with it. She was breaking her own rules, and she never did that. She wanted to believe in Jac, and that scared her. Jac Russo scared her to death.

❖

"What the fuck, Jac," Ray muttered while they stood in line at 0530 to board the jump plane. "You keep pissing James off like last night and you're gonna be screwed."

"Everything is cool," Jac said, lying her ass off. Mallory hadn't come up to the loft until late the night before, and hadn't said anything other than "Tomorrow is your first practice jump. Get some sleep."

"If you say so." Ray looked over his shoulder, then dipped his head. "You nervous?"

"Nah." She grinned. "It'll be just like jumping off the platform. And if it isn't, we probably won't even know when we land."

"Wonderful," he muttered.

"Hey," she said, laughing. "You'll have Cooper with you. He won't let anything happen up there."

"I know, I know." Ray glanced at the open cargo doors and the dark interior of the plane's belly. "I know."

Mallory slowed beside them. "All set, rookies?"

"Fine," Jac said, wishing Mallory would actually look at her.

"Totally," Ray echoed.

"Good. Have fun. Remember to count."

Mallory walked on and Jac swallowed acid disappointment. She'd fucked up and didn't know how to make it right, so she did what she knew how to do. Focused on the mission. She ran the jump sequence again in her head. At least she could show Mallory she deserved her spot on the crew.

"Let's check you out, rook," Sarah said, coming up with Cooper, who joined Ray. The two veterans checked them over to see that their chutes and harnesses were in order, the steering handles clear, and reserve chest chutes in place.

"All set," Sarah said. "Questions?"

"I'm good," Jac said.

They loaded and sat in rows on either side of the cargo bay. When Benny reached two thousand feet, he circled and Mallory pulled open the doors. Frigid wind strafed the interior and Jac's eyes watered. Sarah gripped her arm.

"I'll be right behind you."

"Roger," Jac said, glad they were jumping first. Now that they were about to do it, she wanted to go.

Mallory dropped a pair of streamers to judge the wind speed and direction, watched for a few seconds, then signaled for Jac to come ahead. Jac moved forward in a crouch until she could sit on the edge of the rail, her legs dangling in the slipstream.

"See the landing zone?" Mallory yelled. "About fifty yards of drift."

"Roger," Jac called.

"Ready?"

Jac's pulse kicked once, hard, then settled. Excitement raced through her. "Yes!"

Mallory's hand slapped down on her shoulder and Jac pushed out with all her strength.

Jump-thousand—air whipped around her head and her feet jerked up over her head.

Look-thousand—sky and plane passed over her in a swirling flash and the land disappeared.

Sarah dropped out of the plane, a dark blur against the tilting horizon.

Reach-thousand—Jac grabbed the ripcord. Wait-thousand…wait, wait…

Pull-thousand—her body jerked upright and the chute unfurled. She checked her chute—open, no knots, no twists. Sarah drifted down beside her and her chute popped. Jac grabbed the steering toggles and searched for the landing zone.

Time disappeared. The world became a dizzying dance of lush greens, brilliant blues, and blazing sunlight. She was flying, she was free.

Jac yelled, triumphant.

CHAPTER SIXTEEN

A re you ready for your wilderness adventure?" Sarah asked as she packed her PG bag next to Jac.

"Can't wait," Jac said, hoping she sounded appropriately enthusiastic. She *was* looking forward to the field portion of the training. Being cooped up at base was driving her stir-crazy, and sleeping next to Mallory was torture. Especially considering Mallory had barely talked to her since the jump over a week before. Mallory'd been polite enough, saying good morning just before quickly disappearing down the ladder, offering a bland good night if Jac wasn't asleep, which she usually wasn't, when Mallory finally came to bed in the dark hours of the night. Unless Mallory was a vampire, she was staying up most of the night to avoid retiring at the same time as Jac. Okay, maybe that was being a little paranoid, but the casual, impersonal exchanges were worse than silence. The last thing Jac wanted from Mallory was casual, and admitting it, knowing it, made her feel ten kinds of impotent. Not a feeling she enjoyed. Helplessness made her short-tempered. Even Ray had noticed and asked her what was wrong. She'd told him she was fine. She wasn't about to discuss Mallory with anyone, especially one of the guys. Even one of the good guys.

"Gosh," Sarah said, "someone got out of the wrong side of bed this morning."

"Sorry." Jac sighed. "I really am looking forward to being out in the woods. Climbing a few trees sounds like a lot more fun than throwing myself off a platform onto the ground."

"I always hated that part of the training too." Sarah laughed. "I mean, after all, that's why we jump with parachutes. And you have to admit, the jumping is fun."

"Awesome." Jac couldn't help but smile just at the memory of the last real jump—the exhilaration still swamped her. The parachute could completely counteract gravity, and landing feet first on the ground after dropping thousands of feet was still a shock, no matter how controlled the landing. At least she hadn't landed in a tree—yet. Smokejumpers ended up in trees on one out of three landings and had to drop to the ground on the end of a line. So the continued practice of hard landings off the platform in between plane jumps made sense. Jac knew that, but watching Mallory standing just a few feet away for hours, acting as if Jac wasn't even there, was eating her up inside. Jac had never wanted to be seen so much by a woman, by anyone, before. She'd spent most of her life trying *not* to be seen, not to be noticed, not to be pegged as Franklin Russo's daughter. Anonymity meant not being examined, questioned, scrutinized by her peers, by her teachers, by the ubiquitous reporters—all wondering if she held the same views as he did, if she was really a lesbian like the rumor said, if she was really a right-wing bigot underneath everything. She'd tried so hard to fly under the radar, she was stunned when anyone wanted to get to know her. And Mallory, for a while, had seemed to care about who she was and what she thought. Losing that connection was killing her. She couldn't sleep, she wasn't hungry, and her body was in revolt. The barest glance from Mallory made her heart race. And she was horny and couldn't make herself come. Didn't even want to and most of the time didn't try. None of which helped her mood a damn bit.

"What are you doing for your night off?" Sarah asked.

"I hadn't really thought about it yet," Jac said. She'd been too busy wondering where Mallory had disappeared to. As soon as they'd finished the afternoon's jump training, this time on the slamulator, Mallory had headed to her office with her clipboard under her arm. By the time Jac had helped store gear and grabbed a quick shower, Mallory's desk was vacant and the loft empty. Mallory's bed had been neatly made up with her sleeping bag rolled and tucked at the bottom of the cot, as if Mallory wasn't coming back that night. The idea that Mallory might be spending the night off base with someone made Jac feel as if a hundred knives were sticking in her belly. She rubbed it, but the pinpricks of pain didn't go away. "What are you doing?"

"I'm going dancing. Want to come?"

Jac laughed. "Where?"

"A country-western place in Bear Creek."

"Tell me you're not going line dancing."

"I do a mean two-step. What about you?"

"I don't know how." Jac hadn't gone out with friends since before her last tour, and rarely before that. Suddenly the idea of staying in camp with whichever guys were still around seemed pathetic, but her social skills were feeling a little rusty after the debacle with Annabel.

Sarah nudged her shoulder. "Come with me. I'll teach you."

"Do I need shit kickers?"

"Well, it does help to have a hot pair of cowboy boots," Sarah said, cocking her hip and affecting a Texas twang, "but you can probably get by with any pair of boots that aren't loggers. Do you have anything?"

Jac rubbed her neck. "How about riding boots? I've got some of those that might do."

"Okay. It's a date. I'll meet you about eight? Does that work for you?"

"Are you driving?" No way did she want to sit around thinking about Mallory for another three hours.

"Was planning to."

"How about we leave earlier and I buy you dinner first?"

Sarah grinned. "Absolutely. I'll meet you out in the yard in half an hour. Mine is the '85 Mustang."

"Sweet."

"She is." Sarah squeezed Jac's arm. "Be prepared for a hot time, handsome."

Laughing, Jac headed to the hangar for clean jeans and a shirt. Bear Creek hardly warranted a dot on the map, but the little town offered the only nightlife around. If there was an unattached woman in a sixty-mile radius, she'd be there on a Friday night. Maybe a night out and a little friendly female company was exactly what she needed.

❖

Emily reached across the small round oak table and took Mallory's hand. Her smile was quizzical, her soft brown eyes warm and gentle. "Is there something bothering you? You're awfully quiet tonight."

Mallory flushed, embarrassed. "I'm sorry, Em. Dinner was great. Thank you for cooking."

"You know I love to cook, and you're an appreciative diner."

"Meaning I eat like a lumberjack," Mallory said, laughing.

"You have better table manners." Emily sat back in her chair, resting their joined hands on her knee. Her shirt had a tiny wildflower pattern stitched around the edge of the collar and cuffs. On anyone else the look might have seemed cutesy or out of style, but not on her. Emily's light brown, shoulder-length hair shone with sunny highlights, and her heart-shaped face glowed. She was as fresh and exciting as spring mountain air. Being with her was just the kind of relaxing pleasure Mallory craved after the last few weeks.

"It's really good to see you." Mallory lifted Emily's hand and kissed her knuckles.

"I was surprised when you called. Surprised and happy."

Mallory struggled under a wave of guilt. Emily was a wonderful, intelligent, beautiful woman who deserved more than her half-attention. "Believe me, I appreciate you for a lot more than your excellent cooking."

"I do seem to remember that." Emily colored faintly, and her mouth softened into a seductive curve. "But as much as I enjoy you in and out of my kitchen, I have no expectations."

"Ah God, Em, I'm just distracted. Training camp is in full swing, and I haven't slowed down in weeks." Mallory wasn't defending her lack of attention with the easy excuse of too much work, at least not entirely. When she'd called Emily the morning before and suggested they get together tonight, she'd really thought her only motivation was the desire for an evening with a woman she admired and found attractive. They'd been seeing one another on and off for over a year, although not exclusively and not even all that frequently. Whenever they got together, Mallory relaxed and enjoyed herself. She liked listening to Emily's tales of small-town living, and no one knew a town or its inhabitants better than the postmaster. Emily had always said she was happy being single as long as single included enjoying the occasional attentions of a bright, sexy woman. Mallory had always been pleased to oblige. Tonight, though, as the evening wore on, she began to feel uneasy. Emily offered a welcome, effortless antidote to the constant disquiet that had settled in her depths the day Jac arrived at camp. A night with Emily might let her shake free of the nagging turmoil, but she couldn't help thinking she was using Emily, and that was unacceptable. "I'm lousy company tonight, Em. I'm sorry. Maybe I should go."

"I don't think that's what you need. I remember last year when boot camp was in swing—you were tired, sure, but you were also having a great time. You don't look that way right now."

Mallory shifted her gaze before Emily saw too much. She'd wanted to be a forest ranger since the first time her father took her and her older brother camping when she was four. Her father had instilled his love of nature in both his kids, but only Rob followed Bill James down the academic path and became a botanist. Mallory didn't want to study nature, she wanted to be *in* it, and what better way than to be guarding it against destruction. She loved her work, but after last summer, when she lost her crew, the pleasure always came with a backlash of pain. She couldn't blame that tumult on Jac, even if Jac did make her shaky balance feel even shakier. She smiled wanly. "I'm a year older now. Maybe it's catching up to me."

"Uh-huh." Emily sat forward, radiating calm acceptance. "Mallory, why don't we go out for a little while? We'll relax, have some fun, maybe a drink or two, and if you want to come back here, I'd love for you to do that. If you don't, we will still have had a wonderful night."

Mallory stared down at their joined hands. "I'm sorry, Emily. I'm bad company, and you deserve better."

"I disagree. You're wonderful company, and I enjoy seeing you whether we end up in bed or not."

"Thanks," Mallory said softly, lifting her gaze to Emily's. "You're a fabulous woman, and whoever you take to bed ought to be there a hundred percent."

"Absolutely. I wouldn't have it any other way." Emily scooted into Mallory's lap, put her arms around Mallory's neck, and kissed her. She rested her forehead against Mallory's. "You're an honorable woman, Mallory James. And I appreciate it. But please don't put me on a pedestal, either. Believe me, I can enjoy a no-strings-attached hot romp in the sheets as much as anyone."

Mallory grinned and kissed her back. "I'll be sure to remember that, Ms. Postmistress."

"See that you do." Emily jumped up and tugged Mallory's hand. "Now, take me out on the town."

Feeling lighter than she had in days, Mallory looped her arm around Emily's waist. "Your wish...my command. Where to?"

Emily laughed. "Where else? Tommy's."

❖

"Slow slow quick quick," Jac muttered while Reba wailed in the background. She lost the count and bumped Sarah off stride. Again. "Hell. Maybe you better lead."

"You're doing great." Sarah tugged Jac's arm tighter around her waist and subtly guided Jac through the pattern of a close Texas two-step. "Don't look at your feet."

"I can't help it. I don't want to step on yours."

"You will if you look down. Look in my eyes." Sarah squeezed Jac's left hand. "You've got great rhythm. Go with it."

"I feel like a klutz." Jac followed Sarah's instructions and concentrated on looking into Sarah's eyes. The indigo irises sparked with flecks of gold, hints of fire against an evening sky. "This might not be good idea."

"Why?"

"Your eyes are beautiful."

Sarah blushed. "Thank you."

"That wasn't a line, you know."

"I don't care if it was, it was very nice." Sarah moved a little closer. "Want to try going a little faster?"

"Oh man, you like to live dangerously."

Laughing, Sarah leaned back in Jac's arms and shook her head. "Not usually, but tonight, I'm feeling adventurous."

Jac raised her eyebrows. "Oh?"

"Don't worry, your virtue is safe. I'm not planning on seducing you."

"Well damn, now my night is ruined." Jac grinned and Sarah did something complicated that had her ducking and twirling under Sarah's raised arm before she could think about it and trip herself. "Hey!"

"See? Told you."

Sarah raised Jac's arm, made a mirror-image twist underneath, and then Sarah was in her arms again and Jac didn't think. She just felt Sarah and the rise and fall of Reba's lament about love gone bad. Holding Sarah felt good, comfortable. "Thanks for this."

Sarah rested her cheek lightly on Jac's shoulder. "You're welcome. I needed it too. It's been a crappy spring."

"Want to tell me about it?" Jac asked.

"Nah. He's not worth wasting a good dance on. But thanks for the offer."

Jac dipped her head. "Any time."

Sarah laughed. "Now *that* sounded like a line."

"Busted."

"Oh look," Sarah pointed their joined hands to the far side of the wide dance floor that took up half the rustic bar, "there's some of our crowd over there. I figured they'd end up here sooner or later. Want to join them?"

Steeling herself, Jac looked in the direction Sarah had pointed, and her stomach fell. Anderson, Ray, and Cooper sat at a table against the railing at the edge of the dance floor. Mallory wasn't there. "Sure."

When the song ended, she and Sarah threaded their way through the crowd toward the guys. By the time they reached the table, already crowded with beer bottles and shot glasses, Ray and Cooper had dragged over chairs for them.

"You look pretty good out there," Anderson said to Jac.

"Sarah makes me look good," Jac said.

Ray snorted and handed her a Heineken. "Good thing somebody does."

"Ha ha." Jac pulled up a chair for Sarah and then one for herself. Another song started, and Ray leaned over to Sarah and asked if she'd like to dance.

"Sure," Sarah said, and they went off to the dance floor.

"You'll forgive me if I don't ask you to dance," Anderson said. "Two left feet."

"Me too, usually," Jac said. "Sarah really is good."

"My wife probably wouldn't be overjoyed to know I was out on the town with a couple of gorgeous women, either."

Jac laughed. "You're pretty safe with me, Anderson."

He grinned. "Likewise."

"And just for the record, Sarah isn't my date."

"Not keeping score." He stared across the dance floor, then waved. "Looks like we're in for a real party tonight."

Jac spun in her chair and told herself to breathe. The initial swell of excitement quickly turned to a hard lump of disappointment. Mallory had finally appeared, but she wasn't alone. A very pretty woman had her arm looped through Mallory's as they navigated the crowd, greeting people as they passed. They looked like they'd been here before. They looked like a couple.

"Yeah," Jac said quietly. "I guess we're all here now."

CHAPTER SEVENTEEN

"Hey," Emily said, giving Mallory's arm a tug. "Isn't that Cooper over there?"

Mallory followed Emily's direction and took in the group at the table. Cooper's distinctive gold-blond hair and massive shoulders flashed like beacons even in the hazy glow of the cobweb-coated light fixtures tucked under the heavy pine ceiling beams. But she wasn't looking at Cooper when she muttered, "Uh-huh."

Jac sat at the table next to Cooper, with Sarah beside her. Mallory hadn't expected to see Jac tonight, definitely not here. Jac's head was tilted toward Sarah, who seemed to be whispering something in her ear that was making Jac laugh. Mallory slowed her meandering course around the room, trying to give herself time to figure out what bothered her the most—that Jac had appeared somewhere Mallory thought she'd be free of the confusing and annoying reactions she had every time Jac was around, or that Jac seemed to be having a really good time while she was having a really off night. Jac looked great in a casual white button-down collar shirt with the sleeves rolled halfway up. Mallory was glad she'd chosen her favorite sweater, a black cashmere pullover that she'd bought on a whim because it felt so good against her skin and did nice things for her breasts too.

Instantly she wanted to shake herself for the ridiculous thought. Ridiculous not to have anticipated Jac would show up here. Where else would she go on the one night off before a ten-day stint in the wilderness? Bear Creek was the only town within reasonable driving distance, and Tommy's was the only nightlife.

"Sarah's here too," Emily said, delight infusing her tone. She grasped Mallory's hand and pulled her along the sinuous path created by the haphazard placement of tables around the dance floor. "I haven't seen her since last fall. What a treat."

"Yes, she showed up early for training camp."

"I should say hello, but we don't have to hang with them if you don't want to." Emily half turned, walking backward and studying Mallory with a tiny frown between her brows. "I know you like to get away from work when you're here, so if—"

"No," Mallory said quickly. She wasn't going to be derailed by Jac's presence. She had control of herself, after all. "It's fine. If *you* don't mind."

Emily pressed close against Mallory's side to make way for a couple headed for the dance floor. "I like your crew. I don't recognize some of them, though."

"Three of the new guys." Mallory made a conscious effort to sound upbeat. She was going to be seeing Jac on and off the base every day for the next six months, and she might as well get used to it. The conflicting blend of anticipation and wariness that stirred her insides whenever Jac was around had to burn off eventually. Sooner or later she'd be able to look at her without her heart jumping into her throat and every cell in her body starting to tingle. Hopefully sooner rather than later, because the on-again off-again, totally unwanted sexual charge that went along with everything else was making her damn irritable.

"Um, Mallory sweetheart," Emily said laughing, "one of those guys is definitely *not*. If you haven't noticed, I *am* going to start worrying about you."

"I noticed."

"She is one of yours, right?"

"One of the rookies." Mallory was having trouble putting more than a few words together, and feeling more and more disoriented with every second. Especially when Sarah rose and Jac followed her to the dance floor. Mallory watched them find space on the crowded floor, watched Jac open her arms and Sarah step into them as if she'd done it a million times before. Sarah was beaming. She looked radiant, and Jac, sultry and sexy in the plain shirt and faded jeans, had a gentle amused smile on her face. Damn it, they looked like they were really hitting it off.

"You sure about this?" Emily asked. "Because you've got about two seconds to change your mind."

"I'm sure." Mallory jerked her gaze away from her best friend and the rookie she shouldn't even be thinking about and drew Emily up to the table. "Guys, this is Emily." She pointed to each of the men at the table in turn. "Ray Kingston, Ron Anderson, and you know Cooper."

"The night is definitely looking up," Ray announced. He and the other men hastily rearranged the bottles and glasses on the water-ringed tabletop and commandeered several more chairs from nearby tables. When Mallory and Emily settled at the table, Ray pushed two sweating bottles of beer across to them. "Here. These are fresh."

"Thanks," Mallory said, shifting her seat so she couldn't see the dance floor. Too bad she couldn't as easily dispel the image of Jac and Sarah from her mind.

Emily leaned into Mallory and sipped her beer. "So how are you all liking training camp?" She squeezed Mallory's knee and grinned. "Or maybe I shouldn't bring that up with Mallory here."

The guys laughed.

"Please," Mallory said, spreading her arms to indicate the whole of Tommy's, "feel free to speak your mind. I hereby declare this a penalty-free zone. In here, I'm not the boss."

From behind her, Jac said, "If that's the case, we need to spend more time around here."

Jac's voice feathered down Mallory's spine like warm honey and settled in the pit of her stomach. Heat flowed indolently through her depths, and she had to force her fingers to relax their grip on the bottle she was clutching. "Don't get too used to it."

"Actually," Jac said, sitting opposite Mallory, "I don't know about these guys, but the only complaint I have about training camp is there aren't enough hours in the day to train more."

Ray and Anderson cracked up, and Mallory couldn't help but smile a little bit. "I'm also not giving out any points for kissing up tonight, Russo. So you can save it."

Ray hooted and poked Jac's shoulder. "Busted, buddy. You can forget about impressing the boss tonight."

Jac stared at Mallory, her mouth curved into a smile, but her eyes more searching than amused. "Apparently so."

"Emily," Sarah said with a big grin, crowding next to Jac, their shoulders touching familiarly. "Great to see you. I can't wait for you to catch me up on all the news."

Emily laughed. "That might take five minutes or so." She stretched her hand across the table to Jac. "We didn't get introduced. I'm Emily Sorensen."

"Jac Russo," Jac said, shaking Emily's hand.

"What do you think of Tommy's?" Emily asked.

Jac glanced at Sarah, her eyes sparkling. "I can't remember the last time I had so much fun. Dancing isn't usually my thing, but Sarah is a great teacher."

Sarah draped her arm over Jac's shoulders. "That's not true. You're a natural. I told you that."

A buzz of annoyance swarmed Mallory's throat, and she swallowed back the unexpected surge of jealousy. Sarah was just being friendly. Sarah was a friendly person. In fact, that was one of the things Mallory liked best about her. Right at the moment, though, she would've preferred Sarah being a little less friendly. Sarah touched Jac with a whole lot more than friendliness. They'd obviously been having a great time together all evening. While she'd been out of sorts and unable to connect with Emily the way she wanted, Jac was off painting the town with Sarah. Wonderful.

"Anybody for refills?" Ray asked, rising.

When everyone answered in the affirmative, Sarah got up. "I'll give you a hand."

Emily shifted her chair toward Anderson, who was telling her about his wife and kids and job back home, and Mallory found herself with nowhere to look except at Jac. The conversation faded into the background and Jac was all she saw. Garth Brooks started singing about thunder and lightning and lust, and for a millisecond, Mallory thought about asking Jac to dance. The idea came out of nowhere and hit her harder than a falling tree, but fortunately she came to her senses instead of losing them. Tommy's might be a work-free zone and she might not be the boss tonight, but she couldn't afford to drop her barriers around Jac whether they were at work or not. If she did, she might not be able to get them back up again when she needed them. A body brushed by her arm trailing a cloud of vanilla and sandalwood and complicated florals. Obsession. She knew the perfume, and she knew who wore it.

A busty blonde in tight blue jeans that accentuated her heart-shaped ass and a tight white stretch top that made it very evident she wasn't wearing a bra leaned down and murmured something in Jac's ear. Chantal Burns. Wonderful. Just wonderful.

"I'm not very good," Jac said, subtly shifting on her chair as if trying to put a little space between herself and the breasts that were very close to her cheek.

Chantal put her red-tipped fingernails on Jac's shoulder and smiled across the table at Mallory. "Hi, Mallory. I see you've brought us some interesting new…faces."

The jealousy that had plagued her earlier buzz-sawed back. Chantal was a sometimes bartender at Tommy's, married to a long-distance trucker who was never home. Chantal filled the hours while he was away fooling around with the customers, male and female alike. Mallory squelched the desire to pluck Chantal's hand off Jac's shoulder. "How are you doing, Chantal?"

"Much better now." Chantal cocked her hip, trailed her finger up Jac's shoulder, and twirled a lock of Jac's hair around her fingertip.

"I can see that." Mallory raised her brows at Jac, whose expression vacillated between amusement and disbelief.

Chantal bumped Jac's shoulder with her hip. "Come on. If you need lessons, I'll teach you."

Emily grasped Mallory's wrist as Lady Antebellum started singing "Need You Now." "This is a great song. Want to dance, Mallory?"

"Sure," Mallory said, determined not to ruin Emily's evening.

Jac's smile never wavered but her eyes shuttered closed, locking Mallory out. The sudden change sent a cold blast through Mallory's insides. As Emily pulled Mallory toward the dance floor, Jac's whispered words to Chantal roiled in her depths.

Let's dance. I'm sure you can help me out with whatever I need.

❖

"So," Chantal said, sliding into Jac's arms, "you're going to be up at Yellowrock all summer?"

"I don't know yet," Jac said, trying to inch back and still keep her rhythm. Chantal didn't seem to care if they were actually following the dance steps. She was so close against Jac's stomach and hips there was no way Jac could actually carry off the pattern. "I've still got a lot of boot camp to go."

"Oh, you're a rookie." Chantal managed to lean her head back while pressing her breasts even more tightly against Jac's. She had nice breasts, full and firm and probably not all completely original, but nice all the same. Jac straightened to ease some of the contact. She didn't usually go in for bar pickups, at least not without a little conversation and a bit of connection first, and she was totally not in the mood at the moment. She'd only agreed to dance to get away from the uncomfortable tension at the table.

Mallory obviously wasn't happy to see her, and that hurt. She kept trying to figure out what she'd done wrong. What she'd said, what invisible line she'd crossed. She appreciated boundaries. She respected them. She never would've pushed Mallory… Okay, maybe that wasn't true. Maybe she had pushed. Mallory fascinated her. Mallory was aloof, remote, controlled—everything Jac understood and most of the time emulated. But there were moments when Mallory smiled at her, and the sky opened and sunlight drenched her. Waiting for those moments seemed endless, and then when they came, when she and Mallory connected, every second of waiting was worth it.

"Hey," Chantal murmured, skating her fingertips down Jac's neck. "I hear boot camp is really rough. All the guys complain about what a ballbuster it is. You could probably use a good massage. I've got a great hot tub back at my place. We could—"

"I don't think so, Chantal," Jac said. "Really, I appreciate it, but—"

"Baby," Chantal said laughing lightly, "I don't know if you've noticed, but you're not going to have a lot of choices around here. And trust me, neither Mallory or Emily is really your speed."

Jac stiffened. "I'm sorry?"

"Come on, baby—with a reputation like yours, you need a woman who's been around, and I bet I can show you things even you haven't done before."

"I don't recall us meeting before, and you I'd remember." Jac forced a playful tone. "So how do you know anything—"

Chantal waved her hand dismissively. "A face like yours is hard to hide. Hey, baby—really, it's cool. I think I could really get off doing a celebrity."

"Probably. But not tonight." Jac's guts turned to ice. Maybe she'd been fooling herself that she'd found a safe haven at Yellowrock. Maybe she'd never outlive her past or her birthright.

"Tell me you wouldn't like a little TLC." Chantal rolled her hips into Jac's crotch.

Jac registered the pressure and the surge of sensation shooting through her pelvis and down her legs. Was that what she wanted? Someone to take her mind off what she shouldn't want and couldn't have? She wouldn't mind not thinking, not guarding, not second-guessing everything and everyone for an hour or two. She'd never really been able to do that with anyone, except Mallory. Everything came back to Mallory. "I'm not fond of one-way streets, and I'm running on empty. I think I'm gonna have to take a rain check."

Chantal pretended to pout and gave up all pretense of two-stepping. She wrapped both arms around Jac's neck and cleaved to her, her mouth moving indolently against Jac's neck. Jac just prayed for the song to end. She wasn't made of stone, and Chantal was hot and wanting. She really needed to escape before she gave in and took Chantal up on her offer out of sheer fatigue.

Cooper tapped Jac on the shoulder. "Cut in, Russo?"

Jac could've kissed him, but damn it, her mother's manners kicked in and she hesitated, glancing at Chantal. "Okay?"

Chantal shrugged and gave Cooper a hot smile. "Sure. Coop and I are old friends, aren't we?"

"Not so old, gorgeous." Cooper laughed and pulled Chantal into his arms.

Jac backed away and bumped into Ray. "Sorry."

"No problem." He tapped Mallory on the shoulder as she danced close by with Emily. "Cutting in."

Mallory released Emily, and her eyes met Jac's. "Guess we've been retired."

The fire in Mallory's gaze melted the ice in Jac's belly. "Want to dance?"

Jac held her breath while she waited for Mallory to say no.

"Okay," Mallory said softly, and Jac stopped breathing altogether. When Jac didn't move, Mallory laughed. "Having second thoughts?"

"No," Jac said quickly, sucking in a breath. She willed her feet to move and prayed she could remember what she was supposed to do.

RADCLY*f*FE

Holding out her left hand, she slid her right arm around Mallory's waist. Mallory moved close. Their bodies didn't touch, but heat shimmered between them all the same. Jac licked her lips. "I guess I should warn you now, it's my first time."

Mallory laughed again, free and unburdened, and she was so incredibly beautiful Jac wanted to kiss her throat where the sound echoed.

"Thank you so much for telling me ahead of time." Mallory leaned close and whispered, "I could lead if you need me to."

"I'd like to try, but it's up to you. I do know how to follow."

"Why don't you go ahead and we'll see how you do."

The music changed, slowed, and Jac found she could manage the waltz steps fine as long as she didn't think too long about the way Mallory fit in her arms, the way her hair smelled like honeysuckle and sweet clover, the way Mallory's fingers slid so easily between hers.

"Jac?" Mallory murmured, her cheek grazing Jac's.

"Yeah?" Jac said, ordering herself not to look down at their feet.

"You're shaking."

"I'm terrified."

"Do I scare you?"

Mallory's breasts and belly and thighs glided over Jac's, subtle and so, so sexy. Jac couldn't think, lost track of the people moving around them, forgot her own name. "You have no idea."

"You survived Chantal." Mallory's lips were so close to Jac's ear, Jac could hear each breath, feel the warm exhalations trickle down her neck.

Jac swallowed back the plume of excitement that shot through her chest. "You could've warned me."

"I didn't want to make assumptions. She might have been exactly what you were looking for."

"You know she isn't, don't you?" Jac spread her fingers over Mallory's lower back but didn't pull her closer.

"Jac," Mallory said, her tone a warning even as she trailed her fingers across Jac's shoulders and into the hair at the back of her neck. Her mouth skimmed Jac's earlobe. "We have a rule I haven't gotten around to telling you."

"What's that?" Jac forced herself not to tense. Here it comes. The escape clause, the exit, the line that couldn't be crossed.

Mallory leaned back, the playfulness gone from her eyes. She was still so close their lips nearly touched. "What happens in Bear Creek stays in Bear Creek."

"Wouldn't have it any other way." Jac wondered if Mallory was talking about herself or Chantal.

"Good. I wouldn't want you to get the wrong idea."

"Don't worry, I understand the rules." The song wound down and Mallory pulled away. Jac still had enough sense left to know wherever they were going, Mallory was leading. She let her go.

CHAPTER EIGHTEEN

"Oh my God." Gasping, Emily dropped into the seat beside Mallory, brushed damp hair back from her face with one hand, and reached for her beer with the other. "I don't think I've danced as much in a year."

"I'm sorry, I should have taken you out more often." Mallory drained her own club soda. "I think I've let you spoil me with home-cooked meals and all your attention."

"No complaints from me." Emily leaned against Mallory's shoulder and clasped her hand. "You're a pleasure to spoil, and I've always liked quiet nights in. I'd forgotten what a great dancer you are, though."

"Your dance card seemed to be pretty full tonight," Mallory noted. Ray, then Anderson, and eventually Sarah had all danced with Emily. Mallory had declined several invitations and escaped to the sidelines. She enjoyed dancing, but after she'd almost lost her grip out there with Jac, she decided the safest place for her was with her ass in a chair. Jac was still on the floor, and Mallory studiously avoided looking for her. She still couldn't believe she had come a breath away from kissing her. On the dance floor at Tommy's. Could she possibly do anything more stupid? Well, yes—she could have invited Jac to spend the rest of the night with her at Big Sky Lodge, the only hotel in town. What happens in Bear Creek… God, she'd almost given in to the fist of want pounding away in her belly. Jac had made it pretty clear she was willing. And she smelled so good—mountain pine, clean and sharp—and her body was so tight and hot. Jac would be damn near irresistible under any circumstances, but add in her stubborn determination to excel and her touching honesty and her quiet humor and her gorgeous, intense eyes that looked right through the darkest shields... Oh, she was so, so tempting. Mallory rubbed her eyes, as if that would dispel the images that rippled through her mind like an endless stream of teasing caresses.

"You're not having a very good time, are you?" Emily said softly.

Mallory jumped. "No, I'm having a great time. You were right. I'm glad we came out."

Emily stretched and sighed, looking and sounding content. "I have to work tomorrow. I hate to say this, but I should probably go."

"Okay," Mallory said, hoping she didn't sound too relieved. "I'm ready." She rose quickly and lifted Emily's coat from the back of her chair, holding it so Emily could slide into it.

"You can stay, you know." Emily turned and placed both palms against Mallory's chest. "I think we know each other well enough to be honest about things like this. Wherever your head is, you're not thinking about coming home with me. It's okay."

"Ah God, Em." Mallory looped her arms around Emily's waist inside her coat and tilted her forehead against Emily's. "I'm a jerk. You may not want to be on a pedestal, but I swear you deserve one."

"If I was inclined to be angry with you—which I'm not—your charm would save you." Laughing, Emily kissed Mallory lightly. "If you want me on a pedestal, I'll be more than happy to stay there. All the same, for tonight at least, I think we should leave it at dinner and dancing."

"Thanks," Mallory said, her chest tightening. She should go home with Emily, make love with her, sleep peacefully. Awake content. Content was good, better than crazy with need and want and doubt. Emily might not have her heart, but Emily didn't mind, and with Emily, she'd never risk losing her soul. She would be safe. "I know you might not believe this, but you really are exactly what I needed tonight."

"Good. And likewise." Emily waited while Mallory got her coat on, then took her hand. "Ready to get out of here?"

Mallory looked past Emily to the dance floor. Sarah and Ray were dancing. So were Jac and Chantal. She could stay—Emily would understand. She could make that offer to Jac—spend the night with her, burn with her until the fire burned itself out. But she'd never be safe with Jac—not even for a night. Jac got too close, made her want too much. If she cared, she'd be vulnerable, and she wouldn't be, couldn't be, again.

Mallory looked away, certain of her choice despite the lead weight dragging at her heart. "More than ready. Let's go."

❖

Jac watched Mallory and Emily leave hand in hand, a hard ache filling her chest. Dumb reaction. They came together, of course they were going to leave together. They were on a date.

"Thanks for the dance," Jac said, steering Chantal off the floor. The crowd in Tommy's showed no sign of winding down, even though it was after one. She wasn't tired, at least not physically, but she felt kind of like she did after an afternoon in the slamulator. Bruised and weary. Being around Mallory all night, brushing shoulders with her, trading pleasantries, pretending she didn't want more, had tired her out in spirit. She pretty much just wanted to climb into her sleeping bag, close her eyes, and shut out the world for a couple of hours. Then she'd be ready to face Mallory, the last of boot camp, and a season of being around a woman she wanted so badly to reach, who didn't want her anywhere around. "I've got an early day tomorrow, so I'm going to call it a night."

"The offer of the Jacuzzi and a massage is still open." Chantal wrapped her arms around Jac's neck, stood on her tiptoes, and nipped at Jac's lower lip. Her breath tasted of lime and gin. Her body threw off sex like a coin-operated vibrating bed, relentless and just as impersonal.

Jac knew damn well Chantal's attraction had nothing to do with her, and everything to do with what Chantal saw as a new adventure. Jac was as adventurous as the next woman, but she didn't like the idea of being a notch on anyone's bedpost. And the idea of making love to a woman who wanted nothing more than a thrill, no matter who gave it to her, left her cold. She'd had a lifetime of being chased after because of her name. Her solution had been to surround herself with strangers, and now she'd had enough. If she couldn't do more than slide against a body in the dark for a few mindless hours and wake up as empty as when she went to bed, she'd do without. "Yeah, thanks, but I'd better just get going."

"Some other time, then."

"Good night." Jac escaped into the crowd before she made a remark she couldn't take back and would surely regret. Sarah was back at the table, and Jac squatted beside her. "I was thinking I ought to get back to base. If you're not ready to go, I should be able to catch a ride with one of the guys."

"No," Sarah said, "I'm about done in myself. I don't think I've danced this much in years." She collected her things and stood. "Let's say good night to the guys and get out of here. Mallory left already, I think."

"Yeah, she did," Jac said abruptly. She didn't want to talk about Mallory or Emily. "You want me to drive? I haven't had anything to drink in over an hour."

Sarah shook her head. "Neither have I. God, we're really party animals."

"Yeah," Jac said, not sorry she'd come, but glad to be leaving the relentless hunt for an antidote to loneliness behind. "We're dangerous all right."

Outside, the inky sky was crystal clear and almost painfully bright after the murky light in Tommy's. Splinters of moonlight illuminated the road as Sarah drove back to base. Theirs was the only car on the highway, and Jac could almost believe they were on another planet—remote and void of any other life. The barrenness mirrored the hollow ache in her core, a not unfamiliar sensation. The first time she'd felt that cold isolation had been when she'd been twelve and she'd overheard her father in his study dictating a press statement outlining his position against gay marriage. He'd used words like "unnatural," "amoral," "a sin against God," and she'd known he was talking about her. She'd wondered then if he would say the same things when he learned about her and hoped he would change his mind, because she didn't think she could change herself. When she'd been unwilling to hide and unable to lie, she'd learned that his feelings wouldn't change either. Knowing her, supposedly loving her, had not made a difference. Perhaps that was when she had learned that being known and still being rejected was far worse than being discounted through ignorance and fear. Maybe that was when she'd stopped wanting to be known.

Jac tilted her head back against the seat and stared up at nothing, wishing she knew how to close the door again on longing.

"Tired?" Sarah asked gently.

"A little footsore," Jac murmured. "Obviously, I didn't know what I was in for at Tommy's. I think I danced with every single person in the bar."

Sarah laughed. "I guess I should've warned you that new blood in a place as small as Bear Creek requires everyone to investigate."

"No problem."

"You've really got the moves down now. I don't know what excuse I'm going to use the next time I want to get you to go out with me."

"All you have to do is ask, lessons not required," Jac said. "I'm at your service."

Sarah laughed. "Be careful what you offer, cowboy."

Jac glanced down at her feet. "I guess I'm gonna have to get appropriate foot apparel."

Sarah's eyes lit up. "Oh, let me know when you want to go shopping. There's a great new place in town."

Jac shook her head. Shopping with a straight girl. Turning down an invitation for a night of wild sex with a hot woman. Could her life get any stranger? "Okay, I'll let you know—if I'm still around, that is. I have to get through the last ten days."

"You're not really worried, are you? You're doing great."

"We still have the field training left to do. I haven't exactly impressed Mallory so far."

Sarah glanced over at her, her brows a dark slash across her forehead in the moonlight. "It's not about impressing her, you know that, right?"

"I know. She's totally fair. She's a great training instructor."

"Uh-huh."

Jac's face heated. Sarah sounded as if she was waiting for Jac to say more, but there was nothing she could—or would—say. Mallory had been nothing but professional. Jac was the one out of bounds, and she sure wasn't going to share her frustration with Mallory's best friend.

"You now, Jac—" Sarah's cell rang and she fumbled in the pocket of her jacket. "Hello?...Hey, we were just—"

Jac straightened. Something in Sarah's tone put her on alert.

"About half an hour—maybe a little bit less. What's up?" Sarah nodded silently. "Okay. Jac is with me. Who else is at base?...Figures, everyone's away…Hold on." Sarah looked over at Jac. "How much search and rescue experience do you have?"

"Plenty. I got certified when I worked at a ski lodge in college, and I had more than enough practice in the Guard."

"Jac is good," Sarah said into the phone. "You want me to call Tommy's and see if I can round up anyone else?…Okay, your call. See you soon."

"What?" Jac asked as soon as Sarah hung up.

"A party of climbers are missing up on Granite Peak. No radio contact since this morning, and they've been religious about checking in twice a day. We got called to assist the rangers because we're the closest base. Mallory wants to leave as soon as we get in."

"Okay," Jac said, grateful to bury her personal ghosts as a surge of energy filled her with purpose. She couldn't do anything to change what her father thought of her, or to escape public scrutiny and opinion, or to convince Mallory she was worth letting close. But she could fight for someone else and maybe make a difference—and the charge of putting herself on the line helped fill the empty spaces inside.

CHAPTER NINETEEN

Sully walked into the ops office while Mallory was running checks on the radio transmitters the team would need for the search. Even though he must have been asleep when the call for backup came in from the ranger station in Granite Peak Park, his face was unlined, his shirt unrumpled, and his khaki trousers sharply creased. Mallory had had one leg in her sleeping bag when he'd called her. The adrenaline rush had roused her, but her eyes felt gritty, and her jeans and chambray shirt, though clean, had just come out of her laundry bag, and they looked it.

"I've got this, Sully," she said. "No need for you to stay up."

"Uh-huh." Sully leaned against the doorjamb and crossed his legs at the ankle. "Who are you taking?"

"Sarah and Russo. Everybody else is still off base."

"You want me to set up the field camp tomorrow when the rest of them get back?"

"That works, thanks. I don't want boot camp to carry over into June." Mallory stacked the radios next to a pile of topographical maps. While she worshipped order, if she got bent out of shape every time her schedule got torpedoed by an act of nature, she'd have been committed by now. "Hopefully we'll find these kids in the morning and be back by tomorrow afternoon."

"Who's the lead on the search?"

"David Longbow. He's sending four teams out at dawn. We should have plenty of time to get there."

Sully crossed the room and craned his neck to see out the high horizontal window. "Lotta cloud cover coming in. I doubt you'll be able to get any planes up."

"I know. I just checked the forecast. A cold front coming down from Canada might bring snow in the high country by tomorrow midday. We really need to find them before that."

"It's too early in the season for a climb that high," Sully said, shaking his head.

"David says the rangers tried to talk them out of it, but"—Mallory shrugged—"it's still a free country."

"Yeah, I know." Sully grinned wryly. "And I recall not listening to anyone when I was their age either."

Mallory chuckled. "Sully—I'm not so sure you'd listen now."

"Be careful out there, okay?"

Mallory nodded. "You got it, Chief."

She grabbed the gear and headed into the yard to load the Jeep. Ground searches this time of year were always frustratingly slow and dangerous, as the snow covering the slopes in the high country started to melt underneath the crusted surface. Slides and mini-avalanches were common. She hoped to hell those kids hadn't been caught in one. If they had, the SAR teams might not find them until July. She hoped she wasn't making a mistake bringing Jac along, but she could use the manpower. Jac might be a rookie in terms of smokejumping, but she did have experience on the line, and many search and rescue volunteers had even less experience than Jac. She couldn't explain the anxiety gnawing at her insides, but trying to puzzle out that strange sensation was a lot more comfortable than dealing with the surge of pleasure and relief she'd experienced when Sarah had told her Jac was on her way back with her.

Jac wasn't spending the night with Chantal, and Mallory had absolutely no reason to be happy about that. Not just happy, practically jubilant. Ridiculous. She wasn't about to start keeping tabs on Jac's love life. She didn't even want to think about Jac's love life. She especially didn't want to think about Chantal and her perky breasts and her pouty lips and her hands that were all over Jac every time Mallory looked in their direction. God, Chantal had looked ready for Jac to fuck her right there in the middle of Tommy's.

Mercifully, the sound of an engine dissolved those particular images, and she spun around to watch Sarah's Mustang pull in behind the Jeep. She resolutely did not look at Jac when Jac climbed out of the passenger side and joined Sarah.

"Hey," Sarah called.

"Good to see you." Mallory grabbed her go bag and stashed it in the rear compartment. The gravel crunched under their approaching footsteps, but she kept working. Her pulse tripped when the barest hint of pine wafted to her. The tangy scent made her stomach quiver absurdly, as if she'd never smelled the forest before. She lived in it, for God's sake.

"What do you need us to do?" Sarah asked.

Drawing in a slow breath, Mallory straightened and turned. Sarah and Jac stood a few feet away in a pool of moonlight. She'd just seen Jac a few hours before, and there was no reason for her heart to race, but it did. The tightness in her stomach, the anticipation in her thighs, annoyed her almost as much as it amazed her. Jac hooked her thumbs in the sides of her pockets, rocking ever so slightly on her heels, her gaze steady on Mallory, as if to say, *Here I am. What do you plan to do about it?*

Nothing. She planned to do absolutely nothing about Jac beyond treating her precisely as what she was—a rookie member of the team. Racing heart and sweating palms be damned. Biology—that's all it was—reflex, too long without a little human contact. Like she could have had with Emily if she'd been able to get Jac out of her mind.

"Change if you need to, and then grab your go bags," Mallory snapped. "You'll need ice gear. Everything else is loaded. We've got about a three-hour drive. No reason to have Benny fly with weather moving in."

Sarah glanced up at the sky. Thick swaths of blue-black cloud swirled rapidly across the sky, obscuring the moon and blanketing the stars. "It was clear when we left Bear Creek."

"A heavy front is coming down from the north."

Jac said, "How many are out there?"

"Three," Mallory said. "Two boys and a girl. College kids. They decided to get in a climb before they left for summer break. Only they forgot it's not summer up here yet."

"Experienced climbers?" Jac asked, her tone hopeful.

Mallory shook her head. "One of the boys is. The girl has a little experience. The other guy, none."

"Man," Jac muttered. "We better find them fast, then."

"Roger that," Mallory said. "Hopefully we'll be back here tomorrow."

Sarah headed off to the barracks, stopping in the middle of the yard to talk to Sully.

"I've got EMT experience," Jac said. "Ski patrol."

"Good, I can always use backup." Mallory leaned against the Jeep. "I'm surprised you weren't a corpsman in the Guard, then."

Jac rubbed the back of her neck, her expression distant, as if remembering. "I had that choice, but I wanted to stop troopers from getting blown up, not piece them back together afterward."

Mallory's throat tightened at the image of how close Jac must have come to death so many times. Even though she knew Jac had been trained for the work, the idea of her defusing one of those monsters, alone and vulnerable, scared her in a way she hadn't been scared since the flames roared down on her team a year ago. She shuddered. She couldn't go there again, and to remind herself, she said out loud, "You an adrenaline junkie, Russo?"

"Not so much. Steady hands, remember?"

Mallory said nothing.

"Mallory," Jac said, the levity gone from her voice. "You can count on me. I promise."

Mallory didn't want to. She didn't want to count on anyone, didn't want to need anyone, didn't want to fear losing anyone. "Just do your job, and we'll be fine."

"Just so you know, there's nowhere else I'd rather be tonight than right here."

What was Jac saying? She had to be talking about the job. She couldn't be talking about Chantal. Could she? Could she really be that brave? Mallory knew she wouldn't have been. Wasn't. "Get your gear, Russo. We need to move out."

Jac held her gaze as if waiting for her to say more, and when she didn't, Jac strode away. Mallory ached to call her back—wanted to say she understood. That this was where she wanted to be too—not anywhere else, not *with* anyone else. She kept her silence. Better that way. Safer. Yes. *Yes.* Then why the hollow ache in her chest? Mallory gritted her teeth and double-checked the equipment she'd stored in the back of the Jeep. The sound of another vehicle pulling into the yard put thoughts of Jac and the fleeting pain in her eyes out of Mallory's mind.

Kingston, Anderson, and Cooper climbed out of Cooper's battered Ford 450.

"What's going on?" Cooper called as the men hurried over.

"Missing hikers," Mallory said. "Who's the designated driver?"

"Me," Ray said.

"How are you feeling?"

"Fine," Ray said. "Need another man?"

"Could use one. Grab your stuff. We're ready to leave."

"Give me a minute," he said, and he hurried away.

"Cooper—you'll be with Sully setting up field camp."

"Sounds good."

Sully ambled over. "All set?"

"Yes," Mallory said. "Good luck up at River Rock."

"Don't worry, I'll keep them busy until you show up."

Mallory grinned. "No doubt."

"Keep me updated, and be careful out there."

"Will do." Mallory handed radios to Sarah, Jac, and Ray as they returned. "Okay. Let's go."

"I've got shotgun," Jac said and pulled open the passenger side door.

Mallory got behind the wheel, and Sarah and Ray piled into the rear. She pulled out of the yard, her mind on the upcoming mission, but her senses flooded with Jac. She could still smell her, damn it. She tightened her grip on the wheel and kept her gaze forward. If she didn't look at her, maybe it would be easier to ignore her. "Everyone should try to catch a little sleep."

"I can spell you driving in a little while," Jac murmured, "so you can catch an hour or so."

"I'm fine," Mallory said.

"No doubt. But even superheroes sleep sometimes."

"Anyone ever tell you you were a smart-ass, Russo?" Mallory muttered.

"Not that I can recall."

"Smart-ass with a bad memory."

Jac laughed softly. "Thanks for taking me along tonight."

"I needed a warm body." The instant she said it, Mallory recognized her mistake. Thankfully, the dark hid the blush she felt heating her cheeks.

"I'm going to pretend I didn't hear that," Jac said too quietly for Sarah or Ray to pick up above the sound of the engine revving, "until you really mean it."

"That's not going to happen," Mallory said.

"You never know," Jac said as she leaned her head back and closed her eyes. "There's always Bear Creek."

❖

The murmurs of conversation from the backseat faded away, and Jac figured Sarah and Ray were sleeping. She'd catnapped for a while until the Jeep bumped off the highway and onto a fire trail.

"Must be getting close," she said.

"Another hour or so," Mallory murmured.

"Ready to surrender your cape, Wonder Woman, and grab some sleep?" Jac knew she was taking a chance baiting Mallory, teasing her, but she didn't know any other way to get through to her. When she'd realized Mallory was back at camp and not somewhere with Emily, the flood of relief was so strong she couldn't pretend she didn't care. She cared, and the knowledge slammed through her with equal parts terror and wonder. The last time she'd really cared about a woman she'd been in college, young and naïve and impressionable. Cynthia had been a graduate student, a classic California blonde exiled to Idaho because the college offered a hotel management program that was the best in the West. Cynthia had been a sorority girl, vivacious and sexy and fickle. She'd run so hot and cold Jac never knew whether a dinner date would end up with them in bed or her heading back to her dorm room alone and frustrated. When she'd begun to realize that Cynthia only wanted to spend time with her when she was attending obligatory family affairs with the power people who surrounded her father, she called it quits. Cynthia wasn't interested in her company, but only in the company she kept. Why did she keep forgetting that lesson?

"All right." Mallory pulled over. "You win this one."

From the backseat, Sarah murmured thickly, "We there?"

"Not yet. Go back to sleep." Mallory put the Jeep in Park and got out.

Jac opened her door and crossed in front of the Jeep, slowing as Mallory's figure skirted the cone of light thrown off by the headlights. She waited just at the edge of the shadows for her. "Thanks."

Mallory's face was half in shadow, half illuminated by the slanting light. A furrow creased her brow. "For what?"

"For trusting me. To drive."

"You know," Mallory said softly, "you've never given me any reason not to trust you. It just doesn't come easy for me."

"I know. Me neither." Jac wanted to touch her so badly. Just to graze her fingertips over the top of her hand. As if the slight physical connection would somehow cement the fragile, elusive bond that flickered between them like firelight.

"And, Jac?"

"Yeah?" Jac's chest was so tight she could hardly get words out.

"Wonder Woman had magical bracelets, not a cape."

"I never could keep my superheroes straight."

Mallory brushed by her in the darkness, leaving the lingering hint of honeysuckle behind. When Jac climbed behind the wheel, Mallory had already tilted the seat back and curled on her side facing Jac. Her eyes were closed, one hand beneath her cheek. Strands of dark hair layered across her face. Jac carefully reached across the space between them and brushed the hair away from Mallory's eyes with her fingertips. Mallory's eyelids fluttered open, and her gaze caught Jac's and held.

"Drive," Mallory whispered, tilting her head so her cheek brushed against Jac's fingers.

"Yeah." Jac eased the Jeep back onto the fire road, her hand tingling from the fleeting touch. That soft caress excited her more than Chantal or any woman before her ever had.

Chapter Twenty

A hazy glow in the sky over the mountain peaks ahead told Jac she was getting close to the rendezvous point. She gently shook Mallory's shoulder.

"Mal, we're here."

Mallory jerked, mumbled "okay," and released her seat belt. After she straightened her seat back, she ran both hands through her hair, managing to somehow toss the thick brown waves into sexy swirls that clung to her neck and made Jac itch to catch them on her fingertips.

"What?" Mallory muttered, peering at her suspiciously.

Jac stifled the urge to rub her mouth, hoping she wasn't drooling. "Nothing." She paused. "You look beautiful."

Mallory's lips parted as if she was about to speak, then her eyes narrowed. "Stuff it, Russo."

"Roger that," Jac said with a grin. Mallory had almost smiled, and her husky tone belied the brusque words. That almost-smile settled in the pit of her stomach like a warm, comforting caress.

"And eyes front."

"On it, Boss," Jac said, the warmth kindling to heat when Mallory muttered, "Smart-ass."

The fire trail emerged from the woods into a clearing that bordered a small lake, and Jac parked behind a line of other emergency vehicles and turned off the engine. An hour before dawn, mist hung over the water in tense, gray layers. Three dozen people milled about a bunch of picnic tables pushed together in front of a semicircle of parked 4x4s, a pair of EMT trucks, and one van with a canine unit logo. "Looks like the place. Pretty big crowd already."

"David said he expected another two dozen to show up later this morning if we haven't found them by then." Mallory looked into the backseat where Sarah and Ray were stirring. "Both of you have your radios?"

"It's been digging into my ass all night," Sarah complained.

Laughing, Ray held his up.

"We'll use channel three between us," Mallory instructed. "David will let us know what channel to use to contact the search base."

"How will we be searching?" Jac asked. "Pairs?"

"Probably," Mallory said. "That will be up to David. Depending on how he has assessed the terrain, the risk factors for the rescue teams, the incoming weather—the usual parameters." She looked from Jac to the others. "Remember, we don't want any more victims out there today. Stick with your partners. Be careful."

"Roger that," Ray said.

"Always," Sarah said.

Jac pocketed the keys, climbed out, and grabbed her equipment from the back. Mallory led the way down to the staging area, wending through the crowd of men and women, most of whom were drinking coffee from steaming paper cups. She stopped beside a man who looked to be about forty with collar-length jet-black hair, deep-set dark eyes, and a broad, handsome Native American face.

"Mallory," he said, pleasure in his voice. "Great to see you. Sorry it has to be this way. Thanks for getting up here so fast."

"Hi, David." Mallory hugged him and gestured behind her. "My crew."

He held out his hand, and Jac introduced herself before he moved on to Sarah and Ray.

"What do you have?" Mallory asked, turning to the picnic table where a large topographical map was held down with battery-powered flashlights at each corner.

Jac leaned close to see, her shoulder brushing Mallory's. The air vibrated with the excitement of the search, fed by the low buzz of charged-up rescuers and the familiar stirring in her blood that came with the call to duty. But not even the thrill of personal challenge struck as deep as the excitement of being anywhere near Mallory. Her skin practically hummed when she so much as looked at her, as if she were walking through a force field. Until Mallory, the only time she'd ever felt so alive was when she was disarming an IED. Sometimes she thought Mallory might be just as dangerous, at least to her sanity. Sucking in a breath, Jac ordered herself not to think about Mallory and concentrated on what David Longbow was saying.

"They left from the ranger's station here," he tapped a spot on the map, "Thursday morning to climb Granite Peak. They were carrying the usual gear—tents, water, food. They had cell phones and planned to check in twice a day when they could get a signal, which they did—until last night. They were due to descend this morning, but they haven't been heard from."

"You have their route?" Mallory asked.

David frowned. "We have the course they planned, but I'm not entirely sure that's where they actually were." He traced a line with his finger up the elevation of Granite Peak. "This should have been their path up the southern face." He circled an area. "We had heavy snowfall all winter, as you know. Part of the trail here is in the path of some recent slides, and the warmer days may have softened it up enough to make crossing the snowpack hard work. They might have tried to go around and gotten farther astray than they realized."

"Makes it difficult to determine the search area," Jac muttered.

Mallory nodded and David said, "Exactly. We can't put a plane up. The cloud cover's already too thick. It's going to snow, on top of everything else."

"The north trail intersects here," Mallory said, pointing to an area east of the large snowpack. "They might have come across this trying to get around the snow and thought they'd found the trail again."

"More than likely," David said. "That's what I'm going to assume." He overlaid a clear plastic sheet onto the map where grid sections had been drawn with Magic Markers. The areas had been denoted with numbers and letters. He pointed to one section marked C10. "You've been up this sector a couple of times, Mallory. I thought we'd put your crew here."

"Good enough." Mallory looked at the sky. "It's going to take a good hour and a half to get there, but we can drive partway. You need me here for anything?"

"No—go ahead and get started. Eat first." David pointed to a woman in a USFS uniform working at a table in front of a nearby tent. "Susan has GPS units for you, as well as the rest of the communication information."

Sarah pointed to the canine van. "Are you sending dogs out?"

"Not yet. If it looks like you're gonna have to dig for them, we'll bring the dogs. I want to save them for that."

"Good idea," Sarah murmured. "I hope we don't need them."

Jac studied the van, then looked at Mallory. "Cadaver dogs?"

She nodded.

"If you haven't crossed their trail by midday," David said to Mallory, "make sure everybody gets a break."

"Roger," Mallory said.

Jac followed Mallory's lead, collecting another radio and a GPS tracker, then moving on to the food tent. Civilian volunteers handed out coffee, egg and bagel sandwiches, PowerBars, and packets of trail mix. She filled her pockets with the snacks and grabbed two of the egg sandwiches. The four of them sat at a table out of the way, drinking their coffee and downing their breakfast.

"Anybody have any concerns, questions?" Mallory asked.

Ray shook his head.

Sarah sipped her coffee and folded her sandwich wrapper neatly into a small square. "How do you want to break up the sector?"

Mallory spread out her map and marked the grid section they were to search with a red Sharpie she pulled from her pack. Within that section, she marked four quadrants. "You and Ray will start here"—she made a mark in the lower right-hand corner, then arrowed upward— "and climb here. Jac and I will mirror you and move up parallel."

Jac traced an irregular pale blue line. "Is this a stream?"

"Yes," Mallory replied. "And we'll need to be sure we don't diverge when we hit it or we'll leave an area uncovered. We'll check GPS coordinates every fifteen minutes. Anything I missed?"

No one said anything.

"Everyone feel all right?" Mallory checked each of the team. "Got enough rest? Fuel?"

"I'm good to go," Jac said.

"Me too," Sarah said.

"Yep." Ray stood. "Let's go find these kids."

❖

Jac hiked her ass up onto a boulder, pulled a PowerBar from her pocket, and held it out. "Here."

Mallory regarded the offering as if it were an exotic animal, her dark brows drawing down. "I'm not hungry."

"Yes, you are, you just don't know it."

"You know, Russo," Mallory said, jamming her hands onto her hips, "I think I ought to know what I need."

"I don't think you do. Eat the damn chocolate bar."

"How is it you're an expert on me all of a sudden," Mallory griped, swiping the bar from Jac's hand and peeling back one end of the wrapper. She bit off a piece and chewed vigorously, regarding Jac with a belligerent expression.

"I've been watching you. You don't eat regularly, you don't sleep enough, you drive yourself into the ground in the gym. You need looking after."

"Ditto, ditto, and ditto." Mallory poked herself in the chest. "But you don't see me bugging you about what you ought to be doing, do you?"

"Not yet. I thought I'd give you time."

"Unbelievable." Mallory finished the PowerBar in three bites and stuffed the wrapper into the outside pocket of her cargo pants. "Thanks."

"You're welcome." The rock was dry but cold under Jac's butt, and she tried to imagine what those kids must be feeling if they were stuck somewhere in ice and snow. "You think one of them is hurt?"

"Hopefully that's all they are," Mallory said, dropping down beside Jac on the huge stone slab and leaning back on her hands. "I can't think of any other reason why we haven't heard from them unless they've lost their equipment and are just trying to get down the mountain the best they can."

"Without a plane in the air, I guess it's possible they're on their way down, and we just can't see them."

"I hope."

Jac scanned the mountain looming over them—steep rock faces, patches of dense forest, acres of thick ice and snowpack. Climbing was difficult in daylight even with all the equipment they needed. Winter rescues were tricky—rescuers died every year attempting them. "With this terrain, if we've got injured, it's gonna be tough getting them out. Especially after dark."

"I know. Let's find them before sundown, then we'll figure out how to evacuate them." Mallory checked her watch. "Five minutes. You okay?"

Mallory rested lightly against Jac's shoulder, and Jac wasn't cold any longer. They were in the middle of a dangerous rescue, as dangerous as plenty of the missions she'd been on overseas. She wasn't frightened of injury or even death, but she was terrified of losing the first connection she'd ever found that made her feel as if she wasn't alone. And she was plenty tired of pretending she couldn't feel the heat that sparked between them. She slid her arm around Mallory's waist.

Mallory shifted on the rock and stared at her as if she'd lost her mind. "What the hell are you doing, Russo?"

"Sorry, I just—" Jac blew out a breath and inched closer, nuzzling Mallory's hair. "You smell so damned good."

"Are you out of your—"

"Hell with it," Jac muttered, and framed Mallory's face. When Mallory didn't pull away, Jac eased forward and kissed her. Mallory's skin was cool under her fingers, but her lips were soft and warm. Jac carefully traced the surface of Mallory's lower lip with the tip of her tongue, and Mallory made a tiny sound of surprise in the back of her throat that whispered off into a moan. Jac's chest seized and she couldn't breathe, but she'd rather die than stop. Mallory's mouth moved against hers and heat flooded her. For an instant, Jac glimpsed flames flickering in a hearth on a snowy winter afternoon. The feeling of home, of safety, of contentment wafted over her until the blaze caught and flames shot high and excitement scorched her skin. She groaned softly and slid her hand into the thick hair at the base of Mallory's neck.

Mallory's palm slapped against her chest, and Mallory jerked back. "Stop that."

"Sorry," Jac said, but she didn't mean it. Her breath was coming fast, and all she could see was the hazy reflection of her own desire in Mallory's green eyes. Mallory's mouth said no, but her eyes said something completely different. "I've been wanting to do that since the muffin morning."

Mallory caught her breath, half laughing, half choking. "Since the muffin morning? The *muffin* morning?"

Jac grinned. "That's how I think of that morning when I saw you lying on your cot, your face so soft and sleepy and beautiful. I wanted to kiss you then. And just about every second I've been near you since. The muffin—I get a little excited every time I see one now."

Mallory's mouth curved into a smile, and her face flushed as if she were suddenly very warm. Her tongue flicked out and moistened the surface of her lower lip. She lightly traced the arch of Jac's cheek with her knuckles and then trailed her fingertips along the edge of her jaw. "Russo, you're crazy."

"Not so much right now."

Mallory shook her head. "Wrong place, wrong time—wrong person."

"You said five minutes, so I've still got time," Jac said softly. "And you look just right to me."

"Your judgment is suspect."

"Sometimes," Jac agreed. "But not this time, Mallory. Not this time."

"We've got a big job ahead of us."

"I know," Jac said, her fingers still threaded through Mallory's hair. "That's why I'm not going to kiss you again until later. Until after we find them."

"Pretty sure of yourself, aren't you?"

"No, not always. But I'm certain about kissing you again."

Mallory jumped down from the boulder as if it had suddenly come to life and growled at her. "You're nuts. We are not doing this."

Jac jumped down beside her and shouldered her pack. "Why not?"

"For about a million reasons, starting with the fact that—well— how do you even know I want to kiss you?"

"You do. You brought me a muffin."

"Enough with the muffins," Mallory snapped. She stared at Jac, her eyes bright, nearly feverish. "Damn it."

Mallory grabbed Jac by the shoulders and jerked her forward, her mouth coming down hard over Jac's. The kiss was hard and demanding and hot and so powerful Jac's legs shook. As quickly as it began, Mallory pulled away. Gasping, dizzy, Jac reached out to steady herself on the rock. "Jesus, Mallory."

"Now we're done. I mean it." Mallory grabbed her gear and stormed away.

Jac pressed her hand to her chest as her heart skittered around like a marble in a bowl. She never got this hyped even after she'd neutered a bomb, and she was always pretty damn high then. Maybe she was having a heart attack. She wasn't certain her legs would hold her up, let alone carry her up the mountain, but she forced herself forward in Mallory's tracks. She wasn't foolish enough to hope Mallory wouldn't regret what she'd just done, but Mallory's kiss proved she wasn't alone in her desire, and that was enough. At least she could tell herself that for now.

CHAPTER TWENTY-ONE

Mallory stopped to assess a thirty-foot cleft in the mountainside that fell away into a deep ravine. They'd been climbing steadily for two hours, their progress impeded more than she'd anticipated when they'd needed to traverse fresh snow and rock slides. They had another two hours of good light, and she wanted to reach the edge of their search grid before then. Her hope of finding any of the kids alive was wavering, but she couldn't stop, wouldn't stop, until she knew for certain. Above the five-hundred-foot drop, a narrow ledge, less than two feet wide in places, cut across the rock face at a forty-five degree upward angle. A portion of the outcropping had fallen away, probably eroded by ice and frost. The adjacent rock face was nearly vertical and iced over. She uncoiled her climbing rope from the clip on her pack, tied in to her harness, and handed the free end to Jac. "I'll lead. You'll belay."

Jac secured the belay device to her harness but didn't attach Mal's rope. "Mal, that ledge looks iffy. Use bolts."

"Planning on it," Mallory said. Maybe if Jac hadn't been with her, she wouldn't have. She'd free soloed plenty and was comfortable without ropes, but if she was tied in to Jac, she wasn't going to risk pulling Jac over the side with her if she fell. She'd take the time to screw in the ice screws and attach her line as she made her way across.

"We still might need to find another way around," Jac said as she positioned the line in the belaying device, anchored to an outcropping of solid rock, and adjusted the friction. "That ledge may not hold."

Jac sounded worried, and Mallory knew it wasn't from fear. Jac didn't seem to have a fear bone in her body. They hadn't talked since she'd kissed Jac in a moment of wild, insane abandon. What could she possibly say about that kiss? She might have dismissed Jac's uninvited kiss as meaningless, but she'd kissed her back. And then some. She'd kissed Jac. Even thinking the words made her head hurt. She hadn't intended to kiss Jac. Hadn't known she was going to do it. But Jac's hands on her face had been so incredibly gentle, incredibly tender. Unbelievably powerful. And then Jac's mouth had been exploring hers, careful but not cautious. Testing, asking, but never hesitant. Jac was never hesitant. Even now she wasn't afraid. But Mallory was afraid for her—just a tiny kernel of fear she couldn't let grow.

"We'll take it slow." Mallory grasped Jac's shoulder and squeezed. Right now, she needed to put what had happened between them out of her mind. Somehow. "If we have to backtrack, we will, but if we do, we'll probably have to go halfway down the mountain to find an alternate route. We'll lose the light, and I hate taking the chance they're up ahead somewhere. Possibly close by. We can't leave them out here another night. They won't make it."

"I know that, and I agree with you." Jac leaned close as a gust of wind swirled a cloud of snow around them. Her words came close to Mallory's ear, her breath warm against Mallory's neck. "But I'm not gonna take a chance on losing you. I'm just not."

"I know what I'm doing. You have to trust me on that when we're out here in the field."

"I do," Jac said instantly. "I trust you wherever we are."

Mallory's throat tightened. Jac had to be the bravest woman Mallory had ever met. She'd been hurt, betrayed, abandoned, and still she took risks. Jac didn't hide her heart, she didn't shield herself. What the hell was wrong with her? "Don't do that, Jac, just don't."

"Don't do what? Trust you? Why not?"

Jac sounded so damn reasonable and looked so damn beautiful with strands of wavy dark curls framing her face below her red wool cap, Mallory didn't know whether to shake her or kiss her again. "Because I meant what I said back there. You kissed me and I kissed you back. I won't lie about that." She shook her head. "How could I? But it's not happening again. I don't want it. I don't need it. And if we're going to work together, that kiss needs to stay back there from now on. Let it go. Now."

The brilliant light in Jac's eyes dimmed, as if shutters had slammed closed. "I get it, Mallory. It won't be an issue. You have my word."

"Good," Mallory said, a hollow ache spreading inside her. Finally, her words had gotten through, so why didn't she feel happy? Watching Jac pull away hurt. She hadn't expected it to hurt, though why, she didn't know. She seemed to be without defenses whenever Jac was around—feeling everything as if she had no shields, the slightest touch searing through her, every look, every word striking deep inside her. Now that the invisible connection had snapped, a spot between her breasts burned as if she were bleeding. She sucked in a breath, steadied herself. "Okay. Let's get across and find these kids."

"Right," Jac said, her tone all business. Nothing in her voice, nothing in her expression, indicated that only a few hours ago they had touched like lovers.

"On belay." Mallory put the image from her mind. She couldn't afford to think of it now, she couldn't afford to think of it ever. She inched out onto the ledge, tested the footing with her ice ax, and called, "Slack."

Jac played out some of the rope, and Mallory advanced foot by foot. After she'd gone six feet, she called, "Tension," braced her legs, and pounded in an ice bolt. Once she'd clipped the rope to the protection, she repeated the procedure, slowly making her way across the ledge.

"Off rope," she called when she reached the other side. She untied the rope and fed it through her ATC to guide Jac's climb across. Ice crystals swirled in the air, catching what little light remained and refracting it into tiny rainbows. Jac stood on the far side of the ravine, her features softened by the winter mist. So much more separated them than thirty feet of ice and rock and empty air. Jac was brave, but Mallory wasn't. Two good men had died, men she'd worked with for years, as close to her as brothers. She'd loved them like brothers, and their deaths had nearly crippled her. Even friendship was a risk. Her love for Sarah—the thought of losing her—terrified her now. She didn't want more, and Jac made her want more.

"On belay," Mallory called.

"Roger," Jac said. "On belay."

Mallory adjusted the tension on the line, watching Jac's every move. "Nice and slow, Russo."

"Not to worry," Jac called, flashing a grin that caught Mallory by surprise and set off a small earthquake of shivers along her spine. "Remember, steady is my middle name."

Mallory ignored the sharp slice of frigid air knifing through her chest with every breath. All that mattered was Jac. The second climber was usually the most secure, which was why she had gone first to begin with. But the ledge was tricky and visibility low in the swirl of ice and snow. She wasn't going to be able to shake the slithering dread in her belly until Jac was beside her on solid ground. She swallowed the urge to tell her to hurry.

Jac viewed the narrow ledge as she would an IED—a formidable enemy, but one she knew how to beat. Her vision sharpened, her thoughts crystallized, and the tang of adrenaline filled her mouth. Battle lust. She'd known it all her life in one form or another. Only this time she wasn't fighting alone. Mallory had her back. Confident, ready, she unhooked her ax from her belt, grasped the rope, and stepped out onto the ice- and snow-covered shelf. Her pulse was steady, her breathing regular, her mind focused only on one thing—keeping herself and her climbing partner safe. Mallory's crossing could have loosened the underlying ice and snowpack, creating unstable footing, and she checked each foothold carefully before she moved. When she reached the first of Mallory's bolts, she unclipped her rope. Blinking away tears stirred by the lashing wind, she called, "Tension!"

Mallory took up the slack, and Jac set off again. The surface underfoot was nearly obscured by blowing snow, uneven and slippery. She tapped the ground directly in front of her, sending loose rock and ice skittering over the side. A few seconds later a heavy thud sounded from far below followed by the rumble of a mini-avalanche reverberating up the rocky cleft. She reached the halfway point, and some of the tension in her shoulders eased a little bit. Another few minutes and she'd be on solid ground. She took another step, felt the snow shift under her boots, felt the vibration, heard a grinding sound, and had only a second to tighten her grip on the rope.

"Falling," Jac shouted and the ledge gave way. Her shoulder struck the edge of the rocky outcropping as she dropped, and a searing pain shot down her right arm. Her fingers went numb, and she lost her grip on the guide rope, free-falling until the slack caught and her harness jerked her roughly into a horizontal position, like a fly on the end of a line. She twirled, spinning around, driving her already damaged shoulder into the wall again. She cried out, unable to stop herself, and tasted blood in her mouth.

"Jac!" Mallory called from above. "Jac?"

"Here." Jac swallowed blood, the initial swell of panic fading. She wasn't falling anymore. The rope had held. She kicked her feet around, forcing her torso toward the wall until she found a handhold on a three-inch root sticking out through the ice. She got herself vertical, head up, feet down, and craned her neck to see above her. A dark shadow broke the uniform fall of snow. Jac rubbed her face on her sleeve, clearing dirt and debris, and focused on the shape. Mallory knelt on the ledge, her features stony, the guide rope tight around her hips.

"Are you hurt?" Mallory called down.

"Banged up my shoulder. My arm isn't working quite right, but I think it's just sprained."

"Can you climb?"

Jac braced her feet against the vertical wall and dug her toes into the frozen surface, searching for a foothold as she gripped the rope with her good arm. "Yes."

"Let me know when you're ready, and I'll pull you up."

Snow, rocks, and small pebbles broke free from the gap in the ledge and rained down in Jac's face. She closed her eyes and turned her head away. When the shower stopped, the gap in the shelf was wider, and a fresh gouge in the rock face had appeared just below where Mallory knelt. "That ledge isn't safe, Mal. You need to reposition."

"We need to get you up. Climb."

Jac knew what Mallory wasn't saying. The rest of the ledge could give way at any second, and if it did, they would both fall with very little chance of getting back up again. Once she put her weight against the wall, with Mallory as the fulcrum, that ledge would bear even more weight. "Mal, I don't think—"

"Climb, damn it, Jac. Don't argue."

Jac tightened her grip, pushed down with her thighs, and pulled herself up as Mallory reeled in the slack. More stones fell, a chunk of ice bounced off her back.

"I'm not taking you down with me," Jac yelled.

"No one is going to fall. Keep coming. Another couple of feet and I'll have you."

Jac secured new footholds, flexed her thighs, bunched her shoulders, and shoved herself up. The rope tightened as Mallory worked her end. The crack below the ledge widened. She was close, but not close enough. "Back off to somewhere stable, Mal. I can make it from here."

She was lying, but Mallory didn't need to know that.

Mallory's face appeared through the haze, her eyes dark burning coals. "Don't quit on me, Russo."

Jac tried to flex the fingers of her right hand, searching in the front pocket of her jacket for her knife. If the ledge gave way she could cut loose—Mallory might have a chance.

"Don't you even think it," Mallory snarled, her expression feral. "You get up here, Russo. I'm not letting you go. You got it?"

Jac couldn't cut herself free even if she'd wanted to. The feeling was coming back in her arm, but not fast enough. Her fingers were too numb to grip her knife. If she didn't want to take Mallory down to the bottom of that ravine with her, she had to get herself up. She flexed the muscles in her abdomen, forced her feet into the crevices in the wall, and pushed. Her shoulder struck the wall, and she bit back a cry. Then Mallory was leaning over the edge, grabbing her harness, jerking her up, and she was kicking, pushing, pulling herself onto stable ground.

"I've got you," Mallory gasped, crushing Jac against her body.

"Get off of here, Mal," Jac gasped. "I'll be right behind you."

"Be careful, Russo," Mallory murmured against Jac's neck. "I'm not pulling you up again today."

Jac closed her eyes and breathed the scent of Mallory deep into her chest, letting herself rest in the safety of Mallory's arms. "Can't say as I blame you."

"Shut up, Jac." Mallory's lips brushed over Jac's cheek, so light they might have been snowflakes except for the searing heat that followed. "Just shut up."

Chapter Twenty-two

Jac crawled off the ledge, got her legs under her, and braced her body against the rising wind. Her pulse stopped racing, and her stomach settled with her first step onto stable ground. The snowfall formed a solid wall of white now, and she focused on Mallory's dark silhouette just ahead of her as she pushed forward into the gale.

"Over here," Mallory shouted, pointing to a story-high outcropping of boulders.

Following the brief break Mallory forged in the frozen tapestry, Jac ducked under a slight overhang, hunched against the rough rock face next to Mallory, and turned her head out of the driving wind and snow.

"How do you feel?" Mallory asked. Ice crystals caked her lashes, melting on the dark filaments like weeping diamonds.

"I'm good." Jac saw the words deflected by the stormy surface of Mallory's eyes, but she recognized pain where others saw only cold reserve. Mallory was blaming herself for the accident. "I'm alive. You're alive. All that matters now is the mission."

"We need to turn back. You're injured and I can't leave—"

"No. I can keep going." Jac raised her injured arm to demonstrate. "Strength's coming back. Must have banged the nerve a bit. No harm done."

"My fault," Mallory said tersely. "I shouldn't have let you cross—"

"Mallory, we're partners out here. A team." Jac lowered her arm, giving her aching shoulder a rest. "If I hadn't wanted to cross and hadn't thought it was safe for you *or* me, I would've said so."

"I'm still the boss, team or not. I'm sorry." Mallory stared straight ahead, her jaw set, her cheeks pale beneath the windburn that painted a crimson swath high on each arched cheekbone.

"Look," Jac said, refusing to let Mallory shoulder blame when there was none, "I know the statistics as well as you do. I know how many rescuers are injured or worse. If it wasn't dangerous out here, those kids would've strolled down the mountainside yesterday. We don't have time to beat ourselves up. Deal?"

"You're right," Mallory said, some of the tension easing from her face. She turned until their eyes met and smiled gently. "How's your shoulder really?"

"Hurts like a son of a bitch." Just seeing the shadows recede from Mallory's eyes made Jac's pain fade. "But it's not broken, and the strength is back in my hand. I'm good to keep going, but I don't think I can climb, at least not right away."

"If this snow keeps up, we're not going to be going anywhere for much longer." Mallory brushed the moisture off her face impatiently. "We knew weather was coming, but I hoped we'd at least have today."

"Let's push on. We've still got some time."

"Are you sure? I'm not risking you getting hurt again." Mallory cupped Jac's jaw. "I want to find them, but I can't chance losing you."

The words came out in a low, tortured whisper, as if Mallory didn't want to say them, didn't want to feel the fear that reverberated in her voice. Jac's heart hurt for her, but Mallory didn't need her sympathy. Wouldn't accept it if she offered.

Jac removed her glove. "Give me your hand."

Mallory's brows furrowed, but she took off her right glove and held out her hand. Jac took her fingers and squeezed, not hard enough to hurt but enough to make her point. Mallory's fleeting grin said she'd made the right move.

"Believe me now, Boss?" Jac relaxed her grip but kept hold of Mallory's fingers. The heat of Mallory's hand in hers was welcome in the bitter cold, but the connection warmed her in places far deeper. Mallory was a touchstone, a solid comfort she'd long ago stopped seeking. "Mal, I—"

"All right, Russo, I believe you." Mallory slid her hand free. "But if you have any trouble at all, I want to know about it. No heroics."

Jac nodded, not trusting herself to speak. What had she almost said? Not anything she ever expected to feel and definitely not anything Mallory wanted to hear. Mallory had made it clear over and over—Mallory didn't want anything from her except her best in the field. The same thing Mallory wanted from all the other members of her crew—nothing more. When had she started wanting more—and how quickly could she stop?

Jac shoved her hand back into her glove. "No problem. All I want is to find them and get off this mountain."

"Good enough. Let's—" Mallory's radio crackled.

"Rescue C-ten-two," Sarah announced over the rescue channel. "We have one of the climbers. He said the other two are near the mountain crest. One injured."

David Longbow's voice cut in. "Approximate coordinates?"

Sarah responded with the location, and Mallory pulled out her map. "This is rescue C-ten-one. We're half a mile below their location."

"Can you make it with the weather?" David asked. "We can't get a helicopter up there until morning at the earliest."

Mallory hesitated and Jac knew why. Mallory was still worried about her, but if they didn't get to the other two climbers, no one else was going to until at least the next day when the storm relented and visibility improved. By then, those two kids could be dead.

"Tell him yes, Mal. I'm fine and we can't stay here. Might as well keep moving."

Mallory nodded sharply. "We can make it, David."

"Radio your position every half hour."

"Roger that."

Jac got to her feet and slung her pack over her good shoulder.

"I want to keep a line between us," Mallory said as she stood and attached her rope to her harness.

Jac ignored the rope Mallory held out to her. She was the most likely to fall—even though she felt strong, her balance was a little off from shifting the weight in her pack to one shoulder. If she fell, she'd pull Mallory down with her. "I think I'm better off—"

"That's the only way we're doing this, Russo. Your choice."

Jac didn't see she had much choice. Maybe she was too used to going it alone. When she stared down an IED, it was just her and the bomb. She had teammates, but she took the long walk out to duel with death alone. "Okay."

"Thank you," Mallory said. "I know it goes against your nature, Jac."

Mallory's understanding melted the last of Jac's resistance, and she tied on to Mallory's lead line. "You be careful too. You've still got a few things to teach me."

"Oh, don't worry, rookie. I've got plenty in store for you."

Laughing with a surge of pleasure, Jac pushed off in Mallory's footsteps.

❖

Mallory fought her urge to go quickly. Too many rescuers ran into trouble when rescue fever made them jettison judgment in the rush to get to the victims. Visibility was almost zero, despite at least an hour of daylight left, and the footing was getting more treacherous with every step and every new inch of snow. She checked her GPS again. They couldn't be more than a few hundred yards away from where the lost climber had estimated his friends were located. She gripped the line connecting her to Jac and tested the tension, some of the tightness in her chest easing when the resistance on the line told her Jac was behind her, moving in tandem with her. She didn't try to talk to her. Her voice would never carry over the howling wind. If she turned to look for her, she probably wouldn't see more than a blurry outline in the clouds of snow. Knowing Jac was there was enough to keep the images that haunted her from breaking her concentration. She couldn't afford to see the ledge giving way, couldn't let the memory of Jac disappearing into the void burn a hole in her brain. The terror still skirted the edges of her mind, threatening to cripple her if she couldn't keep the panic at bay.

For a few horrible seconds after Jac had fallen, she'd stopped breathing, her heart threatening to burst from the agony. She'd thought nothing could be as horrible as emerging in the ashes of the blow-over last summer, of surveying her team and realizing she was missing two men. She'd prayed never to feel anything like that excruciating despair again. She'd sworn never to put herself in the position where she might lose everything. She'd do anything, everything, to ensure her team was always safe. She'd guard against personal affection, she'd steel her heart against caring. She would never be vulnerable again. But she hadn't counted on anyone like Jac—so open, so honest, so fearless. Jac pierced her armor as if she were completely exposed and defenseless. She couldn't let herself care this much. She had to find some way to stop it.

Mallory clambered over a rocky verge onto more level ground, dotted here and there with lone scraggly pines and enormous boulders. Jac came up beside her.

"How much farther?" Jac shouted.

"We're close," Mallory replied. "They probably don't have a light by now. Hopefully they found some kind of shelter. Let's check out the rocks up ahead."

Jac gripped Mallory's shoulder. "Let's untie. If we search independently, we'll make the most of the daylight left."

Mallory hesitated. The idea of Jac being out of her sight made her stomach roll. She battled her racing heart and made herself consider their objective dispassionately. Jac was right. She was more than capable. She would be fine. "All right. Double-check your radio now."

Nodding, Jac unhooked her radio, walked a few feet away, and spoke into it. Mallory's radio crackled and Jac's voice came over.

"You're good," Mallory called.

Jac returned, her dark eyes burning through the snow between them. "You be careful too."

"Check in every five minutes." Mallory pointed to a looming rock formation in the center of the field of boulders. "The one that looks like a snowman. That will be our center point. I'll take left of there, you take right, and we'll meet there, all right?"

"Got it. See you soon."

Jac turned away and within seconds was swallowed up by the storm. Mallory's throat was dry, and the coppery bite of fear filled her mouth. She swallowed, blanked her mind. The mission was all. She'd see Jac again soon.

Five minutes later, she checked in with Jac. "Anything?"

"Not yet."

At ten minutes and fifteen, the response was the same.

Mallory reached the far side of the boulder field and circled toward the rendezvous point, battling frustration. When her radio crackled, hope surged.

"Mallory," Jac said urgently, "I've got them."

"Where?"

Jac reeled off the coordinates. Mallory checked her GPS, adjusted her path, and hurried forward as quickly as she could in the rapidly waning light.

She found Jac kneeling over two huddled figures on the lee side of a pile of boulders. The snow-covered climbers were barely recognizable as human forms, and in the dark, Mallory suspected they would have passed right by them. "Are they alive?"

"Yes, but both are unconscious." Jac stood. "We need to get them someplace out of this storm. They're both really cold."

Mallory looked around. No caves, no forest. They were out in the open with nothing but rocks as windbreaks. She pointed to the cliff face. Snowdrifts several stories high rose from its base. "We'll need to dig a snow cave. There's no telling how long this storm will last or how much snow we'll get. You know how?"

"I've never done it, but I know the principles."

"There's a good buildup on that rock face. Dig in three feet before you angle up. We don't need a big cave, just enough for the four of us. I'll call David with our position, and then I'll get these two ready to be moved."

"All right."

Jac set off and Mallory radioed to base. "Rescue C-ten-one. Come in base."

David's voice crackled from her radio. "Go ahead, Mallory."

"I have two injured," Mallory said. "Both hypothermic. We're digging in, David."

"Roger. Will dispatch a helitack at first light if the weather breaks. Check in every hour."

"Will do." Mallory clipped her radio on her belt, shrugged out of her pack, and set it beside the two inert figures. She checked their necks for pulses. The girl's was steady and slow, but the boy's was thin and thready. She fished her penlight from her pack. His pupils reacted sluggishly, and in the dim light a large bruise over his left temple was apparent. Probably he had fallen, and the girl had elected to stay behind with him, sending the third member down the mountain for help. After positioning a soft cervical collar on each victim, Mallory pulled two thermal blankets from her pack and covered them. She didn't want to start intravenous lines until she and Jac moved them to a more stable location. In the few minutes she'd had her gloves off to treat the climbers, her fingers were nearly frozen.

"Can you hear me?" Mallory said close to the girl's ear. "I'm a paramedic. We're going to take care of you."

She got no response from the girl or her male companion. They were both dangerously hypothermic. She shoved her penlight into her pocket, propped the FAT kit as much out of the snow as she could, and trudged through the thigh-high drifts to where Jac dug. Freeing her shovel from her equipment pack, she started to dig in the tunnel Jac had started.

"Hey." Jac backed out of the tunnel and crouched next to Mallory. "I'm about to angle up now. Soon as I make a little room, you can get in next to me, and we can dig together."

"Okay. The sooner we get them inside, the sooner I can get some fluid into them. They're both shocky. And we'll need to get some heat."

"Okay. Just give me a minute."

"How's your shoulder? Why don't you let me dig for a while?"

"I'm holding up. We can switch on and off if we have to."

Mallory wanted to protest, she wanted to take care of her, but she needed to respect Jac's judgment. "Okay."

Jac squinted as snow blew into her face. "How are they?"

"Critical, and not much we can do out here but try to keep them from getting any colder."

"Guess I better get digging. You okay?"

"I'm fine." Mallory touched Jac's face with her gloved fingertips. "Don't play hero if your shoulder wears out."

"Not me." Jac grinned and crawled back into the cave.

After a few minutes that felt like a year, Jac called Mallory into the tunnel. Jac had set her flashlight in the middle of the floor, and they worked shoulder to shoulder in the cramped space, scraping snow from the walls and ceiling, and pushing it out through the tunnel. Within minutes, they had created a domed space just big enough to accommodate four people. The closer they were crowded together inside the cave, the more their shared body heat would help to warm them. Jac used the handle of her shovel to push through the roof and create a vent hole.

"Nice work," Mallory said.

Jac wiped sweat from her forehead, her eyes glittering with fierce determination. "Let's go get them."

Mallory wanted to kiss her—because she was fierce, because she was strong, because she was beautiful. She squeezed her arm. "Good idea."

The distance from the climbers to the cave was only a few hundred feet, but it took them nearly forty minutes to move them, one at a time, bracing their necks and protecting their spines, ensuring that whatever injuries they might have weren't worsened. Once they had them both inside and positioned on their backs in the center of the cave, Mallory started intravenous lines and infused a saline and glucose solution to help counteract shock and provide some minimal nutrition. While she worked, Jac carved out a ledge for the flashlight-sized portable heater.

"There's not much more I can do." Mallory sat back on her heels, her back against the ice wall. "I don't see any obvious extremity fractures, but the boy clearly has a significant head injury."

"Here." Jac passed a nutrition pack to Mallory. "Eat this."

Mallory took the foil pack, her fingers brushing Jac's. The warmth of Jac's skin shot through her arm. "Thanks."

"I have a good internal clock," Jac said. "We should try to get some sleep. I can wake up every hour to check them."

"Make it every two. I'll split the duty with you."

"Good enough." Jac settled down on the far side of the boy, stretching out so her front rested against his side.

Mallory did the same on the other side of the female climber, sandwiching the two victims between them to keep them as warm as possible. Impulsively, she reached over the two and gripped Jac's arm. "You're solid, Jac. I'm glad it's you with me."

"Yeah, me too."

Jac's hand closed over hers, and Mallory didn't have the strength to pull away. She closed her eyes and held on to the comfort she needed so badly.

CHAPTER TWENTY-THREE

Stinging eyes and a dull throb in the back of her head forced Jac from an uneasy slumber. She blinked away sweat from the corners of her eyes, feeling the cloying dampness of perspiration inside her shirt and pants. The cave had steamed up with the four of them inside, and she was hot where her front molded to the boy and chilled everywhere else. The boy beside her lay still and silent, his breathing low and raspy. The girl whimpered occasionally in her sleep but didn't seem to be aware of anything that was happening. The ice beneath Jac's side was hard as marble. She'd prefer the hot gritty sand of the desert to this, but not if it meant being there alone.

Mallory's fingers were entwined with hers, and she didn't want to move. Mal needed to sleep. And Jac didn't want to lose their tenuous connection. Isolation was a state of being for her—normal to be solitary, physically and emotionally. She loved her baby sister to distraction and loved her mother and father as much as she could love two people whose lives were bound to hers, but who did not know her or understand her or even really want her in their lives. She'd never had a relationship with anyone where she'd felt seen, where she'd been known and appreciated for her good points and her bad points, her strengths and her weaknesses, her dreams and desires. After a while she'd come to the conclusion that relationships like that didn't really exist, and if they did, she hadn't run into one and wasn't about to spend her life searching. She had other things to do. Missions to accomplish. When she wasn't deployed, she worked alone at jobs that made a difference. Ski patrol. Forest service. Keeping people safe, fighting nature's dangers, pitting herself against the odds. She'd been satisfied with the work, had a sense of purpose, and that had been enough.

All that had changed when she'd spent a few intimate hours late in the night over hands of cards with a woman who mattered. Mallory could have sent her packing back into the night, or feigned interest as so many others had, without really caring who she was. But Mallory, despite her preconceptions, had given her a chance to prove herself. To show herself. And in the process, Jac had discovered the soul-satisfying experience of *being* herself, without subterfuge or façade, with a woman whose smile lit up her life. Now being alone was a circumstance she could and would tolerate if she had to, but she'd never be able to go back to believing it was what she wanted. She knew what she needed now, and she knew who she wanted. All the same, wanting did not necessarily equal having. She didn't have many cards left to play, and Mallory seemed to be holding the power hand.

"Did you get any sleep?" Mallory murmured.

"Some. You?" Jac waited for Mallory to pull away, and when she didn't, her heart picked up speed. Mallory's thumb played over the top of her hand, and the whispered touch made her thighs tremble.

"On and off. Did you reach David?"

"Not the last time I tried," Jac murmured. "Probably the storm."

"I know. I couldn't get through either." Mallory propped herself on her elbow, regarding Jac across the two unconscious climbers. "We ought to have daylight now. I'm going to go check on the storm."

"Don't go too far," Jac said, her throat husky with sleep and terrifying need. Mallory's hair had come loose and lay tangled around her shoulders. Smudges of fatigue made her darkening green eyes seem endless. Her lips were chapped, her voice raspy. She looked weary and rumpled and so goddamned beautiful Jac wanted to cry. "I wouldn't want to lose you out there. Not after all this."

Mallory studied Jac solemnly, as if she were trying to decipher some hidden meaning to Jac's words. "You think it's that easy?"

"What?" Jac asked, her stomach tightening.

"For people to walk out the door and never come back."

"It's happened." Jac grimaced. "Although, to be fair, most of the time I was the one walking out and never coming back."

Mallory smiled ruefully. "Leave before you get left?"

"Not so much. Just being realistic," Jac said, although maybe Mallory was right. Or maybe she just chose people—women—she knew would never stay. So much easier when there were no expectations, no dreams to be shattered, no desires to be abandoned. So why did she suddenly feel like a coward? "I guess I never found any reason to stay."

"Well, I don't intend to get lost. So you don't have to worry."

Jac wasn't certain if Mallory was talking about their current situation or something far more personal, but she'd never had a conversation even close to this with anyone before. She'd never let her guard down this way, never had any desire to—not so much because she feared rejection as because she had come to anticipate it. So why bother? She'd never considered closing doors around Mallory, never tried to protect herself, and that very fact made everything that happened between them unique and so very important. She just wished she knew what it all meant. She was patrolling a minefield without a map, with no idea where the explosive devices were hidden. She'd never felt so vulnerable, or so helpless to change her circumstances. But she was no coward. "What do you say I buy you dinner when we get out of here today?"

The corners of Mallory's mouth shot up before she schooled her expression to seriousness again. "Russo, you're impossible."

"So far that's worked pretty well for me."

"Yeah, I can see where it would." Mallory squeezed Jac's hand and let go. "I'll be back in a second."

Jac got up to her knees, wincing at the discomfort in her shoulder and the ache in her lower back. "I'll change the IVs while you're gone. They're getting low on both these kids."

"Thanks."

"Dinner?"

Mallory tilted her head as if she were trying to read Jac's mind or see into her thoughts. After a second she shook her head, stymied. "You really are fearless."

"Not really. Just determined."

"Ask me again when we're off this mountain."

"I'll do that."

Mallory wiggled along the side of the cave and disappeared into the tunnel. Mallory had not said no, and a tiny spurt of hope blossomed in the center of Jac's chest. Mallory might hold all the cards, but she was still in the game.

❖

Mallory crawled out of the cave and was assaulted by spears of sunlight arcing off the pristine snow that blanketed the mountainside beneath a flawless robin's-egg blue sky. The ozone-tinged air bit at her nostrils, thin and sharp as knives. Sweat instantly frosted her neck, and she drew her collar up against the bone-deep cold. The mountain rose behind her, majestic and untamable. For an instant she thought of Jac, every bit as strong and wildly beautiful, and every bit as dangerous as the deceptively gorgeous peaks at her back. She put aside the thought of how natural Jac's hand had felt cradled in hers, ignored the heat that had flooded her belly when Jac had warned her not to get lost. She should've said no instantly to the offer of dinner. Why the hell hadn't she? She couldn't think about that now. She needed to talk to David.

Hoping to catch a signal away from the rock face, she pushed through powdery waist-high drifts and struggled to the edge of the narrow plateau where the climbers had sought refuge and nearly found death. They'd gotten far off track, and how the third member of the group had even made it partway down the mountainside alive, she'd never know. Even experienced mountaineers would've had a hard time descending the north face in clear weather, but somehow he had managed, and probably, hopefully, saved his friends in the process.

Shielding her eyes with one hand, she tried David again. "Rescue C-ten-one, calling base, over. Rescue C-ten-one calling—"

"This is base, Mallory. How are you doing?"

"We're all okay, David. What's the ETA—" The ubiquitous rush of the wind abruptly changed, growing heavier, gaining momentum until a thundering beat reverberated in her chest. Victory bubbled in her throat before her conscious mind sorted out the cause. But she knew. She turned quickly from the brink of the precipice, stared into the sky, and saw salvation. "Helitack coming in now, David."

"Roger that. Good work, Rescue C-ten."

Mallory waved in a wide arc, and the rescue helicopter waggled its runners before leveling for the descent. The rotors couldn't have been more than twenty feet from the vertical rise of the mountainside. Mouth dry, pulse hammering in her ears, she watched until the bird touched down and a bearded man in a bright red flight suit jumped out.

"We'll need stretchers for both of them," Mallory called.

He signaled a thumbs up, opened the rear of the helicopter, and reached inside for a stretcher. Leaving him to follow, Mallory plowed her way back to the tunnel and quickly shimmied inside.

"They're here," she said breathlessly.

"I heard them," Jac said, busily capping IVs and checking the cervical collars on the boy and the girl. As she adjusted the collar on the girl, the young climber opened her eyes.

"What? Where—oh God—" The girl's eyes were glazed, barely focusing, and panic rode her voice.

"You're okay," Jac said gently. "You're still on the mountain, but we're getting you home soon."

"Jerry?" She tried to sit up but could only manage the barest movement. "God. Mitch?"

"Your friends are okay," Jac said. "Don't try to move around. Let us do all the work. That's our job."

Mallory stayed out of the way as Jac efficiently prepped the boy and the girl for transport. Jac had obviously done that kind of work before, and there wasn't room for both of them to maneuver in the cave. Besides, she just liked watching Jac work. Jac was intense, focused, efficient. Gentle, but unhesitant. Just like she was about everything else that she did. Jac would make a great smokejumper. So much depended upon attention to detail, good judgment, certainty of will. Jac had all those things.

She'd make a great smokejumper, but on someone else's team. Working with her like this, every day, was going to be torture. Being around Jac threw Mallory's rhythm off, gave her something to think about besides the goal, the mission, and she couldn't. She couldn't afford to do that. She couldn't afford to have anything intrude on her focus. She didn't want a personal life. She didn't want personal feelings. Fortunately, it wasn't that difficult to get smokejumpers moved around from team to team. They weren't, like the hotshots, based in one place or strictly integrated as units. Sometimes they'd finish a fire call in one state, pack out to a pickup point, and end up in a completely different state until they were rotated out again with different team members.

Sometimes she didn't get back to Yellowrock for weeks. She'd work the rotation so she and Jac were on different shifts, and they probably wouldn't see each other for the rest of the summer.

Jac looked over at her. "We're ready."

"Good. Nice work." Mallory grasped the stretcher the helitack crew member had slid down the tunnel behind her, and she and Jac logrolled the girl onto it. On hands and knees, she guided the stretcher out. The man in the red flight suit grabbed the end, and together they lifted.

"I'm Rich Dennis out of McCall. Good to see you."

Mallory grinned. "Likewise. How's the flying?"

"Smooth. Ought to be an hour or so to Gardiner Regional."

They fell silent as they trudged through the drifts to the helicopter. After sliding the stretcher with the girl inside, Rich climbed in and pushed the second stretcher out to Mallory. She dragged it over the snow back to the cave and crawled inside, guiding it behind her. Jac had all the gear packed, and they quickly secured the boy to the stretcher, piled their equipment packs between his feet, and worked their way back to daylight.

"Careful with your shoulder," Mallory said as Jac lifted her end.

"I'm good. Where are we headed?" Jac asked as they maneuvered the stretcher toward the helicopter.

"Medical center at Gardiner."

"How far back to base?"

"A solid half day's drive," Mallory said. "If the weather lets up."

Mallory hoped the trip would be quick. As soon as they got back to base, they'd be heading right out to the field camp to complete the pre-season training. She could settle back into her role as training manager, and Jac would be just one of the rookies again. They wouldn't be partners any longer, and the troubling sense of intimacy would disappear. She ought to be happy about that, but for some reason a cavern yawned inside her, dark and cold and lonely. She so did not need this. Even the satisfaction that usually came from a successful mission eluded her. Ordinarily, rescuing the climbers and getting them to safety would be all she needed to feel complete. The aching sadness in her chest was something new. Something new and unwelcome and, hopefully, something she could quickly correct.

CHAPTER TWENTY-FOUR

Jac watched the red-bordered landing zone on the rooftop of Gardiner Regional Medical Center grow larger and larger as the helitack landed on the white cross in the center. A cluster of white-coated medical personnel rushed forward the instant the helo's runners touched down. The flight tech slid open the door, and trauma team members surged forward to transfer the stretchers onto waiting gurneys. The tech jumped out, calling out status updates as everyone raced toward the building, the injured quickly hidden in the center of the scrum. Within a minute everyone had disappeared, leaving Jac and Mallory still in the belly of the shuddering bird.

"I guess we're done," Jac said, the adrenaline waning and fatigue grabbing her by the throat.

"If it's okay with you," Mallory said, "I'd like to go downstairs and see if I can get an update on the kids."

"Yeah. That would be good." Jac released her shoulder harness and winced as her stiff shoulder objected to the sudden freedom.

"Maybe we ought to have someone check that shoulder too," Mallory said.

"No, it's okay."

"Actually, that wasn't a suggestion." Mallory climbed down and extended her hand back to Jac. "Come on, let's get you looked at."

Jac considered refusing, but if she didn't get medical clearance she knew damn well Mallory would never let her back in the jump plane. Somehow, she feared Mallory might be looking for an excuse to keep her at arm's length, maybe even farther than that. She wasn't going to give her any ammunition. Grasping Mallory's hand, she let herself be guided out to the rooftop. "Okay. But you know how long an ER visit can take, and we need—"

"I don't care how long. Sully has things covered back at base. All that will keep."

"Okay," Jac said again, surprised at how easily Mallory dismissed missing another day of boot camp. A little frisson of pleasure shot through her belly. Maybe she mattered more than Mallory was willing to let on. And maybe she was setting herself up for a fall—one a lot worse than back there on that ledge.

They followed the path of the trauma team and took the elevator to the ground floor. Like in most regional trauma centers, the doors opened across from the emergency room. To the right was the waiting area, where a harried clerk and several admitting nurses shuffled papers, typed on computers, and copied insurance cards.

Mallory stopped in front of a set of gunmetal gray double doors with Emergency Room stenciled in peeling black letters. "I'll see if I can get an update on the kids while you sign in."

"Take your time," Jac said, surveying the stack of charts in the rack next to the window. She crowded closer to the wall as a transport orderly pushed an elderly man in a thin white cotton smock in a wheelchair, trailing an IV pole and oxygen canister on wheels. "You hungry? I'll see if I can rustle us up something while we're waiting."

"Starved." Mallory hesitated. "Maybe you better not eat anything."

"Mallory, I don't need surgery. I probably don't need anything except some anti-inflammatories. But if I don't eat something, I'm in danger of committing criminal acts."

"Really." Mallory smiled a teasing smile. "Are you one of those people who loses all semblance of civility when you need to be fed?"

Jac had a hard time looking away from Mallory's mouth as she spoke. The windburn had faded, leaving her full lower lip looking bruised and just kissed. Kisses she wished she'd put there. She was hungry for a lot more than food and didn't know how long she could hide it. "Yeah. I get pretty dangerous."

Laughing, Mallory tugged on the zipper of Jac's flight jacket. "Well then, go find some food. I'll be out in a minute."

Jac grabbed Mallory's hand and pretended to bite her finger. "Careful. I did warn you."

Mallory's lips parted and her eyes darkened, the shadows of fatigue replaced by glowing embers. "So noted."

When Mallory made no move to pull away, Jac battled the urge to lean forward and take her mouth. She was on the verge of combusting, her fuse lit, burning fast and hot. She shuddered and released Mallory's hand. "See you in a few minutes."

"Don't get lost out there, Russo." Mallory didn't want to let Jac out of her sight, and that crazy reaction propelled her through the automatic doors and down the hallway to the brightly lit nurses' station like her butt was ablaze. The ravenous look in Jac's eyes shimmered through her despite the distance she put between them. What was she doing, flirting with her like that? But she knew, oh, she knew. She liked putting that hungry look in Jac's eyes, liked the way Jac's breath hitched when she teased her, liked the pressure that surged between her thighs when Jac took her hand. Maybe—maybe there was some safe halfway point. She'd never had any trouble separating her feelings from her physical pleasures before. She certainly cared about Emily, enjoyed her company in and out of bed. Why not with Jac? Not until after boot camp, when there couldn't be any doubt the boundaries were nice and clean, but maybe then. Maybe then she could ease this terrible ache she had for her. Maybe.

❖

The doors swung closed and Jac was alone. She looked at her fingers, half expecting to see sparks shooting from her fingertips. Sweat trickled down the back of her neck and under the collar of her shirt, but she shivered as if icy fingers trailed across her bare skin. She throbbed. Damn it. This was bad.

She knew how to get her body into the zone where her emotions had no impact. Breathing slowly through her nose, she filled her lungs, expanded her diaphragm, centered herself the way she did when she prepared to dismantle a bomb. Dismantling the power Mallory held over her would be a hell of a lot more difficult. Maybe impossible, especially when she welcomed it. But at least she could hide it for a while.

When her legs felt steady again, she skirted around the rows of bolted-together gray plastic chairs to the sign-in window and scribbled her name on the clipboard. A middle-aged woman in a painfully bright green velour top on the other side of the sliding plastic partition leaned forward and scanned the length of Jac's body.

"You an EMT?" the clerk asked.

"Firefighter."

"What's the problem?"

"Banged up my shoulder."

"Huh." The clerk swiveled around, muttered something to a nurse who nodded, then swung back around. "Ought to be just a few minutes."

"Thanks. Is there a cafeteria?"

"Down the hall."

The clerk went back to her paperwork, and Jac followed the scent of microwaved burritos and burnt coffee beans. The cafeteria was little more than a vending room, but there were several trays piled high with doughnuts and bagels, a row of industrial-sized coffee dispensers, a few baskets of small plastic containers filled with peanut butter and cream cheese, and muffins. After two days of trail mix, protein bars, and dehydrated meals out of foil containers, this spread looked like a banquet. She glanced at the muffins and smiled to herself. She might never be able to eat another muffin unless she was feeding it to Mallory. Mallory. God. She couldn't stop thinking about her, and the only thing she was accomplishing was to drive herself nuts.

She poured two tall Styrofoam cups of coffee to go, grabbed a cardboard tray along with four bagels and spreads, and paid the cashier. Back in the waiting area, she settled into one of the chairs opposite the silent TV showing a news station and set the supplies next to her. At not quite eight on a Sunday morning, the waiting area was surprisingly crowded. An exhausted-looking young mother with two toddlers and a baby in her arms occupied one corner. A worried-looking older man in a dapper suit sat militarily erect at the end of the last row, his hands on his thighs, his eyes riveted to the closed double doors of the treatment area. Someone very important to him was back there. A young couple in biker jackets and tattered jeans snoozed across from Jac, the girl's hand resting proprietarily on the bearded guy's thigh. The casual intimacy struck Jac in a way she'd never experienced before. She thought of

Mallory's hand in hers throughout the night, and her stomach knotted, replacing the hunger pangs with a different kind of need.

The doors opposite her opened, and Mallory came through, scanned the room, and fixed on Jac as if Jac were the only person in the waiting area. Jac's skin flashed hot. Suddenly the dingy, somewhat desolate room was brighter, the medicinal odor and faint undercurrent of illness faded, and her pulse jumped as if someone had just yelled *incoming.*

"Hey," Jac said.

"Oh my God, you've got food," Mallory muttered, dropping into the seat next to her. "You are a prince."

Jac laughed, trying for casual when she was close to imploding. "Prince? What happened to king? I'd even settle for queen." She handed Mallory one of the cups of coffee. "A touch of cream. No sugar."

Mallory reached for a bagel. "What, no muffins?"

Jac choked in mid-swallow, hot coffee searing its way down the center of her chest like molten lava. Mallory made a sympathetic sound and rubbed her back, which didn't help at all. The press of Mallory's palm burned through her, and her breasts tightened. When she caught her breath, she said, "I thought I'd save that for a special occasion."

"If this isn't one, I don't know what is." Mallory massaged Jac's back in slow circles. "But I don't mind waiting."

Jac had never in her life wished so much for time to stand still. She wanted Mallory never to move her hand, never to look at her with anything other than the tenderness in her gaze right now, wanted never to hear Mallory's voice without the teasing undercurrent of desire. She had no idea how to keep the spell from breaking, and the helplessness made her hands tremble as she spread cream cheese on a bagel with a plastic knife and held it out to Mallory. "Here. Try this for now."

Mallory grinned, leaned forward, and took a huge bite. She chewed, swallowed, licked her lips. Her fingers trailed down the center of Jac's back and moved away. "Mmm. Heaven. Thank you."

"You're welcome." Jac's insides churned and her head swirled. She was hungry, but she wasn't sure she could handle even a bagel. "Any word on the kids?"

"They took the boy right to CAT scan. The girl is a lot more alert now." Mallory sipped her coffee, her knee resting against Jac's. "I think they've both got a really good chance."

"That's great," Jac muttered. "A good day's work, huh?"

"Mmm. Very good," Mallory said, watching Jac over the rim of her coffee cup with heavy-lidded intensity. "Aren't you going to eat?"

Jac's blood surged, and every disparate piece of her life—her work, her needs, her desires—coalesced in the heat of Mallory's gaze. Fuck, she was in deep trouble. "Uh, I think I'll save it for the drive back."

"Not a bad idea. That late spring storm is moving south. We might run into it," Mallory said, "so it could take us longer than I expected. I rented us a Jeep. They're going to deliver it here. Sarah and Ray will have taken ours back to base—hopefully before the storm hit."

"The ER should call me back soon. Sorry about the wait."

"It's no problem," Mallory said. "I'll just work you twice as hard when we get back."

"I knew there was a catch."

Mallory laughed, and her laughter warmed Jac all the way through. She was in no hurry to get back, and Mallory didn't seem to be either. That was strange. She had expected Mallory to be anxious to return to base where she could resurrect the rules and regulations and the distance that came with them. But if Mallory wanted to spend more time with her, she wasn't going to question why.

"And the best news"—Mallory gathered the tray and dumped it in the nearby trash can—"is the ER docs said we could use their locker room to shower. They know we've been out a couple of days. As soon as we get your shoulder seen to, we can get cleaned up."

Jac groaned. "Oh man, I could use a shower."

"Same here." Mallory skimmed her hand over Jac's thigh and squeezed lightly. "It's looking to be a mighty fine morning, all things considered."

"Yeah," Jac murmured, her whole leg tingling from the fleeting touch. "Fine for sure."

❖

"I'm her partner," Mallory said when the ER tech told her to wait outside the treatment area. "I'm coming."

The young Hispanic man raised an eyebrow at Jac. "Up to you."

"It's fine," Jac said.

He led them to a treatment cubicle, pulled the striped cotton curtain back a few feet, and gestured to the narrow, sheet-covered stretcher in the middle of the small space. "Everything off to the waist. There's a gown on the end of the bed. Take a seat and someone will be in in a minute." He dropped the clipboard with Jac's intake information on it into a plastic bin on the wall and walked away.

When Jac looked around the room as if uncertain what to do next, Mallory said, "You need some help getting out of your jacket and shirt?"

Jac blushed, suddenly looking a decade younger, and Mallory's heart swelled. She stepped behind Jac and gently grasped the shoulders of Jac's flight jacket. "Here. I've got this. Just ease your arm out of the sleeve."

"It doesn't hurt unless I try raising it," Jac muttered.

"Sounds like your rotator cuff," Mallory said. "Shouldn't have let you carry the damn stretcher out there."

"It felt fine then," Jac said, a stubborn note in her voice.

"Uh-huh." Mallory understood the macho routine. She would have been the same way. Injuries were part of the job. Unless you couldn't move, you didn't let them get in the way of doing what needed to be done. All the same, the idea of Jac being in pain made her stomach clench. She draped the jacket over a metal folding chair, the only furniture in the room besides the stretcher, and plucked up the standard hospital-issue gown. She opened it and held it out to Jac. "Here you go."

Jac unbuttoned her shirt, shrugged her good arm out of the sleeve, and pulled the other side down her arm without raising her shoulder. She tossed the shirt on the chair, repeated the maneuver with the T-shirt she'd worn underneath, and turned with one hand out for the gown. "Thanks."

"You're welcome," Mallory said hoarsely, unable to prevent her eyes from sweeping down Jac's torso. Jac's nipples tightened and her stomach hollowed, as if Mallory's gaze had been a caress. Mallory would have sworn the image of Jac naked had been burned indelibly in her mind after her first glimpse in the locker room, but she'd failed somehow to register just how incredibly beautiful she was. Tired, rumpled, hurt, Jac was still magnificent.

Jac's breathing picked up, her breasts rose and fell more quickly, and Mallory had to clutch the thin cotton fabric to keep from touching her. "Put this on, it's freezing in here."

"Right." Jac slid her arms through the sleeves.

"Turn around, I'll tie you up."

Jac turned, her naked back to Mallory. Tendrils of Jac's hair lay in dark swirls against her neck, and when Mallory brushed them aside to secure the cotton ties on the back of the gown, Jac shuddered. Mallory rested her fingertips gently on the bare crests of Jac's shoulders and closed her eyes. An inch of air so thick and hot they might've been standing over an open fire was all that separated them. If she applied the slightest bit of pressure, Jac would be in her arms.

"Mallory," Jac whispered, leaning back until she settled into the curve of Mallory's body.

Mallory rested her forehead against Jac's hair. "Jac, I—"

"Hello, hello," a robust male voice announced as the curtain swung back. A very large, very jovial, shaggy-haired redhead in scrubs and a wrinkled white coat stepped into the room. "I'm Dr. Hurley. I hear someone's got a bum shoulder."

"That would be me." Jac pivoted to face the doctor. Her eyes were a little hazy, and she sounded slightly dazed. "But I think it's just a little ding."

"Well, let's have a look," he said.

Mallory stepped back, her hands falling to her sides. Her heart thudded in her chest, and her legs quivered so badly she had to rest her butt against the stretcher to get her balance. When her head stopped spinning, she edged farther around the bottom of the stretcher so Jac could climb up onto it. "I'll wait outside."

Jac shot her a surprised look but Mallory slipped out and leaned against the wall. She had just come dangerously close to crossing a line she'd already moved more than she should have. She didn't trust herself to recognize her own boundaries anymore, and that was ten times more terrifying than any wildfire she'd ever faced.

Chapter Twenty-five

G ood news," Dr. Hurley said with a face-splitting grin. "You really banged up your shoulder, but you didn't tear anything. Your MRI looks great—your rotator cuff is intact, there's no fluid in the joint, just a little soft tissue swelling." He waggled his hand. "Well, maybe a bit more than a little swelling, but a couple of days of rest and anti-inflammatories and you ought to be good as new."

Jac glanced at Mallory when she edged around the curtain and into the cubicle, then back at the ER physician. "I guess I'm going to have to ask. Define 'good as new.' I'm a wilderness firefighter. I need to climb, I need to carry a pack, I need to work with heavy equipment."

His expression grew solemn. "I know what you do. I know what you both did out there in the last couple of days. You're heroes around here." He rubbed his hands together and grinned again. "Seventy-two hours of rest, ibuprofen three times a day, and if you have full range of motion in your shoulder at that point—and, if you're as tough as everyone says you are—"

"She is," Mallory muttered.

"You can work without restriction," Hurley finished.

Jac breathed out a sigh of relief and shifted on the stretcher to face Mallory, who seemed to be looking anywhere but at her. Even though it'd taken almost two hours to get the emergency MRI, to wait for a radiologist who could read it on a Sunday, and then for the ER doctor to review the findings, Mallory had somehow managed to always be busy. After talking on the phone to Sully for a while, she went outside to wait for the rental service to deliver the Jeep—even though it was thirty degrees and already lightly snowing. Jac knew when she was being avoided, and after the feel of Mallory's hands on her, the press of Mallory's breasts against her shoulder, and the whisper of Mallory's breath against her ear, her absence cut deep.

Mallory had pulled away, and Jac didn't know how to reach her. Mallory didn't trust her, and she didn't know how to convince her she wouldn't hurt her. She would have waited with her hand outstretched, urging her to believe, if waiting was what it took. Somehow she did not think time alone would be enough—even though she really had nothing but time.

The firefighting season stretched ahead and hopefully, if she passed boot camp, she would have work to occupy her, but she didn't have anyone expecting her to return at the end of the season to a life that included intimacy and affection. She hadn't really thought ahead to what she would do in the fall. If her father received his party's nomination, which everyone thought was going to happen, she was probably going to be more of a liability in his eyes than she already was—too visible, too controversial, and too at odds with his stance on just about everything. She wondered where he would want her to disappear to next. She was young and healthy, and wars still raged. Maybe it was time to make her reserve status permanent and go active. War she knew. Those enemies she understood. And the bombs, her singular, particular enemy, she did not fear.

"Jac?" Mallory slid into Jac's field of vision, her expression perplexed, as if she had been speaking for a while and Jac had not been listening.

Jac jerked straighter, conscious of the flimsy cotton covering her naked torso, conscious of the tightening of her nipples at the mere sound of Mallory's voice. "Yeah?"

"The storm's coming on fast and we might have a chance to outrun it, but we'll have to leave right away. Do you mind skipping the shower?"

Jac didn't need an interpreter. Mallory didn't want even the slightest chance of intimacy between them. As if stripping down in the hospital locker room was going to be some kind of threat. Her skin chilled, as if snow already fell on her. As if she were already out in the cold. She jumped down from the stretcher, ignoring the jolt of pain shooting through her shoulder. "That's a good idea. We need to get back. We can catch up to Sully and the rest of them in the morning then, right?"

Jac kept her face averted as she sorted through the jumble of her clothes and picked out her T-shirt. She balled it up and tossed it back on the chair. It was stiff with sweat and she wasn't putting it on again. She checked out her shirt. It wasn't in much better shape.

Mallory grasped her arm. "Here. I know it's a little funky, but it's clean and it's warm." Mallory held out a navy blue sweatshirt that read *Gardiner Tigers* above an emblem of the high school.

"Where…?"

"Gift shop." Mallory grimaced. "Sorry, the selection was pretty slim."

"It looks great to me. I don't suppose they had any underwear?"

Mallory laughed. "Not unless you want something in size one that says 'It's a boy!'"

"Sorry. Won't fit the equipment."

Mallory's smile flickered for a second. "No, I don't imagine it would." She hefted a plastic bag. "I've got one, too. I'll go get the Jeep. You—uh—need any help?"

"Nope. I've got it."

"Great. Okay then." Mallory backed toward the curtain. "I'll be right outside in the emergency room parking lot. It's a black Commander. I'll get it warmed up and we can hit the road."

"Be there in a minute." Jac turned her back to give Mallory a chance to escape, which was obviously what Mallory wanted. This time though, Jac was going to let her go.

❖

Mallory sat behind the wheel, clenching the steering wheel so hard her palms ached and the tips of her fingers went numb. Heat blasted from the dashboard vents, but the center of her chest was a solid block of ice. Snow slashed against the windshield, melting into trails of tears that streaked her vision. Irritated, she brushed her fingers over her face and they came away wet. She stared at the glistening moisture on her fingertips. She couldn't possibly be crying. She couldn't remember the last time she'd cried. No, she could remember, she just didn't want to.

The night after Phil and Danny's funeral. The night after four hundred firefighters and two hundred engines, sirens blaring, had formed a long, twisting procession through the mountains carrying Danny and Phil back to base where their bodies had been lifted by a full-color honor guard into a helitack while a regimental band played taps. She had stood with the rest of her team, her arm in a rigid salute, while the bird lifted off for Danny and Phil's last flight. Her eyes had been dry, her throat closed, her heart thudding painfully to each beat of the drum. Inside she mourned to the wail of the sirens. That night she'd driven two hours away, gotten a hotel room and a bottle of Jack Daniel's, and drunk herself to sleep. Sometime before she'd passed out, she must have cried—when she woke, her pillow was wet. She'd dumped the dregs of the Jack down the toilet, showered, and driven back to base.

She never talked about what happened in Idaho, except when the review board had called her in to recount the details of how she had spotted the safe zone, what factors she had considered, what possible dangers she had seen from the position of the fire front, the prevailing winds, the terrain, and what line she had chosen for her team to dig. She had talked about Phil and Danny then, but the words had sounded as if they were coming from someone else. Her words had been precise, concise, clear, and according to them, procedurally correct. Her judgment had been deemed accurate, her decisions right. They had said she was without fault, but she knew they were wrong.

Mallory tasted salt and licked her lips. She rubbed the rough sleeve of her sweatshirt over her face, erasing the signs of her pain and weakness. Enough. Somehow, wanting Jac had opened the doors to all she had buried, and freed every nightmare memory she wanted to obliterate. The only way she knew to close and chain the door again was to build a wall between her and Jac. She knew she was succeeding. She'd seen the flare of hurt and bewilderment in Jac's eyes. But Jac was a survivor. Jac would be fine. She wasn't sure she would be, but at least she was breathing, moving, functioning, and for so long, that was all she had wanted. Enough. She had made those things enough. And now, it had to be.

The passenger door opened and Jac dropped into the seat beside her, bringing a gust of wind and snowflakes with her.

"Sorry," Jac said briskly. "It's really bad out there."

"I know. I was hoping we could get a couple hours in and then maybe grab something to eat when we got ahead of the front."

"Whatever you want, Mal. It's up to you."

Mallory backed out of the parking place and pulled out into the snowy street. Up to her. If it was up to her, she never would've met Jac Russo with her dark, burning eyes and her gentle touch. She never would have fallen in love with her.

Chapter Twenty-six

Mallory pulled into a gas station on 89S a little after nine p.m. Traffic on the two-lane was almost nonexistent. Much of the highway was obscured by drifting snow, and most of the time she couldn't see beyond the tapering cones of her own headlights. Late spring snows, when everyone was prepared for the onset of summer and no one wanted to face yet another whiteout blizzard, always seemed to be the worst of the season. The only positive note was storms like these usually blew in and blew out quickly. With any luck, the morning would bring sunshine and a quick melt. But right now, all she wanted to do was get back to base safe and sound. Her eyes were gritty from staring at the endless expanse of white, the surface unbroken by any other tire tracks. Not even a single set of red taillights glowed ahead to help orient her. The Jeep was quiet save for the rumble of the engine, and at times she felt as if she were alone in the universe. Except she wasn't. Despite the demands of the tricky driving and the terrible visibility, she was always, constantly, aware of Jac.

Jac lay curled up beside her in the passenger seat, asleep. She'd taken a pain pill in the emergency room and drifted off an hour or so after they'd left Gardiner. Wanting her to rest, Mallory hadn't even turned on the radio to help dispel the monotony. She didn't mind the silence. Jac's quiet breathing provided a soothing buffer against the wind that howled outside the windows. She'd never been quite so acutely conscious of another person's presence before. She'd had to stop herself more than once from reaching across the space between them and stroking Jac's hair. She really did not want to think about what that meant.

Easing in next to the snowcapped gas pumps, Mallory parked

and released her seat belt. The bright lights above the pumps blazed in through the windshield, glaring directly into Jac's face. Jac muttered under her breath and shifted uneasily. Mallory leaned over and rubbed Jac's shoulder, settling her. "It's okay. I'm just going to get some gas. Everything is fine."

Jac's eyes flickered open and she frowned, her expression confused and her eyes clouded with sleep and a hint of pain. "Where are we?"

"About a hundred miles from the base."

"Fell asleep. Sorry," Jac said, jerking at the seat belt and pushing herself upright.

"No, don't wake up. I'm going to grab a soda and a couple of candy bars. I'll get you one if you want."

"Hershey's. Dark chocolate."

Mallory smiled. "You got it. I'm going to leave the motor running so you don't get cold. Do you need anything else?"

Jac shifted fitfully, settled against her uninjured shoulder facing Mallory with her cheek against the seat, and closed her eyes. "No. I'm fine. Thanks. Sorry. Lousy company."

"I told you not to apologize." Mallory gave in and feathered her fingers through Jac's hair. The dark wavy strands were faintly damp, and she worried that Jac was sweating and in pain. "You're very good company. How's your shoulder?"

"Achy. Nothing real serious."

"And you wouldn't admit it if it were." Mallory let her fingers linger on Jac's throat for longer than she should have, then eased back into her seat. "I'll only be a minute with that candy bar."

"Hey, Mal?" Jac muttered, her eyes still closed.

"What, baby?" Mallory said softly around the lump in her throat. She'd never seen Jac look quite so vulnerable, not even when she was dangling against the cliffside by a rope, minutes from death. The urge to protect her, to ease her discomfort, to obliterate anything or anyone who'd ever hurt her, was so strong Mallory ached inside.

"You really know how to show a girl a good time."

Mallory laughed, her heart threatening to leap from her chest. "Be careful, you didn't get the chocolate yet."

"I trust you to bring it." Jac's lids rose a fraction and she stretched out one hand, catching Mallory's fingers. "I trust you."

When Jac squeezed her fingers, a wave of heat rolled up Mallory's arm, lodged behind her breastbone, and, with the next breath, radiated outward like a starburst. Her head spun. "Why? Why would you?"

Jac's eyes opened fully, the bright lights outside reflecting in her dark irises like stars scattered across the night sky. "Because I've told you things I've never told anyone else, and you're still here. Whenever I've needed you, you've been right there."

"Oh God, Jac," Mallory murmured, rubbing her cheek against the backs of Jac's fingers. She hadn't known how cold she was until the warmth of Jac's flesh flooded into her. "I don't think I deserve that kind of trust."

"Don't you get it yet, Mal?" Jac traced her fingertips over the corner of Mallory's mouth. "That's one of the few things you can't control. It's not up to you. Trust lives in our hearts. Like love."

Mallory froze. Terror slammed through her, followed instantly by racking, agonizing pain. Not the dull throb of guilt or self-recrimination, but the horrible void left behind by those she'd led into the mountains and stumbled out without. A black hole beckoned, threatening to drag her in and crush her. All this time she'd kept the worst pain at bay by blaming herself over and over so she wouldn't feel anything else. If she let go of her guilt, she'd have to face the bright, lacerating wound of pure and simple loss. "I can't."

"Why not?"

"I'm afraid."

"Of what?"

"I can't, Jac. Please. Don't ask me."

"I want you, you know that, don't you?"

Closing her eyes, Mallory clutched Jac's hand between both of hers and fought the insane urge to give in. She longed to lay her head on Jac's chest, to lay down the suffocating burden for just one night. Could she have one night? Was that even fair? She wasn't a coward, and she wouldn't lie. She dropped their joined hands to her lap and shifted on the seat, facing Jac, knowing her face was unshielded in the relentless glare of the artificial sun. "I know. And I want you too."

Something miraculous passed through Jac's eyes—not the glint of triumph, not the blaze of victory, but the tender softening of desire. Mallory took a breath, needing to be clear. Needing to be honest.

Jac spoke first. "Right this second, I don't want to hear the *but* I know you think I need to hear. So can we just not go there right now?"

"How come you figured me out so easily?" Mallory whispered.

"Ice isn't all that hard to see through if you just look." Jac smiled and gestured to the distance between them. "I'm a little slow maneuvering tonight. Do you think you could find your way clear to kiss me before you seduce me with chocolate?"

"I never said—"

"I know." Jac's wistful longing pierced Mallory's heart. "Just let me dream for a minute."

"Oh, the hell with it." Mallory pushed over into the space between their seats, not caring that the gearshift dug into her ass. She didn't care about the storm, she didn't care about the tiny voice in the back of her brain screaming at her to get a grip. All she saw was the firestorm swirling in Jac's eyes. And fire was something she understood. She cupped the back of Jac's neck, spreading her fingers over the column of muscle that curved in a sinuous arc of strength and beauty to the junction of Jac's shoulder. "You're so goddamn gorgeous."

Jac's lips parted ever so slightly, as if she might speak or laugh, but Mallory didn't give her time to do either. She brought her mouth down over Jac's, gently but firmly. Jac gasped, and Mallory skated the tip of her tongue over the silky-soft surface of Jac's lower lip. She tasted cinnamon and heat. Mallory groaned.

Jac's arm came around Mallory's shoulder, and her fingers gripped Mallory's upper arm, holding her close, as if fearing she might suddenly bolt. Her mouth opened more and her tongue teased out, toying with Mallory's. Jac's teeth grazed her lower lip and Mallory tightened between her legs. She wanted to climb into Jac's lap, straddle her narrow hips, rub herself against Jac's hard belly. She wanted Jac's hands inside her jacket, under her shirt, clasping her breasts, teasing her nipples. Oh God, she wanted to come right here and now. Jac's fingers slid into her hair, tilting her head as she pushed her tongue deeper into Mallory's mouth. Mallory whimpered.

"God, Mal," Jac groaned against her mouth. "I want you so much."

"Your shoulder. The storm…"

"Uh-huh."

"Bad timing," Mallory panted. "Really, really, really bad timing."

Jac laughed shakily. "I don't think I can stop. You're the boss. Do something."

"Just remember you said that, next time…" Mallory marshaled what little strength and sanity she had left and pushed away. Her lips were burning. Her body was aflame. She wanted nothing more than to let Jac's fire consume her. "I have to get out of the car. I can't think."

"Don't go far," Jac whispered. "Please, Mal. Don't go far."

Mallory shoved open the door, bolted outside, and slammed the door before snow could swirl in. She pulled up the hood on the Gardiner High School sweatshirt and zipped her flight jacket up to her throat. Her hands shook so badly she could barely get the gas cap off. Hunching against the blowing snow, she pumped gas as quickly as she could, capped the tank, and hurried toward the station. She refused to think. She refused to acknowledge the trembling in her blood or the pressure threatening to burst her heart into fragments. She touched her bare fingertips to her lips. Three inches of snow coated the parking lot. Ice crystals hung in the air she exhaled. Frozen tears coated her lashes. And her lips burned. *She* burned. What had she done?

A lone attendant manned the counter inside the convenience store. Mallory blinked in the harsh white light that bleached everything to a monochrome. Moving mechanically, her mind a blank, she grabbed several candy bars and two sixteen-ounce bottles of soda, bundled everything into her arms, and started for the counter. A sliver of reason penetrated the fog that clouded her brain, and she took stock of what she had picked up. No Hershey bar. She spun back to retrieve one, and the headline on a newspaper in a stand next to the checkout counter caught her attention. She stopped, reread it, and her stomach plummeted.

IDAHO SENATOR FRANKLIN RUSSO CLINCHES PATRIOT PARTY NOMINATION

Underneath the headline, a picture of Jac's father with arms outstretched, a triumphant smile on his handsome, virile face, took up the rest of the front page. Beneath the image was the caption: "Conservative nominee pledges return to American values."

Mallory almost laughed out loud. American values. What a joke. If people only knew how he treated his own daughter, with so little respect, so little care, he wouldn't be seen as some kind of savior. Outrage swelled just thinking about Jac being shunted aside, made invisible, when she was so brave, so kind, so generous and strong.

Mallory squelched her anger. Her feelings were not what mattered. What mattered was Jac.

"Help you, miss?" the clerk asked, a note of uncertainty in his voice.

Mallory jerked, wondering how long she'd been staring at the newspaper, and went back for the Hershey bar. She piled the sodas and snacks on the counter, hesitated, then picked up a newspaper. Jac ought to know, to prepare for what was coming, if nothing else. As much as she'd love to protect Jac from any hurt, Jac did not need to be shielded. She needed to be supported. "Sorry. Just these things."

He rang up the items with bored efficiency, ran her credit card, and with a short grunt, went back to watching the small black-and-white television perched on the front window ledge. Mallory hefted the bag with the newspaper folded up inside and headed back to the car. Her earlier tracks from the Jeep were already filled with new snow. They hadn't managed to outrun the storm but were barely managing to keep pace with it. She needed to keep her mind on the road and away from the memory of Jac's mouth.

Sliding into the driver's seat, she slammed the door and propped the bag between her thighs. Carefully not looking at Jac, she pulled out the sodas, put them in the cup holders, and extracted the candy bars. She handed the dark chocolate to Jac. "Here you go."

"Thanks," Jac said, straightening in her seat. "I'm more awake now. You want me to drive? You've got to be tired."

"I'm really okay," Mallory said.

"Are we?"

"Sure." Mallory finished her Reese's cup in three bites and washed it down with her soda. She stared at the newspaper sticking out of the plastic bag, and before she could change her mind, yanked it out and handed it to Jac. "I guess you better see this."

Silently, Jac unfolded it and held it up to the light slanting through the windshield. She sucked in a breath. "Well. That's going to make life interesting."

"You didn't know?"

"No. I knew it was likely." Jac grimaced. "That's part of why he wanted me out of sight. Tabloid stories about his queer daughter's escapades were not what his campaign committee wanted to see when he was trying to clinch the nomination."

Mallory stifled her urge to curse. "He could have told you before you read it in the newspapers."

Jac twisted in the seat, grabbed her pack from the backseat, and pulled it into her lap. She dug out her cell and thumbed through the menu. "Nora Fleming, his campaign manager, left a message last night. That's probably what it's about."

"What does she say?"

"Can't tell. No signal."

"What will happen next?" Mallory asked.

"I'm sure I can expect a visit from the press." Jac stared at her phone, willing Nora's voicemail to self-destruct. "God, I'm sorry, Mallory."

"What for?"

"You have no idea what these people can do. The last thing you and the rest of the crew need is some media circus dropping around to see what the next president's daughter—prodigal daughter, I might add—is doing."

"He's not the president yet."

"No, and unseating a sitting president is going to take some doing. Especially one as popular as Powell." Jac's voice was a monotone, eerily empty. "But I know my father, and he knows how to put on a show."

"You really think the press will bother you?"

Jac laughed shortly. "Why do you think I'm here, Mal? He wanted me out of the public eye because if they can't find something to write about him, they'll write about me instead."

"Well, there's nothing much to say about you, now, is there?" Mallory hated the weary, defeated note in Jac's voice.

"That doesn't stop them. If they can't find something, they'll make something up." Jac rubbed her face with one hand. "I don't want you ending up a target."

"I'm nobody's target, Jac," Mallory said. "And I'm not afraid of a little public scrutiny."

"Right. Probably nothing will come of any of it." Jac turned the chocolate bar around in her hands, staring at it as if she wasn't quite certain what it was. "They'll all be too busy following him around for a while, anyhow. If I stay here, out of the public eye, I just might make it through the summer."

"I'm so sorry," Mallory said.

"There's no need to be. I'm used to it by now." Jac refolded the newspaper and buried it in the bag along with the other trash. "I'm complicit to a degree. I went along with my father's demand that I disappear to save my mother the strain of family strife and to give my sister a few more months of a normal life."

"What about your life?" Mallory caught Jac's hand and threaded her fingers through Jac's. Such strong, capable hands.

Jac cradled Mallory's hand between hers, stroking her thumb over Mallory's knuckles. "I'm okay, really. I wanted this job long before my father decided it would be a good place to hide me. I'm just sorry you got saddled with me, and now this."

"You've earned your place," Mallory said. "I'll admit, I was irritated when I thought you had gone around procedure to get a position, but I understand now what happened. You didn't make it happen, your father did."

Jac's fingers tightened on Mallory's. Light glanced off the knife-edge plane of her cheek, shadowing her eyes and casting the line of her jaw in sharp relief. "If I'd known this was coming, I wouldn't have—"

"Wouldn't have what?" A heavy weight settled on Mallory's chest. She'd finally stopped running. Or almost. And now, what if it was all for nothing? "You wouldn't have what, Jac? Wouldn't have kissed me?"

"You don't know how vicious politics can get."

"I don't care about that."

"I do." Jac clasped her hands between her knees, her face averted.

"You didn't answer my question."

"I don't know the answer," Jac said softly.

"Let me know when you do." Mallory fastened her seat belt, put the Jeep in gear, and drove into the storm.

CHAPTER TWENTY-SEVEN

Looks like we have the place to ourselves," Mallory said when she drove into base a little before six in the morning and pulled up in front of the hangar. A single light glowed over the shack door. All the windows were dark and the land vehicles were gone.

"Guess everyone's at field camp," Jac said, trying for a business-as-usual tone. The storm had finally tracked west, giving them clear skies for the final leg of their return trip. There wasn't even any snow on the ground when they reached Yellowrock.

"At least they aren't sleeping in snow out there." Mallory rested her arms over the top of the wheel and rolled her shoulders. "We haven't missed much—they've probably just got camp set up."

"You're not going to head right out, are you?" The last hundred miles had taken almost eight hours, and while Mallory drove, Jac had pretended to nap even though she wasn't sleeping. She was still processing the news about her father, and still reeling from the kiss. She couldn't quite believe she'd asked to be kissed—nothing could be more *not* her—or that Mallory had relented and actually touched her. Damn, what a kiss it had been too, just slow enough to bring her blood to a boil and hard enough, possessive enough, to make her hungry for a lot more than the kiss. If they'd been anywhere other than the front seat of the Jeep she wouldn't have stopped with kisses. She'd been close to not being able to put on the brakes, even though she hadn't gone all the way in a car since she'd moved out of her parents' house and gotten her own place. Mallory lit her up like no woman ever had.

Now she was half sorry she hadn't stopped before the kiss even got started. Knowing how well Mallory teased and taunted with the lazy play of her mouth, how demandingly Mallory's hands skimmed over her, how good Mallory felt in her arms already made her throb for more, and there couldn't be a worse time for her to get involved with anyone, especially someone she cared about. Her life was about to turn into a zoo. She'd been through this before—she was going to be on display every bit as much as her high-profile father, only this time she'd have nowhere to hide.

When her father had first run for the senate, she'd been in her late teens and suddenly been catapulted into the public eye. The whole family had been. Her father was no ordinary senatorial candidate, even then. He'd already been highly vocal and highly visible in the conservative Patriot Party—his family money and a great deal of financial and political support behind the scenes had skyrocketed him onto the national scene overnight. Reporters descended like locusts.

She'd been followed by paparazzi, her high school friends and enemies had been interviewed, and more than a few had been willing to talk about her partying and dalliances with other girls. That had been the beginning of her father's behind-the-scenes campaign to make her conform to the image of the daughter he needed and, barring that, to at the very least make her invisible. Now that he was a presidential candidate, she wouldn't be able to find a hiding place deep enough or dark enough to avoid the spotlight. And anyone close to her was going to be fair game. She didn't want to drag Mallory through the kind of scrutiny she'd experienced for the last decade or so, even if Mallory thought she could handle it. "So what's on the agenda?"

"I'd say we've earned a day of rest," Mallory said. "Sarah and Cooper can handle the training for now. I'll check in with Sully a little later and tell him we'll be out tomorrow morning."

"Okay." Jac climbed out of the Jeep and dragged her pack with her. She slung it over her good shoulder and leaned down to look back at Mallory. "Do you mind if I grab a shower first?"

"No, go ahead," Mallory said slowly.

Jac turned away from the questioning look in Mallory's eyes and headed toward the standby shack. Once she got out into the field, she'd be able to put some space between her and Mallory. Mallory would be busy with the training program, and she'd be busy making sure she passed. She'd come here to work. At least she'd still have that.

Mallory sat behind the wheel, watching Jac stride stiffly across the yard. She could practically feel Jac's pain rippling on the air and clutched the steering wheel, frustrated and more than a little bit scared.

She'd never seen Jac close down this way, draw in on herself, go so cold and remote. "Ice" would suit Jac now, far more than her. She felt completely defenseless, without her usual shields and barricades. That simple kiss had ripped them all away, and she wasn't sure she could put them back even if she wanted to. She didn't think she wanted to. For the first time since she'd carried Phil and Danny's bodies out of the mountains, she didn't feel empty inside. She didn't feel frozen. Jac had done that.

Jac, with her persistent honesty and fiery passion, had thawed the heart of her grief until she'd had no choice but to embrace it, and once she did, the terrible sorrow burned through her and purified her pain. She would never stop grieving, but she didn't feel paralyzed in an endless loop of unrelenting guilt any longer.

The standby shack door slammed shut with a crack that echoed across the still yard like a gunshot. Jac was gone. Retreating, running away, and since Jac was no coward, Mallory could come up with only one explanation. If Jac pulled back, erected walls, she would do it because she thought Mallory needed protecting from the kind of intrusive scrutiny that had forced Jac to distrust everyone.

"I'm not everyone," Mallory muttered. Jac spent altogether too much time trying to protect the people around her at her own expense—her mother, her sister, and, whether she acknowledged it or not, her father. In an effort not to compromise her father's campaign, to spare her sister the kind of embarrassment that most teens would find devastating, and to shield her mother from family strife, Jac had willingly stepped aside. God, she'd even taken herself off to war, where even death didn't scare her.

"Well, enough of that." Mallory pocketed the keys, grabbed her gear, and followed Jac.

The shower was already running, and Jac's clothes were heaped on the end of the bench. Mallory hesitated, took half a second to think rationally, and finally admitted she'd already gone well past the point of logic. She'd kissed Jac. More than once. If she let Jac pull away now, she might as well say none of it had mattered. And she couldn't.

She stripped before she could panic and eased around the corner into the shower room.

Jac had turned on two showerheads full blast and the room was filled with steam. Jac leaned against the far wall, her arms braced, her head down, her back to Mallory.

Water cascaded in sheets over the bunched muscles in her shoulders and along her spine, breaking up into rivulets running over the rise of her ass and down the backs of her thighs. Jac's right shoulder was discolored, a purplish bruise spreading down her arm and back, and Mallory wanted to kiss the hurt away. That hurt and every hurt Jac had ever suffered. Mallory's skin misted with want and her throat closed. She ached to touch her, to trace her fingertips over the crests of Jac's shoulders, along her arms. Her breasts swelled and her nipples tingled and she wanted to rub herself against Jac's back. A tiny fragment of her brain still worked, and she cared too much about Jac to take her by surprise.

"Jac," Mallory murmured, her voice breaking. Jac didn't move and Mallory's heart leapt into her throat. She wasn't sure she could make her legs move enough to turn around and leave, but she would if she had to. She wouldn't be another person Jac couldn't trust. She wouldn't go where she wasn't wanted, but she couldn't leave unless she knew for sure Jac wanted to be alone. "Jac, I'm here."

Slowly, so slowly Mallory thought her heart might stop beating, Jac turned and flung the wet strands of dark hair away from her eyes with a flick of her head. Her tight breasts lifted away from her sculpted chest and the columns of muscles in her abdomen tensed. Her gaze raked down Mallory's body. "There's plenty of room."

"I didn't come to share the shower," Mallory said, still not moving.

"Do you know what you're doing?"

"No. Yes. Mostly." Mallory moved closer. "I know right now I want you more than I've ever wanted any woman in my life. I can't stand not touching you any longer. I can't stand you going away—"

Jac groaned and pulled Mallory close, forcing their wet bodies together, and swallowed the rest of Mallory's words with a kiss so hot and so hungry Mallory stopped breathing. Her thighs turned to molasses, and she wrapped her arms around Jac's waist for support.

"Your shoulder," Mallory gasped, backing Jac against the shower wall on the far side of the stream of water. She steadied herself with her arms against the wet tile on either side of Jac's chest and pressed her hips between Jac's legs. She was so aroused, so swollen, that the little bit of pressure was enough to make her come.

"Shoulder's better already," Jac rumbled, sweeping her hands down Mallory's sides to cup her ass, yanking her even closer. She slid her teeth down Mallory's throat and sucked lightly in the hollow between her collarbones.

"Be careful," Mallory whispered, the first tendrils of pleasure unraveling inside her.

"Doesn't hurt." Jac kissed lower, over the curve of Mallory's breast, until she licked the water droplets from Mallory's nipple. Her tongue was soft, tantalizingly warm.

"Not talking about your shoulder." Mallory arched, her head fell back, and she climbed another notch closer to the crest. "You'll make me come."

Jac laughed and massaged Mallory's ass. "Damn right I will. But not just yet."

"I don't think," Mallory gasped, shifting to straddle Jac's thigh, "that's up to you."

"You feel so good. So wet, hot. Not rushing." Jac's breath came faster. She cradled Mallory's breast in one hand and stroked down the center of Mallory's stomach with the other, feathering her fingertips just above her clitoris.

"Oh God, touch me." Mallory couldn't stop her hips from rocking, couldn't stand up much longer. She dropped her forehead to Jac's shoulder and pushed herself harder into Jac's hand. "Please, I need you. I need you now. There. Right there."

"Soon." Jac spun Mallory around until Mallory's back was against Jac's chest and her ass cushioned in the curve of Jac's pelvis. Mallory moaned, protesting, feeling the absence of Jac's heat against the front of her body like a missing part. And then Jac's hands were caressing the curves of her breasts, cupping them in her palms, dancing her fingertips down Mallory's belly. Making her tremble. Making her crazy.

"Please." Mallory grasped Jac's wrist and pushed her hand lower, guiding Jac's fingers between her legs. "Feel what you've done."

"So, so wet." Jac stroked lightly along her length and buried her face in the curve of Mallory's neck. "You're so beautiful," Jac whispered. "I love the way you feel."

Mallory covered Jac's hand and pressed Jac's fingertips inside her.

"Fill me up. I need to have you everywhere, inside me, deep. Now, Jac."

Jac's arm tightened around Mallory's torso, and her fingers closed over Mallory's nipple. "I want to make you come."

"I'm so close," Mallory moaned, turning her face into Jac's neck. She kissed her throat, dug her fingers into Jac's wrist, urged Jac deeper inside. She felt Jac tremble, heard her groan, and Jac's excitement pushed her over. She cried out, closing down hard on Jac's fingers. "I'm coming."

Jac thrust against Mallory's ass, coating Mallory with her desire. "*Ohh fuuck.* Me too."

Mallory closed her eyes, abandoning reason and logic and caution as she burned in Jac's flames.

"Oh my God, oh my God," Mallory sighed when the waves of fire receded. She was on the floor between Jac's raised knees, still cradled in Jac's arms, her cheek resting on Jac's shoulder. Jac sat with her head tilted back against the shower wall, her eyes closed, her neck and chest suffused with the incendiary flush of passion. Mallory loved knowing she had reduced Jac to exhaustion. She licked Jac's neck. "Mmm good?"

Jac laughed. "No. Terrible. Can't imagine why I want to do it again right now."

"Do you?" Mallory shifted and stroked Jac's chest, toying with Jac's small, hard nipples. She kept it up until Jac's breasts were rosy and Jac was breathing hard. "It's a big hot water tank, but we're going to run out soon."

Jac cracked one eye open. "Think we can make it to the loft for round two?"

"If you move your hand."

"I like being inside you."

Mallory groaned and tightened inside again. "God. I don't want to move. I don't want you to move. But I think we probably ought to."

"In a minute." Jac kissed her again, a slow, languorous exploratory kiss as possessive as it was celebratory. While she teased and taunted and sucked and licked, she eased her fingers from between Mallory's legs.

"I love the way you make me feel," Mallory whispered.

Jac kissed her again. "Yeah. I know. You okay?"

Mallory summoned her energy and got up onto her knees, resting both hands on Jac's shoulders. "I know it sounds corny, but I don't think I've ever felt better."

Jac brushed her cheek against Mallory's breasts and kissed her. "It sounds just great to me."

Mallory rose, held out her hand, and helped Jac up. "We better go. I think I'm getting ready for the next round. Stop touching me for a minute while I wash my hair."

Laughing, Jac held up both hands and moved a few inches away. "Sure?"

"No." Mallory put her hand in the center of Jac's chest and pushed lightly, forcing her back another step. "Rinse off and go away. I'll be out in a minute."

Jac snuck in for another kiss, then jumped back out of range. "Okay. But I'm counting. One minute."

Smiling, Mallory turned her back and reached for the shampoo. If she kept looking at Jac she was going to have to touch her again, and they'd never get out of the locker room.

❖

Mallory found Jac standing motionless in the middle of the locker room, a wet towel dangling from her hand, staring into her locker.

"Jac?" Mallory asked, tightening the knot holding the towel around her breasts. "What's wrong?"

Jac slammed her locker door. "Nothing."

"Do you think by now I can't tell bullshit when I hear it?" Mallory skirted around the bench, grasped Jac's arm, and turned Jac to face her. Jac was pale, the dark shadows beneath her eyes carved deeper by the flat fluorescent ceiling light. "Tell me."

"It's nothing." Jac jerked away, flinching when she pulled her shoulder back.

"I don't want to hurt you." Mallory dropped her hands. "But I'm not letting you get away with this silent treatment, Jac. I don't need your protection. And I'm not afraid of anything that has to do with you." She softened her voice, knowing she sounded like she was on the attack. Carefully, slowly, she cradled Jac's jaw and kissed her. A light brush of her lips over Jac's mouth, just enough to feel her. So Jac would know she wasn't going away. "You touched me and I don't want you to stop."

Jac shuddered and her lids slowly closed. Emboldened, Mallory stepped closer, sliding her other arm around Jac's waist, drawing her near until their bodies connected everywhere. She kissed her again, sliding her lips over Jac's, feeling her heat, tasting her. She murmured against Jac's mouth, "I'm not afraid."

Jac heard the strength in Mallory's voice, felt the certainty in her touch. She needed that—that solid, unwavering certainty. She gripped Mallory's hips, teased her tongue over Mallory's mouth. She needed her. Needed her close. Needed not to push her away, or to run away. "I don't know what to do."

"Tell me, baby," Mallory whispered. She framed Jac's face. Kissed her. "Trust me."

"I've only ever gone it alone," Jac murmured. "No matter what—it was always just me. One-on-one with whatever bomb lay in my path. I never had a partner." She pressed closer, needing Mallory's fire to melt the frozen wasteland of her isolation. "You have no idea what my father is capable of."

Mallory threaded her fingers through Jac's hair and kissed her mouth, the angle of her jaw, the spot below her ear that made Jac tremble. "I know I don't. But none of this is about your father. Only us."

"Not for much longer," Jac said. She forced her fingers to relax their death grip on Mallory's hips and backed away. She unlocked her locker and swung open the door. She didn't want to look at the photograph taped inside, but pretending it wasn't there wouldn't help. Behind her, she heard Mallory gasp. The image was grainy, but it was easy to see her and Mallory about to kiss.

CHAPTER TWENTY-EIGHT

"What the hell," Mallory exclaimed. "Where did that come from?"

"It's a shot from Tommy's that night we all went out. The background has been touched up so you can't tell we were actually only dancing and not in the midst of a clinch."

"I know but—how? We didn't—"

Jac ripped it down and turned it over. She read out the barely legible pencil scrawl. "'If you don't want your girlfriend splashed all over the newspapers, maybe you should take the season off.'" She handed it to Mallory.

Mallory's hands were steady as she held the image and read the words. "Someone from here did this." She flicked the edge of the photograph with her fingernail. "The question is, why?"

"Obviously someone doesn't like us very much. Or maybe just me." Jac leaned back against her locker, looking so damned defeated Mallory wanted to pound something. "God, Mal, this is only the beginning of something bad."

"Jac," Mallory said gently, squashing her fury, "let's get some sleep. We can tackle this later today."

Jac nodded, methodically pulling jeans and a T-shirt from her locker. She tugged them on without underwear, her eyes slightly unfocused, her hands trembling ever so slightly. Mallory would gladly have murdered whoever had put that photo in Jac's locker. The only reason she wasn't raging around the locker room, kicking doors, was because Jac needed her to be steady. She didn't doubt for a second that Jac's fears were justified. She'd heard enough of Jac's past and read more than enough in the newspapers to know that Jac had had precious little privacy in her life. She'd witnessed how Jac's father subtly and not so subtly controlled Jac's life when attempts to turn Jac into some mythical ideal daughter had failed—even though Jac was damn exceptional all on her own. Jac had put her family first time and time again, but not this time. This time, Mallory intended to do whatever she could to see that Jac didn't become a pawn in her father's political game. But right now, Jac needed something a lot more immediate. She needed to be safe, and she needed to be able to let down her guard without fear.

Mallory grabbed sweats and a zip-up fleece from her locker, dressed, packed up their SAR gear, and stowed everything on a shelf. She'd sort the equipment out later. She hesitated, then unclipped her radio and called Sully. "Sul? You copy?"

"You back, Ice?" Sully's scratchy voice replied.

"Yeah, just got in." Mallory watched Jac shove her bare feet into her boots. Jac was either dog-tired or a lot more upset than she wanted to let on. Either way, it didn't matter. Mallory was going to take care of it. "I'm taking me and Russo off call until tomorrow at oh six hundred, Sul."

"Roger that," Sully came back instantly. "We're good here."

"Copy that. See you tomorrow." Mallory turned off her radio and put it with the rest of the gear.

Jac frowned. "How many times have you gone off call during the season?"

"What does it matter?" Mallory slung her arm around Jac's waist. "Time to hit the loft."

"Mal, how many times?"

"Never. Come on."

"Damn it," Jac muttered. "It's already starting. I don't want you—"

Mallory kissed her to shut her up, since making her drop and do fifty push-ups wasn't an option any longer. Somewhere up on that snow-covered mountainside they'd gone from trainer and trainee to partners. And besides, kissing her was so much better. So, so much better. When she'd had her fill of tasting her, luxuriating in the slow burn of Jac's mouth, she whispered, "This is about what I want, Jac. What I need today. You. I need you."

"Okay, yes. Anything." Jac leaned into her, accepting her support. "I should call my father—"

"Later. You're going to get some sleep first. Do you need a pain pill for your shoulder?"

"No, the shower helped a lot." Jac grinned, something of her old spirit flashing in her eyes. "And the rest of the water therapy was pretty effective too."

"Oh, it was, was it?" Mallory kissed her again, just a touch of lips this time, not enough to get them started, and it wouldn't take much. At least not for her. Just looking at Jac made her want to get Jac's clothes off again and touch her everywhere. Somehow, Jac had turned the tables on her, and she still wasn't quite sure how that had happened. She felt fabulous—she still buzzed inside, outside, everywhere. She wanted Jac's hands on her again, inside her again, and a hell of a lot more. "We should go now."

"Oh yeah?" Jac's gaze dropped down Mallory's body and then slowly tracked back to her face. "Why is that?"

"You know damn well why. If you don't, I'm doing something wrong."

"Oh no, you're not doing anything wrong." Jac cupped Mallory's neck and kissed her, harder than Mallory had kissed her, longer and deeper, and Mallory started to melt.

"Stop," Mallory whispered, bracing her palm against Jac's chest. "I want you, damn it. And we need to get some sleep, and then we need to find out who the hell took that photo."

Jac rested her forehead against Mallory's. "I know. I know we do. But God, Mal—I want you so damn much. I've never felt so much with anyone. For anyone."

"No one has ever made me *want* to feel so much," Mallory said, and the terror came racing back. She firmly shoved it aside. She wasn't letting the past in, not for a few hours. All she wanted was the unbelievable joy of being with Jac. Of touching her, holding her, pleasing her. Later, later she could worry about what everything meant. Mallory tugged Jac's bottom lip between her teeth. One more kiss and she'd lose it. She pushed away. "We've got time."

Jac didn't look like she believed her, but she grasped Mallory's hand and set out with her across the deserted yard. The hangar was dark and empty. Mallory could almost believe they were the only two people in the world, and that was exactly the way she wanted it. Today her radio was off, and she wasn't responsible for anyone or to anyone, except the woman beside her. She wasn't going to think about the rest of the season, or Jac's father's campaign, or someone who wanted to harass them—or worse. She was with Jac, with nothing between them, and the sensation was exhilarating, arousing, satisfying, downright wonderful.

"Go up," Mallory said when they reached the foot of the ladder to the loft. "I want to put a message on my phone to reroute emergency calls to another station."

"Don't be long," Jac murmured and kissed her.

Mallory admired the snug fit of Jac's jeans and her tight, tempting ass until Jac disappeared overhead. When she got her brain working again, she rang the regional call center, signed out for twenty-four hours, and climbed up to the warm, dimly lit loft. Jac stood motionless between the two cots, her back to Mallory, as if uncertain as to what to do next. Mallory gripped the back of Jac's waistband and pulled her back into her arms. She wrapped both arms around Jac's middle and kissed the back of her neck. Jac smelled of coconut shampoo and her own unique mix of earth and sun. Mallory felt herself get wet, felt herself swelling, and she loved the feeling. She loved how she came alive whenever she touched Jac. She wasn't cold inside, she was molten. "You don't think you're gonna be sleeping in that cot across from me, do you?"

Jac covered Mallory's hands with hers. "I'm sure hoping not, but I don't think one of those cots will hold both of us."

"Neither do I." Mallory turned Jac in her arms and clasped Jac's butt, rocking her pelvis against Jac's. She watched Jac's eyes darken, loving the effect she had on her. "You could consider today the first day of the final field training. We'll rough it and put the sleeping bags on the floor."

"Roughing it, huh?" Thinking she could sleep on a rock pile if Mallory was next to her, Jac dipped her head to nibble at Mallory's neck. She licked her way up to the tender spot beneath Mallory's ear, teasing with her teeth until Mallory moaned. Mallory's sharp intake of breath struck Jac in the pit of her stomach like a hammer blow. Her legs got weak, and her heart thundered like she'd just finished running the obstacle course with a full pack. "I can't touch you without getting hot, Mal. I'm so wrecked."

Mallory gripped Jac's hips and pushed away from her with a satisfied grin. "Is that right?"

Mute, Jac just nodded, her pulse beating a crazy tattoo in her head, her chest, between her legs.

"I think I can take care of that," Mallory whispered. "Don't move." She reached behind her, grabbed her sleeping bag off the foot of her cot, and tossed it onto the floor. She bent and quickly opened it, pulled Jac's bag down and layered it over hers, and folded back the top to expose the soft flannel lining. "There." Mallory swiveled on her knees in front of Jac and put her hands on either side of Jac's fly. When she looked up, her lips parted as if she were very, very hungry.

"Mallory, come on," Jac muttered, her hips lifting all on their own. She steadied herself with her fingertips on Mallory's shoulders, looking down into Mallory's sparkling, triumphant eyes.

"What? Huh?" Mallory said with a teasing lilt as she popped the button on Jac's waistband. She unzipped Jac's fly, her gaze never leaving Jac's face.

"I'm naked under there," Jac warned, her voice thick and husky.

"Oh, I know." Mallory grabbed the material over Jac's hipbones and tugged her pants down, shoving them to the tops of Jac's boots so she had enough room to spread her legs.

The top of Jac's head threatened to blow off. She was wet, hard, and ready. "If you stop now I'm going to cry."

Mallory kissed Jac's stomach and rubbed her cheek over the base of Jac's belly. She clasped Jac's ass in both hands and squeezed, pulling Jac harder against her face. "Have a little faith," Mallory whispered against Jac's skin.

"Mal," Jac groaned. "I really need you to make me come."

Mallory licked a line from Jac's belly button down to the triangle between her thighs. Jac's thighs rippled and her knees bent. Mallory held her tighter and licked her again. "Don't come right away."

"I'm not gonna be able to help it."

Mallory tilted her head back and shot Jac a boss look. "I know you've got better control than that, Russo."

Dazed, a little desperate, afraid she might come the instant Mallory touched her, Jac shook her head. "I don't. I don't. Damn it, you're killing me."

Mallory laughed. "Oh no, I'm not. I'm going to make you feel so good." She framed Jac's sex with both hands and opened her with her thumbs. She moaned, a hungry moan of approval, and kissed Jac exactly where she needed it.

"God," Jac gasped, tilting her hips, pushing against Mallory's mouth. "Do that again and I'll come."

"Go ahead," Mallory murmured, her lips moving against Jac's center. "I really want you to come in my mouth."

Jac's vision went fuzzy. The little bit of pressure from Mallory's lips passing over her tense clitoris was so exquisite, so perfect, she started to hum inside. "You're gonna make me come."

"Mmm-hmm. So you said." Mallory sucked her, softly, slowly, and then leaned back, rubbing her hands fitfully up and down Jac's thighs. Her lips were swollen and flushed. "You're so beautiful. You taste so good I don't want you to come yet. I want you just like this forever."

"I can't, Mal," Jac groaned. "Just let me come, then you can do anything you want."

Mallory slid her thumbs up the insides of Jac's thighs and parted her again. "I'll remember you said that."

Mallory's mouth closed over her, firm and sure and hot, and Jac grabbed Mallory's head. She worked herself into Mallory's mouth, her knees going loose and her ass tightening. "I'm coming. Oh fuck, Mal, I'm coming."

Mallory took her, all of her, in deep and didn't stop until Jac ceased pumping between her lips. Mallory looked up, her expression soft and sated. "Lie down with me."

Jac stumbled the few feet to the sleeping bag and collapsed as Mallory crawled over beside her. Jac kicked off her pants and boots, wrapped Mallory in her arms, and kissed her. She wanted Mallory, needed her, in ways that should have scared the hell out of her, but all she wanted to do was shout like a crazy person, she was so damn happy. She'd just been demolished by a woman and she'd never felt stronger. The chains of caution fell away and the words burst out. "I love you, Mallory."

Mallory stiffened.

"I know you probably think it's just the great sex talking," Jac said quickly, "but it—"

"I don't think that." Mallory stroked Jac's hair, then cupped the curve of Jac's hip. Pressed tight against her. "But I don't know if I want you to."

"Yeah, I know." Jac kissed her forehead. "But it's one of those things, like trust. You don't get to decide."

"I'm afraid I'll hurt you," Mallory said, a hint of desperation in her voice.

"Loving you feels good, Mal. Don't ask me not to."

"God, I can't." Mallory buried her face in Jac's neck. "Maybe I should tell you not to, but I can't."

Chapter Twenty-nine

J ac surfaced from oblivion to someone shaking her shoulder. Grunting, she tried to pull away but stopped resisting when her brain registered the faint current of honeysuckle wrapping around her senses. The next instant she remembered everything. Mallory's body, warm and pliant beneath her hands, Mallory's head thrown back in abandon. Mallory's mouth on her, taking her in ways she'd never been taken before. Her hips jumped and she groaned. "Mallory?"

Beside her, Mallory sat up quickly. "We've got company."

"What?" Jac's eyes flew open. Judging by the slanting rays of the sun coming through the window high up on the wall, it was only late morning. They'd been asleep two or three hours at the most. "Benny maybe?"

"Not unless he's wearing high heels," Mallory muttered.

Jac heard it then, the rapid-fire strike of heels on cement, and her stomach sank. She knew that rhythm. "Fuck."

"Jac?" Mallory searched around inside the sleeping bag, found her sweatpants, and lifted her hips to pull them on, still lying flat on her back. "What's going on?"

"Stay there." Jac jumped up naked and looked around for her clothes. She'd chucked everything far and wide when she'd taken them off. Just as she spied her jeans, she heard the scrape of shoe-leather on steel. Their company had arrived. She spun toward the edge of the loft, and a familiar coiffed blond head appeared followed by a long, sensuous body sheathed in a tailored plum Prada silk suit. The skirt came to just above Nora Fleming's knees, showcasing her shapely expanse of calf below. The suit jacket was buttoned over a low-cut ivory camisole, exposing a hint of pale creamy cleavage. Sexy without being blatantly suggestive. Nora stopped, sedately deposited her soft calfskin briefcase on the floor next to her lethally thin spiked black heels, and coolly appraised Jac. "You haven't been answering your phone."

"I've been busy," Jac said.

Mallory handed Jac her jeans. "Put these on."

"Thanks." Jac grasped the pants without looking at Mallory and jammed her legs into them. "What are you doing here?"

"Your father has a fund-raiser Friday night. He wants you there."

"I can't make it." Jac zipped her fly and buttoned her jeans. Her stomach felt hollow, as if she hadn't eaten in a long time, but the thought of food made her nauseous. The loft was cool and she was bare-chested. Her nipples tightened.

"Could you excuse us for a few moments," Mallory said, getting to her feet, "while we get decent?"

Mallory spoke with what some might call a pleasant tone, but Jac knew better. The ice in her voice barely disguised the razor edge of temper. Mallory was pissed.

"This doesn't concern you," Nora said dismissively, not bothering to look at Mallory when she responded. "Jac, whatever game you're into here isn't as important as your father's fund-raiser. It's bad enough we couldn't reach you for his *nationally* televised acceptance speech. Your father is going to be the next president of the United States, and it's time for you to grow up."

"Grow up," Jac whispered, thinking of her months overseas, her weeks on the fire line last summer, the last few days doing SAR up in the mountains. She'd faced death, beaten death, wasn't that enough? Wouldn't anything ever be enough? "I'm not playing, Nora."

"Whatever you think you're doing is beside the point. The family needs to present a united front now. You're needed at home."

Jac shook her head. "That would be new. I thought he wanted me MIA."

"Jac," Mallory murmured, grasping Jac's arm.

"It's a little late to feel sorry for yourself, Jac. Most of your problems you brought on yourself." Nora glanced at the rumpled sleeping bags as if indicating the evidence. "Considering you've practically made it your life's work to entertain the media, your father has little choice. He can hardly pretend you don't exist."

Mallory said, "It seems to me he's been doing a pretty good job of that so far."

Fleming flicked arctic blue eyes in Mallory's direction. "Perhaps you'd like to excuse us. This is Jac's business."

"Actually, this is my business too." Mallory retrieved Jac's shirt and handed it to her. While Jac took the shirt, Mallory stepped slightly in front of her, facing Nora. "I'm Mallory James. I'm the ops manager of this station. Jac's not going anywhere."

"Well that's very convenient for you," Nora said. "Is sleeping with your subordinates a regular part of your program?"

"Nora," Jac said sharply. "This is private."

"Not really." Nora bent down, opened her thousand-dollar briefcase, and withdrew a manila folder. She slid out a photograph as she walked to Jac. "I wouldn't exactly call this private."

Jac's stomach curdled. She only had to glance at it for a second to recognize the image. Her and Mallory, apparently about to share a kiss. "Did they ask for money?"

"Not yet." Fleming put the photograph back in the envelope. "Since you've obviously gotten yourself into another"—Fleming raked her eyes over Mallory—"situation, you need to let us contain it. I think you'll be better off at home. Your father agrees."

Mallory slid her arm around Jac's waist. "This is a situation, all right, but one you probably don't understand. Jac's not going anywhere. She's on my team, and unless I say she goes, she doesn't." When Fleming looked like she was about to interrupt again, Mallory held up her hand. "Furthermore, our relationship is our business, and no one is going to tell us what we can and cannot do."

"Mal," Jac murmured, "we ought to talk about this." Mallory might be used to parachuting from a plane into the face of a wildfire, but she had no idea how dangerous it would be taking on Franklin Russo. She wouldn't just get burned, she'd be incinerated.

Mallory spun around, her back to Fleming, and cupped Jac's chin. "Look at me." When Jac averted her eyes, Mallory gave her head a little shake. "Look at me, damn it. You think I'm going to let you walk away after"—she gestured to the sleeping bag—"this? After what we did up on that mountain?" She kissed her. "Sometimes, Russo, you are just without a clue."

From behind them, Fleming sighed loudly. "Well this is all very touching, but what you two play around at in your spare time is of no consequence to the greater issue. The fact remains, Jac needs to get onboard for her father's campaign, and that means not being publicly associated with any kind of unsavory relationship."

Mallory laughed, and Jac looked to be sure Mallory wasn't holding any kind of weapon, although without doubt, she could wring Nora's neck with her bare hands.

"Okay," Mallory said briskly. "We're really done now. You are in a secure area of a government facility, without a pass, and unescorted. That means you need to get out of here. Now."

Fleming's eyebrows rose. She glanced at Jac. "You need to come with me. The car is waiting."

"No," Jac said.

"I suspect a large part of the funding here is state," Fleming said, almost as if she were talking to herself. Then she smiled at Jac, circling like shark to prey. "The same friends of your father who pulled strings to get you here could make your girlfriend's job disappear."

"That's absurd," Mallory snapped.

Jac pulled away from Mallory's grasp, her face blank. "That would be a hell of a lot harder than getting me a position I was already qualified for."

"You think so?" Fleming asked coolly, watching Jac as if sighting down the barrel of a sniper rifle. Focused, unblinking, sure. "Do you really want to take that chance?"

"Don't do this, Nora."

"Don't make me. You know you won't win."

"How long?" Jac asked, her head throbbing.

"Jac, what are you doing?" Mallory exclaimed.

Jac didn't look at her. She couldn't possibly explain to Mallory the power her father wielded, legitimately and maybe, behind the scenes, not so legitimate. Only someone who had felt the pincer crush of his methodical attack for years would believe what he was capable of. He could do more than make Mallory's job disappear. He could probably make this entire station redundant. Nora was more than his campaign manager, she was his fixer—when problems came up, she had free rein to do anything she wanted. Nora Fleming did not make idle threats. "How long do I need to pretend to be the perfect daughter?"

"As long as we need you. Your father is running on a decency campaign. I don't have to tell you what that means." Fleming laughed, completely without mirth. "Powell has a lesbian daughter. Your father needs to show he's done a better job with you. Admittedly, he's got his work cut out for him." She laughed again. "But luckily you clean up well."

"Jac, don't let her railroad you into this," Mallory said urgently. "This is your life, Jac."

Jac wanted to say, *No, it's your life,* but Mallory wouldn't believe her. Or if she did, she wouldn't care. Mallory's life was about responsibility—taking care of everyone else, no matter the cost to her. Jac didn't plan on being another person Mallory sacrificed part of herself for. She wasn't going to drag Mallory into the soul-draining vortex her life was about to become. Besides, with her gone, whoever had taken that photograph would have no more reason to stir up trouble. Mallory would be safe. Jac nodded at Fleming, who smiled, pleased with her victory.

"Jac, no," Mallory said.

"I'm sorry." Jac took a step away. She didn't think she could leave if Mallory was touching her. "Please understand. I need to do this."

The shock and pain in Mallory's eyes almost dropped Jac to her knees. She had to get away, and fast. She slipped around Fleming and vaulted onto the ladder, half falling to the concrete floor. She made her legs work. Hurried out.

She couldn't think about Mallory or she'd break. She had to get home. She needed to convince her father she wouldn't endanger his public image. She needed to play his game, at least while he held the winning cards. Then maybe Mallory would be safe.

❖

Mallory watched Jac disappear from sight, unable to believe she was going. How could she just walk away? From the job, from her. How could she let her father do this?

"She would have left sooner or later, you know," Fleming said conversationally. "I've known her a long time. She's not the type to settle down."

"Get out."

"I can track down the source of that photograph, if you like," Fletcher said, picking up her briefcase.

"I don't want anything from you."

"Although with Jac gone, whoever took it will likely lose interest soon enough. Nevertheless, the offer stands."

"How can you treat her like she's nothing but a chess piece in her father's game?"

Fleming regarded her with an expression of respect. "I like to win. Someone has to lose." She shrugged. "Besides, I'm not the one sleeping with trash and ending up in the tabloids."

"Neither is Jac."

"Maybe not this time." Fleming smiled. "This time she's outdone herself. I'll see myself out. Thanks."

Fleming somehow managed to climb over the edge of the loft in a skirt without showing more than a flash of thigh. A few seconds later the staccato rap of her heels ricocheted across the hangar deck.

Mallory sank onto the edge of the cot. The rumble of a powerful engine filled the hangar and quickly faded away. Jac was gone. She had disappeared as quickly as an ember floated into the night sky and flickered out. Mallory felt the darkness close around her. She was numb. Somewhere, deep inside, she knew she was angry. Angry and hurt. And scared. Jac couldn't keep denying herself and survive. Mallory dropped her head into her hands.

Think. She had to think.

She just needed a few minutes to make sense of everything. Then she'd probably see this was for the best. She'd never wanted a relationship. Especially not with a woman whose absence made her feel as if a part of her had died. She focused on the sleeping bag tangled around her legs. She thought of lying in the soft, warm flannel with Jac wrapped around her. She thought of Jac's fingers stroking her as she drifted into sleep, filling her as they made love, igniting her body and soul.

She hadn't asked for that. She hadn't asked for any of that. She hadn't known she needed it. Now she had to decide if she could live without it.

CHAPTER THIRTY

The hangar was tomb-like. Even the ever-present drip of oil from machine parts and the whine of wind sluicing over the metal roof were absent. The silence Mallory ordinarily found peaceful only made the ache inside harder to bear. She was off call, with a sunny day for the first time in a week ahead of her, and everything was wrong. Jac should be here and she wasn't. They should still be wrapped up in each other, wakening to the sound of each other's breathing, touching and making love. Jac should not have left her. Jac should not have broken her heart. She'd let Jac touch her—let her into her body and her damn heart. Didn't Jac know she didn't need to fight alone, that Mallory would have stood by her? Mallory wanted to kick the joined sleeping bags over the edge of the loft into the mocking emptiness below. *Real mature. What did you expect? You slept together one night. Hardly grounds for an engagement.*

When Mallory hurt, she worked. She straightened up the loft, squared the cots, placed a rolled sleeping bag at the end of each one. Then she headed to the standby shack to sort and clean the gear she and Jac had used on the SAR. The quiet in the cavernous hangar followed her out into the yard, beating at her like so many silent wings, making the air heavy and hard to pull into her lungs. Her limbs were sluggish, her mind vaguely empty. And the ache deep in her core throbbed with every step. The harsh lights in the locker room made her eyes water. She swiped at the moisture on her face and tried not to see Jac leaning against the wall of lockers, naked, water glistening on her smooth, tanned skin. She tried not to feel the heat of Jac's flesh beneath her fingers. Tried not to see the wounded desolation in Jac's eyes when Fleming had handed her that photograph.

Mallory stiffened. The photograph. A tiny click in the back of her brain cleared some of the fog. The click got louder, steadier, and disparate pieces of a fragmented picture started to fit together. How convenient that Fleming had a copy of the photograph—just in time for Franklin Russo's candidacy announcement. Just the kind of ammunition Jac couldn't fight. And then using it to threaten Mallory's job? Maybe the whole station? Fleming knew Jac's history. She had to know what Jac would do—Jac was programmed to put herself in the path of destruction for the sake of those she loved. Mallory paced around the bench between the lockers. Maybe Jac didn't believe she wasn't alone anymore, but that was no reason to let her go on believing it. Mallory considered her options. She might not be able to take on a powerful presidential candidate who chose to use his family as props and sent his rabid watchdog to make threats, but she wasn't helpless, and she wasn't giving up on Jac. The photograph was a place to start.

Energized, she spun around, checked her jacket pockets for the keys to the rented Jeep, and sprinted out to the yard. She tore out onto the highway and headed south. An hour later she drove through a still-sleeping Bear Creek and pulled up in front of Emily's house. She wasn't exactly sure what she was going to say or do, but she knew she had to start here. She checked her watch. Eight a.m. Emily might still be asleep. Maybe she should drive around town until she found an open coffee shop. She ought to at least bring pastries as a peace offering. As she reached to key the ignition, the front door of Emily's small wood-framed house opened, and Emily stepped out onto the porch in a pale blue robe cinched at the waist. Looking perplexed, Emily waved and motioned for Mallory to come in. Mallory pocketed her keys, got out, and strode up the sidewalk. Emily stepped back inside and Mallory followed.

"Hi." Emily stood on tiptoe and kissed Mallory lightly on the lips. "What are you doing here? Are you all right?"

"I'm sorry. I know it's early. My clock is all turned around."

"You've been out on a call?"

"Yes. And then some things—came up."

Emily linked her arm through Mallory's. "Come back to the kitchen. I was just about to make coffee. Are you hungry?"

"No," Mallory said, although her stomach rumbled in contradiction.

"We'll see about that. Take off your coat and tell me what's going on."

Mallory hesitated in the doorway to the cheery kitchen. Emily looked beautiful in the bright morning sun, her hair glowing, her skin fresh, her expression vibrant. She looked happy, and Mallory suddenly felt out of place and guilty for bringing discord into the tranquility.

"You've got something on your mind," Emily said.

"I don't know how to say this," Mallory said abruptly.

Emily finished filling the coffeemaker with water, set the kettle down, and turned to study Mallory. "Come to tell me things have changed?"

"Yes. I'm sorry."

"I can't say I'm surprised after the last time you were here. Change was in the air." Emily smiled faintly. "I'm disappointed, of course. But I'm not going to lose your friendship, am I?"

"Of course not. I—"

"You needn't tell me how fond you are of me. I know." Emily rested her hands on Mallory's shoulders and kissed her again, not a sisterly kiss, but one with no expectations. A gentle, tender, caring kiss. "You've met someone. Someone who's shaking you up. I think that's a good thing."

"There are some problems."

"Of course there are. No one ever comes to a relationship without a past. Can you tell me about it?"

Mallory sighed. "I'll try. You're sure it's all right?"

"Very sure."

They sat at the table, and when the coffee was done, Emily poured two cups. Mallory told Emily about her relationship with Jac and the photograph in Jac's locker. She left out Fleming's visit and Jac's family issues. She wouldn't violate Jac's privacy.

Emily's brows drew down. "You're sure the photo was taken here in town?"

"It had to be. It's the only place we—" Mallory felt her face growing warm. Could she really be blushing at the mention of sex? Unbelievable. "We didn't…we weren't…last night was the first time we were together. The photograph was taken before that."

"Where is she now?"

Mallory's stomach tightened. "Something came up with her family. She had to leave."

Emily didn't look like she believed that was the whole story, but she didn't question. "Well, if the photo was taken at the bar, there are limited options as to who was responsible. After all, who around here would care about you and Jac being together?"

"Motive," Mallory murmured. "That's it, isn't it?" Really, who *would* care? No one she worked with. She had no exes, no one with a grudge or a score to settle. Not unless… The queasy feeling in her stomach sharpened into an agonizing blade to her heart. "Maybe a friend of Phil or Danny? Someone who blames me for their deaths?"

"Oh, honey, I can't believe anyone who worked on the line, or loved anyone who did, would do something like this. What happened last year wasn't your fault, and the only one who blames you is you."

Mallory heard the words, and for the first time, started to believe them. "Why else would someone try to make it look like we were intimate?"

"Maybe the message wasn't for you. Maybe this is about Jac."

"I suppose there are a lot more possibilities there," Mallory said. An old girlfriend? A jealous husband? A political rival of her father? God, anything was possible. "But it still leaves the how."

"Well, that probably could be anyone. The bar is always crowded, and no one is really paying much attention to what's going on outside their own circles. I wouldn't think a stranger would go unnoticed, though." Emily traced a pattern on the cotton tablecloth with her fingertip. "But I can't imagine why a local would do this."

Mallory thought back to that night, of the guys from the station who were there. Then she pictured the room, and the locals, and her jaw tightened. "I think I might have an idea about that. I'll need to ask a few questions."

"You want me to go with you?"

"No." Mallory leaned over and kissed Emily. "Thank you. Can I take you to dinner sometime real soon?"

Emily smiled. "No. But you can come here for a good meal. Bring Jac too."

The pain raced higher in Mallory's chest. Would she even have a chance to see Jac again?

❖

The next morning at dawn, Mallory roared into the field camp set up in a clearing beyond the end of the access road. Campfires smoldered in rock-ringed pits in front of a cluster of tents. She pulled her Jeep in beside the work trucks, jumped out, and pushed through the brush into camp. She smelled coffee but didn't see anyone around. She dumped her gear by the central fire pit and debated announcing her arrival loud enough to wake everyone else up. She recognized Sully's tent, but she didn't want to face him yet. He wasn't responsible for what she suspected, but he'd take responsibility anyhow. Not knowing what to do with herself, she found the coffeepot sitting on one of the boulders facing the fire and felt the side. Still hot. She dug her camp cup out of her gear bag and poured herself a cup of coffee so dark and so strong her eyes watered. The sound of a zipper sliding down on a tent flap brought her twisting around.

Sarah emerged in a sweatshirt and sweatpants, yawning and brushing hair from her eyes. "Hey. I didn't expect you until later."

"Had some things to take care of. Where's Hooker?" Mallory said abruptly.

Sarah frowned, the sleep leaving her eyes and her face tensing. "Why? What's wrong?"

"Long story. Where is he?"

"You sound like you want to chew him a new one," Sarah said, reaching back into her tent and coming out with her own tin cup. She joined Mallory by the fire and poured coffee. "I don't know where he is. He told Sully early yesterday he had an emergency and needed the day off. He's not back yet as far as I know. What's going on, Mallory?"

Fury hazed Mallory's vision. "The cowardly bastard is running away."

"Excuse me?"

"He's not coming back. He's a stalker. Or a goddamn spy."

"Spy? For who?"

"I'm not sure exactly, but I think he's been watching me and Jac." Mallory ground her back teeth. "The bastard had Chantal taking pictures of us."

"Us who?"

"Me and Jac. I think he left one in Jac's locker."

"Chantal told you that?" Sarah sounded incredulous.

"Yep. She couldn't believe I was upset." Mallory snorted, half-angry and half-disbelieving. "Hooker told her the pictures were for a work party—a joke. All in fun."

"What kind of pictures?"

"Fortunately nothing too revealing, since we didn't do anything then." Mallory looked away.

"Wait a minute. Intimate photos of the two of you?"

Mallory flushed. "We were only dancing that night we all went out to Tommy's. The shot made it look like more."

Sarah grasped Mallory's arm. "My God, Mallory—that's awful. Why?"

"I'm not sure. To harass us maybe—maybe it's just an anti-gay thing." That would make sense if it hadn't been for Fleming. Why send photos to Fleming if blackmail wasn't the object, and it didn't seem to be. Mallory kicked a rock into the fire pit. "He's been a little bit belligerent since he arrived, but I thought it was just the typical macho reaction to a woman in charge. Now I'm not so sure. I think maybe he was here to watch Jac."

"You said nothing had been going on between you and Jac when the photograph was taken. Is there more now?" Sarah asked gently. "Between the two of you?"

"I thought so."

"Where's Jac?" Sarah frowned. "I thought she was coming up with you."

"She's not. I'm not sure she'll be back at all."

Sarah's breath burst out. "Oh, I'm really sorry, Mallory. What a mess."

"I don't care about the photos, but Jac does." Mallory sat down on the boulder. "It's a lot more complicated than a little bit of work harassment."

"After all that nastiness with the tabloid photos, I imagine Jac is really gun-shy," Sarah said. "Will you be able to prove Hooker was behind it?"

Mallory laughed bitterly. "I doubt it. Chantal doesn't have the camera card. It's just a he said/she said thing with her claiming he asked her to take some racy candids. If he denies it, there's not much to do."

"Wait a minute," Sarah said. "If you think Hooker was a plant, how the hell did they get him into our station?"

"I pulled his personnel files last night. He was a last-minute applicant when another guy got injured. He was qualified, Sully passed him on to me as a probable accept, and I agreed when I reviewed the applicants." Mallory shook her head. She should have caught that something was out of whack. "He looked really good on paper. Now that I think of it, maybe too good."

"You couldn't have known." Sarah sat on the boulder next to Mallory and wrapped her arm around her. "So what are you going to do now, Ice?"

Mallory stood and tossed the dregs of her coffee into the smoldering ashes. "I'm going to finish up boot camp and see if Hooker comes back and proves me wrong."

"And what about Jac?"

Mallory looked away, afraid if she saw the sympathy in Sarah's eyes she'd embarrass herself. She'd walk through fire for Jac if Jac were hurt, but Jac had left by choice. If they hadn't slept together, she might have gone after her all the same, but they'd blurred their boundaries now. That one night changed everything. Especially for her. "I'm kind of hoping she comes back too."

"If she doesn't?"

"I guess that's the really big question, isn't it. I wish to hell I knew the right answer."

❖

Three days later, Mallory still had no answers, but she was more certain of a few things. Hooker had not come back, and when she and Sully tried to track him down through the regional office, no one seemed to know where he was. When she wasn't supervising the rookies while they climbed trees, cut lines, or assessed and laid out safety zones, she was digging into Hooker's background. She didn't come up with anything except that the paper trail stopped abruptly with the application that Sully had received early in the season. Hooker was a plant, and that had to have been arranged well before Jac was inserted into the team. No doubt, Fleming was a long-range planner.

She got up before the sun and didn't crawl into her tent until she couldn't stand up any longer. Exhaustion allowed her to sleep, but it didn't stop her from dreaming. She could keep Jac out of her thoughts during the day by focusing on the firefighters she needed to train, but she couldn't prevent Jac from invading her thoughts when she lay down to sleep. She saw her quick smile, heard her easy laugh, felt the gentle touch of her fingers on her face. She saw her eyes darken with desire, heard her moans of passion, felt the immeasurable pleasure of Jac filling her, taking her, surrendering to her. She ached for her with every bit of the soul-lacerating pain she'd lived with since she'd lost her men. If she hadn't had her crew counting on her, she might have broken.

"On my mark," she called to the three men set to scale the test trees. She stood at the base of one with her stopwatch. Sully and Sarah were timing the climbs at the others. "Go."

She stepped back, craned her neck, and clicked off the watch when Anderson reached the preset target high up in the air. She took note of his technique as he descended. The other men reached the ground nearly simultaneously. "Nice job."

"Thanks." Anderson released his harness from around the base of the tree, hesitated, and said, "Have you heard anything from Jac?"

Mallory's jaw tensed. "No. Not yet."

"But if she comes back, she can make up what she missed, right?"

"She gets points for the fieldwork during the search and rescue mission we did." Mallory slid her stopwatch into her pocket and sighed. "But she has to make the last jump on Saturday."

Anderson pushed his hard hat back off his forehead, appearing to be fascinated by something in the trees beyond Mallory. Then he dropped his gaze to hers. "Sometimes a person goes AWOL because they don't quite have their head on straight. That's when someone in the squad needs to go get them and drag their ass back to base before they really get themselves into trouble."

"This isn't the Army, Anderson," Mallory said. If Jac had *just* been one of her crew, she would have gone after her already. But Jac hadn't wanted her along. Maybe didn't want her at all. Jac's choice, not hers.

"Close enough," Anderson said. "If you tell me where she is, me and Ray will go collect her."

Mallory studied him. "You know who she is, right?"

"Oh yeah, I know. She's one hell of a wildland firefighter."

"Yes, she is." Mallory tried to set aside her personal feelings, ignore the hurt. Anderson was right—Jac was crew. You didn't abandon crew, ever. Her heart said something even more important, something she couldn't deny. Jac was hers. "I'm the boss. I'll go get her."

He grinned. "Good idea, Boss."

Mallory tucked her clipboard under her arm and motioned Sarah to follow her as she walked away from the group.

"What's up?" Sarah asked.

"I need you to cover for me for a while."

"About time."

"Yes," Mallory said. "It really is."

CHAPTER THIRTY-ONE

"Daddy is going to be upset with you for wearing that," Carly said, closing Jac's bedroom door on her way to flopping down on the bottom of Jac's bed. Her body-hugging white tank top rode up a good four inches above her very low-cut skintight blue jeans, exposing a glittering turquoise piercing in her belly button. That was new and, Jac was willing to bet, *Daddy* didn't know about it.

"Probably right." Jac checked the crease in her dress blues in the full-length mirror behind the closet door and shook a fold out of her pant leg so the cuff fell smartly over her gleaming black shoe. "How are you doing?"

"I'm all right. I guess there's no way we can get out of this, is there?"

Jac carried her uniform jacket to the bed and laid it out. "You know there isn't. How come you're not dressed?"

"I don't want to sit around being uncomfortable any longer than I have to."

"I thought you were the girly-girl in the family." Jac took the regulation measuring guide and checked the placement of her insignia on her collars and over the right breast. Then she hung the jacket on a hanger and leaned her shoulder against the closed closet door. "You want to talk about all this?"

Carly's pretty face, more delicate than Jac's, scrunched up. She kicked her flip-flop rhythmically back and forth against the bottom of her foot. Her hair was as black as Jac's but longer and sculpted away from her face. She didn't have the same dark eyes, though. She'd gotten their mother's blue eyes. She was gorgeous and popular and just as insecure as any other seventeen-year-old. Suddenly being thrust onto national television couldn't be very comfortable for her. Jac's solution to the far more limited level of notoriety she'd faced at Carly's age had been to secretly buy a motorcycle, start running with the rough crowd at school, and find herself a girlfriend, or a string of them. Carly was a lot more tightly wound, which was maybe even more worrisome.

"I sort of thought this was coming," Jac said, hoping to get Carly talking. She'd been back in Idaho four days, and this was the first time they'd been alone. Four days that felt like forty years. She tried to keep her focus on her sister. Maybe it wasn't too late to help her. "The announcement kinda took me by surprise all the same. You too?"

"You think he'll win?" Carly asked.

"I don't know. Sometimes I think the country just votes for the one who's *not* in office, hoping that a change will make things better. Powell is pretty popular, though. I think he's got a fight coming."

"I don't want to live in the White House." Carly sounded defiant, but her lower lip trembled, the way it always had when she was trying not to cry.

Jac was ten years older, and she hadn't been around a lot to help buffer Carly from the fallout of their father's growing popularity. She'd thought staying away was the best thing to do. Maybe she'd been wrong about that. She thought about Mallory, remembered the stunned look of hurt on her face, and felt the air blast out of her chest the way it had when she'd been caught in a concussive wave from a bomb that had gone off on her approach, tossing her thirty feet in the air. Leaving hadn't helped Carly. Leaving had hurt Mallory. Maybe she'd been wrong about everything, everything except the way she felt about Mallory. She was sure about that.

"You okay?" Carly asked. "You kind of spaced out for a minute."

"I'm okay." Jac decided her trousers could tolerate a few wrinkles. She sat down on the bed next to Carly and took her hand. "If he gets elected, you're not going to have to live there. In another year, you'll be going away to college."

"Yeah, but he's traveling all over the place this year to campaign, and he's talking about pulling me out of school and giving me a tutor so I can go with them. It's my senior year. I'm not going to leave all my friends behind."

"Maybe you can work a deal with him—you stay here and go to

school except for the really big events where he wants the whole family to be visible." Jac could hear the defiance in Carly's voice. Carly would run before she'd give up the security of the school and the friends she knew. "You can't get away, Carly. I'm sorry."

"As if I don't know that." Carly snorted. "He's already brought on more security staff, and they're starting to follow me around. You think he'll let me stay here alone?"

"You know the security is for your safety, right?" Jac didn't envy anyone assigned to keep an eye on Carly, and if her father did manage to make it to the White House, pitied whatever Secret Service agent would be responsible for the family.

"You never had anyone following you around," Carly grumped.

"Yeah. You're right. I had it easier than you're gonna have it. He's a lot more visible now. A lot more important."

Carly picked at the comforter on Jac's bed. "Are you going to go back into the service?"

"Were you eavesdropping?"

Carly shrugged. "I don't think you can call it eavesdropping when everybody in the house can hear you yelling."

"We weren't yelling," Jac said, although she didn't really remember all of the conversation with her father. She'd made it clear she wasn't going to become part of his campaign entourage. When she told him she was going back to Yellowrock, *back to Mallory*, although she hadn't said that, he'd informed her in his usual cool, calm, absolutely resolute tone that that situation was untenable now. The changes in his political obligations made it necessary for her to refrain from any questionable interpersonal activities. Apparently, she could get herself into problem situations wherever she went.

She'd argued she wasn't going to be on anyone's radar in the middle of the national forest, but he hadn't been swayed. She didn't trust him not to make it impossible for her to go back to Yellowrock by simply making the entire operation disappear. The one thing he couldn't stop her from doing was reactivating her enlistment. She had a valuable skill, and she knew she'd have no trouble being reposted overseas. She'd almost made the call that morning, but when she did she would be committing herself to at least a year away, and any hope of seeing Mallory again would be gone. Leaving had always been the right decision before, but this time the pain was tearing her apart.

"I don't know what I'm going to do yet, Car," Jac said. "Mostly I just want to get tonight's sideshow over with."

"I wish I were as brave as you, so I could disappear too," Carly said. "But I don't want to be a soldier. No way am I sleeping in a tent with a bunch of guys around and bugs."

Jac laughed. "Just hang in there until you get to college. Things will get a whole lot better then."

"How come you came back?"

Jac looked away from her sister's penetrating stare. One of the things she loved about Carly, and found the most irritating, was Carly's habit of asking personal questions as if it was her absolute right to know the answers. Privacy was not a word in her vocabulary. "This time it was easier than fighting him."

Carly's brows drew down. "That doesn't seem like you. You've always been too proud to let him tell you what to do."

"Sometimes there's things more important than your pride."

"I didn't think there was for you."

Jac nodded. "Me neither."

Carly drew her legs up and wrapped her arms around them, laying her cheek on her knees. "It's a girl. Right?"

Jac couldn't help smiling, even though thinking of Mallory hurt. Thinking of her also made her happier than anything ever had, and for the past few days had been the only thing that kept her going. "Yeah, it's a girl."

"Special one?"

"A real special one."

"So I guess you kind of fucked things up, huh?"

Jac nudged Carly with her elbow. "Language."

Carly rolled her eyes. "Please."

"And what makes you think I fucked anything up? Geez, Carly."

"You're here by yourself. If you're here at all, you must've fucked something up."

Jac sighed. "Probably. Most likely."

"Is she mad at you?"

"She ought to be."

"What did she say when you left?"

Jac flushed. "Not much. We didn't really talk about it."

"Oh boy. You really, really, really did fuck up."

"Yeah. Remind me about it, why don't you." Jac jumped up and pulled her uniform jacket off the hanger. She slid it on, buttoned it, and checked her reflection in the mirror. She pressed down her collar and aligned her tie. "Come on. I'll wait for you to get dressed. I'll be your escort tonight."

"That's kind of queer. But nice all the same." Carly heaved herself up off the bed with loose-limbed grace. "Okay, but you better get between me and the fallout from Daddy when he finds out you're not wearing the dress you were ordered to wear."

"He'll have to shoot me before I wear that."

Carly slid her arm through Jac's. "I know it sucks for you, but I'm glad you're here. It sucks a little bit less for me."

The ache in Jac's chest spread down into her belly, and she wondered how much longer she could stay standing. She kissed Carly's temple. "Then I guess I did one thing right."

❖

Mallory didn't have any trouble finding the ballroom where Senator Franklin Russo's presidential campaign fund-raiser was being held. She just followed the crowd of tuxedo-clad men escorting elaborately coiffed women bedecked in expensive gowns and glittering jewels down the carpeted hallway of the mezzanine of the Four Seasons Hotel. Twenty minutes on the Internet when she'd gotten back to base the night before had given her the location and time, and she'd covered the 450 miles to Boise in the morning with plenty of time to get checked into a hotel, shower, and change. She wasn't wearing a gown or a bank vault full of jewels, but she looked presentable enough in the black suit she'd borrowed from Sarah—she didn't yet know why Sarah felt the need to bring a Donna Karan suit into the north woods—and heels she'd purchased herself that afternoon. Fortunately, the fund-raiser was not an invitation-only affair, and she hoped she'd pass as press corps or even hotel staff. She didn't really give it much thought—Jac was here somewhere, and she was going to see her no matter what. If she didn't do this, she'd drive herself crazy for the rest of her life wondering what might have been.

Two young guys in off-the-rack black suits flanked the double doors into the noisy ballroom. Both had close-cropped blond hair, square jaws, broad shoulders, and the flat stare common to bouncers and cops and security guards the world over. Mallory wasn't intimidated. She worked with tough guys every day. She smiled at one, said hello to the other as if they were best friends, and walked past them into a brightly lit room filled with white linen covered tables beneath crystal chandeliers. Buckets of Domaine Chandon sat in the center of every table, ringed with china plates, silver flatware, and crystal glasses, all glittering as brightly as the jewels adorning the donors.

At the far end of the room, two long tables flanked a speaker stand bristling with microphones upon a raised dais. Franklin Russo, a vigorous, youthful-appearing fifty and even more handsome in person than his photos suggested, sat to the left of the speaker stand with a dark-haired, middle-aged, patrician woman who was beautiful if a little detached, as if her thoughts were elsewhere. Even from the far side of the room, Mallory could see the woman's resemblance to Jac. Mallory swiftly searched the rest of the faces of Russo's entourage, almost passing by her before registering the dark eyes that captured hers like none ever had. In the few days since she'd seen her, Jac had changed. Her cheekbones slashed above sharply hollowed cheeks, as if she'd dropped weight on a forced march. Her thousand-yard stare was remote, removed, impenetrable. She sat erect, her shoulders squared, her hands invisible, probably folded in her lap in keeping with the rest of her militarily rigid posture. The uniform was perfect, not a crease out of alignment, not a wrinkle. Jac was so still she might not even have been breathing, her gaze fixed at some distant point as if she were absent from the room in all ways but physical. Jac had effectively disappeared herself.

Mallory's heart seized. The red sea of Jac's pain wafted over her, nearly suffocating her. She fought for her next breath and steadied herself with her fingertips against the pristine white linen covering the table next to her. She couldn't look away from Jac, even though she bled to see her this way.

"Jac," she murmured. "I'm here, baby. I'm here."

CHAPTER THIRTY-TWO

J ac drifted in the zone between hyperacute awareness and total detachment. The murmur of the audience, the speaker standing a foot away from her extolling her father's virtues, all receded into the background the way the sound of the ocean pounding outside a seaside cabin becomes white noise. The rapt faces of the men and women clustered at the tables and crowding the edges of the room blurred into pale, flat caricatures. Even as she separated herself from everything around her, she was exquisitely aware of the slightest change. Carly shifting impatiently in the chair beside her. The pop of a champagne cork. The rising tide of excitement as the time for her father's speech drew closer. Her gaze was unfocused but missed nothing—the rotation of the security guards at the front doors, Fleming passing behind the stage giving orders into her Bluetooth headset, a waiter approaching the dais with a fresh pitcher of water.

A heat signature ignited at the back of the room, and her focus honed in on it. Her pulse skyrocketed at the flare of recognition, and her right hand clenched on her thigh. She drew in a sharp breath. Mallory.

From across the sea of faceless bodies, Mallory smiled at her, and the shield Jac had set between herself and a world in which she had no place shattered like crystal on stone. Sensation flooded her. Joy. Worry. Guilt. Need.

"I have to go," Jac whispered as she pushed her chair back.

Carly stared at her. "Are you freaking kidding me? He'll kill you."

Jac shook her head and ran her knuckles along the edge of Carly's jaw. "No, he won't."

Carly grabbed her hand. "Jac—don't leave, okay?"

"I won't." The constricting band around Jac's chest relaxed, and she breathed deeply, finally freed by the chance to stop running. "Behave for the rest of the night. I'll see you soon. I promise."

Jac slipped from her chair, jumped down from the back of the stage, and maneuvered through the electrical cords and sound equipment on the floor.

Fleming stepped into Jac's path, her finger at her ear, probably clicking off her microphone. "Where do you think you're going?"

"I need to take a walk."

"Not now."

"I've done my duty for the evening. Everyone's had a look at me. The only thing anyone cares about now is his speech."

"You don't leave until his speech is over and everyone has pledged their donations. Then you work the room, making nice. You know the drill, Jac." Fleming half turned away and muttered something into her headset.

"Good night, Nora." Jac stepped around her, and when Fleming tried to get in front of her again, she grasped Fleming's elbows, lifted, and moved her aside. Anyone watching would've thought she was just steadying Fleming as she passed by. Fleming sucked in her breath, but she was no physical match for Jac, and Jac strode away.

Everyone in the room was focused on the stage, and Jac quickly made it to the back of the ballroom. When she reached the spot where she'd seen Mallory, Mallory was gone. Panic surged until Jac smelled honeysuckle and turned, captured by the scent. Mallory had moved into the shadows away from the tables. Jac hurried to her, still a little bit afraid she might disappear.

"Hi, Jac." Mallory smiled softly.

Jac ran her hand down Mallory's arm. Mallory was real. Mallory was here. "I thought I might've dreamed you."

"Nice dream?"

"It is now."

"Feel free to dream about me anytime," Mallory whispered.

"I will." Jac's brain was fuzzy, her heart racing so fast she was dizzy. "You look incredible. I miss the work boots, but the heels aren't a bad substitute."

Mallory laughed and ran her fingers over Jac's chest. "This is all pretty impressive. You look amazing yourself."

"What are you doing here?"

"Don't you know?" Mallory asked, her voice low and husky.

"Mallory," Jac groaned, her chest an agony of need. "God, I want to touch you."

"I was afraid you wouldn't want to." Mallory's eyes never left Jac's. "I was afraid I'd lost you. I don't want to lose you, Jac."

"I'm sorry, I'm so sorry. I never wanted you to feel that way. I didn't know what to do. I didn't want this"—Jac jerked her head toward the crowded room—"this monster dressed up to look civilized to suck you under."

"You ought to know by now I don't go down easy." Mallory drew a deep breath and traced Jac's name tag with her finger. "I love the uniform, but it scares me a little. You're not going back, are you?"

Mallory trembled, and knowing she was the cause about broke Jac's heart. She clasped Mallory's shoulders and pulled her close. "No. No, I'm not. I'm not going anywhere."

"Baby." Mallory pressed her hands to Jac's chest and pushed back from her. "I don't think this is a good place for public displays of affection."

"I don't care." Jac reached for her.

Mallory smiled crookedly. "I believe you, but we're about to have compa—"

Fleming appeared next to Jac, her face an icy mask of fury. She glared at Mallory and gestured to one of the security guards, who immediately strode toward them. "I'm going to have to ask you to leave."

Jac put herself between Mallory and the guard. "You're gonna want to tell him to back off, Nora, or we're going to have a scene."

"You wouldn't," Fleming said dismissively.

"Oh, I would."

Fleming narrowed her eyes at Jac, then abruptly waved off the guard. "All right, we'll do this quietly. But I need you back up on that stage, Jac." She pointed at Mallory. "And I need you gone. I thought you understood that the other day."

"No," Mallory said conversationally, taking Jac's hand. "I don't believe I ever agreed to that. And if I'd had a chance to talk to Jac, she wouldn't be here alone."

Fleming made a very uncultured sound. "You don't really think we're going to let Jac's squeeze-of-the-moment be part of this, do you?"

"Well, actually, no, I don't." Mallory smiled. "Jac and I will be very busy this summer on the line. And as to where Jac travels or who she travels with, that's up to her." Mallory leaned against Jac's shoulder. "But if she wants me to come with her, I will."

"You're willing to risk your career for a fling?" Fleming canted a brow. "You should know I can't be bluffed."

"You should ask Hooker about me." Mallory stepped closer and Fleming stumbled back, her lips parting in surprise. "He'll tell you I never bluff. And I never lose."

Fleming stared, her expression stony. "You don't know what you're talking about."

"Don't I?" Mallory grinned. "You know, I'm not afraid of a little publicity. How about you, Nora? Think you can weather the public fallout of having your little scheme to railroad Jac into line come to light? Are you that essential to the senator's campaign he'd let his image be tarnished? Because I think he'd throw you under the bus."

Fleming turned her back to Mallory and jerked Jac's arm. "Don't be ridiculous. You know better than this."

Jac glanced at the enraptured crowd as her father walked to center stage. His messianic aura overshadowed everything around him, including her sister and mother. His family was the pale accessory to his brilliant star. "He doesn't need me here. He never has."

"That's not the point."

"That's exactly the point." Jac put her arm around Mallory's waist. "Let's get out of here."

"Are you sure?" Mallory asked softly. "Because I'll wait."

Jac drew Mallory out into the hall, and Fleming didn't try to stop them. "I don't want to wait. I need you now." She stopped, suddenly aware of her surroundings. "Damn it. I came in the limo with my family. I don't have a car here."

"You don't need one," Mallory said. "I have a room."

Jac kissed her. "I knew there was a reason I loved you."

Mallory pulled Jac to the elevators. They had to get out of public view before she didn't care who saw them. The hungry, needy way Jac looked at her—as if she wanted to devour her—was driving her crazy. Mallory, her legs suddenly trembling, leaned into Jac. "Stop before I can't."

"No," Jac muttered, her teeth grazing Mallory's throat.

Laughing, about to burst into flames, Mallory punched the button to the elevator, praying for rescue. She was so out of control she was light-headed. Miraculously, the elevator slid to a stop almost instantly, its doors opening soundlessly on an empty car. They tumbled inside and she pushed twenty-seven. Mallory didn't recognize herself, and for once she didn't care. She'd had no plan when she'd walked into that ballroom, and she never did anything without a plan. She always knew where the safe zones were. She never engaged without an exit strategy in play. But tonight she'd only had a goal, and that goal was Jac. And now Jac was beside her, and nothing had ever felt so right. She pressed Jac against the back wall as the doors closed. Lacing her arms around Jac's neck, she kissed Jac until Jac was everywhere—until she was filled with Jac's crisp, bright smell, her strong firm body, her sweet fiery mouth. "I love you."

Jac groaned and pulled her closer. Their lips met, and Jac skimmed a hand up Mallory's thigh and under her skirt. Flames scorched her senses and Mallory let the inferno rage. With Jac she could let go. She kissed Jac and kept kissing her, tasting her mouth, molding to her body, ablaze for her. "God, Jac, God. I'm dying for you." The elevator pinged and she wondered where they were. She had to let go of her, but she didn't think she could. "I want you."

Jac's eyes were hazy, her chest flaring with every breath. "We need to get to your room. I'm half-crazy out of my mind for you."

Mallory pushed away and Jac grabbed her, yanking Mallory back against her chest. Mallory ground her ass into Jac's crotch. "Not helping. *Not* helping." The doors slid open. Twenty-seventh floor. "Oh thank God."

Mallory dragged Jac into the deserted hall. Everyone in the entire hotel was probably downstairs on the mezzanine. Her room was only a few doors down from the elevator, and she had her key card out before they reached the door. She slid it into the lock, jabbed the handle down when the little green light came on, and shoved the door open. Then Jac was crowding her inside and slamming the door behind her.

"The lock," Mallory gasped.

Jac engaged the deadbolt, flipped the security lock, and gripped her shoulders. "Fast or slow?"

"Slow." Mallory stumbled backward toward the bed with Jac's mouth roaming over her throat. "I want to undress you."

"Anything you want, Mal." Jac edged her hands inside Mallory's jacket and traced her thumbs along the arch of Mallory's hipbones through her silk camisole. "Anything you want. It's yours. Take it."

"You," Mallory said urgently against Jac's mouth, working the buttons loose on Jac's uniform by feel. "I want you, Jac. You."

"You have me. Always." Jac caught Mallory's hand and drew it to her heart. "Always."

"You can't change your mind now."

"I won't," Jac whispered.

Mallory started on the buttons on the crisp white shirt, her breathing stuttering to a stop as the fabric parted over smooth golden skin. She edged her fingertips beneath the material and brushed Jac's nipples. They hardened instantly and Jac moaned. "Off with the jacket."

Jac shrugged the coat down her arms, and Mallory pushed Jac's shirt open, bending her head to catch a nipple between her lips. Jac jerked and clasped the back of her neck, pressing Mallory's mouth harder into her breast. Jac's fingers were hot, burning on her skin.

"Mallory," Jac moaned, her hips rocking into Mallory's. "I'll never stop loving you."

"Mmm," Mallory crooned, kissing her way to the other breast as she opened Jac's pants. "I won't let you." She slid her hand inside Jac's briefs and her stomach somersaulted. "You're so wet, baby. So hot and ready." She kissed her way down the center of Jac's board-hard abdomen, pushing Jac's pants down as she moved lower.

"Wait, wait," Jac gasped, lifting Mallory up and twisting so they fell together onto the bed. "I'm too close. I want you naked first."

"Clothes," Mallory muttered, kicking off her heels, yanking her arms out of her jacket. She pushed onto her back, shimmied out of her skirt, and threw it toward the growing pile of Jac's clothes by the side of the bed. She couldn't stand not having her hands on Jac, craved skin on skin, ached to taste her, consume her. The second she was nude she grabbed for Jac, but Jac was faster and rolled on top of her. When Jac's thigh wedged between hers, she clenched and pulsed. She couldn't stop herself from rubbing on Jac's leg, and her clitoris jumped. She clutched Jac's shoulders. "Careful. Be careful, you'll make me come."

"Oh yeah." Jac kissed her and slid her hand between their bodies, filling her in one smooth, deep plunge.

Mallory arched, her mind exploding with heat and color, her breath blasting out with a short, hard groan. She came hard, wave upon wave, riding Jac's hand until she'd given all she could give.

"I love you," Jac groaned, her face buried in the curve of Mallory's neck. She trembled, her hips thrusting between Mallory's legs.

"I love you," Mallory whispered, and Jac came with a broken cry. Mallory cradled Jac in her arms, content to know she could always keep Jac safe there, in the shelter of her heart.

CHAPTER THIRTY-THREE

Jac woke spooning Mallory, her face buried in the curve of Mallory's neck and her arm wrapped around Mallory's waist. Mallory's ass was snugged into the curve of her hips, their legs entwined. She kissed a spot below Mallory's ear, and Mallory murmured, drawing Jac's hand higher, curving it around her breast.

"You awake?" Jac asked.

"Mmm, yes. Sort of." Mallory turned her head and kissed the corner of Jac's mouth. "What time is it?"

Jac leaned over to check the clock on the bedside table. "Close to midnight."

Mallory burrowed closer, rolling her rear against Jac's crotch. Jac's stomach tightened, and she rubbed Mallory's nipple, her breath catching when it hardened instantly. She skimmed her mouth over Mallory's neck and kissed the angle of her jaw. "You feel great in my arms."

Mallory chuckled. "Good thing. I like being here."

"How much time do we have?"

"Tonight?" Mallory asked. "I think that's your call, baby. We're on your turf here."

"What was all that about with Hooker and Nora?" Jac asked.

"Hooker wasn't just your garden-variety jerk," Mallory said.

As Mallory recounted what she'd deduced from Chantal's story, Jac nearly choked on her rising fury. If she'd been the only target, she might have shrugged it off as one more assault by her father's rearguard, but this had been aimed at Mallory too. "We ought to go public and take Nora down with her own ammunition."

"We could," Mallory replied, "but there would be collateral damage. Some of the media bloodletting would overflow onto your family."

"Yeah, and my little sister is already freaking out." Jac swore. "I hate to let Fleming get away with this, but even if my father fired her, the press would have a feeding frenzy."

"It's okay, baby. I vote we claim victory for the battle and worry about the war later."

"Okay," Jac said, "but we better leave before Fleming has time to think up another way to put the screws to us."

"Whenever you say, we'll head back to Yellowrock."

"And then what?"

Mallory shifted on the bed, turning over to face Jac. "What do you want to happen, Jac? You're the one who left."

Jac rested her cheek against Mallory's hair and closed her eyes. She'd missed most of the last week of boot camp. She cared about that, but she cared a lot more about where she was going with Mallory. She opened her eyes and met Mallory's gaze. "I want to be with you, Mallory. I love you."

Mallory slid her leg over the outside of Jac's thigh, gliding her center against Jac's hip. She was wet, and Jac forgot all about Hooker and Nora Fleming. Mallory kissed Jac, and she was in no hurry. She traced her tongue over the contours of Jac's mouth, darting inside, nibbling, sucking and savoring. When Jac was breathing like a freight train chugging up the mountainside, Mallory drew back and smiled. Her eyes glinted with unmistakable triumph. "I sort of planned on keeping you. You think I drove all the way down here to turn around and go back without you?"

"I'll come back even if you cut me from the team. I sort of fucked that up, didn't I?"

"No, baby, you didn't." Mallory kissed her again, gently. "You more than made up for any time you lost this week up on the mountain, getting those kids out. We've got a jump tomorrow. Are you ready for it?"

"Yes, I am," Jac said.

"Are you ready to walk away from all of this? It's probably not going to be easy."

Jac grimaced. "I've walked away from this before on my father's orders—this time it's on my terms." She shifted closer, pulling Mallory against her belly, needing her everywhere. "I want to see my sister. After that, I'm ready to go."

Mallory ran her hand over Jac's ass. "You want to get dressed and find your sister now?"

Jac grabbed Mallory's wrist and guided Mallory's hand between her legs. Mallory's fingers found her instantly, stroking her exactly right. Jac pushed into her palm, wanting to let go, wanting to hold on, wanting to be connected forever.

"In a minute," Jac gasped. "I need you first. I need you."

Mallory smiled, stroking her deeper, taking her right up to the edge. "Baby, anytime, anything you need."

❖

Jac knocked on Carly's door, and after a few seconds, Carly called, "Who is it?"

"It's me," Jac said.

The door opened to the length of the security lock, and Carly peered out. "Wow, you're in so much trouble."

Jac grinned. "Yeah, yeah. Let us in?"

The door closed, the lock rattled, and then Carly pulled the door wide. She was wearing a ribbed pink tank top and white drawstring pajama bottoms with red hearts, her hair was down and loose, and she looked about twelve. Jac's heart turned over. Man, she didn't want to leave her. She drew Mallory into the room by the hand, keeping it in hers. "Carly, this is Mallory."

Carly dropped down on the bed next to her open computer and drew her legs up cross-wise. She cocked her head and blatantly studied Mallory. "Hi."

"Hi," Mallory said, hooking her thumb over the back of Jac's uniform pants. "Sorry I dragged Jac away tonight."

"It's okay. It was just more of the usual, anyhow." She picked at the hem of her pajama bottoms and looked up at Jac, her face partially shielded by her hair. "So, you leaving, Jac?"

"I'm going back to Montana. I'll be there for the season," Jac said. "But I'm not gonna be that far away, Carly. If you need me for anything, I'll come. If I'm out on the line, I'll come as soon as I get free."

"Yeah?" Carly glanced at Mallory.

Mallory nodded. "We can get pretty busy. Sometimes we're out in the field a couple weeks at a time. But Jac can leave instructions with the base that if you call, someone will get through to us. If you say you need her to come, I'll get her here."

Carly sat up straighter. "Yeah? Like, you're the boss or something?"

Jac laughed. "That's pretty much it."

"Cool." Carly grinned at Jac. "So I guess if you fuck up again, you'll really be in trouble."

"Language," Jac said, still laughing.

"Yeah, whatever."

Carly grabbed her cell phone off the table. "Okay. Give me your numbers."

Jac and Mallory gave her their cell numbers, and Mallory gave her Sully's.

"That last one," Mallory said, "that's Chuck Sullivan. He runs our base. Tell him who you are and that I said to relay to me, and he will."

"I won't use it unless I have to," Carly said, suddenly serious.

Jac knelt in front of the bed and tugged Carly into her arms. "You need me, you call. I'm not leaving."

Carly squeezed her hard, rubbing her cheek against Jac's shoulder. "I love you," she muttered into Jac's shirt.

Jac whispered, "I love you too. Talk to you soon, okay?"

"Okay. You can always text me. You know, if you get lonely."

"I will. Promise." Jac kissed her forehead, straightened, and looked at Mallory. "Ready to go home?"

"More than ready." Mallory looped her arm around Jac's waist. "It's good to meet you, Carly."

"Yeah. Same." Carly drew her computer onto her lap, then looked up at Mallory. "So you'll take care of her, right?"

"I will," Mallory said. "I absolutely will."

CHAPTER THIRTY-FOUR

The klaxon blare jerked Jac upright out of a sound sleep. In the second she took to orient herself, Mallory had already slipped out from behind her and was jumping into her pants.

"Call out, Russo," Mallory said, yanking a sweatshirt down over her head. "We're at the top of the jump list. Let's go."

"With you." Jac tossed back the top of the sleeping bag and hopped out of the warm cocoon of their bed onto the cold floor of the loft. Her heart was pumping hard, her belly coiled with sweet anticipation. First call out as a real smokejumper. First jump with Mallory as her partner. She dove into her clothes, grabbed the PG pack she'd left by the ladder, and slid down, hands curled around the side rails, her feet barely hitting the rungs. Benny had the hangar doors open and was climbing into the plane. She sprinted after Mallory and hit the yard running, the sound of the engines firing up behind her. In the equipment room, they grabbed chutes and equipment crates, and ten minutes later, they were airborne. Cooper was the designated spotter, and Jac settled next to Mallory on one of the benches running along the side of the cargo space. Anderson and Kingston and a couple of the veterans sat across from them. She leaned close to Mallory and shouted, "What do you know?"

"Small burn up in Marten Canyon. No access roads, so we'll be it for a while."

Jac nodded. Too hard to talk above the noise. Not much else to say. That's what they did—got there fast, got there first, and contained the burn before it really had a chance to get started.

She was glad to get started. Ready to test her skills. The best part was she didn't have to prove anything, not to herself, not to Mallory.

She mattered to Mallory, no matter what she did—she knew it in her bones.

Mallory squeezed Jac's arm. "What are you smiling at?"

"Just thinking about the last couple of days."

Beneath her visor, Mallory blushed. Jac grinned. She'd passed her last practice jump and made the team along with everyone else. Mallory had given everyone a two-day pass, and except for a skeleton crew, the station had been pretty deserted. They'd driven to Bear Creek, rented a room in the only hotel in town, and spent the entire two days' leave in bed. She couldn't think of a better way to spend whatever time off they might have in the next few months. The rest of the time, she'd be working with Mallory, and that was pleasure in itself.

Cooper signaled he was about to open the doors, and Jac braced for the onslaught. Cooper slid them back, cold air rushed in, and he dropped the streamers out the opening and gauged the wind direction and drift. Whispers of smoke wafted into the cabin, and Jac's skin tingled. Soon enough, they'd be on the ground and the fight would be on. She glanced at Mallory. Her face was calm, her eyes fiercely focused. Following Mallory into battle was easy. Jac trusted her completely—fighting forest fires, fighting her personal war—she'd never be alone again.

Cooper motioned for them to line up. Mallory was incident commander, so she and Jac would jump first. When Jac dropped into the sky a few seconds before Mallory and counted down, she knew with absolute certainty Mallory would be right beside her. When she pulled her chute and looked back to check it, Mallory's chute opened, and they steered down together, landing almost simultaneously. Jac rolled, disengaged her chute, and quickly stowed it. She joined the others clustered around Mallory, who was directing the crew to collect the equipment crates and assigning posts. When everyone moved off, Jac was the only one remaining.

"You'll be here." Mallory indicated a spot ahead of the fire front where they were going to cut. She pointed in another direction, then tapped a spot on her map. "The safety zone is here. You clear on that?"

"I am," Jac said.

"I'll be down here." Mallory circled a spot at the end of the line. "Not far. If you need me."

"I know." Jac touched Mallory's cheek with her fingertips. "I know you'll never be far. Neither will I."

"Then I'll see you when we beat this one," Mallory said.

"You can count on it," Jac said.

Mallory nodded briskly, tapped Jac's helmet, and turned away.

Jac shouldered her pack and pulled out her pulaski. Time to cut and dig.

Mallory turned back. "Hey, Hotshot."

"Yeah?"

"I love you."

The flames dancing in Mallory's eyes had nothing to do with the fire, and Jac felt the burn in every inch of her. She touched a finger to her chest in a silent salute. "Roger that, Ice. I love you too."

Keep reading for a special preview of BLOOD HUNT, Book Two in L.L. Raand's Midnight Hunters series.

Sylvan, the Wolf Were Alpha, forges an uneasy alliance with Vampire Detective Jody Gates, heir to a powerful Vampire clan, to battle a shadow army of humans and rogue Praeterns bent on destroying any hope of legal acceptance of the non-human species. With outside forces threatening to destroy the Praetern Coalition, several female Were adolescents turn up missing, and chaos descends upon Sylvan's personal guards when Sylvan and her new mate are overtaken by breeding frenzy. While Sylvan struggles to protect her Pack, Jody fights her destiny as well as her growing hunger for human reporter Becca Land.

Blood Hunt
by L.L. Raand

Drake's nostrils flared at the stench of torn flesh and congealing blood. The dirt floor of the abandoned warehouse soaked up the splattered body fluids of the dead wolf Weres, the corpses gleaming wetly under the slivers of silver moon lancing through the holes in the dilapidated roof. Her mate panted beside her, Sylvan's dusty blond hair matted with sweat and her bronze skin streaked with blood. Sylvan's lean, muscular body glistened with a damp coating of adrenaline and pheromones. Four deep, ragged claw marks gouged her side. Ragged rents from the rogue's teeth covered her chest and shoulders. The rogue leader had not died easily.

How bad is it? Drake didn't speak aloud. She wouldn't let the others know of her worry, but she didn't need to. Their mate bond connected them emotionally, physically, and psychically.

They'd all been in pelt during the battle and had shifted back to skin at the end of the fight. Sylvan's wounds should have healed already, but she wasn't at full strength. Not twenty-four hours before, Drake had plunged her claws into Sylvan's abdomen and extracted multiple silver-bullet fragments. The silver still circulated in Sylvan's system, poisoning her. Drake shuddered. She'd come so close to losing her, and her mate wasn't out of danger yet. Someone still wanted Sylvan dead.

Sylvan? How bad?

The muscles in my side are torn. He missed my hip joint. I'm already healing.

You need to shift. You'll heal faster. Drake leaned against Sylvan, needing the contact. Needing much more than that, but waiting until Sylvan had given her orders to the hunters. The *centuri*, Sylvan's elite guard, formed a semicircle behind them, protecting their flanks. Sylvan had led them on a hunting raid in retribution for the assassination attempt against her that had nearly killed Lara, one of her *centuri*. She'd accepted the rogue Were's challenge and fought to the death.

Drake understood why Sylvan had accepted the rogue's challenge and why she had faced him alone, but standing by and watching the larger, mad wolf rip and tear at her mate had nearly driven *her* mad. She'd wanted to throw herself into the fight, to put her own body between Sylvan and the rogue, to tear his heart from his chest. She'd done nothing. Sylvan was Alpha, and she could not rule her Pack if she could not stand to a challenge. The Timberwolf Pack respected her, loved her, but they would not follow an Alpha who could not protect them. Without a strong leader and a clear hierarchy, a social order of predators that was ruled as much by instinct as intellect would descend into chaos. Drake knew all that, but her instincts, her very soul, railed at her to protect her mate. The urge still made her guts churn. *You should be healed by now. Shift, Sylvan.*

After I get my hunters home.

Niki will safeguard your centuri. *Please, love.*

Trust me, mate. I am more than strong enough to do what needs to be done. For my wolves, for you. Sylvan clasped the back of Drake's neck, her still-extruded claws lightly scratching the thick muscles along Drake's spine.

Drake suppressed a shiver of pleasure. Battle released a flood of neurotransmitters that blocked pain, but once the threat had passed, the chemicals morphed into sexual stimulants. All the hunters with Sylvan were aroused. So was she, even more than the others. She and Sylvan were newly mated, and the mate bond demanded near-constant physical connection and sexual release in order to fuse the chemical and hormonal markers that defined them as a mated pair. *Then hurry and finish. We don't know how many more rogues may be on their way, and you've fought enough this night.*

You worry too much. Sylvan's thoughts held a hint of laughter and the pride that ran in the blood of a long line of Alpha Weres. With no hint of a limp, Sylvan strode to the two cowering rogues who knelt in pools of blood and submissive urine, their heads bowed, limbs trembling. Drake and the hunters had killed the other rogues, leaving these two alive to bear witness to the outcome of the challenge and to spread the message that Sylvan was alive—not only alive, but deadly and without mercy.

"Tell your masters the Alpha of the Timberwolf Pack says these streets are mine. This city, this territory is mine. If you sell drugs to poison my wolves, I will come for you. If you threaten my Pack, I will come for you. If you break the laws of my Pack land, I will come for you. The challenge is issued." She kicked the lifeless corpse of the rogue whose throat she had torn out. "And I will not be as quick as I was with this cur. Now go."

The two hesitated for an instant, then spun around, still on their knees, and crawled out of sight. Within seconds, the sound of fleeing footsteps echoed through the cavernous building. Sylvan turned to Niki, her second and the leader of her *centuri*.

"Burn it."

"Yes, Alpha," the auburn-haired Were said. Smaller and fuller-breasted than Drake, Niki's muscular body was a fighting machine. The Pack *imperator*, Sylvan's enforcer, she lived to protect Sylvan. "Andrew—get the Rover. Jonathan—the accelerant is in the compartment under the floor. Max—take Jace and patrol the access road. We don't want this mongrel's lieutenants taking us by surprise if they come looking for him." She spat on the naked body of the dead rogue.

Jonathan, one of the newest *centuri*, rushed off with Andrew. Max, a craggy-faced, shaggy-haired Were, grunted his assent and loped away with Jace, a lithe blond female and Jonathan's twin.

Sylvan slid her arm around Drake's waist. "Happy now?"

Sylvan was trembling, and Drake instinctively drew her as close as she could without appearing to be supporting her. Watching Sylvan dominate the rogues aroused her even more than the fight, and she hadn't thought that possible. Her skin tingled with pheromones and shimmered with sex sheen that mirrored Sylvan's. Her clitoris pulsed and her sex clenched rhythmically. Her inner muscles pounded, and her sex glands, the olive-sized nodes buried deep at the base of her clitoris that produced the unique Were sexual neurotransmitters, were hard and ready to burst. "I won't be happy until I have you alone and under me."

Sylvan laughed. "Not until I've had you under me, and I've come in you."

"You're not strong enough for that yet."

"I was strong enough a few hours ago."

Drake needed Sylvan so badly her blood burned. "That was before you had to fight, and now you're injured again. We'll wait to tangle until you've shifted and finished healing."

"I'm strong enough to take my mate." Sylvan nipped Drake's neck, her bite searing through Drake and making her hips jerk. "And I'm going to come on you very soon."

"I'm ready."

Sylvan kissed her, her hand in Drake's hair, tilting her head back. She thrust her tongue deep into Drake's mouth, her kiss a claiming, a demand—hot and hard and furious. Heat flared in Drake's belly, tightening her clitoris, filling her pelvis with blood and *victus*, the Were life-essence. Her glands pulsed, and she growled into Sylvan's mouth.

Niki said from behind them, "The incendiaries are set, Alpha."

Sylvan's blue eyes shimmered to wolf-gold and bored into Drake's with the promise of their mating. "Do it."

Leaving the *centuri* to ignite the blaze, Drake and Sylvan headed out to the heavily fortified black SUV. Drake filled her lungs with the cool, clean scent of the night—animals in the brush, pollen on the breeze, fish in the nearby river. Life. "I want you in the infirmary as soon as we—"

"No." Sylvan stopped and gripped Drake's shoulders. "I told you that's not what I need."

"I know—"

"No, you don't." Sylvan yanked Drake close, her mouth against Drake's throat. "You. I need you."

Heat roared through Drake's blood, spiking her clitoris so hard she almost came. She needed to claim Sylvan as badly as Sylvan needed her. She ached to touch her, taste her, and know in her bones that Sylvan was alive and well and hers. Groaning at the surge of need, she pressed against Sylvan, rubbing her bare chest over Sylvan's. Her nipples hardened, her breasts tensed, and her skin sparked. Her claws and canines extruded. Before she surrendered to the mating call, she pulled away, whimpering at the painful separation. "No, you're injured. We shouldn't—"

Sylvan snarled and her face shifted, the starkly beautiful planes edging into the sharp edges of her wolf. She was an Alpha Were, and denying her was dangerous.

Drake caressed Sylvan's chest until Sylvan's taut muscles eased. Too softly for anyone else to hear, she whispered, "Don't snarl at me, love. You don't scare me."

The corner of Sylvan's mouth twitched. "That was one of the first things I noticed about you when you were still human. You should have been afraid. Even now, you should be. But you never have been."

"I love your fury. I love your strength." Drake ran her fingers through Sylvan's hair. "I love your power. I'll never fear it."

"But you won't let me control you, either, will you?"

Drake opened the rear door of the Rover and they settled onto the benches bolted lengthwise to the sides of the compartment. "No."

Sylvan laughed.

❖

"I'd like to speak to Detective Jody Gates, please," Becca Land said when the phone at police headquarters was answered by a laconic voice she recognized as the night dispatcher. For crying out loud, was he the only one who ever worked nights?

"Like I told you last time, lady, she ain't working. And no, she ain't called in for the five messages you already left. Maybe you should take the hint."

Becca flushed. *As if.* "My interest is professional—" And why was she explaining something that was no one's business to a man she didn't even know? "Can you tell me when she's scheduled—"

"She was due in at twenty-two hundred. Yesterday. She's late."

By about twenty-four hours. "Surely you have procedures for—"

"Her lieutenant don't seem too worried. Maybe *she* should take the hint and look for another kind of work." He snorted. "Don't really need Vampire cops, now do we?"

A click was followed by empty air. Becca stared at the silent phone. Since when was it okay for city officials not to even pretend to hide their prejudices against Praeterns? Or had the discrimination always been this blatant, and she was just now noticing? God, she hoped she hadn't been that blind.

This plan to track down the elusive Detective Gates wasn't working—time to try something else. She'd been watching Jody's town house almost nonstop since someone shot the Were Alpha there following a meeting with Jody. Jody had given her own blood to revive a dying Were guard and nearly died herself. Talk about a huge scoop, and she hadn't called it in. She'd been right there—really right there. Kneeling in blood and praying that someone didn't die. She'd held off reporting the shooting because she didn't have the bigger story—she wanted to know what was behind those gunshots. And if she reported an assassination attempt on the U.S. Councilor for Were Affairs, the AP would bury the city in TV newscasters and there'd go her chance at the *real* story. Nope, something big was brewing and Jody was her best source. Sort of a sad statement, considering how the Vampire detective wasn't speaking to her at the moment, but hey, a reporter worked with what she had. Detective Jody Gates. God, what a pain in the ass.

She didn't even like the damned Vampire, but she hadn't wanted to see her die either—or whatever living Vampires did before they reanimated as Risen Vampires. She hadn't even known that a Vampire could die from giving up too much of her own blood, but then who knew what the rules were anyhow? It wasn't as if the Vampires—or any of the Praeterns—let humans in on their secrets. Well, okay, maybe that was understandable, considering that humans had done a pretty good job of wiping out the Praetern species something like a millennium ago, and they'd all gone into hiding and hadn't resurfaced until two years ago, when Sylvan's father more or less announced to the world, "Hey, everybody, there are a whole lot of preternatural species who have been living among you for forever, and we are tired of hiding." The great Exodus had pretty much turned the world upside down, and humans, outnumbering the Praeterns by thousands to one, weren't so sure they really wanted to share living space with species like Vampires and Weres who just might consider them prey, or the Fae who had all kinds of magical powers, or the Psi who might be influencing minds, or the Magi whose incantations and spells and wizardry were better weapons than anything humans had been able to construct. Humans, despite their numbers, often built their cultures based on fear, as Becca came to realize more every day.

Well, she wasn't afraid. She was pissed off. She'd tried to help Jody—she'd offered her *blood*—and what did she get for her efforts?

Jody had practically tossed her out on her ear. She'd left Jody's house, but she wasn't going to stay gone.

She was an investigative reporter, and she wanted to know who had taken shots at someone as high profile as Sylvan Mir, and while she was at it, she wanted to know what was going on with the mysterious girls who were showing up in ERs with deadly fevers no one wanted to talk about. Not quite true. *Someone* wanted to talk about them because he—she thought it was a he, she couldn't really tell from the muffled voice on the phone—had been calling her to tell her about these cases. Why? Why did someone want to alert the press to these infections? Were they, as the caller claimed, instances of Were fever being transmitted to humans? If that was true, she needed to alert the human population. Didn't she? Wasn't that her responsibility—to report the stories that made a difference, to expose the dangerous secrets that ultimately cost lives? She hadn't written anything about it yet. She told herself it was because she didn't know enough, but how could she know enough if no one would tell her anything?

Feeling like a stalker, she'd waited and watched and waited some more, from before dawn the day before until well after sunup, for Jody to return. When the Vampire hadn't shown, she'd figured Jody was spending the daylight hours somewhere else, and she'd gone home for a few hours' restless sleep, then back on watch before sundown. As the hours passed with still no sign of Jody, she'd started to worry. Maybe Jody hadn't recovered from nearly bleeding out, or the Vampire equivalent of it. Maybe Jody was at the hospital, although come to think of it, she'd never seen a Vampire patient in the ER. Like Weres, they didn't seek conventional medical care. After giving the Were her blood, Jody had said she'd needed to feed. And she'd said to Sylvan Mir, *You may not thank me when your* centuri *wakes up hungry. I need to be there when she does. When I've taken care of my needs, I'll come.*

Becca pulled her laptop from underneath the front seat and ran a Google search on Sylvan Mir. She'd read enough exposés and editorials about the Were Alpha and the Adirondack Timberwolf Pack to have a general idea where their Compound was located. After scanning a few articles, she clicked Google Maps and punched in the coordinates on her GPS. Time to hunt. First stop—the private headquarters of the most powerful Were Alpha in the Western Hemisphere.

About the Author

Radclyffe has written over thirty-five romance and romantic intrigue novels, dozens of short stories, and, writing as L.L. Raand, has authored a paranormal romance series, The Midnight Hunters.

She is an eight-time Lambda Literary Award finalist in romance, mystery, and erotica—winning in both romance (*Distant Shores, Silent Thunder*) and erotica (*Erotic Interludes 2: Stolen Moments* edited with Stacia Seaman and *In Deep Waters 2: Cruising the Strip* written with Karin Kallmaker). A member of the Saints and Sinners Literary Hall of Fame, she is also a 2010 RWA/FF&P Prism award winner for *Secrets in the Stone*. Her 2010 titles are finalists for the Benjamin Franklin award (*Desire by Starlight*), the ForeWord Review Book of the Year award (*Trauma Alert* and writing as LL Raand, *The Midnight Hunt*), and the RWA Passionate Plume award (*The Midnight Hunt*). She is also the president of Bold Strokes Books, one of the world's largest independent LGBT publishing companies.

Books Available From Bold Strokes Books

Firestorm by Radclyffe. Firefighter paramedic Mallory "Ice" James isn't happy when the undisciplined Jac Russo joins her command, but lust isn't something either can control—and they soon discover ice burns as fiercely as flame. (978-1-60282-232-0)

The Best Defense by Carsen Taite. When socialite Aimee Howard hires former homicide detective Skye Keaton to find her missing niece, she vows not to mix business with pleasure, but she soon finds Skye hard to resist. (978-1-60282-233-7)

After the Fall by Robin Summers. When the plague destroys most of humanity, Taylor Stone thinks there's nothing left to live for, until she meets Kate, a woman who makes her realize love is still alive and makes her dream of a future she thought was no longer possible. (978-1-60282-234-4)

Accidents Never Happen by David-Matthew Barnes. From the moment Albert and Joey meet by chance beneath a train track on a street in Chicago, a domino effect is triggered, setting off a chain reaction of murder and tragedy. (978-1-60282-235-1)

In Plain View by Shane Allison. Best-selling gay erotica authors create the stories of sex and desire modern readers crave. (978-1-60282-236-8)

Wild by Meghan O'Brien. Shapeshifter Selene Rhodes dreads the full moon and the loss of control it brings, but when she rescues forensic pathologist Eve Thomas from a vicious attack by a masked man, she discovers she isn't the scariest monster in San Francisco. (978-1-60282-227-6)

Reluctant Hope by Erin Dutton. Cancer survivor Addison Hunt knows she can't offer any guarantees, in love or in life, and after experiencing a loss of her own, Brooke Donahue isn't willing to risk her heart. (978-1-60282-228-3)

The Affair of the Porcelain Dog by Jess Faraday. What darkness stalks the London streets at night? Ira Adler, present plaything of crime lord Cain Goddard, will soon find out. (978-1-60282-230-6)

Conquest by Ronica Black. When Mary Brunelle stumbles into the arms of Jude Jaeger, a gorgeous dominatrix at a private nightclub, she is smitten, but she soon finds out Jude is her professor, and Professor Jaeger doesn't date her students…or her conquests. (978-1-60282-229-0)

365 Days by K.E. Payne. Life sucks when you're seventeen years old and confused about your sexuality, and the girl of your dreams doesn't even know you exist. Then in walks sexy new emo girl, Hannah Harrison. Clemmie Atkins has exactly 365 days to discover herself, and she's going to have a blast doing it! (978-1-60282-540-6)

Darkness Embraced by Winter Pennington. Surrounded by harsh vampire politics and secret ambitions, Epiphany learns that an old enemy is plotting treason against the woman she once loved, and to save all she holds dear, she must embrace and form an alliance with the dark. (978-1-60282-221-4)

78 Keys by Kristin Marra. When the cosmic powers choose Devorah Rosten to be their next gladiator, she must use her unique skills to try to save her lover, herself, and even humankind. (978-1-60282-222-1)

Playing Passion's Game by Lesley Davis. Trent Williams's only passion in life is gaming—until Juliet Sullivan makes her realize that love can be a whole different game to play. (978-1-60282-223-8)

Who Dat Whodunnit by Greg Herren. Popular New Orleans detective Scotty Bradley investigates the murder of a dethroned beauty queen to clear the name of his pro football–playing cousin. (978-1-60282-225-2)

Ghosts of Winter by Rebecca S. Buck. Can Ros Wynne, who has lost everything she thought defined her, find her true life—and her true love—surrounded by the lingering history of the once-grand Winter Manor? (978-1-60282-219-1)

Blood Hunt by L.L. Raand. In the second Midnight Hunters Novel, Detective Jody Gates, heir to a powerful Vampire clan, forges an uneasy alliance with Sylvan, the Wolf Were Alpha, to battle a shadow army of humans and rogue Weres, while fighting her growing hunger for human reporter Becca Land. (978-1-60282-209-2)